He was her boss...

A few orgasms—earth-shattering or not—were not worth playing Russian roulette with her whole life.

"If we're going to be working together," she said, "this thing between us has to end. No candlelit dinners, no late-night phone calls... No sex."

In response, Griffin threw back his head and laughed.

She set her jaw stubbornly. "I'm not joking."

He pulled her toward him so she was standing between his outstretched legs and took her lips in a soul-searing kiss. The kind that almost ended up with him ripping off her clothes and devouring her until she came apart in his arms.

He smiled. "Well then, you let me know how that goes for you."

Dear Reader,

When I first envisioned Griffin Cain, he was no more than the charming second brother in the Cain family. Characters often start like that for me, very one-dimensional. Still, I knew that he would have to become the CEO of the company one day. My critique partner, the fabulous Robyn Dehart, told me early on that he needed a goal beyond wanting to escape the mantle of responsibility. Of course she was right. She usually is. So I decided that this charming, seemingly irresponsible man was secretly involved with an international aid organization, just the kind of thing his father would disapprove of.

Of course, then I had to decide which international aid organization to model his imaginary charity after. My good friend Tracy Wolff suggested Water.org, a charity with which Matt Damon is heavily involved. I did a little research (i.e., wasted hours and hours online). I'm tremendously impressed with Water.org. That's what inspired me to create Hope$_2$O for Griffin.

I hope that a few of you who read this letter will check out Water.org and find out what great work they do. I made a donation in honor of the book and think it would be pretty cool if others did, too. If you want to give, too, you can check out my website or theirs for more information.

As always, I hope you enjoy this book and love Griffin and Sydney like I do!

Emily McKay

ALL HE
REALLY NEEDS

BY
EMILY McKAY

Published in Great Britain 2013
by Mills & Boon, an imprint of Harlequin (UK) Limited,
Eton House, 18-24 Paradise Road, Richmond, Surrey TW9 1SR

© Emily McKaskle 2013

ISBN: 978 0 263 90471 0
ebook ISBN: 978 1 472 00596 0

51-0413

Harlequin (UK) policy is to use papers that are natural renewable and
                                                    nable forests. The
                                                    environmental

Emily McKay has been reading romance novels since she was eleven years old. Her first Mills & Boon® book came free in a box of Hefty garbage bags. She has been reading and loving romance novels ever since. She lives in Texas with her geeky husband, her two kids and too many pets. Her debut novel, *Baby, Be Mine,* was a RITA® Award finalist for Best First Book and Best Short Contemporary. She was also a 2009 *RT Book Reviews* Career Achievement nominee for Series Romance. To learn more, visit her website, www.EmilyMcKay.com.

For the men and women involved with charitable organizations around the world. They give their time, their work and their money to improve the lives of others. They are the real heroes.

One

Griffin Cain certainly knew how to make love to a woman.

This was not the first time that thought had flittered through Sydney Edward's mind. Indeed, it wasn't even the first time today she'd thought it. Oh, the things he did to her body—the decadent, sinful, exquisite things he did.

But that was Griffin all over. Decadent. Sinful. Exquisite.

And so completely, totally opposite from her. Even now—four months into their clandestine relationship—she could hardly believe the things he did to her. The things she let him do to her. No, to be fair, the things she begged him to do.

Begged. Her, Sydney Edwards.

The most staid, conservative, responsible person she knew. And she was putty in his hands. One of which was, even now, tracing enticing swirls across her naked hip.

"I should go," she muttered, attempting to roll away from him.

"No." The sound that emanated from Griffin's throat was low and possessive, more of a growl than a word. His hand slipped over her hip to rest low on her belly as he pulled her back against him. "Not yet."

"I'm already late for work." But even she didn't believe her protestations. Not when his fingers were slipping down into the curls between her legs. Not when her back was automatically arching so that the moist center of her desire tilted toward him.

"Then be late," he grumbled, nipping at her shoulder with his teeth.

They had had sex twice last night and once already this morning. Normally, she didn't stay over at his condo. So, normally, she was back at home, showered and de-Griffined, long before she had a chance to be late for work.

But Griffin had just returned from an overseas trip the night before. He'd had a different trip just prior to that one. In short, lately he'd been gone entirely too much for her taste.

Not that she needed him.

Not that she even really missed *him*.

It was just that…well, she craved his touch. Which was not at all the same thing as missing him.

Sydney knew that her relationship with Griffin was odd. Contrary to her very nature, even.

They spent very little time together outside of bed. In bed, he lavished her body with attention. So much so that she might have worried she'd become addicted to his touch—if she was the kind of person who allowed herself the weakness of having addictions.

Besides, she was twenty-seven. She was young and healthy. It would be unnatural for her not to be attracted to someone like Griffin. She wasn't the least bit worried that she might become too attached. After all, this was Griffin Cain. Charming playboy. Office flirt. The heir to one-third of the Cain fortune. All in all, an unlikely match for her.

So she wasn't worried that, last night, as soon as she'd gotten his text that he'd landed at Houston International Airport, she'd climbed out of bed and come straight to his downtown

condo to meet him. And it had been late. So of course she'd
bent her personal rule about staying over. No one wanted to
drive home at three in the morning.

And she wasn't even particularly worried about her inability to muster anxiety about being late to work.

Still, she tried to fool him, even if she couldn't fool herself.

"It's all well and good for you to be late to work. You're
Griffin Cain. Your family owns the company. People will forgive you anything."

"And I just got in from Norway."

"I thought it was Sweden." As if it made a difference. He
was always getting back from some exotic location or heading off to some other.

"Your boss isn't even coming in today," Griffin murmured.

His fingers found the nub of her desire, stroking her in a
way that made her tremble and ache all over again.

The rational part of her brain lodged a vain protest. She
should be stronger than this. She should have some shred of
willpower where he was concerned. But she wasn't and she
didn't.

Besides, once more wouldn't hurt.

The heat of his erection stroked her moist folds. He was so
close. All she had to do was rotate her hips and wiggle to ac-
commodate him from behind. He'd take her fast and hard. One
movement from her and they could both have what they needed.

She arched her back, ready to give herself over to her desire, but instead, he rolled her over onto her back. He pinned
both her hands over her head with one hand and stroked her
folds with the other, making her arch and moan.

"Open your eyes." The gentle tone of his voice didn't make
it any less of a command.

She kept her eyes firmly closed, willing his fingers to move
more quickly, to push her over the edge.

But he stilled. She knew he was teasing her until she gave
him what he wanted. She rocked her hips, bumping against

his hand and against the length of his erection. Digging her heels into the mattress, she pushed her hips up, wanting to drive him in.

"Open your eyes," he said again, somehow touching her, teasing her, yet staying out of reach.

She gritted her teeth as she opened her eyes. She wanted to glare at him for forcing her hand, but sexual desire made her languid and weak. Her protestation came out as a groan of satisfaction.

Griffin leaned over her, his usually relaxed smile stretched into a grimace of restraint. He'd teased her, but it had cost him. He was torturing himself, too. It made her smile, that fierce expression—knowing how hard it was for him to restrain himself.

He muttered a curse and plunged into her. She met his every thrust, her gaze on his the whole time, until she felt his control shatter and his own eyes closed. Only then did she let her climax wash over her.

His body was hot and heavy on hers, but the sensation was not unpleasant. She was satisfied. Not just her body but her pride. She may need him, but he needed her just as badly.

He rolled off her and this time, when he pulled her against him, she didn't resist. He was right. Her boss, Dalton Cain, wasn't coming in today. He had had nothing on the schedule today anyway, no meetings to move around, no appointments to jostle. For once, her plate was blessedly bare. No one would miss her.

Even though she was late for work already, even though she still needed to shower and eat before heading in, she let herself fall asleep. Partly because she was exhausted and sated as she rarely had been and partly because her realization brought her a sort of peace.

Griffin should have been exhausted, but he wasn't. Just as he should no longer have the energy to desire Sydney, but he did.

Despite his fatigue, Griffin couldn't sleep. He was still on Norway time. Or was it Sweden? He'd traveled so much recently, he barely knew where he was or where he'd been.

So he did what he always did when he couldn't sleep. He turned on the TV and poured himself a bowl of cereal. The marshmallows in his Lucky Charms were just starting to soften when the doorbell rang. For the life of him, he couldn't guess who it might be.

He opened the door to see his brother, Dalton, standing in the hall. Dalton, who normally looked like he'd wandered straight out of a Brooks Brothers' ad, was dressed in a slightly wrinkled shirt and jeans. Jeans, for Christ's sake. Griffin hadn't even been sure Dalton owned jeans. But there he was. And the poor guy looked worn-out. Like the past few days had beaten the crap out of him and left him in an alley somewhere.

Unsure how else to greet his brother, Griffin said, "Hey, you're up early."

Dalton's gaze drifted from Griffin's bare feet to the pajama bottoms he'd pulled on not five minutes ago before finally landing the cereal bowl on the table in front of the TV.

"I'm not up early," Dalton said drily. "It's nearly noon."

Nearly noon. Crap, he really had kept Sydney here way longer than he should have.

At the thought of Sydney, Griffin's gaze jerked to Dalton. Dalton was her boss. And—as far as they knew—Dalton didn't know that his brother and his assistant were sleeping together. Griffin didn't *think* that Dalton would mind, but hell, what did he know?

Feigning casual, Griffin leaned back to glance at the clock on the TV, then he scoffed. "It's 11:05 a.m. That's not nearly noon. And I just got back from the Middle East last night." Or was it Norway? Or Sweden? Crap.

He could only hope that because he didn't remember where he'd been, Dalton didn't, either. Sweden—or Norway—first for a meeting with Bergen Petro and then down to Yemen for another meeting. No more than a day for each of those trips. Then he'd taken two personal days for a long weekend down to Rwanda. No one from Cain Enterprises knew about Rwanda, but for him it had been the most important part of the trip.

He was secretly involved with an international aid organization called Hope2O. He'd been in Rwanda on behalf of Hope2O working to set up a water district there.

He traveled all over the world for his job. Of course, no one at Cain Enterprises knew he worked with Hope2O. The Cains were allowed to donate to certain charitable organizations, but the family members rarely came into contact with actual poverty. That kind of dirty work was beneath them. To the Cains, compassion was weakness. He didn't want anyone in the family—not even his brother—to know just how "weak" he was.

He walked back toward the sofa. "Hey, you want something to eat?"

"No, thank you." Dalton shut the door and followed him in.

"You want some coffee?" Griffin asked.

"Yes. Please."

Griffin headed for the coffeemaker. Though his condo boasted a gourmet kitchen, mostly it went unused. It was galley-style, open to the living room, outfitted in honed black granite and hickory cabinetry. His housekeeper kept it stocked with the essentials. Coffee, cereal, fresh milk, cold cuts and bread.

He punched a few buttons on his Saeco Espresso machine and let it work its magic. It made a single, perfect cup of coffee at a time, but it was damn slow.

Glancing out into the living room, he saw that Dalton had his elbows propped on his knees and his head in his hands. The guy looked whipped—which was something Griffin would never have thought possible.

Dalton had spent his entire life dancing to their father's tune, and until today, Griffin would have sworn he was fine with it.

Cooper was the opposite. He was Hollister's illegitimate son. He had almost nothing to do with the family at all.

The closest he himself had come to bowing to Hollister's will was accepting the job he currently held at Cain Enterprises. Because Cain Enterprises—a conglomerate of oil, land development and banking—operated mostly in the United States, there wasn't a lot of international marketing to do. It was a cush job. One that Hollister had created solely to lure Griffin to work for him. Hollister liked having his sons firmly under his control. Griffin liked the fat paycheck and the international travel. And he'd never once envied Dalton his position as heir to the family business.

Dalton was the company leader, Cooper was the family outsider and Griffin was just the guy who met everyone's lowest expectations. Until recently, everyone had been happy with that.

A little more than a week ago, Hollister—who was practically on his death bed—had called them all to his side. Apparently news of his impending demise had reached the outside world. Some lover he'd scorned long ago had sent him a nasty anonymous letter informing him that he had a daughter he'd never known. The woman who'd written the letter wanted him to die knowing he'd never find the girl.

A letter like that wasn't something Hollister would take lying down. So, he'd issued a challenge: whichever of his sons found the missing heiress would inherit all of Hollister's wealth. If no one found her, all his money and his share of Cain Enterprises would revert to the state.

Yeah, Griffin was pissed off that their father was trying to manipulate them all like this, but he wasn't particularly worried. The way he saw it, Dalton was highly motivated to find the heiress. He had the most to lose.

If Dalton's weary appearance now was any indication, the search for their long-lost sister was not going well.

As far as Griffin knew, Dalton had been working full-time

the past week to try to find the heiress. That was why he'd texted Sydney that he wouldn't be coming in today.

Ah, crap.

For the first time since Dalton showed up on his doorstep, Griffin considered how Sydney would react if she realized her boss was there. Though they'd been together for four months now, she'd insisted they keep their relationship a secret.

Especially from Dalton.

And here he was about to serve Dalton coffee. As if the machine could read his mind and make coffee, it emitted a series of seductive beeps to indicate Dalton's drink was ready.

Griffin came out of the kitchen and set a mug on the table in front of Dalton. "So," he said, clapping his hands together to hide his nerves. "What brings big brother D to my humble abode in the middle of the day?"

Jesus. Big brother D? Why had he said that? He sounded like a jerk. Thankfully, Dalton didn't seem to notice.

Dalton reached for the coffee. "I think the real question is why you're not at work in the middle of the day."

"Hey, jet lag's a bitch." Suddenly it occurred to him that as long as Sydney didn't come out of the bedroom, he had no reason to be nervous. It wasn't as if Dalton would wander in there on his own. Griffin purposefully stretched his mouth into a salacious grin, just to make sure Dalton knew he wouldn't be welcomed into the condo's private quarters.

As if on cue the shower cranked on in the other room.

"Oh," Dalton said, finally putting together what should have been perfectly obvious.

Griffin glanced at the bedroom door and then back at Dalton. This was the moment of truth.

Sydney took quick, efficient showers. She was efficient about everything except sex. Five minutes max. Another two to dress. Which meant in seven minutes or less, she'd wander out of his bedroom with damp hair, dressed in clothes that had spent the night crumpled on the floor.

Then, one of two things would happen. Dalton would be cool with it, and Sydney would realize their being together just wasn't that big a deal. Or she would freak. And that would mean the end of their relationship. No more enthusiastic welcomes home. No more warm body beside him in bed. No more mindblowing sex. He wasn't willing to give up any of those things.

When he noticed Dalton looking at him, he forced a smile. "Give me a second, will you?"

Dalton nodded. "Take your time."

Griffin crossed the bedroom, made a quick detour through the closet to change clothes and grabbed his keys before heading for the bathroom. Sydney had the hot water cranked all the way up, and steam churned out of the glass-brick shower. The wavy glass distorted the killer curves she normally kept hidden beneath conservative clothes. She wasn't the kind of woman who showed off her body, but she didn't seem to mind being naked, either. He loved watching her shower. Unfortunately, this time it couldn't end with them going back to bed.

Still he couldn't resist propping his shoulder against the doorway of the walk-in shower and enjoying the open sensuality of her movements and the heavy, relaxed, deep breaths she took as she scraped her nails over her scalp. She gave her hair a final rinse and turned off the faucet, reaching for a towel.

As she dabbed the towel over her face, she realized he was watching, and her lips tipped upward in a smile. "Stop it. You know I have to get to work."

"I know."

She wrapped the towel around her chest, tucking the corner in to secure it, and then grabbed a second towel off the rack before edging past him into the bathroom proper.

Even though her smile was relaxed and her words teasing, there was something guarded in her expression. But maybe that was to be expected. She'd made it clear when they first got involved that this was a just-sex kind of relationship. Nothing more. Which was perfect because he was a nothing-more kinda guy.

Still, leaving before his girl even got out of the shower was a little harsh, even for a nothing-more kinda guy.

She bent over at the waist to wrap her shoulder-length auburn hair into one of those turban things only women seemed to be able to manage, then straightened, frowning. "What's up?"

He fished a house key out of his pocket and set it on the bathroom counter beside the contact case and tiny toiletry bag she carried in her purse. "I have to head out. Lock up when you leave?"

Her frown deepened. "Wait. I don't want… I mean, why…"

He didn't give her more time to protest but gave her a quick peck on the lips. "Don't worry. You can give it back to me the next time you see me. Stay as long as you want. There are muffins or you can find something in fridge. Marcella always leaves stuff like that."

"But…" she tried to protest again.

He pretended to misunderstand. There was no point in her getting upset before he knew what Dalton wanted. "Text me later tonight and let me know what your plans are."

She caught up with him just shy of the bedroom door and stopped him with a hand to the arm and an unwavering stare. "What's going on?"

Her stare did him in. Something about her warm brown eyes made it impossible for him to lie to her. "Dalton stopped by. We're going to lunch."

"Dalton? Dalton, my boss?"

He grinned, partly hoping to disarm her and partly because her shock was amusing. "You know any other Daltons?"

"Do you think he's here because he knows about us?"

"No," he said, perfectly honestly. "I think he's here because he's up to his neck in this crap our dad has dumped on him. He may be your boss, but he's also my brother." He dropped another kiss on her mouth. "Don't worry, he'll never know you were here. I'll take care of it."

Then, because he just couldn't resist, he gave her ass a squeeze beneath the towel before leaving the room. She had a great ass. He only hoped that Dalton showing up today hadn't spooked her so badly he never saw it again.

She was going to kill Griffin. What the hell did he mean, *he'd take care of it?* Was he going to take care of it like he took care of that pothos ivy that had been slowly dying in his living room? Or like he took care of... Well, crap, she couldn't even be properly indignant because she couldn't very well rant against his lax attitude toward taking care of things because as far as she knew, he had absolutely no responsibilities in life other than keeping that damn potted plant alive. And he appeared to be failing at that.

For several stunned minutes, Sydney stood there beside the door, listening to the murmur of voices from the other side. She could distinguish none of the words and barely registered the tone. But she tried because somehow it seemed deathly important that she hear every nuance of their conversation.

Which was ridiculous because this probably had nothing to do with her. Dalton had a lot on his plate right now. She knew that better than anyone. She was one of the few people with whom Dalton could even discuss the missing heiress. For the previous week, he'd asked her to hand her normal workload off to someone else on the support staff so that she could devote her time to doing legwork in the search.

She and Griffin had never discussed the missing heiress, but it made perfect sense he'd be worried about it. His livelihood was also at stake. The entire company was at risk. Her job, too, now that she thought about it.

So of course Dalton would need to talk to Griffin. That made perfect sense. Totally, completely logical.

Still, she kept her ear pressed to the door until she heard Dalton and Griffin leaving the apartment. After that, she dressed quickly, barely giving herself time to towel dry her hair and apply a quick, but necessary, coat of mascara before grabbing her purse on her way out. But she stopped short with her hand on the front door of Griffin's apartment.

Crap. The key.

Going back to the bathroom her steps were slower. The key to Griffin's condo sat on the marble countertop, the brass gleaming against the black-veined white marble. She stared at it for a long minute.

"Ugh. Stop being such a wimp. It's just a key."

She grabbed it and stalked to the front door, carefully locking the door before dropping the key into the change pocket of her wallet as she walked down the hall to the elevator. She pointedly did not put it on her key chain. It wasn't that kind of key. She and Griffin didn't have that kind of relationship.

No, they had a very casual, sex-only kind of thing. A no-key-exchange kind of relationship.

She punched the down button with a tad more force than was necessary. She was just being responsible. Like when they'd first started sleeping together and he'd presented her with the test results of his most recent physical, proof that he was drug and disease free. At first, she felt weird about it. Like it was wrong having that kind of information about someone she barely knew—even someone she was sleeping with. Sure, the information was nominally about sex. But there was other information in there, too. She now knew his cholesterol number and that his last tetanus shot was in 2010—from the time he'd gotten snagged with a hook while deep-sea fishing, she'd later learned.

But she hadn't wanted to know about the tetanus shot any more than she'd wanted to know the origin of the tiny scar on the side of his neck. Any more than she'd wanted a key to his apartment.

Which was why, when she got out to her car, she sat there for several minutes, sucking in deep, panic-reducing breaths.

What was she doing?

When was she going to stop fooling herself?

Sex with Griffin was a bad idea. Very bad.

When they'd first started sleeping together, it hadn't seemed like a bad idea. It hadn't even seemed like an idea. More like… an accident. Like when she'd accidently adopted her cat, Grommet. She'd come home to find the poor, malnourished kitten huddled on her front porch to stay out of the rain. She couldn't just leave the pathetic tabby there, so she brought him inside. But he was wormy and sick and even had to have part of his tail amputated. The vet had recommended putting him down instead of taking him to the shelter. A thousand dollars plus weekly allergy shots later and she was the proud owner of the ugliest cat on earth.

Sleeping with Griffin was kind of like that.

Except not at all. Because Griffin wasn't pathetic and he wasn't tame and she most definitely was not allergic to him.

But when it came to adopting Grommet, she hadn't meant to keep him. It was supposed to be just for one night. That's what she'd told herself about Griffin, too.

Last summer, in the middle of a record heat wave, fresh on the heels of an awful breakup with her fiancé, Brady, she'd slept with Griffin.

It was Brady's fault, really. Nine months before their wedding—a date it had taken him two years to agree upon — he'd reconnected with his high school girlfriend on Facebook. He'd apologized profusely for breaking up with Sydney. But how could she feel anything past the burning indignation of finding out the guy she'd been with for six years was in love with another woman? So much in love that he quit his job and moved halfway across the country to be with her, when he hadn't even wanted to sell his condo to move into Sydney's house once they were engaged.

She'd wanted to punch him. It was the first and last time in her twenty-seven years of life that she wanted to do physical violence to another human being.

Instead, she'd calmly emptied the single drawer he'd allotted her in his condo and done the same for the few items he kept at her house. The whole exchange had required only two empty cardboard boxes. She hadn't even had to take a day off work. And she'd told herself she was fine. Fine.

She'd continued being fine right up until the point she'd stumbled onto a Facebook post about Brady's wedding through a mutual friend. Then, all of a sudden, she hadn't been fine anymore. Less than thirty-six hours after Brady married another woman, she did the unthinkable. When she'd run into Griffin Cain in the coffee shop half a block from Cain Enterprises, she'd typed her number into his cell phone. Yes, he'd been flirting with her since she'd hired on at Cain Enterprises. He flirted with everyone. She'd never dreamed she'd be one of his conquests.

Griffin was handsome and charming. With his shaggy, dark-blond hair and ocean blue eyes, he looked better suited to professional surfing than international business. His crooked smile and sexy dimples had all the women in the office swooning.

Still, she'd been sure she'd be able to resist him, despite all the times he wandered into Dalton's office and propped his hip on the corner of her desk to flirt with her while he waited for Dalton to come to or from some meeting. Despite the way he'd occasionally bring her gourmet coffee and drop it off at her desk with a salacious wink as he headed for Dalton's office. Despite all that, she knew she could resist him because she knew he treated all the women in the office that way.

And she hated that kind of crap. And she hated people who coasted by on their good looks almost as much as she hated people who got by on their family name. Griffin was the triple-whammy of things she despised in the business world.

Of all the men she knew, he was the guy she was least likely to get romantically involved with. Which was precisely what made him appealing to her after Brady dumped her. She'd been emotionally bruised and battered. When she ran into him that morning at the coffee shop, when he turned on that classic Griffin Cain charm, she did the unthinkable. She decided to sow her own wild oats.

She hadn't really believed she had any wild oats in her. They certainly had never floated to the surface of her psyche before. But Griffin had somehow gotten the damn things to sprout.

The one night she'd planned on allowing herself with Griffin had turned into a weekend. And then into a month. And then into four.

The brief sexual encounter was no longer brief. She'd managed to keep it purely sexual, but it was no longer uncomplicated. A mere call from him had her leaving her house in the middle of the night for a rendezvous. She'd stayed over at his place. Showered in his shower. Missed a morning of work. And now she had a key to his frickin' condo.

It was time to stop fooling herself. She wasn't just having sex with Griffin. She was acting like an addict. And it was time to go cold turkey.

Two

Griffin took a sip of his coffee, looking from the file in front of him to Dalton sitting across the table. He'd coaxed Dalton out of his condo and down the block to his favorite little Argentinean café. Once their coffee had arrived, Dalton had pushed a file folder across the table to him. And then he'd dropped a bomb.

"What do you mean, you're done?" Griffin asked.

"Done." Dalton leaned back against the booth's red vinyl upholstery.

"Like, done? Like, you're not searching for her anymore?"

"Exactly."

"What, you want me to take over?" Hollister expected them to search for the heir separately. But he hadn't expressly ordered them not to work together. "I've got a trip scheduled for next week, but after that—"

"I'm done." Dalton leaned forward. "I'm not looking for her anymore. I'm not jumping through any more of Hollister's damn hoops. I'm out."

"Fine. You need me to handle this, I'll handle it. You know how I feel about Hollister's games. I'll pass on to you whatever I find."

"When I say I'm out, I mean I'm out for good. I'm not searching for the Cain heiress. I don't want Hollister's damn prize. I'm stepping down as CEO. I'm passing the torch to you."

"To me?" Griffin dropped the folder like it had caught fire. "I don't want Cain Enterprises."

"Neither do I."

"Of course you do. This is what you've wanted your whole life. Every—"

"Right. Everything I've ever done has been for Cain and what has it got me? Nothing. So this morning I submitted my resignation."

"You what?" Griffin recoiled from Dalton's words.

"I resigned," Dalton said simply. "I recommended the board name you interim CEO. I can't guarantee they will, but I talked to Hewitt, Sands and Schield personally. I think they'll be able to sway the others. Now—"

"You quit?"

"I resigned." Dalton looked like he might bust out laughing. "Try to keep up."

"You can't quit." Great. His brother finally developed a sense of humor and it turned out to be sick and twisted. "Cain Enterprises needs you. More than ever with Hollister sick."

"I agree. Cain Enterprises needs a strong leader. But you can be that leader just as easily as I can."

And that's where Dalton was dead wrong.

Dalton had been preparing for this job his whole life. Griffin, however, had spent his whole life waiting to take his inheritance and get out of the business. "Even if I wanted to, I'm not prepared to be the CEO. I don't—"

"My assistant knows everything that goes on in the office. If there's anything you don't know, she can bring you up to speed. I know you haven't worked much with Sydney in the past, but she's top-notch. She'll take good care of you."

Shock must have made his esophagus seize because the sip of coffee Griffin had just taken went straight into his lungs, damn near choking him.

"I don't… You can't…" Griffin shook his head. Dalton was stepping down? And he was saying that Sydney would take care of him? The irony was just too much. For years he'd been phoning it in for his job at Cain Enterprises. Just biding his time until he could walk away free and clear. He'd stayed with the company out of duty and because if Hollister knew where his interests really lay, he'd be cut off without a dime. And now, after all this time, Dalton wasn't just giving him more responsibility, he was handing him the entire damn company. "What the hell brought this on? And what on earth are you going to do if you're not the leader of Cain Enterprises?"

"I'm going to win the heart of the woman I love."

Okay. So Dalton had officially gone crazy.

"You're what?" He sat back, waving aside his question. "Never mind," he said darkly. "I know who's to blame for this. Laney."

Dalton's mouth curved into a sappy smile. "Yeah. Laney."

Griffin muttered a curse. "You're throwing away everything for a woman?"

"Laney's not just—"

"Yeah. I'm sure. Laney's delightful. Frickin' wonderful." He leaned forward and tapped the center of the table to emphasize his point. "I've always liked Laney. And even when we were kids I saw that she was special to you. So if you want to be with her, then be with her. But don't throw away everything you've worked for all your life over it."

Dalton shot him a look that was somewhere between annoyed and amused. "I never thought I'd say this, but you sound remarkably like our father."

"God, I hope not." Griffin leaned back and blew out a frustrated sigh. "It's not that I don't want you to be happy, it's just that…"

He had a lot on his plate right now. In the next month alone, he had two trips to Guatemala planned and one more to Africa. The project in Rwanda was at a critical stage and it was the first in that country. On Griffin's most recent visit, he'd made inroads to get the project financed by a local bank, but if he didn't get back down there soon, it might all fall through. The simple truth was, he didn't have time to be CEO.

Griffin set down his coffee cup to see Dalton watching him with that slightly dazed look people in love usually wore. Griffin wanted to leap across the table and strangle some sense into his brother. "Did it ever occur to you that I might have better things to do?"

For nearly a full minute Dalton just stared at him. Then Dalton burst out laughing, and didn't speak for another minute until he stopped. "Better things. Nice one."

Griffin unclenched his jaw. "I'm serious. I just happen to be busy right now."

Dalton took a lazy sip of coffee and shrugged. "There's nothing you do as VP of International Marketing that can't be done by someone else."

That was probably true. His job at Cain required very little. He liked it that way because it left his hours free for his work with Hope2O. And the occasional dalliance with a beautiful woman…such as Sydney.

But Dalton wasn't buying his busy schedule as an excuse, so Griffin changed tactics. "Look, you don't really want to step down at CEO. It's who you are. You're the guy who takes care of business. You're the guy who's going to find this missing heiress."

And until this moment, Griffin had believed that. He hadn't had even a shadow of a doubt that Dalton would find the heiress and, as a result, win the entire Cain fortune as his prize. But he knew his brother. Dalton was fair to a fault. He wouldn't take the money and run. Once Dalton had secured the Cain fortune, he would carefully divide it up among the three—or four—of them. However, if Dalton backed out of things now, then they were all screwed, Griffin included.

Dalton smiled. "Well, it's time for you to step up and become that guy because I'm not him anymore."

The problem was, he wasn't that guy, either. Ever since he was a kid he'd been hiding his true nature from his family.

He was—and this was a direct quote from Hollister—a pansy-assed do-gooder with a heart of gold. That was a hell of an insult to hear at age nine, especially from the father he worshipped like a god.

So—since he was nine—Griffin had been hiding who he was, had been hiding the fact that he cared about the quality of life of other people in the world. Even the people who didn't contribute to Cain Enterprise's bottom line. And he would continue to hide it.

The bleeding-heart liberal born into a Texas oil family. The ugly duckling had nothing on him.

Before now, all he had to do was keep his head down and try to blend in. Now, Dalton expected him to take over. He was going to do the only thing left to do. He would find the heiress. If he controlled his father's fortune, he could walk away from the day-to-day running of the company. He could devote himself full-time to Hope2O or anything else that struck his fancy. In short, he could do whatever the hell he wanted.

By the time Sydney arrived at the office, she'd managed to calm herself down enough to pass for normal. Now more than ever, she wanted to continue impressing Dalton with her competence and trustworthiness.

If her experience with Brady had taught her anything, it was that she had to depend on herself. When it came down to it, she was alone in the world. She had herself and whatever stability her job provided. That was it. She couldn't afford to let herself get distracted by a man again.

Certainly not one of the Cains.

She spent the afternoon at her desk, answering what email of Dalton's she could, and then catching up on the work she'd missed that morning.

It killed her knowing that Dalton and Griffin were out together at lunch, even if she never came up in their conversation. It was a bad omen, like a comet flitting across the sky to herald the impending arrival of a horrible natural disaster.

The two halves of her world were on a collision course and she wasn't sure how to brace herself for impact.

So she should have been relieved when two o'clock rolled around and the door to the office finally creaked open. Hoping Dalton had decided to come in after all, Sydney leaped to her feet, ready to greet her errant boss.

But it wasn't Dalton who walked into the room. It was Griffin.

Her heart thudded and she had to fight the sudden and completely irrational urge to bolt. There were three doors in her office. One led to Dalton's office, another to the conference room. Griffin now blocked the door into the hall, but she could easily flee through the conference room. And, yeah, she knew how ridiculous it was that she wanted to.

But the simple truth was, Griffin wasn't supposed to be part of her work life. He was the stuff of fantasies, and fantasies should have the common courtesy to stay out of the workplace.

As if Griffin knew exactly what was going on in her head, he flashed her a wry smile. He was carrying a thick manila folder and he looked like he'd spent considerable time running his hands through his hair. "Hey."

"Hi." Then she cringed at how breathless she sounded. *Hi* seemed too informal. Too reminiscent of the way she'd greeted him last night when she'd thrown herself into his arms. She tried again, aiming for cool professionalism. "I mean, hello. Can I do something for you?"

He could clearly tell she was flustered because his smile widened. This was just like him. He loved to tease her.

But then his smile faltered as he reached back to close the door to the office. "Did you talk to Dalton before I showed up?"

"No." Something about the way he held himself made her nervous. Like maybe this was more than him just messing with her. "What? Is something wrong?"

"Not wrong exactly…. Have you checked your email?"

"I did when I first got in, but that was a couple of hours ago." Most of the emails that needed her attention came through Dalton's in-box, so she didn't check her own email nearly as often.

"You should check again." He flash a wry smile as he said it, but he looked pained rather than amused—like the one man on the *Titanic* who knew how few lifeboats there were.

Without another word, she pulled up her email on her computer. Ten new emails since she'd last checked. She opened only the one from Dalton. She had to read it twice. And then read it again just to be sure.

Then her eyes found Griffin. "He's resigning?" Then her gaze dropped back to the email and she read it again, sure she'd misread it. *Sure* she had. "He can't resign! This is crazy." Then she looked back at Griffin. "Did you know he was going to do this?"

"Not until lunch."

"He can't resign," she repeated, this time more numbly.

Of course, he could do whatever he wanted. It wasn't like he was legally obligated to come to work. He wasn't a prisoner. But still…Dalton was completely devoted to Cain Enterprises. In the eight months she'd worked with him, he'd worked eighteen-hour days. Weekends. Holidays. Cain Enterprises was his entire life.

"Maybe he's earned it," she said, barely aware she was speaking aloud. And then her eyes saw the tiny detail that they'd glossed over until now. "Wait a second. It says he's recommending you for the position of interim CEO."

"Yeah, that's what he said."

"And that he wants me to retain my current position. So that I can fill you in."

"Yeah. He assured me he was leaving me in good hands."

Her gaze sought his. "He's leaving you in my hands?"

Griffin grinned. "Yeah. Ironic, isn't it?"

Feeling suddenly jittery, she shot to her feet. "No, it's not ironic! It's…" But she couldn't think of the word for what it was.

Unthinkable.

Disastrous.

Humiliating.

Griffin held out a hand as if to ward off her growing panic. "Hey, calm down. This is no big deal."

"No big deal?" Her voice came out a little squeaky and high-pitched. "My boss—the leader of this company—just quit and left me in charge."

"Technically, he left me in charge."

"Oh, really? And what exactly do you know about the day-to-day running of the business?"

"Not much because—"

"Exactly. You don't know much because you're always jaunting off to some exotic location to do 'business.'" She put the bunny ears around the word. But then she immediately felt like a bitch. She was acting horribly. It was just that she didn't like change and she hated having the rug pulled out from under her. She was stressed and scared and she was taking it out on Griffin.

She dropped back into her chair and ran a hand over her face. "I'm sorry. That was…"

"Uncalled for?" he offered helpfully.

"I was going to say really bitchy." She softened her words

with a smile. "I'm sorry. I'm freaking out, but I shouldn't take it out on you."

Griffin crossed over and sat on the corner of her desk, stretching his legs out in front of him. "Hey, it's okay. You're nervous. But don't worry. We'll work it out."

"How're we supposed to work it out? Dalton has left a billion-dollar company in the hands of an overpaid psych major and a playboy." She glanced up at him quickly. "No offense."

"None taken."

"Neither of us is prepared to run this company." But then she broke off and studied Griffin. Really looked at him. Oh, sure. She looked at him all the time. He was her lover. They spent an increasing amount of their spare time together. She'd gone from the point of being in awe of his sheer masculine beauty to being comfortable with his easy grin and smiling eyes. But today she looked at him through a different lens. Today she looked at him as a potential leader.

He'd been raised with wealth and privilege beyond her imagining. He was the second son in a powerful and influential family. But there was the rub. Second son.

She knew from her dealings with Dalton and the other Cains—and from gossip around the office—that the family largely considered Griffin something of a slacker and screwup. Oh, Dalton himself never said that. But everyone knew Griffin had a cushy job. The company paid him insane amounts of money to travel and be charming.

For the first time, she wondered if the cushy job was really the one he wanted.

Cocking her head to the side, taking in his unexpectedly serious expression, she said, "You haven't had a lot of choice before now. You don't want to be CEO, do you?"

Because for all she knew, maybe he did. They never talked about work. Or family, for that matter. Or personal ambitions. Maybe he'd always wanted to be CEO but being Dalton's younger brother had held him back.

Then his face spilt into a grin and he laughed. "Me? CEO?" He shook his head. "No. I've never wanted to be CEO."

She bit down on her lip. "So what is it you do want to do?"

"I want to find the missing heiress. If I do that, all of these problems go away." His blue eyes gleamed with a satisfaction she wasn't used to seeing from him outside of bed.

Which was good—it was nice to see him caring about something, even if it was just finding a way to shirk his familial responsibility. But at the same time, it made what she had to say so much harder.

"You know that isn't actually going to happen, right? Your father has slept with dozens of women. Hundreds. All over the world. Your half sister could be anywhere."

"Not necessarily. My dad's usually pretty careful about the whole birth control thing, so if I operate under the assumption that the woman who got pregnant is someone he was in a relationship with—"

"Wait a minute. That in itself is a huge leap. How do you know your dad was a stickler for birth control?" Even as the question flew out of her mouth, she couldn't believe she was asking it. The absolute last thing she wanted to think about was Griffin's father's sexual habits.

"Where do you think I got my paranoia?" His lips twisted in a faint smile that somehow wasn't. It wasn't an expression she was used to seeing from him. "He drove it into me at an early age."

"And this is going to help how? I mean, you have an illegitimate brother, so obviously he did get a woman pregnant."

"Exactly. But probably not the first time—he's way too much of a control freak to let that happen. I think he'd actually have to be in the middle of an affair with a woman before he ever got sloppy enough to risk her getting pregnant. Which means—"

"Which means the field of hundreds just got narrowed down

to seventy or eighty?" Which still wasn't great odds, but she had to admit it was better than what she'd originally feared.

"More like fifteen or twenty. The old bastard's pretty damn careful about who he lets close to him." His voice was carefully devoid of emotion, but it made her hurt for him in a way she'd never expected to.

After all, she was the orphan in this equation, the one who had grown up with nothing as she was bounced from foster home to foster home. He was the golden boy, the glib son of a billionaire who had never expected anything from him. So why then did she suddenly feel sorry for him?

Not that she could let him see that. Griffin didn't do pity, self or otherwise.

"So you want to find your sister." She dragged herself back to the conversation at hand. "And then what? Saddle her with the CEO job?"

He sighed. "You need vision, Sydney. Work with me here. I find Hollister's missing daughter, I get the money and Dalton is left with nothing. Which isn't going to sit real well with him, no matter what he says. So when I sweep in and offer him a fat CEO salary plus major stock options in the company, he's going to jump at it. Especially if he doesn't have to deal with Dad's BS. I'll put him in charge, let him run things the way he wants to." He dusted his hands together like it was a fait accompli. "Everybody wins."

"It's not always about winning."

"Don't kid yourself, Sydney. It's always about winning. It's only the stakes and the game that change."

Which summed up all the reasons she couldn't be with him anymore. When there was nothing on the line, it was easy to spend time with him and not care about philosophical differences or his lifestyle or the fact that everything really was a game to him.

But now that he was her boss, she couldn't afford to wear those blinders anymore. She couldn't afford to let a few minutes'—okay, a few hours'—satisfaction get in the way of her job. She liked her job, needed her job for the money and the sense of self it gave her. There was no way she was going to become one of those women who slept with the boss, her survival dependent on the whims of a man she had no hope of holding on to.

No, a few orgasms—earth-shattering or not—were not worth playing Russian roulette with her whole life.

"You really think this is going to work?" she asked Griffin.

"It's absolutely going to work. Plus, the good news is Dalton is handing over all his research so far and he thinks he has a lead. So we're golden." He winked at her. "Trust me."

As if. She took a deep breath, blew it out slowly and tried to ignore the fact that she suddenly felt like she was making a deal with the devil. "Fine. I'll help you find your sister. But that's it."

"What do you mean, that's it? That's all I need."

"I mean, if we're going to be working together, if you're going to be my boss, this thing between us has to end. No sex, no candlelit dinners, no late-night phone calls. We—" she waved her finger back and forth between them "—are officially over."

For long seconds, Griffin stared at her like he couldn't quite comprehend what she was saying. Then he did the most amazing thing. He threw back his head and laughed. And laughed. And laughed.

Three

It was cute really, how annoyed she looked.

She set her jaw as bright pink flushed her cheeks. "I'm not joking."

He tried to clamp down on his laughter. He really did. "*I'm* not joking."

"Then stop laughing." As if to give herself a better angle from which to glare at him, she pushed to her feet.

But from his point of view, it only brought her closer. She'd been sitting not far from him but still out of reach. Now he was easily able to lasso her arm and pull her toward him so she stood between his outstretched legs.

"I'm serious," she insisted, but there was no force to her words and—as if she could read his mind—her gaze dropped briefly to his mouth.

"I know you are. That's what makes it cute." He widened his stance and pulled her close enough so that she was pressed against the vee of his legs, the juncture of her thighs against the hard length of his erection.

It felt so good having her there, so right. He inhaled sharply and was immediately hit with the scent of her. Sydney never wore perfume, but she favored a shampoo that smelled like coconut and lime. He was used to the smell of her hair, the way it mixed with the naturally sweet smell of her own skin and made him think of eating pancakes in bed on a perfect, lazy Saturday morning. But today she'd showered at his place and instead of her normal tropical, fruity smell, when he inhaled, he got a hit of Sydney layered under the smell of his own soap. Maybe it shouldn't have been sexy, but it was. He felt it like a punch in the gut. She'd been in his shower mere hours ago. The smell of her only reinforced every instinct he had. She was *his*. Whether she knew it or not, she belonged to him.

Which made her edict that they stop sleeping together all the more funny.

He gave in to the urge to slip his hand along her jaw and to pull her closer.

Her mouth parted and she sucked in a quick breath. Anticipation. But instead of kissing her, he buried his nose in the hair right behind her ear and drew in a deep breath, just taking in the scent of her because he wanted to remember forever how she smelled in that instant. To burn it into his memory.

He felt a little shudder go through her and then he couldn't resist running a trail of kisses up under her ear and across her cheek to her mouth. Then his lips were moving over hers in a soul-searing kiss. The kind that almost ended up with him ripping her clothes off and devouring her until she came apart in his arms.

Unfortunately, he didn't think sex with his assistant would be a very efficient way to spend his first afternoon as CEO. Besides, even with the door closed, there was always the risk they'd be interrupted.

It was a struggle, but he mustered enough restraint to lift his mouth from hers and nudge her hips away from his before he lost all control. For a long moment she just stood there, face tilted up, lips moistened and parted, like she was so dazed she hadn't even realized he was no longer kissing her.

He smiled again, purposefully making light of the irresistible pull she held over him. "Well, then, you let me know how that goes for you."

She blinked. "How what goes?"

"That whole not sleeping together thing you have planned."

The space between her eyebrows furrowed in confusion. Then she backed up a step and jerked her hands away from his hips. "Well, this was hardly a fair test."

"Right, sweetheart." He bopped the tip of her nose with his finger. "Let me know if you devise a fairer test than that. Meanwhile, I'll be in my new office."

He loved seeing her shocked expression as he sauntered into the office that used to be Dalton's and shut the door behind him.

Once he was alone in the room, however, he blew out a long, slow breath.

When it came to running Cain Enterprises, he wasn't nearly as confident as he'd let Sydney believe. He wasn't worried about the day-to-day stuff, but the prospect of dealing with the board damn near had him breaking out in a cold sweat.

The board of directors that Hollister had amassed for Cain Enterprises was a bunch of vultures. If they knew what had happened in the past couple of weeks, they'd be circling for sure. First, Hollister—who had never displayed any sign of weakness to his business opponents—had made a very irrational decision when he'd sent his sons on this quest. The whole company hung in the balance as a result.

And now that Dalton had resigned, from the outside, it had to look like they'd all lost their minds. The board members weren't fools. If they knew how unstable things really were, they'd start swooping down to peck out bits of flesh from what remained of his inheritance.

Right now, the company needed strong leadership more

than anything. The company needed someone who could command respect. Unfortunately, Griffin knew he wasn't that man.

He was all too aware of his limitations as a leader. He lacked his father's cutthroat business tactics and his brother's stolid determination. Perhaps even more importantly, he had no interest in running Cain Enterprises.

At the moment he had two interests: completing his work for Hope2O and the very tempting new assistant that came along with the CEO job. Apparently, being CEO was going to interfere with both of those pursuits. Which was why he had to get this yoke off his neck so he could get back to his real life. He had to find this damn missing heiress.

He dropped into the chair. Testing the springiness of the seat, he rocked back but there was very little give. Damn, even Dalton's chair felt stiff and unyielding, much like his brother was.

Griffin glanced down and saw that the chair was actually the same model as the one in his office down the hall. Thanks to an array of knobs and levers, he could easily adjust it to suit his taste. Instead, he rolled the chair closer to the desk, flipped open the file Dalton had given him and started going over the notes Dalton and Laney had made. He left the chair exactly as it was. He wouldn't be sitting in it long enough to bother changing it.

Sydney stared at the closed door to Dalton's office, trying to squelch the sinking feeling in her gut. Except it wasn't the door to Dalton's office anymore. It was the door to Griffin's office now. This was not good.

Oh, this was *so* not good.

Feigning a calm she didn't feel, she turned back toward the computer at her workstation and mindlessly pulled up her email. If someone came into the office, she wanted it to look like she was busy. And competent. And not sitting here fantasizing about her boss.

Her boss.

Ugh.

She was absolutely not going to be that woman.

Her mother had been that kind of woman. The kind who casually slept with men to get favors from them. As far as she knew, her mother had never strayed into actual prostitution. She'd traded sex for rent, or car care or so her boss would overlook the fact that she was late for the seventeenth time that month. Even if that wasn't real prostitution, it had cast a pall over Sydney's childhood. Poverty, drug use and bad decision-making had dominated her life until she'd been taken away from her mother at the age of six. From there, she'd bounced from foster home to foster home for years before finally settling in at Molly Stanhope's house when she was eleven.

Molly's house had been a haven for the last seven years she was in the foster care system. In fact, Molly was still the closest thing she had to a mother. It was Molly who had been her moral compass since then. It was Molly who would not approve of Sydney sleeping with her boss.

Well, who was she kidding? It's not like Molly would have gushed with approval over Sydney sleeping with Griffin Cain in the first place.

Sleeping with her boss compromised her position in the company. It meant he wouldn't respect her. Her coworkers wouldn't respect her and, worst of all, it destroyed her job security. It threatened not just her heart, but her livelihood.

As far as Sydney was concerned that sort of carelessness was a luxury she couldn't afford. As a product of the foster care system, she had no one to depend on but herself. If the unthinkable happened and she lost her job, she was on her own. There were no loving parents for her to rush back to. There was no safety net. Hell, she didn't even have a kindly uncle who could lend her a couple hundred bucks if she needed it. All she had was her cat, Grommet. And even he was kind of grouchy. If she was lucky, he might deign to curl up on her lap if she bumped the air-conditioning up.

She was completely on her own.

If she lost her job, she could lose her savings. Her house. Even her foster-siblings would feel it, because she'd been helping a couple of them with college tuition.

Just to give herself the kick in the ass she needed, she dug through her purse for her cell phone and scrolled through their numbers. Five of them had sort of stuck together because they'd all been at Molly's at about the same time. She passed over Marco and George. They were both good guys if she needed advice on car care or barbecue, but they'd be useless at this sort of thing. Jen was studying abroad this semester and who knew what time it was in Spain. So Sydney pulled up Tasha's number.

Tasha answered on the third ring. "Hey, what's up?"

"Nothing." Sydney aimed for a breezy tone but landed somewhere near strained. "Just thought I'd call and see how you're doing."

There was a pause of obviously stunned silence. "On a work day? Are you sick?"

"No. Of course not. I'm fine. What, I can't call you just to check in?"

"On a work day?" Suspicion strained Tasha's voice. "I mean, sure, I guess you can. You just never have in the past. Oh, my God, were you fired?"

"No! I mean…" Sydney forced a chuckle. "Calm down. Nothing's wrong. Dalton's not in today, that's all."

Thank goodness she had a handy excuse because apparently Tasha saw right through all her half-truths.

"I just…" Sydney fought the sudden urge to spill the beans. To tell Tasha everything. To share her burdens. Get a second opinion. The problem was, people usually came to her for help, not the other way around. So instead, she asked, "How're your finals going?"

And thankfully Tasha let herself be distracted.

"Ugh. Just awful. Political Theory is knocking me for a loop."

"I thought you liked that one."

And distracting Tasha was as easy as that. Fifteen minutes of griping later, Sydney was wrapping up the conversation when Tasha inadvertently delivered the wakeup call Sydney needed.

"I just can't wait for this semester to be over so I can blow off a little steam."

"Just don't do anything too crazy, okay?" Sydney said, that familiar need to protect her sister rising up inside her.

"Don't worry, I won't do anything you wouldn't do."

Tasha's words were like a stab in the gut. If that was the barometer, then Tasha could be in serious trouble.

"Just be safe."

Tasha chuckled. "I know the drill."

"Yeah, I know you do."

"Hey, are you sure you're okay?" Tasha asked her out of the blue.

"Yeah. Great."

"Because you just missed an opportunity to remind me to call you if I needed to."

"Oh. Sorry. You know you can always call. Anytime, day or night."

But of course, Tasha never did call. Like Sydney, Tasha was über-responsible, superpredictable and determined to make a better life for herself than the one fate had handed her. She was also the last of Molly's foster kids Sydney felt really close to. And soon Tasha would graduate from college, get a job and maybe move away. Maybe she wouldn't need Sydney anymore.

Sydney didn't like to admit it to herself, but she still needed Tasha. She still needed to be needed.

She'd known this day was coming. She'd even thought she'd been prepared, back before her boss up and quit, back when her job was stable and her life still made sense. Now? Well, in the past few hours her life had unraveled at an alarming rate. But Griffin was right: panicking wouldn't help anything. What she needed was a plan. Part one: stay out of Griffin's bed. At least until this was all over with. Part two: find the missing heiress.

Of course, both of those things were going to be harder than they sounded. She'd been helping Dalton look for the missing heiress before he'd gone off the deep end. She'd already scoured hospital records and county court records. So far, she'd found diddly.

And then there was the matter of Griffin. If she had any resistance against him at all, she wouldn't be in this mess in the first place.

She didn't need a plan. She needed a miracle.

Four

Miracle or no, she wasn't going to sit around here just waiting for…for what? For Griffin to come out of the office and pounce on her?

She needed a little emotional distance. A way to remind herself that Cain Enterprise's new CEO was now her boss. Not her lover. A way to reestablish the professional footing of the boss/executive assistant relationship.

Her very first boss, for example, had always insisted she call him sir or Mr. Thornton. And she'd never once made out with him at her desk. Never mind that Mr. Thornton was seventy-four, humpbacked and mean-spirited. Still, maybe there was something to this formal professionalism.

Maybe if she just focused on the job, she'd be able to push aside her personal desires. So she did the only thing she knew how to do in a situation like this. She did her job.

She started with the basics. She contacted Marion, Griffin's former assistant, and had her send over his schedule. Marion clearly hadn't heard anything yet from Griffin because she seemed to think the request came from Dalton.

After that, Sydney generated a short action list. Things that had to get done to ease this transition. When Dalton came back, she wanted him to be impressed as hell by how smoothly everything had run in his absence.

She sent everything over to her iPad and marched to the office door, knocking only briefly before letting herself in.

She found Griffin sitting behind Dalton's desk, a file open on the blotter in front of him. He didn't look up when she walked in. His hair—which always looked a little scruffy—was even more disheveled than usual. He held a pencil in his hand, tapping the eraser end against the desk at a frenetic pace. His expression was a mask of intensity and she felt a little shiver go through her. Despite his blasé attitude, he took this very seriously.

Did she know him at all? Sure, she knew many things about him. Like that he had a scar on his neck and that he didn't like chocolate but would eat anything with caramel. And that he watched the *Star Wars* trilogy every year on Christmas. But was knowing all of that stuff the same as really knowing him?

Confused, she automatically took a step backward, intending to sneak out and then knock, but his head snapped up and he saw her standing there, clutching her notes and her iPad in front of her. She was struck again by his expression. By the fierceness of it.

Then his countenance cleared, a smile slipped back onto his lips and he looked like himself again—all easy, laid-back charm. Nevertheless, she was left with the feeling that perhaps the Griffin she was used to seeing was the mask and the intensely focused Griffin was the real man. God, that was an unsettling thought.

"You need something?" he asked, his voice oozing that kind of breezy cool that she'd been aiming for on the phone with Tasha.

"No...I mean, um, yes. But I can come back later. Dalton never minded if I just walked in. Is that okay? If it's not, I can just—" *Stop talking!* she ordered herself. Jeez, she'd never been the type to vomit words when she was nervous. So what was up now? She blew out a breath. This was just another first day with a new boss. Nothing to worry about.

Except, no matter how she sliced it, this was not just another new boss. This was her lover. A man who knew her body intimately. A man who'd driven her to the heights of passion over and over. She'd been vulnerable with him in a way she'd never been able to be with another man. She'd only allowed herself that vulnerability because he wasn't a part of her real life. He was part of her nighttime fantasy world. Now, the two disparate parts of her life were becoming inextricable intertwined and, frankly, it terrified her.

"Sir—" she began, thinking of Mr. Thornton "—just tell me what you expect from me."

Griffin slowly leaned back in his chair, stretching his legs out in front of him and bringing one hand up to stroke his thumb thoughtfully across his mouth, giving her the impression he was trying to hide the fact that he was laughing at her expense.

"Sir, huh?" he asked in a mocking voice.

She ground her teeth. He was definitely enjoying this. "How would you like me to address you?"

A slow smile spread across his face. "I'll think about that and let you know."

"Shall I come back later?"

"It's fine. Come in whenever you want."

"I can knock first. Next time I'll just knock first." Again with the babbling! What was wrong with her?

"Whatever makes you comfortable."

Humph. If only that were possible.

She flipped open the cover of her iPad, causing it to flicker awake and reveal the page of notes she'd made at her desk.

"First off, sir, there are—"

"Okay, I've thought about it. Stop calling me sir."

She gritted her teeth, swallowed and tried again for the formal professionalism. "Whatever you wish, Mr. Cain."

As if he was purposefully baiting her—and he probably was—his smile broadened. "I'd like you to call me Griffin."

"Fine. There are some things we should go over to ease the transition."

"Okay. Hit me."

He flashed her another one of those amused smiles and she cringed. She wished now that she hadn't made such a big deal about the name thing. Instead of impressing him with her efficiency and professionalism, she was acting like a total dork. "First off, I'd, um…like to go over Dalton's schedule for the week."

"I thought Dalton had been focusing on finding our sister."

"He was, but he still had to run the company." She looked down at the calendar app. "The weekly officers' meetings and the—"

"But," Griffin interrupted her, "I don't have to be able to do everything Dalton did. No one's going to expect that of me. At least not at first—and maybe never."

Sydney had to swallow a laugh. He was right, of course; everyone would expect less of him because of his reputation as a dilettante and playboy.

As if he could read her mind, he flashed her one of his charming grins and gestured modestly to his chest. "*I* wouldn't even have this job if it wasn't for my family connections. So nobody is going to expect much. Everyone knows I'll need help, especially these first few weeks. I can hand off most of the daily running of the company to someone else while I focus on finding the heiress. Once we find her, the pressure will let up a bit."

She'd only been thinking about Dalton's resignation in terms of how it would affect her. She hadn't skipped ahead yet to the broader ramifications of how it would affect the whole company. When she did think about it, it terrified her. Cain Enterprises was a billion-dollar company. It employed countless people. He'd not only thought about all those ramifications, but also had thought of them quickly enough to start working on a plan.

She nodded. "Okay. In that case, shall I arrange a meeting between you and..." She let her words trail off as she waited for him to supply a name.

"Merkins."

"Merkins?" She shifted her shoulder as she considered. "Not DeValera?"

Joe DeValera was the chief of operations, so he was the more natural choice.

"No, Merkins has a better head on her shoulders."

"DeValera won't like that you're handing over responsibility to the CFO instead of to him. As COO, he'll expect to handle things while you get your feet under you."

"All the more reason he doesn't need more power. Write up a memo to all the executives explaining the decision. Make sure it sounds like DeValera's current responsibilities are too important and that no one else can do his job."

Sydney nodded, quickly taking a few notes for the memo she'd later write and send to Griffin for approval. As she did so, she couldn't help being impressed by his light hand when it came to managing the executive staff.

Something of her surprise must have shown in her expression because Griffin asked, "You disagree with my decision?"

She finished writing her notes as she shook her head. "No. On the contrary, I think it's a brilliant strategy." Griffin looked at her with his eyebrows raised, like he wanted her to say more, so she kept talking. "DeValera is very much your father's man. He's a good COO but a bit of a narcissist." As soon as the words were out of her mouth, she cringed. "I shouldn't have said that."

"I agree completely. And I don't trust him. With Hollister's health failing and this stupid quest of his—which, thankfully, no one outside the family knows about—the company was vulnerable enough before Dalton decided to step down. I don't want DeValera getting any ideas."

"That's very smart." She cringed a little, realizing she sounded like a yes-man.

"Then why do you look doubtful?"

She tilted her head, considering her next words. Just how honest did she want to be here? She never hesitated to give her opinion when Dalton asked for it, but he rarely asked.

"Out with it," Griffin ordered, his playful grin never slipping from his face.

"I just didn't expect you to have such insight into the inner workings of the company. That's all."

The smiled that twisted his lips suddenly looked just a little bitter. "Right."

"The strategy is brilliant," she hastened to reassure him.

"You just didn't think I was capable of it."

"It's not—" But she fumbled, unsure how to finish her sentence. And feeling just a smidge annoyed at him. "Look, you give off an air of…privileged indolence. I'm not the only one in the company who thinks this. Anyone would tell you the same thing." But suddenly she found she couldn't quite look him in the eye. Disconcerted by the idea that she didn't know him at all, she flipped the cover of her iPad closed, running her finger across the smooth blue leather. "But clearly you're not that guy. Obviously you haven't been ignoring the daily office politics of the company. Otherwise you wouldn't have noticed that Merkins has amassed a really great team or that DeValera is a power-hungry narcissist."

"Hey, narcissist is your word, not mine."

Her gaze snapped back to his and she saw that his smile hadn't changed at all. But perhaps his eyes were crinkling just a tad around the edges.

"All I'm saying—" her voice took on a defensive edge, but

she didn't try to hide it. It wasn't her fault he was that good at
hiding his true nature "—is that you can't spend all that time
and energy creating a persona to fool everyone and then be
annoyed when you actually do fool everyone."

Griffin knew Sydney was right. He also knew her annoyance with him was totally justified. He'd kept a lot of things
from her. There were sides of himself he shared with almost
no one. Things he hadn't ever meant to share, even with her.

When he'd first started working for Cain Enterprises, he'd
been pegged as the slacker in the family. At first, he hadn't
courted that image on purpose. He simply hadn't wanted the
job. But he had wanted the inheritance that would one day be
his, and his father had made it clear that he'd never have one if
he didn't accept the other. As it turned out, being a piss-poor
executive left him plenty of time to work for Hope2O. Being
known as the lazy one had made his life easier. Everyone he
knew thought him either incapable or unwilling to work, so
no one ever expected jack from him. No one within Cain Enterprises, anyway.

Generally speaking, he was okay with people thinking he
was an ass and a playboy. So why was he annoyed that Sydney believed that, too?

Did he honestly think she somehow looked past the image
he'd carefully cultivated to the man beneath? Would he want
her to if she could?

It was hardly a fair question.

And Sydney was still standing before him, waiting for his
response. And also looking rather nervous. She kept rubbing
the pad of her thumb across the edge of her iPad cover as she
frowned down at it as if she couldn't quite figure out where it
had come from.

Finally, she straightened her shoulders and said, "If that's
all?"

He pushed himself to his feet and sighed. "You're right.

And I'm not annoyed." Maybe if he said it often enough, he'd
believe it. "I have no reason to be. If I act like a jerk, I have no
one to blame but myself if that's how people see me."

Her expression was guarded, so he couldn't tell whether or
not he'd placated her when she said, "Fine. I'll make that appointment for you with Merkins and have a draft of the letter
to the officers."

"And let's see if we can get the board up here for a meeting by this evening. They've all seen that email from Dalton
this morning. I don't want to give them too much time to think
about things."

She had her iPad out again, making notes. After a second,
she glanced up. "You might not realize this, but Dalton usually gives at least one week's notice because several of the
board members—"

"Are out of town? Yes, I know. We'll video conference them
in. Before we do anything else, we need to get me confirmed
as interim CEO. Promise them it'll be a short meeting. I don't
want to give them time to debate the alternatives."

"Very good."

"Also, I'll need to meet with Marion this afternoon and let
her know I've changed positions."

"Will she expect to move up with you?"

"Probably not. She's used to coasting by without doing too
much work. Besides, we'll need her to hold down the fort in
the office of the VP of International Marketing until we can
find someone else to fill that job."

She nodded, then closed the iPad again.

"Sydney—" he coaxed before she could vanish for good.

But she ignored the tone he'd used.

"Shall I schedule the meeting with Merkins for first thing
in the morning? Say, eight o'clock?"

He did a quick mental review of his personal schedule.
"Make it nine-thirty."

"Nine-thirty?" Sydney asked, frowning. "By then, everyone

will have been at work for several hours. Gossip will already be spreading. You need to get her on your side straightaway."

She was right, of course. Except he had a virtual meeting with a bank in Nairobi set up for eight in the morning. It had taken him two weeks to get the financial officer of the bank to even agree to the meeting. Rescheduling it would be a nightmare.

"I have another obligation at eight," he said, hoping she wouldn't argue with the note of finality in his voice.

He should have known better. Sydney set her jaw at a stubborn angle and flipped open her iPad again. "You don't. I took the liberty of having your assistant, Marion, forward your schedule to me earlier. Your morning is free."

"Marion doesn't have my complete schedule. I have a phone call to make at eight."

Sydney blew out a breath as though she was trying to muster her restraint. "Can you push it back?"

"No." It would be four in that part of Africa as it was. This was the best he'd been able to do.

Sydney pinched her mouth shut but then seemed unable to contain her ire. "You really don't want to blow this. DeValera will be looking for a way to shut you down. If he gets too much time with Merkins first—"

"Okay, eight-thirty. I'll try to move my other meeting forward." And he'd talk really fast.

She must have realized she'd gotten as much as she was going to because she gave a tight little nod. Then she added, "If you want to send me your personal schedule also, then I can put everything on a master schedule. Might make things easier for you."

"No. Marion never had access to my personal schedule. You don't need it, either."

"How can I function as your assistant if I don't know when or where you'll be?" she asked, frowning.

"Just run everything by me before you firm things up. That's how I did it with Marion."

Her frown deepened and her jaw clenched even tighter. "But I can't—"

"Marion made it work. So will you. It's just how I like to do things."

"Fine." But he could tell from the narrowing of her eyes that it wasn't fine at all. She spun on her foot to leave and he was pretty sure he heard her mutter, "If your personal life has to be that mysterious…"

He nearly called her back and explained the truth about his work for Hope2O but instead he kept his mouth shut.

Marion had been hired for him by his father's assistant. He'd liked Marion without ever really trusting her. And to be honest, as wily and cunning as Hollister was, Griffin wouldn't be surprised if the whole CEO office suite wasn't bugged.

Still he didn't want Sydney to think he was purposefully shutting her out—even if that was what he was doing.

"Wait a second." Instead of letting her leave, he stood and crossed to where she hovered near the door. He held out the folder he'd gotten from Dalton. "Here are all the notes from Dalton about his search for the heiress. Make copies for yourself and take an hour or so to look it over, then we'll talk more."

She looked from him to the folder and then back, finally meeting his gaze as she took the folder. Her expression was cautious but less openly distrustful than it had been just moments ago. "Okay."

"Look, I know I'm difficult to work with. And I know the company's in trouble. I'm going to do my damnedest not to screw it up any more than it already is. Let's just get through this. Together. Okay?"

"Okay." She tucked the folder on top of her iPad and left the office.

Alone in the room, Griffin was all too aware of the overbearing décor, the heavy French furniture and massive mahogany desk that had been in the office since Griffin's own childhood. The very walls seemed to close in on him.

Juggling the disparate elements of his life was typically something he excelled at. He kept his work for Cain separate from his work with Hope2O and his love life separate from both. He functioned best with everything compartmentalized.

He hadn't been lying to Sydney when he'd told her was going to try his damnedest not to screw anything up. That was true for the company and for his relationship with her.

Sydney worked furiously for the next couple of hours setting up the board meeting. The fact that every single member of the board was willing to rearrange his or her own schedule to be there—either in person or virtually—was either a good sign or a very bad one.

A half hour before the meeting she went across to the big conference room on the other side of the building to verify the folks in the IT department had gotten everything working for the board members who couldn't be physically present. She double-checked that catering had done their job, and she even removed one limp lily from the floral arrangement on the sideboard. Now everything was perfect.

This meeting had to go well. If the board didn't approve Griffin as interim CEO, she'd probably be out of a job. Yes, she'd find another one, but this was a good job, especially for someone as young as she was. She'd lucked into it. She'd first been hired as a temp when Dalton's previous assistant had knee surgery, but he'd kept her on when Janine had decided not to come back.

If she lost this job, her next position wouldn't pay nearly this well. Which meant making her mortgage payment would be a strain. It was already steep, but when she'd first bought her house, it had seemed like such a good investment. It had represented all the security she'd desperately wanted. Now, it just represented all that she'd lose if this didn't go well.

She left the conference room and hurried down the hall to her office. Griffin was leaving his as she walked in.

"I was just checking on the conference room. Everything looks good there."

"Thanks." He smiled that same breezy smile she was used to, the flash of white teeth and deep dimples. Suddenly the nerves she felt for the meeting morphed into a pleasant fluttery sort of anticipation that had nothing to do with efficient IT and catering departments.

She handed him the folio folder from her desk. "Here's your copy of the agenda. I kept it simple."

He flipped it open and read over it as she spoke. "Looks good."

He was about to walk out when she stopped him. "Wait a second. Is that what you're wearing?"

"Yeah." He glanced down as if seeing his jeans and shirt for the first time.

"You don't look the part of the business executive."

"I haven't exactly had time to go home and change."

She held up a hand to ward off a protest. "Just give me two minutes." She dashed into Dalton's office and dug around in the coat closet for a minute before returning. She held out what she'd found. "Here, put this on."

Griffin held it out in front of him. "A sweater?"

"Come on, trust me."

"A sweater?" he repeated, even as he pulled it over his head.

"I didn't have a lot to work with here." She helped him with the hem, tugging it over his hips. "Dalton keeps a couple of jackets here, but your shoulders are broader than his, so you couldn't wear one of those." Griffin stilled as she fussed over him, adjusting the sleeves of the V-neck sweater so a half-inch of cuff showed. Then she grabbed the two ties she'd found and held them up. "What do you think? Yellow or green?"

His lips twitched, dazzling her with a hint of white teeth and dimple. "How about no tie?"

"A tie says powerful and important," she argued.

"A tie with a sweater says Mr. Rogers," he countered, still smiling.

She rolled her eyes. "Trust me, nothing about you says Mr. Rogers."

Still, she conceded the point and set the ties aside, but she couldn't stop herself from reaching up to straighten his collar. Her fingers lingered on the warm skin of his neck and the faint bristle of growth along his jaw. He hadn't shaved this morning, she knew, but he must have shaved the night before. She thought about what the past twenty-four hours had been like for him. He'd called her as he'd left the airport—that had been around midnight. He must have shaved as soon as he'd gotten home, just before she showed up. She'd never thought about that until now…the way he always shaved just before they saw each other. The way his jaw was always smooth when he kissed her on her neck. And anywhere else.

Suddenly she realized they'd both gone completely still. Her breath caught in her chest as she looked up into his eyes, which were the exact same shade of blue as his shirt. Heat swirled through her body, turning her insides to mush and her knees to jelly.

Was he thinking about it, too? About the way he'd nuzzled her breast just last night? About the way he'd spread her body out before him like a feast and kissed every inch of her? How she'd done the same to him?

Abruptly, she dropped her hands and stepped away from him.

And this was why it wasn't a good idea to sleep with her boss. Up until now, she'd been so worried about the financial implications, she hadn't considered the emotional ones. How sex colored every interaction. How it could distract her. How it could mess with her priorities.

She grabbed a folder off the desk and thrust it toward him. "Here's the agenda."

He waggled the folder already in his hand. "You already handed me one."

"Oh." She glanced down. "This is a spare. In case you need it."

She looked up to see him watching her, the smile on his face broad, his eyes twinkling with amusement. As if he knew just how much he distracted her. "I think I'm good."

Oh, yeah. He was good. So damn good it damn nearly killed her.

"Okay then," she said, her tone overly bright. "Go hit it out of the park. Or whatever sports analogy fits."

"Don't worry. I've got this."

As he headed off to face the board, she had no doubt. He did have it.

He would win them over. He would convince them that he was fully qualified to be the CEO, just like he'd convinced her in the past few hours. He clearly understood how the company operated and what it needed. He even grasped the finer details of the personalities involved. He got people in a way that even Dalton had not. In that regard, he might even be a better CEO than Dalton had been.

But that didn't change any of her plans. She still needed to find the heiress because she needed to get Dalton back. If the past few minutes had shown her anything, it was that she couldn't do her job effectively if she was working for Griffin, not just because he distracted her and muddled her senses, but also because he made her doubt her own judgment. And because he was dangerous to her in a way no other man ever had been.

Five

"What do you think?" Griffin asked as he strolled into the conference room.

Three days had passed since the board had named Griffin interim CEO. As she had predicted, he'd won them over with little difficulty. They were not having the same luck with the search for Griffin's missing sister.

Sydney had laid out all her research on the conference table. In addition to the notes that Dalton had passed on to Griffin, she had stacks of her own notes and forty-two cardboard boxes Griffin's mother had had sent over. She hadn't even touched those yet. Frankly, she was hoping something like an actual lead would come along and she'd be saved the trouble.

Now, she glared up at him. "Seriously? Why are you out here again? You've checked on me every thirty minutes."

A mischievous smile spread across his lips. "This is how I work."

"Oh, really? When you were in your office down the hall, you'd come out every five minutes to distract Marion?"

His grin broadened. "Well, I do love Marion—and she does make a fantastic chocolate bread pudding for me every year on my birthday. But still—" he gave a hey-what-can-you-do kind of shrug "—come on."

"Right." She sighed. He didn't even have to finish the sentence. But she said it aloud anyway. "You've never slept with Marion."

"Of course I've never slept with Marion. I've known her since I was ten. She's like a mother to me."

Sydney scowled at him, even though it was herself she was irritated with. This was not the time to be flirting.

He must have taken her scowl to heart because he said, "Just to be clear, in addition to not sleeping together anymore, are we not supposed to talk about the fact that we slept together? Are we pretending it never even happened?"

She nearly snorted. If only it were that easy. How could she order him to pretend it hadn't happened if she couldn't do it herself?

"Let's just try not to talk about it, okay? My point is," she said sternly, or rather shooting for stern but landing somewhere vaguely in the area of disconcerted, "that even though you have every woman in this building wrapped firmly around your little finger, you'll find I am not so easy to—"

She broke off before she could get the rest of the sentence out of her mouth because she could practically see the innuendo forming on the tip of his tongue.

She waved aside his comment. "Yes, yes. I heard it. Can we just skip over all the jokes relating to the word *easy*?"

His grin broadened to the point he looked like the damn Cheshire cat.

"Look," she continued. "I'm trying to do the right thing here. Stop making this so difficult."

"But I'd hate to be the one accused of being easy." Before she could protest, he held up his hands in surrender. "Okay, okay. I'll let it go. I promise."

Although a smile still teased his lips, there was nothing malicious in his gaze. He wasn't teasing her to be mean; he just enjoyed the game too much to stop.

It was one of those unexpected things about him that she found so hard to resist. And this constant exposure to his charm made her feel...nervous. Off balance. Pursued in a way she never had experienced when they were merely sleeping together. Why was it so much easier to be around him when all his energy was focused on making her climax rather than on making her smile?

"Look," she said, "just stay on your side of the conference table and this will all go a lot more smoothly."

He frowned. "So it's not going well?"

She flipped closed the file in front of her. "You know this is insane, right?"

Griffin nodded with mock solemnity. "I do."

"Your father spent his entire life building this company and now he's threatening to throw it all away based on some anonymous letter he got."

"Exactly."

"And he's pitting you and your brothers against one another to try to find this girl."

"He is."

"Has it occurred to any of you that this girl might not even be real? I mean, obviously, whoever wrote the letter did it just to drive Mr. Cain crazy. She—or he—obviously—"

Griffin interrupted her. "He? The letter was written by a woman."

He reached over her to flip the folder back open and tapped his finger on the first page—a photocopy of the letter.

She picked it up and waved it around. "No, the letter was written by someone claiming to be a woman. Someone claiming to have had an affair with Hollister and claiming to have bore him a daughter. But there's no proof. No real evidence." She put the letter back on the top of the folder and considered it. "Which brings me back to my point. Whoever wrote the letter knew him well enough to want revenge and to know this would drive him crazy. But that doesn't mean that the person who wrote the letter was actually the girl's mother. Or that there even is a girl."

"Hmm." Griffin stood, stroking his chin as he paced the length of her office and back, considering her words. "Good point. But it's irrelevant."

"How so?"

"It doesn't matter who wrote the letter or even whether or not there's a girl to find. Proving there isn't a girl would be harder than finding one. It's like proving there isn't life on another planet. It'd be damn near impossible."

"Well, it might be damn near impossible to find her even if she does exist."

Griffin gave her a level look. "So you think Laney's theory was wrong? You don't think this nanny, Vivian, is the one?"

Sydney flipped back through the file to find the color copy she'd made of the photos Laney had found. The first picture was of two women and a girl standing on the beach somewhere. As Sydney understood it, the older woman was Matilda Fortino, Laney's grandmother. She'd been the Cain's housekeeper for Dalton and Griffin's entire childhood. Dalton had gone to see her because he'd thought that if anyone had the dirt on his father, it would be her. His search had brought him to Laney, whom he'd apparently been in love with when he was younger. As hard a time as Sydney had imagining Dalton—her serious and stoic boss—falling in love at all, she was glad that he seemed to have found happiness, even if he hadn't found his missing sister.

But Laney had believed the girl in this photo might be the missing girl. There was another picture of the girl's mother stapled behind the first. In that picture, she was still pregnant and she had her arm around the shoulder of another pregnant woman—Laney's mother. More importantly, the picture had been taken in the Cain's backyard.

Laney's grandmother had Alzheimer's and could tell them nothing about the young woman or the girl. However—according to Laney's notes—Matilda's incoherent ramblings had led Laney to believe that the woman had a connection to Hollister, a connection that might have put her in danger.

Was all this conjecture, or was this a real lead?

Sydney looked at the two pictures and frowned. "I don't know," she said finally. "The connection seems specious at best."

"I know. It isn't a lot to go on."

Sydney looked up to study Griffin, but once again she was frustrated by his chameleon charm. His mouth was twisted into a smile, but she couldn't read his emotions. Was he as doubtful as she was, or did he believe this girl on the beach was his sister?

Glancing down at the picture, he said, "It would help if whoever took the picture was close enough to see the girl's eyes."

"Why?"

"Well, if she had Cain-blue eyes, then we'd know for sure Hollister was her father."

"Cain-blue?" Sydney asked.

"Sure. Didn't you ever notice that my eyes and Dalton's are the same color?"

"No" She couldn't keep her skepticism from her voice. "Blue eyes are blue eyes. But you and Dalton look nothing alike."

"Maybe not," Griffin chided. "But our eyes are almost identical."

Before she could scoff, he grabbed her hand and tugged her gently to her feet, positioning her to stand between his outstretched legs.

"Look," he gently urged her. "Tell me Dalton and I don't have the same eyes."

She had no choice but to gaze into Griffin's eyes. Standing this close, she was hit with the scent of him. All fresh and minty. His hand, warm and dry, still clenched one of hers. His thumb rubbed idly across the back of her hand. She was struck by how gentle his touch, but how rough his skin, was.

She had been touched by him enough—and intimately at that—that she knew the skin on his hands was roughened as if by hard manual labor, but for the life of her, she'd still couldn't imagine what he might be doing in his spare time to earn those calluses.

Giving her head a little shake, she tried to focus on his eyes.

"Well, for starters, the shape of your eyes is totally different. His eyes are rounder. Yours are more almond shaped. And crinkly."

"You're saying I squint?" he teased, his hands releasing hers to settle on her hips. With nowhere else to put them, she dropped her own hands to his waist.

"No," she harumphed. "I'm saying you laugh. Dalton never laughs. Besides, Dalton has this way of looking right through someone. His eyes have this soulless quality. It's not disdain or annoyance. Just disinterest."

Griffin chuckled. "Exactly. So what about me?"

And this was what stumped her.

"You…really look at people," she began slowly. Sometimes, when he looked at her, she felt as though he could see into her very soul, but she wasn't going to say that aloud. "And I'm not entirely sure that's a good thing because sometimes I'm still not sure if you smile because you enjoy being with people or if human nature amuses you."

The smile slowly faded from his expression and she felt the tension in his hands. Like he was trying to decide if he should push her away or pull her closer.

Part of her knew she should probably stop talking right then and there, but instead she finished her thought.

"But you're not a cruel man, so I don't think it's that you're laughing at people. It's more like…just another way of keeping people at a distance."

She kept her gaze pinned to the top button of his shirt while she spoke, all too aware that she was just guessing about him but that her guesses revealed as much about her as they did about him. If he was really paying attention. And maybe he wasn't.

He gently cupped her chin and tipped it up so she met his gaze. "Is that what you think? That I push people away?"

It's what I do.

But she didn't say that aloud. Instead, she asked, "Do you?"

"Doesn't everybody?"

"Yes, I suppose everybody does."

Suddenly this whole conversation felt way too intimate. Even more intimate than the time they'd spent in bed together because that had been about sex, not emotion. And if there was one thing she was good at, it was separating her physical needs from her emotional needs.

So—though she'd told herself that she wasn't going to sleep with him again now that he was her boss—she gave into every urge she'd been suppressing for the past twenty-four hours. She threaded her fingers up through his hair, luxuriating in the feel of the thick, long strands. She let herself lean into him. And she inhaled deeply, letting the warm spicy scent of him invade her senses.

His hands clenched on her hips and this time she had no doubt about his intention because he pulled her close to him, rocking his hips against the juncture of her legs. He dipped his head down to her neck and left a trail of kisses along the sensitive skin there.

His breath was hot against her skin as he murmured, "Isn't this crossing that line you drew in the sand?"

"Yes, damn it." She wished he hadn't brought it up, but she couldn't fault him for it, either. She was the one who'd set the boundary. She couldn't begrudge him for respecting her wishes, even if he was ignoring her desires.

She gave his waist a quick squeeze, relishing the way his muscles clenched in response to her touch, and then she stepped back.

She smoothed her hands down her sleek tan sweater and gave the hem a tug. "What were we even talking about?"

"Cain-blue eyes," Griffin said easily, apparently less befuddled than she was.

Right. The Cain eyes.

That was the discussion that had led her astray. And—she now realized—she'd never even really responded to the comment. She'd gone and rambled on and on about the shape of his eyes and the character of his smile, but she'd never really admitted that, yes, he and Dalton had eyes that were exactly the same piercing shade of blue. Not bright sky-blue or deep indigo-blue, but an eerie sort of sea-blue, turquoise almost, pale in the center with a dark ring of contrast.

She knew intimately the shade of Griffin's eyes—just as she knew their shape. But she was only vaguely aware of what Dalton's eyes looked like.

"Well," she said brusquely, "even if we could see her eyes, that would tell us nothing. The girl could have brown eyes and still be Hollister's daughter."

"Nah. If she's Hollister's daughter, she has blue eyes."

"You're just assuming the girl's mother didn't have a brown-eye gene to contribute to the pool?"

Griffin waggled his hand in a maybe/maybe not gesture.

"My instinct tells me that whoever she was, the girl's mother would have had blue eyes. My father definitely had a type. My mother, Cooper's mother and his other longtime mistress all looked like they could have been sisters."

It took a second for the full meaning of his words to sink in. When they did, she raised her eyebrows in question and asked, "Seriously?"

He gave a dismissive shrug. "Yeah. He liked waifish blondes. The more fragile-looking the better. And they were all blue-eyed."

She kept looking at him, waiting for him to pick up on her train of thought. When he didn't, she gave his shoulder a playful shove. "Not that, idiot. I mean, your father had a long-term mistress and no one thought to question her?"

"Sharlene doesn't know anything."

"Sharlene? Why does that name sound familiar?"

"How should I know?"

"Sharlene is a pretty unusual name. You're not talking about Sharlene Sheppard, are you?"

"She was Sharlene Davonivich then, but yeah. Why?"

"And this was before she married Jack Sheppard, your father's business rival?" she asked.

"Actually, this was before Jack Sheppard was his business rival. They used to be partners. Things went bad sometime after Sharlene and my father broke up."

Sydney let out a low whistle. "Sometimes the history of Cain Enterprises reads like an Italian opera."

Griffin looked slightly abashed. "Yeah. Heartache. Epic rivalries. It's like *Les Misérables* but without all the singing."

She chuckled, then asked, "Are you sure she's not involved? How long were they together?"

Griffin shrugged. "Ten years, maybe."

"Ten years? Forget what she knows. Forget this wild goose chase after a pregnant nanny who may or may not have even slept with Hollister. If this Sharlene person was your father's mistress for ten years, then she could be the girl's mother."

"No."

"But you said yourself that your father was selective about who he let get close to him."

"Sharlene doesn't have any children."

"Maybe she gave the baby up for adoption." She was really warming to the idea now. It just made sense. "And if she did, that would certainly explain the bitterness in the letter."

"No," Griffin said. "Sharlene was never pregnant."

"You can't know that for sure. Sometimes when women don't want people to know they're pregnant, they hide the pregnancy for as long as they can. They go away for the last few months, give birth in private. They—"

"Sharlene wasn't the type. She and my father never hid their affair."

"As far as you know."

Griffin's hands rested low on her waist and he rubbed his thumb across her hip bone absently as he spoke. "You're right. I'm not a hundred percent certain. But Sharlene was like another mother to me."

He seemed completely unaware of what his hands were doing, but it drove her crazy.

She tried to step away, but his grip on her was surprisingly strong. "So it's only natural you don't want to consider that she might have been the one to write the letter."

"Actually, what I was going to say is that when I was a kid, I saw her at least once a week, sometimes more often. If she'd been pregnant, I would remember it. If she'd gone away, even for a few months, I would have noticed."

Sydney frowned, realizing he was right. He probably would have remembered it.

"Besides," he continued, finally letting her go. "When they broke up, it was nasty. If she'd had the kind of leverage a kid would have given her, she'd have used it then."

"You don't know—"

"I do know." His tone was harsher than she'd ever heard it before; all traces of the easygoing charmer she knew so well were gone.

For a moment, all she could do was stare at him blankly. Then she nodded. "Okay. So Sharlene isn't the girl's mother. But we should still talk to her. She might know something."

He stared at her for a long moment before finally nodding. "Okay. I'll give her a call. See if she knows anything."

Before she could say anything else, Griffin disappeared back into his office and she was left standing beside the conference table, wondering exactly what she'd said that had driven a wedge between them. And what she'd gotten herself into.

If she was honest with herself, it wasn't the family drama that surprised her; it was Griffin's reaction to it. She'd been with him for four months, for goodness sake. They'd had sex countless times. Spent entire weekends in bed eating takeout and watching cheesy monster movies on Syfy.

So how was it there were so many things she didn't know about him?

Before she could ponder that question anymore, her phone buzzed. She glanced down to see a text from Jen.

As she typed in a quick response, she shrugged off the question altogether. There were plenty of things he didn't know about her, either. Things she would never tell him. That wasn't the kind of relationship they had.

Suddenly, that made her sad, even though she wasn't quite sure why.

It felt as though their relationship had shifted inexplicably in the past few days. Yeah, sure, there was that huge obvious shift. He was her boss now. They weren't sleeping together anymore. Yeah, all *that* stuff had happened. But there was something else going on, too. She was seeing a side of Griffin that she'd never seen before. Something beyond that surface charm she'd originally been attracted to.

The problem was, now that she knew there was more to him than that, could they ever go back to the relationship they'd had before? She didn't think so. Now that she'd seen this Griffin, this guy who cared about the company and who worked as hard as he played, she'd never be able to forget he existed. Even if Dalton did come back and she was no longer working for Griffin. She'd never be able to go back to just sleeping with him, either. So where did that leave her?

Even before Griffin had taken over as CEO, she'd worried she was in over her head. She blamed that damned key. Why had everything become so complicated? Working with him every day constantly strained her willpower. She didn't know how much longer she'd be able to keep him at arm's length.

She could only hope they found this girl soon. Once Dalton reclaimed his position as CEO, she'd have a little distance from Griffin. Going cold turkey would be so much easier without having him tempt her constantly. But what if Dalton never came back? It was a possibility she couldn't let herself consider. They would find the girl. Dalton would come back. Griffin wouldn't be her boss forever.

She just had to make damn sure they found her soon.

Six

"How's it going?" Griffin asked from the doorway to the conference room.

Sydney looked from the stack of papers in front of her to Griffin and back with her eyebrows raised. "How does it look like it's going?"

That signature smile of his crept across his face. "Slowly. It looks like it's going slowly."

She gave an indelicate snort. "Exactly. Your powers of observation are astonishing."

It had been two days since the conversation about Sharlene. That conversation that she'd been so sure had changed everything. And yet…nothing had changed. By the time she'd left work that day, Griffin had returned to his normal self. The next morning, she'd briefly considered asking him whether he'd actually called Sharlene, as she'd suggested. Instead, she gritted her teeth and started going through the Cain household records. Forty-two boxes in all. Sydney had dug into the boxes and started looking for any references to a nanny named Vivian.

Part of her said she was being a coward. The other part pointed out calmly that she was just doing her job. This was what Griffin had asked her to do, so she was doing it. If he wanted her doing anything else, he'd tell her.

The part that thought she was being a coward noted that Griffin was stubbornly ignoring the obvious. That he needed to go talk to Sharlene—and possibly his mother also—because a real conversation with an actual human would get him further than countless hours searching through boxes would.

The problem was, as much as she wanted to pretend otherwise, Griffin wasn't just her boss. He'd been her lover first. She knew his personal needs and his professional ones. If this was Dalton she was dealing with, there'd be no question. She would just trust her gut. But with Griffin, she had no idea if her gut was telling her to do what was right for the company or what was right for her man. Or maybe it wasn't her gut doing the talking at all. Maybe this was unfulfilled sexual tension speaking. Because once she found the heiress, maybe she could justify getting back in Griffin's bed.

She looked at him, trying not to appreciate his broad shoulders or the little bit of stubble scattered across his jaw. Since taking over as CEO, he'd traded in his rugged jeans for twill slacks and his linen shirts for crisp, pressed cotton. Somehow the fact that he still left the shirts untucked until right before he went into meetings made the look that much more appealing. The result was that he always came across as just a little rumpled and disreputable. It lent an air of intimacy to the office. And, frankly, it made her want to rip his clothes off.

To keep her hands occupied—and off his buttons—she flipped the lid off box number nineteen. "I've been at this for days now. I'm not even halfway through these records. And so far, all I can tell you is that your mother spends too much on shoes and your parents' accountant pays the bills on time."

"I could have told you that," he said with a smile.

"We're never going to make any progress here."

"You think the information is buried too deep?" he asked.

She picked up a sheaf of papers. Printouts from the early eighties. Old reams of accordion-style paper. The ink from the dot-matrix printer was faded and damn near impossible to read. In addition, the pages were so damn musty, she was pretty sure an entire colony of dust mites was vacationing in her sinuses. She lifted the bottom edge of the stack with her thumb and let it fan through the hundred or so pages.

"I've been through every page of your parents' household records. From the year Laney was born and for two years in either direction, just to be sure. There is no mention of anyone named Vivian. Not anywhere in these records."

Griffin was watching her in that way he had, quietly attentive. The way that made her think he caught all the subtleties going on beneath the surface. That he knew that her eyes ached from staring at the blurred ink. That her back twitched from sitting too long. And, most especially, that every time she'd gotten sleepy from just sitting there going through the pages, she'd given herself a two-minute break to fantasize about locking his office door and doing crazy things to his body. And about the way he liked to drive her completely crazy with lust before taking her. And the powerful way he drove into her. And the way he hooked her ankles up over his arms so her hips were at just the right angle.

And she knew, instantly, that she should not have let that image flit through her brain because she could feel her cheeks heating up. And damn it, now he would definitely know what she'd been thinking, even if he was only guessing before.

Hoping to distract them both, she pushed her chair back and stood, walking over to the water cooler beside the credenza on the far side of the conference room and pouring herself a tiny cup of water.

But when she turned back around, it was to find him watching her. His gaze was hot and she could feel the weight of it against her skin as potent as a physical touch. Crap, she'd distracted him all right, but not in the way she'd meant to.

She swallowed most of the water in one gulp, nearly drowning herself.

"Is it too hot in here for you?" he asked, his voice pitched low with innuendo. "'Cause I could turn the air-conditioning back on for you."

"No, thanks. I know right where the air-conditioning controls are."

"Oh, I know you do." He grinned wickedly and she knew he was thinking of the time he'd all but begged her to pleasure herself while he watched. The resulting earth-shattering sex was no doubt seared into both of their minds. "I was just offering to take care of it for you. If you wanted me to."

Damn, but she did want him to take care of it for her. Right here. Right now.

But that was the very last thing she could do. Because the only thing worse than sleeping with your boss was sleeping with your boss in the middle of the day on the middle of the executive board table.

"Ugh, this is so frustrating. It feels like we're never going to get anywhere like this." Especially because the only place she wanted to get was into Griffin's pants. Yeah, *frustrating* was the perfect word. Unfortunately. "I wish we could just talk to your mother about it."

Griffin gave a bark of shocked laughter. "Why?"

She shrugged. Wasn't it obvious? "Presumably she could tell us exactly who this nanny is."

"I doubt that."

"You don't think she'd remember?"

He gave a snort. "I'd be shocked if she ever knew the woman's name to begin with."

"I find that hard to believe." What kind of woman wouldn't know the name of her children's nanny?

"Do you remember Mrs. Fortino?" he asked.

"Yes. She's Laney's grandmother. She was your housekeeper for years, right?"

"Exactly. Thirty years. I was fourteen when I realized my mother had been saying her name wrong. With an *A* on the end instead of an *O*."

"So? That's an easy mistake to make."

"Yeah, sure. So I corrected my mother. We fought over it. My mother refused to admit she was wrong. Finally, my mother called Mrs. Fortino in and told her that regardless of what her name actually was, from that moment on she was to go by Mrs. Fortina in my mother's presence. She told the poor women that if anyone addressed her by her real name, she would be instantly fired."

"That's absurd. You can't fire an employee over something like that," Sydney protested.

"When you're a self-indulgent narcissist you can do whatever you want if other people let you get away with it. Mrs. Fortino merely nodded and asked if that was all. As soon as she left, my mother told me to never again interfere with the way she ran the household."

"You think she did it to punish you?"

"She did it because she wanted me to know she was in charge."

His cold conviction unsettled her. She knew, of course, that he wasn't particularly close to his family, but she'd written it down as a peculiarity of the rich.

"Well, that's certainly not very nice, but it has nothing to do with this."

"I didn't tell you the story to elicit your sympathy. I told you to explain why I don't think talking to Mother would make any difference."

"Surely she's not that bad."

"I think they said the same thing about Nero's mother."

"Oh, come on." She sent him a teasing smile. "You're comparing her to one of the most reviled women in history? Did she commit murder? Are there plots to overthrow the government I don't know about?"

"Wow, you really know your Roman history."

"What can I say? I liked *I, Claudius*. My point is, a simple conversation with your mother might answer many of our questions."

"First off, there's no such thing as a simple conversation with my mother. And second, a conversation with her has never made any situation better."

Sydney stared down at the open file in front of her, gnawing on her lip as she considered her next words. Sure, just asking him was the most straightforward course of action, but she was definitely treading on new ground here. They didn't have the kind of relationship where they talked about their families or their childhoods. He'd already revealed more to her now than he ever had before. And if it was just human curiosity driving her, she would have let it go. But there was far more at stake here than her fascination with this man. If they didn't find the heiress, the future of the entire company was at stake. Thousands of people would be out of work, herself included.

"You really don't like your mother, do you?" she quipped, trying to make light of an obviously difficult situation.

"What gave me away?" He smiled at her. It was an expression very similar to his normal charming grin but without any warmth in his gaze. "Was it the comparison to Nero's murderous mother?"

She ignored his glib words and asked, "Why?"

He blinked in surprise. "What?"

"Why don't you like her? Or more to the point, why are you so angry at her about this?" She gestured to the mess of papers in front of her, partly to indicate the mass of files his mother had sent over, but also referencing the mess with his father. "This thing with the missing heiress? That's your father's mistake, not hers. She's the victim here—"

"My mother is never a victim," he interrupted.

"She's just as much a victim as you. Maybe more so. The way I understand it, in his original will she was going to receive ten percent. Now, no matter what happens, she gets nothing."

"You think I'm being too hard on her?" His voice was flat.

"I don't know. I guess I just…" She stared down at the page in front of her. One of the corners curled up, and she ran her fingers back and forth over it so it rolled and unrolled. "I get why you're angry at your father over this. I get that. But I don't understand why you seem to be mad at your mother, too."

Without really meeting her eyes, he rounded the board table that dominated the room and crossed to the antique bar that stood in one corner. In her months here, she'd never seen Dalton—or anyone else for that matter—pour themselves a drink in the middle of a meeting. However, Dalton kept the bar there because that was the kind of businessman his father had been. Apparently, among Texas oil men of that generation, a deal wasn't considered sealed until you'd shared a drink over it. It all seemed very *Dallas* to her.

Even though she'd never seen Griffin drink before now, he poured himself a Scotch and tossed it back quickly before pouring himself another.

Finally, he turned and faced her, the glass cradled in his hand, his legs stretched out in front of him as he leaned back against the bar. "You're right. My father is a lying, cheating bastard and he always has been." He took a drink before continuing. "But at least he never pretended to be anything other than what he was. He never hid the fact that he'd do anything to increase Cain Enterprises profits. He never lied about the other women. He's a bastard, but he's an honest bastard. My mother, however, spent our childhoods alternately pretending to be the perfect loving mother and ignoring us completely."

She studied him with a tilted head. "What makes you think she was pretending? Maybe she really was a loving mother."

"Let me ask you this. What would you have done in her shoes?"

His question surprised her so much, she blinked in surprise. "What do you mean?"

He pushed himself away from the bar and took a slow step toward her. "What would you do in her shoes? What would you do if your husband cheated on you?"

"I don't know. I've never thought about it." But everything inside her recoiled from the idea. She wouldn't tolerate it. Still, every woman was different. "I guess if I still loved him, I might try to make it work. Marriage counseling. Something like that."

"No," Griffin said, and at first she thought he was arguing with her logic. But he took another step toward her. "No. Pretend you don't love him at all. That you only married him for the money. Would you stay with him? Just for the money?"

"I would never marry someone just for the money."

"Pretend for a second that you would. Pretend that you were rich already and could have married anyone, but you chose someone so ambitious and ruthless, you knew he could make you rich beyond belief. And then pretend he turned out to be just as ruthless in his personal life. Pretend he slept with whoever he wanted and humiliated you in public and in front of your friends. Would you stay?"

"No." She felt the flame of embarrassment for his mother just listening to him. Not just embarrassment, but anger, too. At Griffin, for so ruthlessly displaying his mother's shortcomings. Anger made her meet his gaze as she defended his mother. "But everyone is different. I can't judge her for staying. I don't know her well enough."

"Well, pretend for a second that you would stay with a man you abhorred. Pretend you'd put up with his cheating and his mistresses. Pretend you'd put up with it for more than a decade because the money was just that important to you. Pretend you're just that stubborn or proud or greedy. Now pretend that the same man who stomps all over you every chance he gets treats your kids just as badly as he treats you."

She dropped her gaze as she felt the bottom drop out of her

stomach. She licked her lips because her mouth had suddenly gone dry. Suddenly she understood why he harbored so much anger toward his mother. Suddenly she got it.

"No." Her voice came out as a whisper. She didn't have kids. She didn't even know if she would ever have kids—at least, not biological kids. She'd always had the idea of doing the foster kid thing someday. If she did have kids—biological or foster—she would do everything in her power to protect them. "No, I wouldn't."

Griffin nodded, then tossed back the rest of his drink and set the glass down with a thud. "Yeah. That's what I thought."

With that, he turned and walked out.

He didn't have to say anything else. Because now she got it. His father may be a bastard, but that didn't really bother him because he'd never really cared about his father. He'd loved his mother. He probably still did. Despite everything, he would love her. That, more than anything, explained why he harbored so much anger and resentment. He loved her, but he was constantly disappointed by her.

She felt the same way about her own biological mother. She'd lived with her for the first six years of her life. Of course she'd loved her. And, of course, all kinds of negative emotions were mixed in with the love, but it was the love that made all of it hurt.

She understood that maybe better than anyone else.

But she was also an outsider in Griffin's relationship with his mother. She could see, perhaps more clearly than he could, just how complicated this was. Unfortunately, none of this insight into the Cain family solved anything. None of this got her any closer to finding the heiress.

One of Griffin's lifelong goals was to never be as much of an ass as his father. In fact, his goal was to never do anything like his father. Yet here he was, bullying his subordinate, bitching about his mother, Caro Cain, and drinking in the middle of the morning. In short, he was acting just like his dad. Funny how that had worked out.

Back in his office—Dalton's office, really—he plunked himself down in Dalton's chair, scrubbed a hand down his face, swallowed back his regrets and tried to think of how to dig his way out of this mess. First step, naturally, was to find something to eat. It was only ten, but breakfast had been a bowl of oatmeal five hours ago. He could feel the Scotch eating its way through the oats right now.

One of the peppermints Dalton always kept in his desk would do for starters. He unwrapped one of the Brach's candies and plopped it in his mouth. Then he started pulling open drawers looking for some nuts or a granola bar or something. He knew Dalton well enough to figure that the guy had probably eaten about half his meals right here at this desk.

Tucked into the back of the second drawer, he found something far more interesting than a pack of almonds. Behind the stack of files was a nine-by-eleven manila envelope with the word *Confidential* stamped on the front. The return address was from a company out of L.A. that Dalton sometimes used to do employee background checks. Not the normal HR kind, either. The hardcore kind. Panic spiked through Griffin. This company did the kind of background check that would reveal a VP's involvement with an international charity. Did Dalton know about Hope2O? If he did, then why the hell had he left Griffin in charge of Cain Enterprises?

In the bottom drawer, he found a jar of almonds and he poured a few out into his hand before opening the manila folder and pulling out the pages it contained. It took him several minutes of staring at the file before he realized what it contained— that was how surprised he was by the envelope's contents.

It wasn't a file on him. It was information about Sydney.

Dalton must have subcontracted the work when he'd decided to hire her full-time. Yeah, HR would handle all the reference checks and job recommendations, but it wasn't uncommon for Dalton to hire out a more in-depth background search for someone in a position of authority at the company. And now that Griffin thought about it, that certainly described Sydney's position. She knew everything about the company and had access to some very high-level stuff. She had more influence than most of the junior VPs. Certainly more than he had. So it only made sense. Still, he hadn't been expecting it, so seeing the file surprised the hell out of him.

He mindlessly popped a few almonds into his mouth as he flipped through the pages. He hadn't meant to read it. If he hadn't been hungry and tired and just drunk two shots of Scotch in quick succession, he would have had the foresight to shove the pages back into the envelope and let it go.

Instead, his gaze scanned the pages almost without realizing he was doing it. And once he'd read some of it, he couldn't stop. In fact, he had to read parts a second time, just because it all seemed so damn hard to believe. So completely out of character with the woman he knew.

Finally, he shoved the pages back into the envelope and buried it at the back of the drawer. He ate more nuts, hoping the salt would quell the queasy feeling in his stomach. It didn't.

If he hadn't felt like a total jackass before, he certainly did now. Here he'd been bitching about his sad childhood as the poor, ignored rich boy, and Sydney had real tragedy in her background. She was one bowl of porridge short of being a character in a Dickens novel. And he'd had the gall to complain to her.

He was surprised she hadn't thrown his drink in his face and walked out on him right then.

Naturally, his first impulse was to apologize. But to do so he'd have to admit what he'd done, which would relieve his own guilt, but she wouldn't be happy about it. Somehow, he didn't think this was the kind of information she'd share with just everyone. After all, they'd been sleeping together for months and she hadn't mentioned that she'd been a foster child.

That Child Protective Services had removed her from her birth mother when she was six. Of course, before this morning, he hadn't trotted out his pathetic tortured past, either. He hated being the object of pity and he suspected that Sydney felt the same way. No. It would be much better if he didn't tell her at all. If he just buried the information in the nether regions of his brain and forgot all about it.

Which still left him with the issue of how to make it up to her for acting like an ass earlier. But that was an issue easily resolved.

He pushed back his chair and dropped the now empty almond container in the trash. On his way out of the office, he stopped back by the conference room. Sydney looked up as he stuck his head in the door, her expression wary.

Before she could ask, he said, "I'm going to follow your advice and go talk to my mother. See what she knows."

Surprise flickered over Sydney's face. "You are?"

"Yeah. I figure maybe you're right about her. Maybe she can help."

"Do you think she will?" Sydney closed the file in front of her and leaned forward eagerly. "I mean, she has nothing at stake in this. If she's anything like you've described, maybe she won't want to help."

Strangely, that idea hadn't actually occurred to him. "She might not be able to help. Her help might be more of a hindrance—" He gestured to the boxes to make his point. "But I'm sure she'll want to help."

"Even if finding the heiress gets her nothing?"

"She won't see it that way. If I find the heiress, she knows I won't cut her off cold. Dalton would never have done that, either, though I'm not sure if she'd have thought it through. It's Cooper she has to worry about. Well, that and the whole shebang reverting to the state. No, she and I may not have a great relationship, but she knows I'll treat her fairly. She'll help if she can." Sydney smiled so brightly, he added, "I'm still not sure how helpful she'll be, but I'll try."

Sydney's grin didn't diminish a bit. "Thank you!"

In that moment she looked so lovely that he wanted to cross the room, pull her into his arms and kiss her. Not the kind of soul-searing kiss that would lead to her spread over the conference table naked, but a simple kiss. The kind that would honor the delicacy of her beauty. The kind that would salve the wounds of a broken childhood. The kind that would promise her a lifetime of safety, security and emotional support.

But he didn't know how to make those kinds of promises, let alone how to keep them, so instead he just nodded and walked away.

Seven

Traffic in Houston sucked. It always did. But for once, Griffin didn't curse the snarl of cars slowing his trip to his parents' house. He did not relish the upcoming conversation or the maternal theatrics that were sure to accompany it. The traffic on the loop was practically at a standstill, so instead of getting on, he pulled into a nearby parking lot and used the Bluetooth in his car to put in a call to Carl Nichols, his second in command at Hope2O.

He hadn't yet told Carl about what was going on with Cain Enterprises. Until now, some part of him had genuinely believed that this would all blow over. That after a couple of days of crazy sex with Laney, Dalton would come to his senses and ask for his job back. But apparently, a little sanity on his brother's part was too much to ask for. And because finding the heiress was proving more difficult than he'd expected, Griffin figured it was time to come clean with Carl so that things at Hope2O wouldn't devolve too much while his own attention was elsewhere.

After Griffin explained, Carl was silent for a long minute. Then he said, "That sounds more like something you would do."

Griffin snorted. "Right. I'll just walk away from a half billion dollars."

"Why not? Dalton did."

"Dalton also got offers from ten other Fortune 500 companies within about five minutes of quitting."

"Do you want to work for another Fortune 500 company?"

"Don't be an ass," Griffin said lightly. "You know I don't want a job somewhere else. I barely do the job I have, even though it's practically part-time. The only reason I've stayed at Cain Enterprises for as long as I have is because I want to get my hands on my inheritance so I can put it to work at Hope2O."

"Right. And now your practically part-time job has turned into a full-time position as CEO."

"Interim CEO," Griffin interrupted.

"Interim or not, you're going to have a hell of a time keeping up with that job and this one."

Griffin glared at the sea of red brake lights still clogging the loop. "You're right. But I don't see any way around it. Either I do this job or I forfeit a fortune."

Carl was silent for a long moment, then spoke with disappointment in his voice. "And you just can't give up the money."

"You know the money doesn't mean jack to me. Hope2O needs the money. Not me."

"No, Hope2O needs you on board all the time. It's your expertise we need, not your money."

"You think I should walk away like Dalton did?"

"Hey, I can't tell you what to do. I've never had a carrot worth half a billion dollars, but ask yourself this—what has the promise of all that money ever gotten you?"

Griffin didn't have an answer to that. The conversation moved on to other Hope2O business, and he stayed on the phone with Carl taking care of obligations he'd been neglecting for a week until long after the traffic on the loop cleared up. It was well after noon when he finally got back on the road and finished the drive to his parents'. All the while, in the back of his mind was the question Carl had posed. What had all the Cain money ever gotten him?

Because Griffin was going to talk to his mother, Sydney felt no compunction abandoning her drudgery to head back to her desk so she could catch up on her normal duties as EA to the CEO. After a morning away from her work, things had started to pile up. The whole EA thing hadn't exactly been the career path she'd imagined for herself when she'd done her undergraduate work in psychology. She'd always imagined she'd do postgraduate study and one day get her therapist's license. She'd taken her first job as an assistant on a whim. Just something to pay the bills while she'd waited for the next semester to start. But she was good at it. The money was great, and she found being in the thick of things in an office surprisingly rewarding. Today was no different. Fifty fires had sprouted up during her morning away from the computer, and she doused them with her usual speed and efficiency. Her inner therapist laughed at her. The joy she took in her job was an obvious attempt to fill her need to be needed. To feel like none of it could function without her. She knew that's why she loved it and she didn't even mind.

She was cruising through her work when the phone rang. "Griffin Cain's office. How can I help you?"

"Is Griffin available?" asked a woman's cool voice.

"He's not in right now. I may be able to transfer you to his cell phone. May I ask who's calling?"

There was an annoyed huff as though the caller had expected Sydney to recognize her voice. "This is Caro Cain. I am allowed to call my own son, aren't I?"

"I'm sorry, Mrs. Cain. I'll patch you through." But the phone rang and rang and Griffin never picked up. Sydney switched back over to the original call and apologized again. "I'm sorry, Mrs. Cain. I'd be happy to connect you to his voice mail or take a message. Was this in regard to the conversation you had this morning?"

There was a pause and then, with a touch of uncertainty in her voice, Caro asked, "The conversation?"

"Yes. The conversation," Sydney repeated, feeling dumb. "Griffin left the office, oh…nearly three hours ago." Surely that was enough time to get to his parents' house. If he hadn't gone there, then where had he gone? "He said he was going to your house to talk to you." Unless Caro wasn't at home. That explained it. "Are you at home? Perhaps he missed you?"

"You may be my son's assistant, but I hardly think I need to clear my schedule with you." There was a pinched quality to Caro's voice. "What did he want to discuss with me?"

Sydney hesitated, her mind flooding with all the negative things Griffin had said about his mother. But he was the one who'd said he planned to go talk to her. Surely no harm could come from her just giving Caro a glimpse of his cards.

"He wanted to talk to you about the missing heiress. We've hit a little roadblock in the course of our research and he thought you would be able to help him narrow down the search."

"He did?" Caro sounded surprised, but she recovered quickly. "Well, of course he did. I was at the house all morning. I wonder why he didn't come."

Sydney nearly harumphed. Caro wasn't the only one with questions. It wasn't that Griffin had to tell her where he was going to be every second of every day, but his disappearing act was getting old. As his assistant, it was her job to know his whereabouts, and frankly she was getting tired of feeling left in the dark.

"I wish he had just called. I've already left the house and won't be back until this evening." Apparently, Caro felt the same way as Sydney. The other woman sighed and then continued in a confidential tone. "We could have talked this morning and been done with it. As it is, it could be sometime tomorrow before he catches up with me. Valuable time is wasting and he's off doing God only knows what."

Sydney hesitated a moment before asking, "Then you would be willing to answer any questions he has? You'd be willing to help him find his sister?"

"Willing? Well, of course I'm willing. What sort of mother do you think I am that I might not be willing to help my sons complete this quixotic quest my husband has sent them on?"

"That's very generous of you. I'll make sure I pass on the message to Griffin." When she could reach him. Where was he?

"Or..." Caro let the word dangle there suggestively. "If you happened to know what he wanted to discuss with me, you could join me for lunch and simply ask me yourself."

"I..." Oh, God. How was she supposed to answer? "I..." On one hand, Griffin was nowhere to be found and, as his mother had pointed out, they were on a time crunch here. On the other, Griffin must have had his reasons for saying he was going to his parents' house and then not going.

Maybe the same reasons he didn't share his schedule with her and made bizarre phone calls that he didn't want her listening in on. If he were a different kind of guy, she might think he was stepping out on her. Maybe she was being naive. Sure, Griffin was a playboy and a charmer, but in the time they'd been together, he'd seemed to curb his outrageous flirting. Plus, the sheer scorn in his voice when he discussed his father's philandering made her think he just wasn't a cheater.

What would it hurt for her to go see Caro Cain and just talk to her? Maybe it would even be for the best. After all, Griffin obviously didn't have a great relationship with her. Perhaps a neutral party could more easily get an honest answer from her.

"I would love to meet you for lunch," she found herself saying.

She quickly jotted down the address, even though she and nearly everyone in Houston knew the location of the River Oaks Country Club.

As she packed up her bag, she even told herself she was doing the right thing. She didn't really believe Griffin would do anything to hurt Cain Enterprises. Not intentionally. But clearly he was not objective here.

Sure, there was a line when it came to respecting a boss's decisions. But if he wasn't available to make the decision, that line was blurry. And if he wasn't being one-hundred percent logical and responsible, then maybe the line even wiggled a little bit.

By the time Griffin pulled up in front of his parents' house, he still hadn't decided what do to about Hope2O. He was so lost in thought he almost didn't recognize the Jaguar XK parked at the curb. Only when he saw the sticker for the rental car company did he remember that the same car had been parked there nearly three weeks ago when Hollister had made his big announcement. Which meant Cooper must be visiting. Of all his father's possible visitors, only Cooper was enough of an adrenaline junkie to rent a Jaguar every time he came to town.

Ever since their father's first heart attack, Hollister had been sleeping downstairs, in the room at the front of the house that had once been his office. Now, all the furniture had been replaced by a hospital bed and enough medical equipment to sustain a surgical ward in a third-world country. Griffin knew this because he'd actually visited clinics in Africa that got by with less.

Today, he peeked into the room and saw that his father was sleeping. He briefly considered waking his father up, but instead he quietly closed the door just as a nurse bustled around the corner. She was one of three who cared for Hollister around the clock. Patting her mouth with a napkin, she said, "I'm sorry, sir. I was just taking a lunch break."

"You don't have to apologize," he assured her. "You're allowed to eat."

The nurse, a pretty woman in her mid-twenties with curves and twinkling eyes, giggled a little. "Thank goodness," she said with a smile.

Instead of hurrying back to her food, she lingered. There was something coy in her posture and expression that let him know that she'd stay and chat if he wanted her to. It'd be easy enough. He could ask how her lunch was, tease her about being away from her station, listen sympathetically about her grueling hours. There'd been a time he would have chatted her up, gotten her number and a few days later probably taken her to bed. There'd even been a time when he would have thought that the break he and Sydney were on meant he was free to do just that. Today, he wasn't the least bit interested.

Instead of flirting with the girl, he just asked, "His condition is still stable?"

Her expression faltered, but she quickly rallied, nodding professionally and saying, "Yes, sir. One of us will contact you if there's the slightest change."

Which answered the question at the back of his mind. She knew exactly who he was—the heir to the fortune. The man with his hands wrapped around a golden ticket.

That was always the problem with women who knew about the money. And, somehow, they always knew about the money. Except with Sydney. Sydney had never seemed remotely interested in that.

He nodded politely to the nurse. "Thanks."

Then he made his way down the hall toward the back of the house, only to see Cooper leaning in the doorway to the kitchen, his hands shoved into the pockets of his jeans and a smug grin on his face.

"Boy, you're slipping." Cooper liked nothing more than to get a rise out of him or Dalton.

"I don't know what you're talking about," Griffin said.

Cooper nodded in the direction of the hall down which the nurse had disappeared. "Come on, a prime piece of ass like that? Normally you'd be all over that."

"I think I have a little more restraint." He couldn't resist adding a subtle dig. "And a little more class."

Cooper pushed away from the door. He flashed a toothy, humorless grin. "Which is your way, I suppose, of saying I have none."

"Hey, that's not what I was saying. But the fact that you heard that is a bit of a Rorschach test of your insecurities, doncha think?"

Cooper had the long and lean build of an Olympic snowboarder, which is precisely what he had been before he started his own company designing and manufacturing snowboards. He was the kind of athlete who was as good in front of the camera as he was on his board. All in all, Cooper was an expert at playing the game, whatever the game was.

Which was one of the reasons why Griffin couldn't get a read on Cooper's mood, not until Cooper was close enough to give Griffin a friendly slap on the arm and say, "So how've you been?"

"Fine." Griffin resisted the urge to rub at the spot on his arm. "So what're you doing here?"

"I just came by to have lunch with the old man."

"He's asleep," Griffin observed.

"He was tired after eating."

Griffin held up a hand palm out. "Hey, I'm not criticizing, I'm just surprised. I would have thought you'd be headed back to Colorado by now. It's been, what, a couple of weeks since Dad's big announcement?"

"I was busy doing..." Cooper's voice trailed off as he apparently fished around for the right word. "Stuff."

"Business stuff?" he asked, even though it was none of his concern. If Cooper could give him a hard time, then he damn well better be willing to take it, too. Besides, if Cooper was also searching for the missing heiress, Griffin wanted to know about it.

"No," Cooper said simply. Then his mouth spread into a wide grin.

"Any chance you're still in town because you're looking for the heiress yourself?"

Cooper's smile broadened without necessarily softening any. "Do you really think I'd tell you if I was?"

No, he didn't. They'd never been close, so why would Cooper share information, even if he had it?

"Are you leaving soon, though?" Griffin asked as Cooper headed for the front door.

"My flight leaves tomorrow morning." Cooper pulled his hand out of his pocket, extracting his keys. He sent a last look back through the door to the kitchen, which he'd just walked through a few minutes ago. "But I'm considering changing my plans. Extending my stay a little longer."

Cooper had almost made it out the front door when Griffin said, "Hey, if you're going to be in town, we should get together." Cooper turned to stare at him, his mouth slightly agape, his surprise so obvious, Griffin felt obliged to add, "You know, hang out or whatever."

That cynical smile flirted across Cooper's lips again. "And not talk about the heiress at all."

Griffin laughed. "Yeah. I can see why the offer looks suspicious. But I mean it. You're not in town that much. Dalton and I don't see you often enough."

"Oh, but you and Dalton hang out all the time?"

"I wouldn't say all the time. But after the divorce he moved into my building, so, yeah, I see him. Not that he'll be around much this week."

"Right. 'Cause of Laney."

Because Cooper had lived in their house for a couple of years after his mother had died, he knew Laney, too, and, as far as Griffin could tell, they'd even been close back in high school.

Cooper had looped his key ring on one of his fingers and he gave the ring a jostle so the keys flipped around his hand and he caught them again. Griffin smiled because he did that same thing with his keys.

"What do you say? There's a great sushi place not far from the office."

Cooper shrugged, though he still looked surprised. "Sure. We should do that."

But, in truth, the invitation had surprised Griffin, too. He'd never before had the impulse to bond with Cooper. Neither he nor Dalton had ever been particularly close to Cooper. Yeah, they'd lived in the same house for Cooper's last two years of high school and during summers before that. They'd wrestled and fought. They'd played touch football more roughly than they probably should have. But had they ever really talked? About anything?

For the first time in his life, that bugged Griffin.

It occurred to him now that once Hollister died, Cooper might never again come down to Texas. Unless there was some major shift in his relationship with his brother, once Hollister was gone, he might never see him again.

Suddenly, he thought of Sydney and all that he'd learned that morning from that damn file. Of the foster mother she still kept in touch with. Of the other kids who'd grown up with her in that foster home with whom she still kept in touch.

It wasn't the kind of thing Sydney talked about. Hell, he shouldn't even know about it, but he did. And he couldn't shake the impression that if Sydney knew just how lazy he was in his relationship with Cooper, she'd be disappointed. Why that mattered, he couldn't say. All he knew was that if Sydney had a half sibling, she'd damn well have done more than have her assistant send a card at the holidays.

He didn't stop to ask himself why it mattered what Sydney

would do. Instead, he followed the faint sound of clattering dishes into the kitchen, where he assumed he would find his mother. Yes, it was rare for her to cook and even odder for her to clean, but he figured that must be where she was because the house was otherwise quiet.

However, instead of his mother, he found Portia at the sink, quietly loading glasses into the dishwasher. Portia had been married to Dalton for nearly a decade before their divorce a year ago. Though Dalton never complained that Portia still flitted about the edges of their family, Griffin found it bizarre as hell.

She looked up when he walked in and gave a jump as if he'd startled her out of deep thought. "Oh, it's you."

He stopped on the far side of the kitchen, not wanting to get too close to Princess Portia. "I was looking for my mother."

Daintily drying her hands on a dishtowel, Portia sighed, making it clear that speaking to him was a burden. "She's having lunch at the country club."

He glanced at his watch. "Perfect. I'll check there."

"You should call first and have her add you to the guest list," Portia said in her most *helpful* voice. "Otherwise they might not let you in."

Like all good Southern women, Portia's helpful voice was designed to eviscerate unsuspecting victims.

"Just out of curiosity, why are you here at all?" he asked. "I mean, you do know that you're not actually part of this family anymore, right?"

Her hands clenched on the towel before she tossed it aside. "I'm here because your parents are going through an extremely difficult time and none of you boys has the common sense to check in on them."

Ignoring the sting of truth that accompanied that barb, he said, "I'm here now."

"And I'm guessing you came to harass your mother about what she knows about Hollister's illegitimate daughter."

"I—"

"She knows nothing. And I can't begin to tell you how distressed she is by this mess that whore stirred up."

The vehemence in Portia's voice nearly rocked him back a step. "Wow, that's an awfully harsh word, Portia. Did it tarnish that silver spoon on the way out of your mouth?"

She ignored his jab and strode forward to the massive island that divided the kitchen and separated them by a good eight feet. She planted her palms down on the granite and leveled a stare at him.

"You may not give a damn about this family, but I still do, even if Dalton and I are not together."

"Yeah, can we circle back around to that? Because I'm still not sure I understand what you're doing here now when you and Dalton are divorced."

"I'm here because Caro asked me to come."

"I had no idea you two were so close." There was a sneer in his voice and he didn't bother to hide it. It irked him a little, that she and his mother were close. Nothing he'd ever done had been good enough for his mother. But she'd welcomed Portia like a long-lost daughter.

Portia must have heard the bitterness in his voice because she shrugged without really meeting his gaze. "Your mother and I have a lot in common. We were both pressured into marriages with powerful men who didn't give a damn about us. I think she admires me for having the courage to walk away. Besides, she was like a mother to me for ten years."

For the briefest moment, he wondered if it really was cowardice rather than greed that had kept his mother by Hollister's side all those years. Then he decided it didn't matter. She could have left. At any point in her thirty-plus years with Hollister she could have walked away. She could have done what was best for her kids and left an emotionally abusive man. Instead, she'd stayed. Maybe it was callous of him, but he resented her for it.

He snorted his derision. "Right. You came running to be

with her because she was like a mother to you for a decade, but that's about ten years longer than she was ever like a mother to me."

Portia's expression softened and she blew out a sigh. "Look, I know she wasn't a perfect mother to you or to Dalton, but try to see this from her point of view. She never asked for this. She's the victim here as much as you, Dalton and Cooper are."

"I'm sure she's hoping either Dalton or I will win the company and throw her a bone or two."

Portia gave him an assessing look. "And will you? If you find your sister, will you give your mother some of Hollister's fortune?"

He answered without even having to think about it. "Yeah. I will. But don't tell her that."

"Her husband is dying," Portia said. "You could show a little sympathy."

"More to the point, her dying husband is cutting her off. If she's crying, I think I can guess why."

Portia stared hard at him and then tossed down the dishtowel she'd held clutched in her hands. "You know, Griffin, you really are a piece of work. You act so superior. You criticize your parents for caring more about money than people, but when it comes down to it, you're scrambling after Hollister's money, too."

"That was the point of this challenge, wasn't it?" Griffin said past the hot knot of anger choking him. "He wanted us scrambling after him."

"Maybe he just wanted your attention," she countered.

"I suppose you think I'm a worthless son for not caring."

Portia shook her head in exasperation. "Look, it's not my business."

"Well, at least we agree on that." He moved to walk out but then stopped at the last minute. "You never told me who she was having lunch with."

Portia had turned away from him to face the sink, and before she turned back he noticed that the tail of her shirt was untucked from her pants. And the twist in her hair had come loose and then been hastily repinned. Looking at her from behind, he realized she was more rumpled than he'd ever seen her. Before he had a chance to wonder why, she turned around and offered him a cold smile.

"I thought you knew. She's having lunch with Sydney Edwards. Your assistant. I'm surprised you didn't know." His shock must have shown on his expression because a broad smile cracked the icy beauty of Portia's face. She looked at her watch with an exaggerated gesture. "In fact, they should be sitting down for lunch right about now."

Eight

Sydney knew she was outclassed the second she set foot in the River Oaks Country Club. Actually, she knew she was outclassed the second she pulled her aging Civic up to the security gate. River Oaks County Club was one of the most exclusive in the country. The sprawling antebellum clubhouse was built of pale bricks, its grandeur reinforced by oil fortunes and a century of social climbing. None of that intimidated Sydney. She'd spent her whole life being outclassed. The way she saw it, in terms of class and social prestige, pretty much everyone was higher on the totem pole than she was. No point in getting upset about that. When it came to interacting with people beyond her means, she was used to faking it.

When the maître d' showed her into the dining room where Caro Cain was already waiting, Sydney had to clench her hands around the strap of her purse to hide the faint tremble in her fingers.

But Caro stood up and, rather than shake Sydney's hand,

gave her an air kiss, which somehow managed to be welcoming and dismissive at the same time.

Taken aback, Sydney awkwardly reached out to return the hug, but Caro had already stepped away.

"Um, thank you for inviting me to lunch," Sydney said.

"Of course!" Caro enthused. "I want to do anything I can to help."

"I see," Sydney said as she lowered herself to the cushioned edge of the seat. The second her bottom touched fabric a waiter was at the table filling up her water glass.

"Would you like a glass of wine?" Caro asked, as though she was a hostess rather than merely another guest at the country club's restaurant.

"Just tea, please," Sydney answered.

Caro gave the waiter a distant smile. "Another wine then for me and a sweet tea for my guest."

"Unsweetened," Sydney quickly corrected her. "I like to keep things simple."

"Very well." Caro nodded. "An unsweetened iced tea," she said to the waiter. Her tone was beleaguered, as if Sydney's choice was a personal affront to her.

"So," Caro said when they were alone again. "Now you're helping Griffin with his search for the girl."

"Yes."

"I'm certainly willing to do anything I can to help."

"Yes, well, the forty-two boxes of household records you sent over have been very informative."

"I'm so glad," Caro said, and though her tone was effusive, it lacked true feeling. "Though I'll admit I was a bit worried about just handing over so much personal information. But I suppose it can't be helped."

Caro gave a fragile smile accompanied by a fluttering hand gesture. Sydney had the odd impression that she wasn't really having lunch with Caro, but rather that she was attending a stage performance. Maybe something by Tennessee Williams, something with a lot of wispy Southern women dripping with family drama. Sydney had never cared for Tennessee Williams. She was more of a Mamet girl, herself.

She couldn't help wondering if Caro Cain was truly as fragile as she appeared. After the waiter dropped off the drinks, Sydney pulled out her iPad and prepared to take notes.

"I'd like to ask you a few questions," she began.

Caro pressed her fingertips to her chest, feigning surprise. "Were the household records not enough?"

"There is a lot of information in those forty-two boxes. Searching through them is quite a job. Because we are a bit short on time, I'm sure you can appreciate the need for efficiency."

Caro delicately brought her napkin up to her eyes as if blotting away fresh tears. "Of course. My dear Hollister could pass at any moment."

The phrase "my dear Hollister" gave Sydney pause, especially after what Griffin had said earlier about Caro abhorring Hollister. *Abhor* was a pretty strong word. And perhaps his failing health had softened her emotions.

"Erm…yes, of course," Sydney hedged, fiddling with the settings on her iPad as she wondered how best to steer the conversation. "If we could just—"

"You don't like me much, do you?"

Sydney snapped her gaze to Caro's face. She cringed. "It's not my place to—"

"I supposed Dalton told you all sorts of horror stories about me."

"Dalton never really discussed his personal life," she was able to say honestly.

"Hmm." Caro took another sip of her wine while pinning Sydney with a cool, assessing gaze. "Then I suppose you've just formed your own opinion based on what you think you know about me."

"I…" Christ, what was she supposed to say to that? "It's really not my place to have an opinion about you."

"Nonsense. Everyone has opinions." Caro waved a dismissive hand and then studied Sydney shrewdly. "I suppose you think I brought this on myself. That I'm as much to blame as Hollister because I turned a blind eye for so many years." She sighed, staring off into space for a moment. "And maybe I should have left, but I knew he loved me in his own way. Hollister is a great man. But even great men never accomplish great things without the right support system. I told myself I could be that support he needed. Perhaps I fooled even myself."

Slowly, Caro's gaze swiveled back to Sydney. Though Sydney met the other woman's gaze, she had no idea what to say. Honestly, she couldn't pretend to be sympathetic, but she also couldn't deny that she understood what Caro meant. Hadn't she just had a similar thought herself at the office? Not exactly, of course. But similar. That's what being an assistant was all about. Taking pride in someone else's work. Helping someone else achieve greatness while being content to stay in the background.

It seemed she could see Caro's faults so clearly, but perhaps that was because they mirrored her own.

Caro seemed to be waiting for some response, so Sydney spoke, hesitatingly at first. "I can't speak to your relationship with Hollister. That's not my place. But I can say this—Griffin also has it in him to be a great man."

"Griffin?" Caro asked.

"Yes, Griffin." The surprise in Caro's voice annoyed her.

"Oh, I'm not disagreeing," Caro added hastily. "I'm just surprised. You worked for Dalton for much longer. I expected you to be touting his greatness."

Heat rose in Sydney's cheeks as she realized her mistake. She had only been Griffin's assistant for a handful of days, and that's how Caro would see it. "Of course Dalton is also great," she fumbled for a response. Something, anything to hide the depth of her involvement with Griffin. "Dalton is incredibly intelligent. And ambitious. And…" Now she was overplaying it. She paused to take a sip of her tea. "I merely meant that I can see greatness in Griffin, too."

"Yes. I agree." Caro leveled another one of those cool, assessing stares at Sydney, giving her the feeling that she'd hidden nothing from the other woman but exposed entirely too much.

"Well," Sydney said with forced confidence. "About those questions I had…"

"Yes," came a voice from right behind her. "I have some questions, too."

Sydney's heart gave a little jump. She knew his voice without having to turn around.

Griffin was here.

She slowly looked over her shoulder. He was standing behind her, just to her right. How much had he heard? More to the point, why was he here? Was he angry with her?

She pasted an ingratiating smile on her face. "Hello, Mr. Cain."

Her use of his last name must have irritated him because his gaze narrowed slightly. "Ms. Edwards," he said with a nod. "Mother." He crossed to Caro's side and brushed a kiss across her cheek. "You look beautiful, as always."

Caro offered him a restrained smile. "Hello, dear. I assume you want to join us. We haven't ordered yet. Shall I have the waiter pull up a chair?"

She was already gesturing when he stopped her with a hand to her arm. "No. Thank you. I'll take Sydney's chair. She can't stay."

"I can't?"

"No. You can't. I need you back at the office."

"You do?" Nice try, but she wasn't going to let him bully her, not when she was just starting to feel like she was making real progress with his mother.

"Yes." He gave her a pointed look. As if she was too dense to get the point. "There's a lot of work to do today."

"Then I'll stay late." She smiled back at Caro. "Your mother was nice enough to invite me to lunch. It would be rude to leave her now."

"You can go back to the office and I'll have lunch with her."

"But—" Sydney began, but then broke off. Glancing back at Griffin, she said, "Perhaps we should discuss this in private."

Griffin looked like he'd rather discuss it back at the office, but instead he gave a tight nod. "Mother, if you'll excuse us?"

"Yes, of course," she murmured.

"Come on, then."

Sydney stood, leaving her shoulder bag at the table because that way he couldn't just show her out. However, instead of taking her out the front of the club, which she'd feared he would do, he guided her out the back, through one of the many glass doors, onto the sprawling patio that overlooked the expansive golf course.

Even though it was late October and theoretically the temperatures should be dropping, it was still in the eighties and the persistent humidity made the air feel sticky. The view of the pristinely manicured lawns of the River Oaks golf course was stunning. It was almost oppressively beautiful. Too beautiful, actually, like the photo on a postcard that's been touched up so much it no longer looks like a real place.

And she knew that was true of the River Oaks Country Club. There was nothing here that was real. Nothing solid. It was all surgically taut skin and chemically brightened grass.

But perhaps she was prejudiced, her opinions colored by her status as an outsider.

Beside her, Griffin said, "Don't pretend you came here to lunch with my mother just to admire the view."

She glanced up at him, taking in the lean lines of his face. Griffin also had that otherworldly quality to him. Not false, exactly, but still too pretty to be real. Unbelievably handsome.

She turned to face him fully. No, she was done pretending.

"Of course I'm not going to pretend. I'm here to talk to your mother, just like you are."

"The question is, why are you here when you're supposed to be back at the office?"

"Your mother called *me*. She offered to help in any way she could. I tried to get a hold of you, but you weren't available. When she offered to talk to me instead, I accepted. I wanted to strike while the iron was hot. I didn't do this to undermine you or go behind your back. I was trying to help. That's all."

He opened his mouth, his hand raised like he was about to jab a finger toward her to emphasize his point. Then he snapped his mouth shut, spun around and paced about five steps away. Only to turn back around, fists clenched at his side, and glare at her. "You do not need to be here."

"I feel like she's really starting to open up to me. Maybe I—"

"If you feel like she's starting to open to you it's because that's what she wants you to feel."

"You're saying she's manipulating me?"

"That's what my mother does best." Suddenly, there was no belligerence in his tone. No frustration. Just exhaustion. "Just go back to the office and let me handle her."

She responded with as much honesty as she could. "I don't think I should," she answered simply. "I'm supposed to be helping you find the missing heiress. Your mother obviously has information that we need. If she'll open up to me—"

"We don't know that."

"She must! And I'm sorry, but the fact that you can't see that makes me question your judgment."

"My judgment?"

"Yes, your judgment. This argument we're having is ridiculous. I'm trying to do what's best for Cain Enterprises and I really believe your mother will open up to me. You've admit-

ted to me that you don't get along with her. Maybe I'll have
more luck. Shouldn't you at least let me try?"

And this, Griffin realized, was why sleeping with his assistant was a dumb-ass idea.

Marion might be nearing fifty and matronly, she might be
a little slow to navigate the latest software and she might even
be still reporting to his father—which he'd long suspected, but
never had any firm evidence of—but at least Marion followed
directions. If he'd sent her back to the office to dig pointlessly
through boxes, she'd have done it with a cheerful smile and
brought him cookies later.

But no, not Sydney. Because Sydney knew him too well to
fall for his bull.

"Look, there is nothing wrong with my judgment. Let me
question my mother."

Her brow furrowed with doubt. Hoping to push the argument over the edge, he ran a knuckle across her cheek. Her
eyelids dropped a fraction and she swayed just a little. And
this was the advantage of sleeping with your assistant. At least
when she was as responsive as Sydney was.

"Trust me," he coaxed.

Her eyes snapped open. "Trust you?" She stepped back, putting more distance between them. "I'm supposed to just trust
you? That's really rich coming from a guy who won't even let
me glance at his Day-Timer."

Where the hell had that come from? "That has nothing to
do with this."

Her gaze narrowed slightly. "Try to see it from my point of
view. How am I supposed to trust you when you never explain
anything? Do you deny that you're hiding things from me?"

He turned away from her and stared out at the lush green
lawns of the golf course. He gritted his teeth. "I was just trying to protect you."

"I don't understand...protect me from what?" Her expression was blank with confusion.

"I'm trying to protect you from my parents. They're not nice people," he admitted. "Bitter. Angry. Manipulative. Pits of nuclear waste are less toxic. And things at the house have only gotten worse since this crap with the heiress started. Why the hell would I want to expose you to that?"

He heard her steps behind him, felt the air shift as she propped her hip against the limestone. The rock was cool beneath his palms. Solid and strong. Everything about the country club, everything about this entire neighborhood was designed to convey strength and power. It was designed to intimidate and exclude.

He waited for her to speak, but when she didn't say anything, he finally looked up at her.

Though her body was facing him, she'd turned her head to stare out over the lawn, too. "So you think...what? That she would intimidate me?"

There was confusion in her voice, but also something else. Something he couldn't quite identify. Like she was hurt maybe.

"It's not just you. My mother intimidates everyone. Except for the people she manipulates. One day she'll treat you like she's your best friend, the next she cuts you out entirely. Friendship, affection, love...for her, those aren't emotions, they're currency. It's not that I didn't think you could handle her, but..." He straightened and turned to face her. "You're not used to this world. You grew up in a world where people cared about each other. Took care of each other."

She gave a snort and he instantly regretted his words. Because he now knew that wasn't entirely true. Her own mother was worse even than his. But horrible in a different way. It was only after Sydney had been removed to foster care that she'd had anyone to take care of her. Only then had she lived in a world where people loved one another.

If he'd thought it through first, he would have phrased it

differently, but he couldn't very well apologize now. Not when she didn't even know he knew about her birth mother.

Still, he said, "I'm sorry. I never meant for this to be a big deal."

She cocked her head to the side again. "Then why is it such a big deal?"

He shrugged, suddenly feeling self-conscious. He wasn't used to talking about his family with anyone. He didn't like to play the poor little rich boy card.

"Next time," she said, "if you have a logical reason for doing something, just tell me. You don't have to be so damn secretive about everything."

"Neither do you," he pointed out, thinking about all the things she hadn't told him. Things he knew only because of that damn background check.

She nodded, slowly. "Okay. It's a deal. From now on, we talk more. We're in this together, right?"

"Right." And suddenly, he found himself smiling at her.

Right up until she added, "If we don't get better at sharing information, we're never going to find this girl."

"Right," he said again. Of course that was what she talking about. "Come on, let's get back in there and finish up with my mother."

He walked a few steps before he realized she hadn't followed. When he turned back, he saw her watching him, her mouth twisted into a wry smile.

"What?" he asked.

She gave a self-conscious shrug and crossed to his side. "I've never had anyone try to protect me from anything, even if it was misguided," she admitted in a soft voice. "Thank you."

All he could do was nod because if she knew the truth, she sure as hell wouldn't be thanking him. If she ever found out how much he knew about her past, she'd be furious.

But, as she pointed out, they were only in this together until they found the heiress. After that, all this talking, and sharing and intermingling of their lives would end. So that was something to look forward to. After that, he could go back to having sex with Sydney instead of sharing all this emotional crap.

Nine

Sydney tried to keep a silly smile off her face as she walked back into the dining room to rejoin Griffin's mother. Everything she knew about the woman, everything Griffin had said and her own instincts told her that Caro Cain would not be pleased if she knew her son was involved with anyone's assistant. She was the kind of woman who would want her sons to date and marry debutantes.

Plus, they'd been out on the patio talking long enough that she was probably already suspicious. Despite all that, Sydney was unexpectedly pleased by Griffin's words. They filled her with a warm fuzziness that had nothing to do with the afternoon's high temperatures. By the time she reached Caro's table, Sydney made sure her expression was carefully professional. Polite but distant.

She wished inside she felt the same, instead of the disconcerting torrent of emotions that were rushing through her.

Caro Cain raised her eyebrows coolly as Griffin held out the chair for Sydney. "Well, you were certainly gone a long time. That must have been quite the discussion you had."

"Just some business we had to clear up from the office," Griffin answered smoothly.

"Anything I can help with?" Caro asked.

Griffin offered his mother a tight smile. "Certainly not, Mother. You know how you hate talking business at the table."

Caro sniffed. "As if that ever stopped your father." Then she blotted at her eyes again. She made a sound like a strangled sob. "What I wouldn't give just to share a meal with him now."

"He's not dead yet," Griffin said wryly as he sat down.

Caro's gaze sharpened. "Do not disrespect your father to me."

Griffin shrugged, but Sydney could tell he was about to launch another volley, so she leaned forward and interrupted the familial sparring. "Mrs. Cain, let's get back to those questions I wanted to ask you."

"Yes, of course. But I will say I was surprised that you're working for Griffin now."

Sydney wondered just how much Caro had deduced of her relationship with Griffin.

"Of course I am," she said quickly. "The CEO needs an assistant. And when Dalton left—"

"Yes, of course." Caro smiled benevolently at Griffin. "I'm sure this won't shock you, but I can't say that I'm sorry Dalton has stopped looking for the girl." Caro leaned close and dropped her voice. "If only one of you can inherit everything, then I'd much prefer it be you."

Sydney watched the revulsion flicker across Griffin's face as his mother patted his hand conspiratorially, but Caro didn't seem to notice it.

However, she did turn her assessing gaze to Sydney. "What I meant earlier was that I was surprised you're still involved. If Dalton has indeed left the company, then why are you still around?"

Caro's questions made one thing clear: she was on to them. She may not know for sure that they were sleeping together, but their long discussion out on the balcony—or perhaps her earlier fumble—had tipped their hand. Caro knew something was up.

Before Sydney could answer, Griffin peeled his mother's hand off his arm and said, "Sydney is working for me now. I needed someone to help me transition to interim CEO."

"And you didn't want to bring your own assistant with you?" Caro asked.

"No." With each question, Griffin's tone cooled. "I needed someone who was familiar with every project on Dalton's plate."

Caro's lips turned down in disapproval. "And besides, you've never really trusted Marion, have you? After all, she worked under your father too long for that, didn't she?" Instead of waiting for him to answer, Caro turned her cool gaze on Sydney. "You, however, haven't worked at Cain Enterprises long enough to have any alliance."

Sydney blinked in surprise at the icy chill in Caro's voice. "I don't... I'm not sure what you mean."

Griffin replied instead of Caro. "She's implying that you're not qualified for the position."

Caro's lips twisted in an unpleasant smile. "Nonsense. I'm sure that the only qualification that Dalton cared about was that she had never once worked for his father. Naturally that one quality prepared you for a position of tremendous power within the company. Unless there are other qualifications I'm unaware of."

"Enough, Mother," Griffin said sharply. "That's a line you don't want to cross."

Caro looked from Griffin to Sydney and back again with her eyebrows raised in feigned innocence. "Oh, I'm sorry." She patted the back of Sydney's hand. "Have I offended you, dear?"

Sydney forced a smile past the bitter taste in her mouth. "Not at all."

But she was starting to see what Griffin had meant about his mother.

"Excellent. I knew you were made of sterner stuff. Now, tell me what you need to know that you haven't been able to find out from the files I sent over."

Well, that was tricky because she'd learned precisely nothing from the files at all. In fact, after Caro's comments about Dalton, Sydney was beginning to wonder whether Caro hadn't been deliberately unhelpful before now. After all, she'd just admitted that she wanted Griffin to find the heiress instead of Dalton. Dalton had been the one who had originally requested the household documents be sent over. Perhaps Caro had simply sent over forty-two boxes of useless papers just to waste Dalton's time.

Of course, demanding answers about that would gain her nothing, so instead Sydney said, "I don't know if Dalton explained why he wanted the household records from that time period, but—"

"He did," Caro interrupted with a sweeping gesture. The wine in her glass sloshed precariously. "Something about a nanny."

"Yes." Sydney paused, wondering if Griffin was going to take over, but he remained silent. "Dalton and Laney had a theory about one of Dalton's nannies. Apparently, she worked for you when you were pregnant with Griffin. Her name was Vivian. She was pregnant when she worked with you. And they know for sure the child was a girl."

Caro took another sip of wine and Sydney couldn't tell if she was stalling for time or if she was merely disinterested.

Griffin lost patience with Caro before Sydney did. He leaned forward. "Do you remember the woman or not?"

"Not off the top of my head."

"I have pictures of her, if that would help." Sydney pulled the file from her bag and pushed the pictures across the table to Caro.

Caro glanced at them without a flicker of surprise or recognition.

"Do you know this woman?" Griffin asked.

"Perhaps. I don't know." Caro waved dismissively. "If there was a pregnant girl who worked for us, she certainly didn't stand out. That is the point, isn't it? That they were the help. Good help isn't seen or heard."

Her tone fairly dripped with derision, making it perfectly clear she thought Sydney was well outside her bounds.

Yeah, Sydney got the point. But she hadn't clawed her way out of poverty by feeling the sting of every subtle insult. Caro would have to work a lot harder to scare her off.

Sydney took a long sip of her iced tea. As she set down the glass she said, "You're a smart woman, Mrs. Cain. I can't believe there could be anyone in your home, help or otherwise, who could make a play for your husband without you knowing about it."

Caro's expression froze into an icy mask, and for one long moment she neither moved nor spoke. Then, abruptly, she smiled with smooth ease. "Well, there's your mistake. You seem to be under the impression that there was only one nanny making a play for my husband."

"There was more than one?"

"Of course. They *all* made a play for him. Hollister has always been quite charming. Add in his personal wealth and his power, and he was virtually irresistible. Every secretary at Cain Enterprises, every female geologist in R&D, every young nanny who cared for the boys—every last one of them was susceptible to his charms."

"*Every* single one of them? That's hard to believe."

"Really?" Caro tilted her head to the side, her expression all innocence. "Can you honestly not imagine that a smart and beautiful young woman might try to use sex to align herself with a wealthy and powerful man?"

Aha. And there it was. The cutting jab she'd been expecting ever since they'd returned to the table. Sydney opened her mouth, readying her own defense, but before she could speak Griffin leaned forward. "That's enough, Mother."

Caro blinked innocently. "Excuse me?"

"Enough with the thinly veiled barbs. Do you remember the name of the nanny or not?"

For a long moment, Caro studied her son, her gaze cunning in her assessment. Then she cut her gaze to Sydney for an instant before her lips turned up in a coy smile, leaving Sydney with the impression that Griffin's defense of her had revealed precisely the information Caro had been digging for.

"In the months she worked for us, I barely spoke to her." Now that Griffin had called her on her attitude, Caro's tone was clipped and irritated. She was obviously a woman who liked to play with her food but didn't like it when her food swatted back. "How am I supposed to remember her name?"

Sydney found herself frowning. "You barely spoke to her? How long did she work for you?"

"Maybe five, six months."

"You had no interaction with her in six months? When she had sole responsibility of caring for your children?"

"She was competent and kept the children out of my hair. Why on earth would I speak to her?"

"Because they were your *children.*"

Caro just waved her hand dismissively, clearly as disinterested in her progeny now as she had been then.

Sydney glanced at Griffin, expecting to see pain flash across his face at his mother's matter-of-fact dismissal. Instead, his expression was shuttered, his eyes unreadable. If his mother's carelessness hurt him, he didn't show it.

Somehow, his carefully hidden reaction made her ache even more deeply. She didn't want to see him openly in pain, but she would have understood that. She could have pitied that. But this? This emotional distance? This careful detachment with which he held his emotions in check? This was much harder for her to see. Because it was achingly obvious that he had expected his mother's reaction. Not because that was how she really felt, but because she'd obviously crafted the barb to punish him for standing up for Sydney.

And suddenly, she got what he'd been trying to tell her earlier about his family. About how ill-equipped she was to deal with their mind games.

She understood something else, too. He hadn't been protecting only her. By keeping her away from his mother, he'd also been protecting himself. However clever they were at hiding their relationship while they were at work, his mother had seen right through the ruse. She now had information about Griffin that she could use against him. He was now vulnerable to his mother's manipulations. Because of her.

Just like that, all the warm, fuzzy goodness that had been coursing through her veins seemed to seep into her belly and congeal into a mass of nerves.

Despite that sick feeling in her gut, Sydney wasn't going to back down, either. Caro knew more than she was saying. Sydney had no doubt about that.

"Okay," Sydney said, keeping her tone diplomatic. "If you don't remember the girl's name, surely you can think of someone who might. There's got to be someone else who can help us find her. How did you hire the nannies?" Sydney asked. "Did you use an agency of some kind?"

Suddenly, Caro's eyes lit up. "Yes. There was an agency. They sent nanny applications over."

Griffin sat back in his seat and gave Sydney an appreciative grin. "Great. Then all we need is the name of the agency."

"I don't have it."

"You what?"

"I don't have it. But Sharlene Sheppard should. Hollister asked Sharlene to help find the nanny. She contacted the agency herself."

"Okay then," Griffin said, pushing back his chair. "We go talk to Sharlene."

Sydney pushed back her chair and stood. She waited until they'd said their goodbyes to Caro and were out of hearing range before asking, "We?"

"Yes," he said grimly. "In for a penny, in for pound, right? Now that you've met my mother, you might as well meet the rest of the cast in this Greek tragedy."

The whole situation made Sydney sad. She'd always felt like she'd gotten the short end of the stick when it came to family. No father in the picture. A mother more interested in scoring her next hit than in parenting. No extended relatives to take over.

But the tangled mess that was the Cain family made her realize just how lucky she'd actually been. She'd landed with a great foster mom. She had foster siblings she cared about. And at the end of the day, she knew she had people who cared about her. Did Griffin have that? Had he *ever* had that?

She thought not. And it simply made her want to cry.

Ten

Griffin had always loved Greek mythology, particularly Homer's *Odyssey*. That bit about Scylla and Charybdis…that was pure gold. The way Griffin saw it, Homer's family life must have been about as fun-filled as his own because anytime he had to deal with both his mother and his father's former mistress, that's how he felt—like he was trapped with a horrible six-headed monster on one side and a treacherous whirlpool on the other.

Was it any wonder he hadn't wanted Sydney to accompany him through those particular straits? Even Odysseus lost good soldiers on that trip.

Though Sharlene looked like a defenseless waif—much as his own mother did—Sharlene was strong. If Caro's personality sometimes seemed as formidable as a six-headed monster's, then Sharlene was the vortex that unwittingly sucked people in. At heart, Sharlene was nice, a rarity in his childhood, but good intentions hadn't stopped her from creating countless problems and endless grief. He'd spent ten years of his life trapped between Scylla and Charybdis.

When he was a kid, he'd actually preferred spending time with Sharlene. Whenever they'd gone to the offices of Cain Enterprises, it had always been Sharlene who had taken care of them. She'd kept crayons in her desk—a hundred and sixty-four count crayons, too, not the measly sixteen count—and she always made sure she had paper to draw on. And when he'd had an emergency appendectomy when he was seven and his mother was out of town, it had been Sharlene who had stayed with him at the hospital.

Of course, as an adult, he could see that the emotional vortex was its own kind of monster. None of which explained why the thought of seeing her again after all this time made him feel sick to his stomach. But of all the women Hollister Cain had seduced and used badly, Sharlene had deserved it the least.

It wasn't until he'd pulled the car onto the loop and was heading for downtown that he felt Sydney's gaze firmly on him.

He glanced over at her, frowning. "What?"

She looked at him with her head cocked slightly to the side. "You're nervous."

He scoffed. "No, I'm not."

"Really?" she asked, looking pointedly at the spot on the steering wheel where his fingers tapped out a frantic beat.

"Okay." Why had he lied in the first place? So he was nervous about seeing Sharlene again. No big deal. "Maybe a little."

"You want to tell me why?"

No, he didn't.

She shrugged as if she didn't really care either way. "I just thought it might help. Talking it out might make you less nervous. If she's as formidable an opponent as rumor has made her out to be, you might be better off not displaying any signs of weakness."

"Rumor? What rumors?"

Sydney shrugged a shoulder. "I've just heard stuff around

the office. Sharlene Sheppard is now, what? The COO of Sheppard Capital? She's supposed to be an amazing business-woman."

"So?"

"And she's supposed to hate the Cains. And now you're supposed to face her down and try to get information from her? This is like braving the lion in her den. It would be nor-mal to be nervous."

"She's really not like that."

"Are you sure? Because I've never seen you nervous be-fore." Her shoulders shifted as she gave a little shrug. The movement did nice things for the little sweater stretched tight across her chest, but even that couldn't distract him enough to take his mind off her words. "True, we haven't been together that long, but I've never seen anything phase you. When you found out Dalton was resigning and leaving you in charge of a billion-dollar company, you didn't even blink. You faced down the board and convinced them to name you interim CEO and you didn't even break a sweat. Frankly, they were eating from the palm of your hand so contentedly, I think you could have asked them to toss out the interim and just be CEO and they would have done it."

"Your point?"

"My point is, neither of those situations made you nervous." She softened her words with a smile. "But you obviously are now. So I don't really know what to do with that."

"You don't have to *do* anything with it," he muttered, even though he knew it wasn't the answer she wanted.

He was silent for a long time. Long enough for Sydney to give another one of those shrugs and to finally turn and look out the window. Like she'd accepted that he just wasn't going to answer. The truth was, even he didn't think he was going to answer. But then she sighed. The noise was almost inaudi-ble over the sound of the car's engine and the ambient hum of traffic, but he still heard it.

Her sigh was as soft as a whisper but filled with regret.

Before now, their relationship had been perfect. Great sex untouched by complications, free from the angst and anguish that emotional involvement brought to the table. He'd thought Sydney was perfectly happy with that arrangement. Why would she—why would any woman—want to listen to him whine about his past?

But then there was that sigh. That regret-filled murmur that sounded like a trumpet's blare. He hated knowing that she regretted being with him. Hated knowing that she was sitting here in the car, wishing she was with the kind of guy who opened up and talked about his feelings. Never mind whether or not there actually were any guys like that in the world. Never mind that he had never, in any of his previous relationships, been the kind of guy who talked about his feelings.

He didn't like to think that she regretted being with him. So, as he pulled off the highway toward downtown, he admitted, "Sharlene isn't a formidable opponent."

"She isn't?"

"No. Sharlene is—or at least was when I knew her—a genuinely nice person. She's a good woman. And she never deserved to be involved with anyone like my father."

Sydney was quiet for a long moment. When she finally spoke, all she said was, "I see."

He hadn't meant to say anything more than that, but something about Sydney's quiet acceptance made his words come out of him in a rush.

"She was his secretary and his mistress for nearly ten years when I was a kid. Sometimes, during the summer or on school holidays, he'd bring Dalton and I up to his office. She was the one who would keep us entertained. She gave us crayons and printer paper for drawing. She even had a little stash of Brach's candies in a jar on her desk just for us."

"Let me guess," Sydney interrupted. "Peppermints."

He shot her a sideways glance. "The peppermints were for Dalton. How'd you guess?"

"He keeps Brach's peppermints in his desk drawer. I used to think of it as his one human weakness. You know, before he quit his job and ran off to be with the woman he adored." Sydney considered him for a minute. "So what kind did you like?"

"The white nougat ones with little jellies inside."

"I liked those, too, when I was a kid." She nodded seriously. "So if you have all these great childhood memories of Sharlene—and for the record, she does sound pretty awesome— then why are you so freaked out about going to see her?"

"I'm not freaked out."

"You're a little freaked out."

"I'm not—"

"Do you need me to run through the list again of the things that didn't make you this nervous?"

Sydney was looking at him with raised eyebrows and an arch expression. Her tone and words were teasing, but he could see in her eyes that she wasn't about to back down on this. He was struck by the sudden urge to pull over the car and…and what? Demand she get out and mind her own business? Or maybe just kiss her senseless so that they'd both remember where the boundaries of their relationship were. This was supposed to be about sex and pleasure. Not about prying painful childhood memories out into the light.

When he didn't say anything—because, God, what could he say?—she kept talking.

"You know, if it was me, I might feel guilty that my father treated her so badly."

"Who said he treated her badly?"

"I inferred it from the fact that your father hates Sheppard Capital and has tried to destroy them financially. If that's not horrible treatment, I don't know what is."

"Yeah," he muttered, his voice gruff. "Good point."

She had him so distracted he'd actually forgotten the conversation they'd had less than an hour ago. Or maybe he'd just blocked it out. He wasn't used to talking about his family with other people.

"Yeah, that's a nice theory, but I'm well past the age where I feel like I have to justify my father's behavior. He's an ass. There's no point in me apologizing for that."

"And yet you clearly feel guilty for how Sharlene was treated. If you're not apologizing for his behavior, then for whose?" She was silent for a minute, then abruptly she swiveled in her seat so that she was looking at him straight on. "You can't feel badly about how you treated her when she broke up with your father."

He shrugged, not entirely sure what to say, partly because it hadn't occurred to him until just then that he even felt guilty about it.

"She was like part of the family. Like my stepmom or something. Then, all of a sudden, she was gone from our lives."

"You were, what? Nine?"

"Ten."

"Look, Griffin, your father's love life is clearly all kinds of messed up. It was wrong that he had a mistress for all those years and acted like it was normal for her to spend time with you and be your friend. It was wrong for them to put a kid in the middle of all that. You were ten. You shouldn't have even known what was going on between them, let alone felt guilty for not sticking up for her or something."

"Maybe not. But I knew she'd been treated badly. Maybe I shouldn't have done something when I was kid. But I've been an adult now for twelve years. That's long enough that I should have found the time to apologize."

She seemed to be considering him seriously, but then she gave a snort of derision. "If you were acting like an adult at eighteen, then you're a better person than I was at eighteen."

He thought about what he knew about her—the things she'd told him and the things he'd learned on his own. "Yeah, I don't believe that for a minute. At eighteen, you were what? In college, taking eighteen hours a semester and working two jobs to pay your way."

He knew he'd slipped up the second the words were out of his mouth. Suddenly he found himself wishing the traffic would clear. Mere moments ago, he was glad for the traffic because it allowed him to postpone the inevitable. Now he wished he was already there.

She hadn't seemed to have realized his gaff yet, but she was smart and—unlike so many people he knew—she actually listened to what others were saying. He figured he only had a few more seconds before—

"Wait a second."

And there it was.

"Okay, I know I've mentioned college. But I never said anything about two jobs."

He faked causal. "I was guessing. You're not the type who would want to incur a lot of debt. You're not the type who would have let your foster mom pay for you." He glanced in her direction, but her gaze was still narrowed and suspicious. "It was a lucky guess."

"Were you guessing about me having a foster mom, too? If you had to 'guess'—" she made air quotes "—what college do you think I would have attended while I was working these two jobs?"

Five semesters at Houston Community College and another four at the University of Houston. "How would I know?"

"Yeah. That's what I'm wondering. How would you know?"

He kept his gaze on the bumper of the white Ford in front of him. Damn traffic.

After a second, he glanced over at her. "How much trouble am I in here?"

She seemed to be considering him, but there was a playful gleam in her eyes. "I haven't decided yet. I guess it depends on how invasively you've invaded my privacy."

"What would you consider invasive?"

"Well, I know Cain Enterprises did a background check when I was hired full-time. So, did you just abuse the privileges your name offers you and get access to my file?"

"I didn't do it on purpose."

"How do you accidentally read someone's background check?" That teasing light in her gaze had dimmed.

"Dalton had the file in his desk. I saw it this morning. I shouldn't have read it, but I did."

And now the details of her life seemed to have lodged themselves firmly into his brain, even though he'd only read the file once. He'd felt vaguely sick to his stomach. His disgust had been partly aimed at her mother because no one's parent should put their kid through the things Sydney had gone through. But mostly, he'd been disgusted with himself because he should never have even looked at the damn thing. Somehow, despite having been neglected and then abandoned by her mother, despite having bounced around the foster care system before finally landing in a good home, somehow, despite all that, Sydney had developed into a decent human being. And she'd deserved better than to have her past dug up.

She clenched the strap of her purse in her hand. It was a classic navy shoulder bag made of fine leather, just large enough to hold her personal belongings and the company-issued iPad. She massaged the strap with such intensity he half expected to see a wear mark on the leather.

"Do you know about Sinnamon?" she asked abruptly.

"I do."

Sinnamon was the name Sydney's birth mother had given her. Her foster mother had filed a petition to have it changed with she was eleven, which was a few years after she'd ended up with Molly Stanhope.

"Do you know about Roxy?" she asked after a moment.

"Your birth mother? Yes."

"What else do you know?"

"More than I should," he admitted, keeping his gaze glued to that white bumper as if he could will it out of his way. "The background search that Cain Enterprises did was pretty extensive. After all, you were hired to be the CEO's assistant. It doesn't get much higher up the chain of command than that."

He glanced at her, fully expecting her to be angry; instead, she looked a little bruised but mostly curious. "Do you read the company background checks on every woman you date who works for Cain Enterprises?"

"No! Jesus, this was nothing like that. It was a mistake." She nodded slowly, but she didn't lose that hurt look. He was so focused on the background check and her reaction to that that he almost didn't catch it. "Wait a second. What do you mean, every woman I date at Cain Enterprises?"

"Well, you know…" She gave a little shrug and looked embarrassed. "I've seen how you are with women around the office."

"You think I sleep with everyone at the office I flirt with?" He laughed. "I wouldn't get anything done at work."

She pursed her lips as if lost in thought. "What about Jenna Bartel?"

"Down in marketing?"

"Yeah."

"She's happily married with five kids."

"But she's always flirting with you!"

"Well, yeah. Five kids. She's desperate for adult conversation."

"Okay." She seemed to be scrounging for another name. "How about Peyton in HR?"

He nodded appreciatively. "Oh, she's great."

"So you dated her?"

"No, she's a lesbian. And in a long-term relationship."

"Okay, what about Chloe Young in R&D?"

This time he cringed just thinking about the disaster that would be. "She's engaged to Ryan Thomas."

"Really?"

"Absolutely. And he's one of those medieval Ren Faire types. Owns a broad sword and everything. No way I'm messing with that. He'd kill me."

"Hmmm," she mumbled.

"So have I convinced you?"

"Yes."

"The real question is why you needed convincing."

Sydney hesitated. Well, the answer to that was transparent. It was easy to believe they were having a no-strings, just-sex relationship when she thought she was one conquest out of many. She wanted to be the rule, not the exception.

She felt her cheeks turning pink, and she refocused her attention on the bumpy spot on her purse strap.

"I can't be the first woman you've dated who works for Cain Enterprises."

"Why not?"

She blew out a breath of frustration. Why not indeed? Because it implied she was more important than she thought she should be. Because it meant maybe this was something special. And she so didn't need those kinds of thoughts in her head. Instead of going down that twisted path, she asked, "So you've honestly never slept with someone from Cain Enterprises before me?"

He snorted derisively. "I'd have to be an idiot to make a regular practice of it."

"Why do you say that?" Sure, she knew why she thought sleeping with coworkers was a bad idea—despite the fact that she was doing it—but she'd also worked enough places to know a lot of people did it anyway.

Instead of answering outright, he asked, "Do you have any idea how much money I'm worth?" Then he muttered a curse. "Or rather, how much I would be worth if my father hadn't lost his mind."

She didn't know any precise numbers. "Not really. But I can guess, based on what the company's worth and how much stock your father owns. From working with Dalton, I gather that, before your father's little trip to fantasy land, he intended for your mother to get ten percent of the company stock and for each of his three sons to get thirty percent."

Which would officially put Griffin into the crazy, stratospherically rich category. Something that made her really uncomfortable if she thought about it too much.

"Exactly. Everyone I work with can make a guess and get within a couple million dollars of my potential worth. Would you want to date someone under those circumstances?"

"Good point."

"Besides, it's not just the money. If I made a mistake and trusted the wrong person, it wouldn't be just me paying for it. It would be the whole family. The entire company."

She couldn't help asking, "Have you made a mistake like that?"

"Once. I was young and stupid. It could have been a lot worse than it was." His hands clenched on the steering wheel and he gave it a little twist, like he was stretching out his arm muscles while he was trying to decide what else to tell her. "But mostly I just learned from watching the way my dad operated. He had women he slept with all over the world, but he rarely let any of them close. Of course, after Sharlene left him, that's when it got really bad. He didn't trust anyone after that."

"Is that why you think this affair he had with the heiress's mom must have been before he got involved with Sharlene?"

He seemed to ponder that for a second. "Yeah, I suppose so, though I didn't think it through before now."

"Here's what I don't get—I've worked with Dalton for nearly a year now, and I've never seen any indication that he's even half this paranoid."

"He's not," Griffin agreed. "But Dalton's different. It's like what you said about the way he looks at you."

She nodded, knowing what he meant. "Like you're a resource, not a person."

"Exactly." He drummed out another beat on the steering wheel. "It's not even that he really thinks that. That's just the perception he gives. But no one would ever look at Dalton and think that he was vulnerable. If you're going to invade a castle, you don't try to blast your way through the front gate—you look for the weakest spot in the defenses. You try to find the back door and sneak in that way."

"Wait a second. You can't think that's how people see you!"

"Of course it is." He shrugged. "I'm the second son. I've never been a serious contender for power within the company. I don't have a real job there."

Even though she'd had the same thought, she bristled in his defense. "You have a real job!"

"Do I?"

"Of course you do. You're the CEO."

He raised his eyebrows in mocking question. "Really? I've been interim CEO for about five minutes."

"And before that you were a VP."

"A VP of what, precisely?"

"You were the VP of International—" But then her memory failed her and she couldn't remember what exactly he did internationally.

"International…" he prodded.

"International something."

"Any idea what I do—or rather did—as VP of International Something?"

"Well, you…travel a lot. And I'm sure you…have a lot of meetings. And…"

"Come on. Seriously, can you describe my job?"

"Well, no. But I'm sure *you* could."

"Look, I don't do a lot at Cain Enterprises. I'm the first person to admit it. If it wasn't a family business, there's no way I'd actually work for Cain Enterprises."

Interesting. And it made her wonder what he would do if he had picked his own profession.

"But you do actually care about the business. You clearly pay attention to what's going on. Otherwise, you wouldn't have even had opinions about how to handle the change in leadership."

"Of course I *care* about it. If Cain Enterprises' stock tanks, it's my inheritance that goes down the drain."

"That's really what you care about? The money?"

"Hell, yeah."

"I don't believe that." Or maybe she just didn't want to believe it. When he didn't say anything in response, she felt a growing sense of unease. Finally she prodded. "You can't be serious about that."

"Why not?"

"I just don't believe you only care about the money."

"Really? You need me to tell you again how much money it is?" he asked glibly. "Because I only need to care about each dollar a tiny amount for it to really add up."

"You're not that guy. You don't even drive a flashy car. You drive a sensible hybrid."

"Maybe I just care about the environment."

She frowned. Yeah, okay. She could see that. If he cared about the environment and worked for a company that did land development and oil exploration, maybe that was how he balanced it out. "Still, it's a sedan. It's like the least fancy car ever."

"Hey," he said, his voice all mock offense. "Don't diss my car. It's a great car."

"But surely there are other hybrids that are a little more—" she mentally fished around for a word that wouldn't be dissing his car "—stylish."

"Sure. That's why I have a Tesla parked in the garage under my condo, but it's not like I'm going to drive that puppy to work every morning."

She didn't even know what a Tesla was, but she could guess. Somehow, knowing he owned a fancy sports car annoyed her, even if she didn't know jack about fancy sports cars. Even if it fit every preconception she had about him.

Yeah, when she'd first met him—hell, even when they'd first started sleeping together—she'd thought he was just some charming playboy type. But in the past few days, her opinion of him had shifted. And the truth was, she kind of liked the guy who cared more about Cain Enterprises and who drove an unimpressive sedan.

That charming playboy? He was a great guy to sleep with. Fantastic in bed. Loads of fun to hang out with. But that other guy—the guy who worried about the family company and drove a sensible car? That was a guy she could really care about.

Not that she wanted to care about him. That was just a heartache waiting to happen.

The truth was, she was perilously close to caring way more about him than she wanted to. The last thing she needed was more reasons to like him.

No matter what else happened, no matter how their relationship seemed to have changed in the past few days, it was just an illusion. The relationship had taken on this false sense of intimacy. The no-strings, just-sex relationship they'd started out with four months ago had gotten very muddled. Things went downhill the second they stopped having sex. Now that they were sharing their histories and emotions, this felt like a real relationship. Like something that might last.

But she knew that was an illusion. He needed her right now. His entire life had been thrown into turmoil over the past six weeks. First with his father's proclamation and then again when Dalton quit. Griffin needed her right now because their affair was the last vestige of normalcy in his life.

But she had to be careful. She couldn't let herself forget that this emotional attachment he seemed to feel for her was temporary. Once his life got back to normal, he wouldn't need her anymore. She just had to make sure that she didn't still need him.

Eleven

Griffin couldn't stand the unnatural calm that had overcome Sydney. "You're being awfully quiet."

"There isn't anything to say."

"That sounds like code for you're pissed off at me," he surmised. "You must be mad at me about the background check."

"No. I'm not."

"Of course you are. Why wouldn't you be? I've invaded your privacy."

She tilted her head to the side as she seemed to consider. "Well, yes. I suppose."

He watched her carefully. "So then you should be mad."

She frowned. "Possibly."

"Possibly?"

"Sure."

"Possibly?" he repeated.

"Actually, I'm more than a little curious as to why you want me to be mad." There was puzzlement in her gaze but no real emotion. It was like she was purposefully distancing herself from him.

And frankly, it *did* piss him off. What the hell was wrong with her?

"You want to know why I want you to be mad? Do you have any idea how crappy I felt about reading that file?" They'd finally reached the downtown exit, and he maneuvered the car onto the exit ramp. "The least you could do is be pissed off at me."

She arched an eyebrow, speculation in her eyes. "Let me see if I've got this right…you're mad at me because I'm not mad?"

He fumed for a moment while he formulated an answer. The building that housed Sheppard Capital was only a block off the loop; driving into the parking garage bought him a few minutes. He pulled into one of the visitor parking spots and killed the engine before answering.

"I just don't get it. You should be pissed."

"It's not a big deal."

"It should be."

"No," she snapped. "It shouldn't be. Don't you understand?"

Now her words were laced with the kind of indignation he'd been expecting all along.

"Apparently not."

"That girl that I used to be, that terrified seven year old, she has nothing to do with me."

"I don't believe that."

"But it's true." Sydney flung her car door open and jumped out. She slammed the door shut and waited until he'd climbed out, too, before saying, "That girl, the one who refused to talk to anyone at school because she was terrified that she'd be taken away by Child Protective Services. That girl, who used to Dumpster dive just to get enough food to eat. I am not that girl anymore. I haven't been that girl since I was eleven."

He watched her carefully from across the roof of the car, taking in the steely determination in her eyes, the firm line

of her mouth, the furrow of her brow. The gentle slope of her
neck, the way her ample chest rose and fell as she sucked deep
breaths into her lungs. He might not have guessed she was
upset at all, if those deep breaths didn't hint at a racing heart.

Sydney was such a crazy bundle of contradictions. Hard, but
not inflexible. Vulnerable, but not weak. And so completely
different than anyone he'd ever met.

Her outburst—brief though it was—had told him more about
her than any other conversation they'd ever had. As strong as
she looked, as smart and competent as he knew she was, he
had seen a totally different side of her. He had now glimpsed
the child she'd once been. Alone, defenseless and afraid. The
idea of that girl was burned into his brain, like the afterimage
of a flash of lightning. It streaked across the sky with wicked
speed, but it was still strong enough to burn the retinas. The
very idea of that young girl was going to stay with him.

And even though he wasn't the kind of guy who coddled
his girlfriends, even though he wasn't big on displays of emotion himself, he had the undeniable urge to pull her into his
arms and comfort her.

As strong as that instinct was, equally strong was the warning bell roaring in his head that if he so much as tried it, she'd
bolt. So instead, he just stood there, waiting for her next move.

Over the next minute, she incrementally got herself back
under control. Then she straightened and gave the hem of her
sweater a tug. A single strand of red-gold hair had slipped free
from the knot at the base of her neck and she tucked it back
behind her ear.

Finally, she slung the strap of her purse over her shoulder
and headed for the parking garage elevator. "You coming?"
she asked over her shoulder.

He nodded, following her. Would she ever stop amazing
him? He didn't think so.

The funny thing was, with every other woman he'd ever
been with, sex had been the most interesting part of the rela-

tionship. But with Sydney he found her as fascinating outside of bed as she was in it. Maybe more.

For a relationship that had started out being just sex, it was getting surprisingly complicated. He had never meant to be this involved with her. He could only hope that because his awful invasion of her privacy hadn't scared her off, then dealing with his complicated family garbage wouldn't, either, because the truth was this new side of Sydney intrigued him. He wanted to see more of her. He just hoped he got the chance to.

As they took the elevator to the tenth floor offices of Sheppard Capital, Sydney was painfully aware of Griffin beside her, watching her carefully. She had the definite feeling that she'd failed some sort of test during their conversation in the car. She didn't know what Griffin had expected of her.

Had he been itching for a fight? Was he looking for a reason to end things between them? She just didn't know.

She honestly hadn't been upset that he'd dug around in her past. She was a little disconcerted about what he'd learned because that was information she didn't share with anyone. Those were things not even Tasha knew about her. She'd worked hard to put that all behind her. It had taken years of therapy to make peace with her past. But she honestly felt like she had moved on. She was a competent adult now. Not that child. No, her life wasn't perfect, but she had a good job—one that paid well and challenged her. She had her own house. She had the stability she'd never had as a kid.

Everything in her life was fine. Fine.

And once they found the heiress, things would go back to normal. They had to because she wasn't sure how much more upheaval she could take.

For now, she just wanted to get through this meeting with Sharlene without incident.

But as the elevator doors opened, she could still feel the tension in Griffin. She could feel him watching her carefully.

To smooth things over, she gave Griffin a playful nudge in the ribs as they walked into the reception area of Sheppard Capital. "Wow. Clearly breaking up with your father was a good move for Sharlene."

"Yep. Unless she preferred to be penniless and powerless," Griffin quipped as he guided her farther inside.

She was acutely aware of the feeling of his hand at the small of her back. Even though he was barely touching her, she felt each fingerprint like it was a brand on her bare skin.

To distract herself, she asked, "What exactly was she doing as your father's assistant that she managed to go from that job to this one? Because suddenly I feel like I'm not pulling my weight."

Griffin chuckled. "Don't worry. I seriously doubt Sharlene had any skills as an assistant that you don't have. But you have to remember Sheppard Capital was in serious trouble when Jack Sheppard died unexpectedly. The company needed anyone they could get. Sharlene stepped in to get it done. I don't think she had any special skills or knowledge. She's the CFO because she's earned it. Because she's fought tooth and nail to keep it going."

"You almost sound like you admire her."

"Almost?" he asked with an arched eyebrow. He then approached the desk of Sharlene's assistant, introduced himself and Sydney and asked to see Sharlene.

At the mention of Griffin's last name, the assistant's lips curled away from her teeth a little, like she found him distasteful, even though she felt obliged to offer him a seat. For the first time since they'd set off on this little adventure, it occurred to Sydney that it might be strange for them to just show up at Sharlene's office without an appointment. It was like opposing armies in a great battle. One didn't just show up in the enemy's camp without first sending an envoy to establish safe passage.

"Have a seat," the assistant said, her voice dripping with disdain. "I'll see if she's available."

In her head, Sydney translated: *have a seat while I verify that my boss would never stoop low enough to see you.*

Just a few days ago, Sydney might have thought Griffin didn't even notice the woman's unpleasant reaction, but she knew him well enough now to realize that he probably did but wasn't showing it.

Sydney stood there, feeling suddenly nervous, knowing that the assistant was no doubt sending an instant message to Sharlene, wherever she was. It was what she had done whenever someone showed up unexpectedly and wanted to see Dalton. It was an easy and silent way to find out if he wanted to see the person or have them sent on their way.

Whatever response Sharlene had given was not what the assistant expected because a moment later she glanced from her computer screen over to them, her expression equal parts confusion and suspicion. Before she could say anything, the door to Sharlene's office flew open.

"Griffin, dear!"

The woman who stood there—Sharlene, presumably—looked to be in her early fifties. She had platinum-blond, carefully styled hair. Everything about her, from her hair to her flawless skin to her elegant pantsuit, spoke of a woman who knew how to take care of herself and spared no expense in doing so.

She took a few steps into the front office, then held out her arms wide. With obvious affection in his expression, Griffin stood, then met Sharlene halfway across the office. Despite the sizable heels on Sharlene's pumps, the woman barely came up to his shoulder.

Sydney was reminded all over again how very tall Griffin was. At just over five-nine, she wasn't a small woman herself, but she'd quickly gotten used to the fact that Griffin was at least five inches taller than she. Griffin was the first man she'd ever dated who had made her feel delicate and feminine. However, beside Sharlene, Griffin looked like a giant. He even lifted her clear off her feet for a moment before setting her gently back to the ground.

Sydney glanced over at Sharlene's assistant, who looked as shocked as Sydney felt by the unexpected display of affection.

Finally, Sharlene released Griffin—but kept a motherly hand on his arm. "Come in, come in."

Griffin started to follow Sharlene into the office, then glanced back at Sydney, giving her a nod to indicate that she should follow.

Sydney watched Sharlene's expression as she rose to follow them. Disapproval flickered over the woman's face but was quickly replaced with a distant but polite smile.

"And you are?" she asked.

"This is my assistant, Sydney Edwards. She's helping me with a project I'm working on."

"Interesting," Sharlene murmured as she gestured toward the love seat and pair of chairs nestled in the corner of the room. "I believe the last time I was over at Cain Enterprises, your assistant was Marion Green. I didn't hear that she'd been let go. What a shame. She was with the company for so long."

Griffin sat in one chair, so Sydney claimed the other. Sharlene sat on the loveseat, crossing her ankles to the side and draping her arm over the furniture.

Griffin smiled, as if he didn't find Sharlene's line of questioning odd. "Marion is still with the company. I suspect that even if we let her go, she'd keep coming to work every day."

Sharlene laughed. "Yes, I suppose so. Well, come in, come in and sit down. My assistant will get drinks. Griffin dear, the last time you visited me at work you were still drinking chocolate milk. Somehow I suspect your tastes have changed. Let me guess." She tapped one perfectly manicured nail against her chin. "Your father was always a Scotch man, but you don't strike me as the type to drink during the day. Shall I have her just bring coffee?"

Griffin nodded stiffly. Sydney got the impression he didn't

want the coffee, but he also didn't want to be rude. He went on to explain the situation with Hollister and his missing daughter before ending with, "We think we know who the woman who wrote the letter might be."

"You do?" Sharlene asked in surprise. "Then you've narrowed it down from a fairly extensive pool."

Griffin ignored Sharlene's comment and said, "We had a nanny who lived at the house from the time just before I was born to when I was an infant. Apparently, she was pregnant and she had some sort of relationship with Hollister. My mother remembered that you helped hire the girl. Or at least found the service that sent her over."

"Hmm…" Sharlene tilted her head to the side and tapped her cheek. "I might have. But I need more to go on than that. What else can you tell me about her?"

"Not much," Sydney admitted. "But we have her photo. Would that help?"

"Certainly." Sharlene smiled broadly.

Sydney pulled the folder out of her bag and handed it to Sharlene, but at that moment, Sharlene's assistant came in to offer drinks, and Sharlene didn't even look in the folder until the assistant had left. Then she made a great show of flipping through the pages within it.

"Is that photo supposed to be in here?" she asked.

"Yes," Sydney said. "It should be on top." She took the folder back from Sharlene, riffling through it herself before admitting, "I'm sorry, the photo must have fallen out in the car. I'll go get it."

Sharlene grabbed her arm. "Nonsense. Griffin was raised better than that. He'll go." A feline smile spread across her face. "Besides, this will give us a chance to talk."

Griffin's gaze narrowed. "Be nice."

Sharlene blinked innocently. "I don't know what you mean."

"She's my assistant. Be nice."

"I'll be fine," Sydney assured him.

As soon as the door closed behind Griffin, Sharlene tilted her head coyly and said, "So. His assistant?"

"Just his assistant," Sydney bit out.

"Oh, my dear." Sharlene laughed. "I know exactly what that means. Don't forget I was just Hollister's assistant for nearly a decade."

"I am truly just his assistant."

"Yes. I'm sure you are." Sharlene's voice dripped with condescension, but there was a knowing gleam in her gaze.

Strangely, it wasn't the condescension that bothered Sydney. It was that look. That look implied a kinship between them. That look implied they were one in the same, both part of the sisterhood of assistant-mistresses.

It was exactly that sisterhood that Sydney had never wanted to belong to. She'd never wanted the kinship or the glimpse into a future filled with bitter resentments.

That look made her all the more determined to convince Sharlene that the relationship she thought she saw was a figment of her imagination.

Needing to convince Sharlene—even if she couldn't convince herself— Sydney gave the other woman the truth. "I've only worked for Griffin for a few weeks. Before that I worked for Dalton. Griffin sort of inherited me. I came with the office."

"I see." Sharlene's eyes narrowed slightly as she studied Sydney.

It took every ounce of self-control she had not to fidget and squirm. Years of being interviewed by CPS officers served her well here. She was used to faking it.

"Well, then," Sharlene said after a moment. "If you know both brothers, all the better."

"All the... Excuse me?"

"You claim you're not involved with Griffin. Despite his obvious interest in you, I might add. Very well. That is your own business. But if you've worked with both Dalton and Griffin, then you suit my needs perfectly."

"Suit your needs?" Syndey sprang to her feet. "Whatever you're—"

"Calm down, calm down," Sharlene cooed, with a dismissive flutter of her hand. "All I need is a little information."

"Information? I will not betray Cain Enterprises!"

"Betray Cain Enterprises? Oh, goodness no." Sharlene gave a trilling laugh. "I have more information on Cain Enterprises than I know what to do with. Corporate secrets are the last thing I need. No, I need information about the boys. Personal information."

"And you think I'm going to give it to you?" The woman was crazy. Stark-raving mad. And quite clever. Sydney could clearly see that Sharlene had gotten Sydney alone exactly for this purpose.

"Calm down," Sharlene said again in that soothing tone. "My interest is not malicious, I assure you."

"Then what is your interest?" Sydney demanded.

"Is it really so hard to believe that I might be curious about them? Concerned even? Are they happy? Is either of them in a well-adjusted, long-term relationship? Is either of them doing what he really wants to do in life?"

Honestly, Sydney didn't know if Griffin was happy. If he was "doing what he really wanted to do in life." So she gave a noncommittal shrug. "Well, who does get to do that?"

"But it's a shame, isn't it? That Griffin's stuck at Cain Enterprises, when that's not what he really wants to do."

"And I suppose you know all about what he really wants to do."

Sharlene gave a self-effacing shrug. "I wouldn't say that I know all about it. I contribute enough to get the monthly newsletters but not so generously as to attract anyone's attention. And I can tell he's not spending as much time as he wishes he could down in Africa."

"What?" Okay, maybe she was just really tired, but the con-

versation seemed to have gone off road into the realm of very
bizarre. "Newsletters? Africa?"

"For Hope2O."

"What?" Sydney said blankly.

"Hope. 2. O," Sharlene repeated slowly. "The international
aid organization Griffin runs."

Twelve

"The what?"

Sharlene recoiled slightly. For the first time since Sydney had walked in, she got the feeling that Sharlene wasn't putting on a show. Her surprise was as real as Sydney's shock. "He didn't tell you?"

"Tell me what? That he apparently runs an international aid organization in his spare time? No. He didn't mention it." Sydney could hear her voice getting all shrill and squeaky. "I'm sorry. Can we backtrack a bit? Start at the beginning maybe?"

Sharlene blinked rapidly. "Yes. Of course." Then she stood and crossed to her desk and began to rummage around in her file folders in one of her drawers. "A few years ago…or more than a few now, I guess, Griffin got involved in an organization called Hope2O. They provide assistance to impoverished villages that are trying to start up water districts in Africa and Central America. They help with organization and arrange financial backing."

"And Griffin is involved in this?" Again her voice sounded squeaky.

Sharlene looked up. "I'm sorry. This has come as a shock to you."

"I just...I had no idea."

Sharlene must have found what she wanted because she straightened and walked back around the desk. She held out a glossy, tri-fold pamphlet. "Griffin is not just involved. As of four years ago, he's their major financial backer. In addition to being on their executive board."

"Of a charitable organization."

"Yes."

"In Africa."

"Yes."

"And he came to you asking you to donate?"

Sharlene gave a trilling laugh. "Oh, goodness no. As far as I know his involvement in Hope2O is his most closely guarded secret. I doubt any of the Cains know about it. Certainly no one at Cain Enterprises knows, but I just assumed you'd have to know about Hope2O, being as close to him as you are. It appears I really was wrong about your relationship with Griffin."

Sydney gritted her teeth, but didn't comment. She refused to confirm or deny Sharlene's suspicions.

"Then how do you know?" she asked instead. Was Griffin really so close to Sharlene? He'd given Sydney the impression that he hadn't seen Sharlene in years.

"I found out about it purely by accident. A few years ago I was having lunch with some of the women I'd worked with at Cain Enterprises. Griffin's assistant happened to be there and she complained about how difficult it was to manage his schedule. How secretive he was. How he appeared to spend far more time vacationing than actually working. This description of him seemed very unlike the boy I'd known. So I looked into the matter."

Sydney didn't know what to say. She was all too familiar

with complaints made by Griffin's former assistant. He was difficult to work with. He did have a reputation for playing more than he worked. But she had just assumed that was who he was.

"You looked into the matter?" Sydney repeated dumbly.

Sharlene sighed, a sound full of guilt and regret. "I know I shouldn't have. I should have trusted that the Griffin I knew as a boy would grow into a decent man. More than decent, in fact. Extraordinary. But I didn't trust what I knew of him. I nosed around in his business and uncovered just how generous and selfless he is. Believe me when I tell you that I'm not proud of myself for doubting him."

Sydney tried to squelch the sick feeling in her stomach. Sharlene felt badly? That was nothing compared to how Sydney felt. Sydney hadn't just doubted that Griffin might be generous and extraordinary. She'd fully believed he was a self-absorbed playboy. She'd slept with him—for months—without ever knowing the person he truly was.

Finally, Sydney willed herself to take the pamphlet that Sharlene was holding. She glanced down. There was a logo at the top of the page, with the word *Hope* and the letter *O* written in nice big letters and the *2* done in subscript, the way you'd write the chemical name for water. Beneath was a picture of a beautiful young African girl carrying a jug on her head along with the statement "Women spend 200 million hours a day collecting water." She flipped open the pamphlet, not reading it, just letting it soak in. Not really believing that Griffin would have anything to do with this organization.

It was too noble a cause for her charming playboy to be involved in. Too far outside the realm of their lives. She could picture him attending charity galas at the country club dressed in a tux, but not drilling water wells in Africa.

Then on the back, she saw it. A picture of a ribbon-cutting ceremony somewhere. In the background, standing just behind the man cutting the ribbon, was Griffin. The picture was small and cluttered with people. If she didn't know every line of his face, she wouldn't have even recognized him. But she did.

Sydney flipped through the pamphlet again, her eyes scanning all the words without really reading them. She looked for any reference to Griffin at all. Any mention of Cain Enterprises. She wasn't particularly surprised when she found none.

Still, when she looked up, she couldn't help voicing her question. "Why would he keep this such a secret?"

Sharlene sighed. "Why does anyone keep anything a secret? I suspect he's ashamed of it."

"Of doing charitable work? It's not like he's a drug addict. He's not laundering money or hosting dog fights."

"Yes, yes, for someone like you or me, charity is a virtue." Sharlene shook her head. "But in Griffin's world, wanting to help others is a sign of weakness. One that Caro and Hollister worked hard to stamp out of her boys from a very young age. Griffin especially."

"Why Griffin especially?"

"He was always much more sensitive than Dalton. He cared about other people. I remember once, in the mid-eighties when the famine in Africa was getting a lot of coverage in the news, Griffin had the nanny bring him up to the office so he could talk to his father. He asked Hollister why they couldn't just give all their money to the people in Africa. I never heard Hollister's full answer because he shut his office door, but by the time Griffin left, he was in tears. Caro was furious. She fired the nanny the very next day."

"That's awful."

"It was. And whatever Hollister said to Griffin, it must have made an impact because I never heard him talk about helping other people again until I found out about Hope2O."

Sydney tried to imagine what Hollister must have said, but she couldn't. Griffin had only been a child. In the mid-eighties, he would have been six or seven. Eight or nine at the oldest.

That was awfully young to have human compassion stamped out of you.

She glanced up to find Sharlene watching her. "Why show me this?" She waved the pamphlet between them. "Why tell me this at all? What do you want from me?"

"I would think that's rather obvious."

"Well, it isn't. Either you're still hiding something or you've gone to a lot of trouble to satisfy your curiosity."

"Fine," Sharlene said, staring across the office to look out the window. "When I was with Hollister, Griffin was like a son to me. So was Dalton, for that matter. I genuinely care about both of those boys, but when things ended with Hollister, he cut me out of all their lives. I've tried to keep tabs on them, but they're both very private men." Sharlene turned her gaze back to Sydney. "Is it so hard to believe that I simply want to know whether or not Griffin is happy?"

For the first time since walking into the office, Sydney felt as though Sharlene was truly being honest. As though she was seeing the real woman beneath the facade.

"No," she answered honestly, sitting back in her seat. "No, it's not so hard to believe. So why not just ask him?"

Sharlene laughed bitterly. "It's been nearly twenty years since I've seen Griffin. Do you honestly think he'd just talk to me? That he wouldn't be as suspicious and guarded as you've been? More so, even."

Sydney didn't know how to respond to that. Two weeks ago, she would have said that Griffin was an open book. That there were no hidden depths, no deep secrets. The perfect wild-oats guy.

Now she knew differently. She'd never met a book more tightly closed or carefully locked. Now she knew the truth. She'd never known the real Griffin. He'd never once showed her the man he really was.

Well, she could hardly blame him for that. She'd kept her

share of secrets herself. The problem was, his secrets concealed the man he truly was.

Four months ago, she'd gotten involved with a jet-setting playboy. A man who delighted in physical and sensual pleasures but seemed to care about little beyond his own amusement.

In the days since becoming his assistant, she'd realized that man was an illusion. The illusion had tempted her body. The real man beneath tempted her heart, her mind. Her very soul. She could fall in love with a man like Griffin Cain.

"I'm sorry."

Sydney looked up to see that Sharlene had come to sit beside her. Sharlene placed a gentle hand on Sydney's arm. Her lovely face was creased with lines and revealed a concern that was almost motherly.

"Pardon?" Sydney asked, not sure what exactly Sharlene was apologizing for.

"I didn't mean to drop this bomb on you. Honestly. I assumed he'd told you about Hope2O. He seemed so protective of you. You seemed so close. I just thought…" Sharlene's voice trailed off, and for a second she seemed near tears herself. "Well, I know what it's like to love a man who doesn't let you in."

"I—" But Sydney cut herself off. Maybe it was easier to let Sharlene believe she was hurt by Griffin's inability to trust her with the truth. It was an explanation that Sharlene would understand, whereas the truth—her fear of loving Griffin— was something she barely understood herself. Finally, she said simply, "Yes. It is hard."

And it wasn't even an outright lie because nothing about this situation was easy.

Fortunately, she was saved from having to say more because Griffin walked back in. She wanted to curl up inside herself and hide. Instead, she had to sit there and sift through Sharlene's conversation for clues to the identity of this girl. She *so* didn't want to be here anymore.

"Did you find the photos?" Sydney asked to hide how disconcerted she felt.

"No. I didn't. I searched the entire car. We either lost them or accidently left them with my mother."

"Oh, look." Sharlene pulled some papers out from between the cushions of the love seat and held them out toward Griffin. "Is this them?"

He glanced at the photos as he took them from her. "Yes. Surprisingly, this is them," he said wryly.

"Well, then," she said as she took them back. "Let me have a look."

Sharlene held both photos, looking from one to the other. After a few moments, she crossed to her desk and put on a pair of discreet reading glass, then flicked on a desk lamp and studied the pictures under the light. After a moment, she nodded, flicked off the light and returned to the seat, handing the photos back across to Griffin.

"So?" he asked, obviously choosing to ignore her blatant manipulation. "Do you recognize the woman? Or the girl?"

"Of course I do. The woman is Vivian Beck. She was Dalton's nanny and yours, too, after you were born."

"Are you sure Beck was her last name?" Sydney asked.

Sharlene's smile cooled as she returned Sydney's gaze. "Quite."

"What else can you tell us about her?"

Sharlene thought for a moment and then shook her head, either feigning regret beautifully or perhaps truly sorry that she couldn't help more. "Nothing. But you should talk to your mother about this. Surely she knows more."

"She said she didn't remember the woman at all."

Sharlene arched an eyebrow in apparent surprise. "Really? I find that hard to believe."

"Why's that? She was pregnant with me and claimed she

barely had contact with her. She thought Vivian might be the woman's first name, but she seemed to know nothing else about her."

Sharlene's mouth curved into an unpleasant smile. "Well, isn't this just like old times, what with your mother's selective memory and her transparent attempts to control everyone?"

"Sharlene, if you know something, just tell me now." Griffin's voice was terse, his impatience obvious.

"Well, it's interesting, isn't it? That your mother claims to barely remember her."

"Why is it interesting?"

"Well, because she simply *must* remember her. She came to the office to see Hollister after she fired the girl. She was furious. Practically hysterical."

If Caro was really that upset about it, then wouldn't Hollister remember the event, too?

Griffin must have been thinking the same thing because he leaned forward and asked, "Did she actually see my father? What did he have to say?"

"She never saw him. He had meetings all that day, but I mentioned it to him." Sharlene smiled mischievously. "But perhaps I downplayed it a bit."

"So he never even knew what happened?" Sydney asked.

"Oh, of course he knew. Everyone at the company knew. People gossiped about it for months. The police were called. There's no hiding something like that."

"The police?" Griffin asked. "Was she violent?"

Sharlene waved a hand. "Oh, no. Nothing like that." She cocked her head to the side, her expression a mixture of curiosity and sorrow. "Your mother really never told you about this?"

Wincing, Sydney glanced at Griffin. Not surprisingly, Sharlene's sympathy—faked or real—only made this worse for Griffin.

"Can you just tell us what happened?" Sydney asked.

Sharlene smiled vaguely. "Of course. The police were summoned because Caro insisted the girl had stolen something from the house when she left. I think your mother knows who the girl in that photo is just as well as I do, but she just didn't want you to know that she knows."

"Back to the nanny. She stole something?"

"Yes. Caro was livid. She'd fired the girl the day before, but when Vivian left she took something of Caro's. As soon as she discovered it was missing, she stormed down to Hollister's office and demanded I help track her down. I tried, but none of the contact information I had worked. Caro claimed I was to blame because I'd recommended Vivian."

"Do you remember what she stole?"

"A ring. Caro's wedding ring, if I remember correctly."

"What?" Griffin asked, leaning forward.

"Excuse me? She stole Caro's wedding ring?" Sydney asked at the same time. She didn't bother to keep the shock out of her voice. She'd faced Caro down and knew how formidable the woman could be. And she wasn't exactly a fluff ball herself. She couldn't imagine having the guts to steal Caro's wedding ring. "I mean, that's hard core. Who would do something like that?"

Griffin blew out a breath. "I think the bigger question is, why would my mother let her get away with it?"

"She did try to look for the girl," Sharlene pointed out with an elegant shrug. "But I don't think she looked that hard. Caro's wedding ring was not very remarkable. It had been in Hollister's family for generations. It was a simple gold band with a few unimpressive diamond flakes. I'm sure if it had been Caro's engagement ring, they would have called out the national guard. Frankly, the weird thing isn't that Caro didn't get the police involved—it's that Caro even noticed it was missing."

"Still, it was her wedding ring. Don't you think that's bizarre?"

Sharlene smiled coyly. "Of course I do. It's bizarre enough that I remember the incident after all these years. I think the real question you should be asking yourself is why Caro claims she doesn't remember it. It's obvious to me that your mother is lying to you."

Thirteen

The charming playboy had vanished.

He was gone. Completely.

Which she should have been okay with. After all, it wasn't as though she actually wanted to talk to him herself. She was too emotionally fragile for that. Too vulnerable.

Still, Griffin's silence unnerved her. He had said absolutely nothing since they'd gotten back in the car. She didn't ask where they were heading. She didn't have to. He was whipping the car through the streets of Houston like a stunt driver on a closed course.

Clearly, he was pissed that his mother had manipulated him. Hey, Sydney couldn't blame him for that. By the time he pulled onto the loop at about sixty, she figured she had to say something.

"Do you think that—?" she began.

"No. I don't." His tone was hard as nails and his gaze didn't even flicker from the road.

"Maybe you should wait until—"

"No."

"Look, I know you're upset, but—"

"Give it a rest, okay?"

She twisted in her seat to face him. "No, I'm not going to give it a rest. Pull over."

"What?" Finally, he looked at her. Just shot a glance in her direction, but at least he was loosening his death grip on the steering wheel.

"Just get off the highway." When he didn't so much as turn on his blinker, she added. "Look, you're pissed off. I get it. You're in no shape to drive, let alone talk to your mother."

"I'm fine." But then, as if to prove his point, a car darted in front of them and he had to slam on his breaks. Muttering a curse under his breath, he eased his foot off the gas.

She watched in silence as his hand twisted on the steering wheel.

"I'm not..." He broke off, muttering another curse.

He didn't finish the sentence, but he didn't have to. She could think of about ten different ways to finish it for him. He was not fine. He was not ready to talk about it. He was not nearly as in control as he wanted to be.

Tension practically radiated from him. His control was whisper-thin and it was all she could do not to rub her hand across his thigh. To try to soothe him. Maybe she would have if she hadn't feared that he would snap altogether.

He flicked on the blinker, eased across the road and a second later exited the highway and pulled into the mostly empty parking lot of a strip mall near the off-ramp. He parked at the back of the lot, under the shade of a sprawling oak. He killed the engine and just sat there for a moment, his hands clenched so tightly around the steering wheel, she thought it might snap under the pressure.

She watched him struggling for a long minute, trying to give him the space he needed to process everything they'd learned in the past few hours. Obviously, his mother knew who the girl's mother was. She'd known and she'd deliberately misled them. Caro Cain's behavior was incomprehensible to Sydney. She couldn't imagine why the woman would purposefully throw roadblocks into Griffin's path, but she did know this. As frustrated as she was with Caro's behavior, it had to be a hundred times worse for Griffin. Who didn't want this job or this responsibility in the first place. Who had been sick of his family's manipulation before this even started.

And the truth was, she didn't know what to say to make any of this better. She didn't know if there was anything she could say to make it better. So instead of trying, she reached out and put her hand on his leg. She felt the muscle twitch beneath her palm. His hands stilled on the steering wheel. Every muscle in his body seemed to freeze. Then he slowly turned and leveled a gaze at her.

She felt stripped bare by the intensity of his Cain-blue eyes. Naked and vulnerable. Completely at his mercy.

"Griffin, I—"

Before she could finish the sentence, before she even knew what she was going to actually say, he threw open the door, unclicked the buckle on his seat belt and propelled himself out of the car.

"Damn it," she muttered before fumbling with her own seat belt buckle and scrambling out of the car.

She rounded the hood and just stood there for a minute, watching as he paced restlessly. He traversed the distance from the car to the tree and back again in long, restless strides. He clenched and unclenched his hands as he prowled, giving the air of a caged beast. But where the panther in the zoo was trapped by the fence and the electric current pumped through the wires, he was confined by his anger.

"Griffin, this isn't as bad as it seems."

He whirled to glare at her. "Are you kidding? I always knew my family was a mess of crazy, but this? This is beyond crazy."

"You don't know that." Yeah. Maybe he did know that.

Maybe it was as bad as it seemed, but she figured, for now, her best bet was to get him calmed down before he did something he really regretted.

"What? You think this isn't bad? You think there's any scenario in which my mother deliberately lied to me, deliberately misled me that's not bad?"

"I didn't say not bad, I just…." Damn. She didn't know what the right response was here. All she knew was that if Griffin went to see his mother now, he'd say or do all kinds of things he regretted. "Look, no matter how bad it is, confronting her now gets you nothing."

Finally, he stopped pacing and whirled to face her. He stood, stone-still, maybe ten feet away, and just stared at her.

Suddenly nervous, she babbled, "I'm just saying maybe you should wait a bit. Calm down first."

"What exactly," he said slowly, his voice pitched low, "do you recommend that I do instead of confronting my family?"

His gaze was hot enough to damn near burn the clothes right off her body.

She swallowed hard as a shiver skittered across the surface of his skin. "Um…maybe some yoga?"

"Yoga?" He gave a bark of laughter and a smile spilt his face. It was a fierce and wild smile, but at least he no longer looked like he wanted to rip something apart with his bare hands.

"Like, meditate or something," she suggested, even though she knew meditation was the last thing on his mind.

He stalked slowly toward her. "I'm not really the type."

She swallowed again, but it got harder and harder to do past the lump her pounding heart had pushed up into her throat.

Oh, dear, she was in so much trouble here. Because, obviously, Griffin wasn't the type. She doubted he'd ever meditated a single instant of his life. He wasn't a guy who could sit still at all, let alone meditate. The only time she'd seen him relaxed—ever—was in bed. And only after they'd both climaxed more than once. Even sex he treated like an Olympic-level sport.

She should not be thinking about sex right now. They weren't supposed to be sleeping together anymore. She couldn't sleep with him, because... Why was she supposed to be holding him at arm's length again? Oh, right. He was her boss. Her boss!

And she was already dangerously close to getting her heart broken as it was.

She needed to remember that. Because after a week of being in his company nonstop, she was like an addict jonesing for a hit of Griffin.

Even though he was the last thing she should have, he was still what she wanted. What she needed.

Geez, she needed to check herself into some sort of rehab program. She just couldn't imagine twelve steps of any kind that would give her the ability to walk away from him.

She couldn't even think when he was looking at her like this. She glanced around, hoping to spot something to distract them, but they were essentially alone. This end of the parking lot was empty. Cars zipped by on the access road without slowing down enough to notice two people talking under a tree. "Um...what were we..."

"About to do?" he asked, his voice pitched low and seductive.

"No." The last thing they needed was to do something. "Talking about. What were we talking about?"

He smiled like he knew exactly what she was thinking. And he probably did. "You were telling me how to meditate."

"Right. Meditate. It's really not that hard. I hear... Um, I think you need to visualize a happy place."

He stopped a fraction of an inch away from her. So close she could feel the heat sparking off his skin. "Okay," he murmured. "Some place happy. I've got a place in mind already."

His lips twitched into a smile and she felt the last of her reserve of willpower melt away.

When he reached for her, she went right into his arms. He buried his hand in her hair as she tipped her mouth up to meet his. Despite the teasing smile that had been on his lips just moments ago, there was nothing light or playful about his kiss. His lips were firm against hers. His mouth hot. His hand possessive. His body hard.

He kissed her as though he needed her desperately. As though there was nothing else in the world but her. As though he was trying to sear this moment into his memory forever, just as it would be seared into her.

She felt the back of the car bump against her legs. She arched against him, opening her mouth even wider as his tongue slipped in to brush against hers. Then his hands were on her hips and he was lifting her up onto the trunk of his car. She wrapped her legs around his waist, pulling his groin against hers. Even through his jeans and her pants, she felt the length of his erection. It was perfect. Divine.

They seemed perfectly fitted to one another. He rocked against the very core of her and pleasure rocketed through her body, making her tremble. Her hands greedily tugged at his clothes, hungrily trying to find bare skin. He pressed her back down onto the trunk of car, following her inch by inch until he was lying fully on top of her. She bucked against him, desperate to be closer.

She felt his hand slipping up under her sweater and her back arched up off the car.

"Wait," she gasped out.

He stilled instantly. Then he groaned and dropped his head down to her collarbone. She felt his breath hot against the skin of her chest.

"Please don't tell me to meditate."

"No. I just think we should go slowly."

He chuckled. "Yeah. Me, too." Then he pulled up, bracing his forearm beside her head as he looked down at her. "But you're right. We can't do this here."

"What?" But then his words sank in. He was right. They

were in a parking lot. A parking lot, for goodness' sake. And it was the middle of the day. "Right. Not here."

He smiled, a slow, sexy smile that showed off his dimples. Obviously he loved having her this disconcerted. She might have been annoyed with him, but she was too distracted by the heat pounding through her.

He levered himself off her and pulled his iPhone out of his back pocket. "Give me ten minutes to find a hotel nearby."

She put a hand on his arm to get his attention and pointed at the nearby building. "You don't have to look far. There's a hotel right here."

It took less than ten minutes for him to get a room. He had her wait in the car—thank goodness because she wasn't sure she'd have been up to the embarrassment of getting a hotel room in the middle of the day. Within fifteen minutes, he was swiping the pass key and letting them into the room. He was kissing her before the door even shut behind them.

He spun her around, pulling off her clothes as he walked her backward toward the bed. His hands were greedy, desperate even. It seemed he couldn't get her naked quickly enough. He yanked back the covers. She kicked off her shoes just as he pulled her pants off her legs. Then he knelt in front of her, first rubbing his cheek against her bare belly, inhaling deeply, like he needed the very scent of her. Then he parted the curls, burying his face between her legs. Pleasure coursed through her body, making her legs wobble beneath her. Weak-kneed and trembling, she tumbled back onto the bed. He followed her, devouring her with greedy strokes of his tongue. Her climax rushed through her, pushing her over the edge as she screamed out his name.

It took him mere seconds to strip completely and then he was on top of her. He plunged right into her, moaning her name, raining kisses on her skin. His intensity overwhelmed her. His desperation thrilled her.

He made love to her like he never had before. Every other time they'd been together, Griffin clung tightly to his control until the last second. He was a master at driving her to distraction while remaining in control. It made him an incredible lover, but she always felt at a disadvantage.

But not this time. This time, he couldn't get enough of her. He couldn't control himself.

Pounding into her over and over, he cried out her name, burying his face in her neck. His need was palpable. He didn't just want her. This was more than mere desire. He needed her. Desperately. And that thought alone sent her tumbling over the edge again as he thrust into her one last time.

Even as she was crying out, she was also crying. Tears streaming down her face because at last she understood. She couldn't have him. She couldn't keep him. And it had nothing to do with the fact that he was her boss. It had nothing to do with work at all.

She needed him to need her. No one had ever needed her before. Not really. And she wanted that—no, needed that— more than she'd ever realized.

And that was precisely why she had to walk away.

He may need her now, but this was only temporary. Of course he needed her now. His life was in turmoil. Everything he knew or thought he knew had been overturned. She represented the last remnant of the life he'd lived before all this nonsense had started with the missing heiress. She was like a security blanket.

Until this moment, she hadn't realized how desperately she wanted him to need her. But now that she did know, now that she understood, she had to get out. Because even if he needed her now, he wouldn't need her forever. But she…she would always need him. Because she loved him.

Only a few minutes later, Griffin rolled to the edge of the bed and sat there, elbows on his knees, head in his hands for several minutes without speaking. Finally, she wiggled up behind him and placed her hand on his back. He flinched away from her touch, stood and stalked over to where his jeans lay on the floor near the door and yanked them on.

"Griffin—" she began.

He looked at her. For one long moment, his expression was completely unreadable. He studied her with such intensity that she slowly sat up, crossing her legs and tucking the sheet up under her arms. "What?"

He crossed back to the bed, sat on the edge and cupped her face in his hands.

"Sydney, I'm so sorry."

Disconcerted, she pulled back, smoothing down her tousled hair and tucking it behind her ear. "Why are you apologizing?"

"I promised you we wouldn't sleep together while I was your boss and—"

"You didn't really promise," she hastened to correct him, trying to lighten his mood. "You scoffed at the idea and tried to control your laughter."

"I knew this wasn't what you wanted. I betrayed your trust."

He looked guilt ridden. Tormented.

A few weeks ago she would have assumed this was all an act, but now she knew better. Now she knew that despite everything, despite his upbringing, despite the arrogance that was so much a part of him, despite his natural charm and easygoing nature, he was an astonishingly decent man. Maybe even the most decent man she knew.

She understood that now in a way that she could not possibly have understood a few weeks ago. Or even twenty-four hours ago.

It nearly broke her heart to think that—in the middle of all he was going through—he was worried about whether or not he'd betrayed her trust. With all he had on his plate right now, with the fate of a billion-dollar company resting on his shoulders, with his family life in turmoil and with his dreams of running Hope2O at risk, he was worried about her. Because that was how compassionate he was. It awed and amazed her. It humbled her.

Pulling the sheet with her, she climbed onto his lap, straddling him. She kept the sheet wrapped around her, so that the only thing separating them was luxuriant cotton. Thin though the barrier might be, she needed it because without it, if they were skin to skin, they would be too close. Pressed against his body, her words would get lost in the intimacy. It would be too easy for this to become about sex. Besides, she'd be too vulnerable.

Instead, she cupped his jaw in her palms and tilted his face so he met her gaze. Beneath the remorse in his eyes, there was the spark of heat. The passion that was always so close to the surface. The passion that had distracted her far too often from the man he really was.

"You didn't betray my trust," she said soothingly. "This was what I wanted. It was what we both needed."

He studied her for a long minute before nodding slowly. His arms snaked around her, one behind her neck, the other cupping her buttocks. He pulled her closer, but rather than kissing her, he bumped his forehead against hers.

"I'm still sorry. I—"

"It's okay." But she could see that the regret in his gaze was still there. The lingering doubts. "I get it," she reassured him. "You don't want to be that guy. The pushy obnoxious guy who manipulates and controls people to get what he wants. I understand now why you don't want to do that. It's because you don't want to be like your father. But trust me. You're not that guy. You're nothing like your father. You're nothing like anyone in your family. I—"

"You're wrong," he said sharply. Then he stood abruptly, picking her up and turning around to deposit her on the bed before pacing over to the sliding door that overlooked the balcony. "I'm more like my father than you know. I have lied to you. I've misled you."

Her heart seemed to catch in her chest. For a moment, she wondered if this had something to do with Hope2O, but he was so serious, so distraught, she couldn't believe that it did. Then she forced out the word, "How?"

Instead of answering outright, he kept talking as if he hadn't even heard her question. "All this mess in my family, this stupid quest our father has laid out, this complicated web my mother has woven, all of it could have been avoided if they would just tell the truth. If just one person in the family would stop lying about everything, would stop trying to manipulate and control the situation to get what they want. If either of them had been honest about anything, their marriage would have been different. I don't want any part of their legacy of lies and deceit and one-upmanship."

She climbed off the bed, wrapped the sheet around her body like a toga and crossed to stand right behind him. The view out the window overlooked the parking lot and the downtown cityscape. She wasn't worried about anyone seeing her because during the day it would be nearly impossible to see into the hotel room from outside, even if there were buildings nearby.

She didn't say anything, but just let him talk. Whatever lie he'd told, whatever deception he'd perpetrated, she didn't believe it was as serious as he was making it out to be. She knew him too well now for that.

"I want to be totally honest with you." He turned around to face her. His hands were propped on his hips, his jeans slung low with the top button undone. His head was slightly ducked, so she almost couldn't read his expression. "I don't have any intention of staying on as CEO for Cain Enterprises."

"I know. You never claimed you did."

He let out a faint groan of frustration. "No. I mean, I've never really had any intention of even working at Cain Enterprises. I've been trying to get away from it since I accepted the job when I was twenty-four. The only reason I even took the job is because my father threatened to cut me off if I didn't work for Cain Enterprises for at least a decade."

"Yes." Again she cupped his cheek. "I know. It doesn't take a genius to see that you're not really happy at Cain Enterprises. You clearly don't fit there. That's why—"

But before she could admit to knowing about Hope2O, he cut her off. "No, it's more than that. It's not just that I don't want to work for Cain Enterprises." His expression still looked so miserable. "It's that I have other plans entirely. Things I've put on hold for the better part of a decade because—"

Finally, she couldn't take anymore of it and she pressed her fingers to his mouth. "I know."

"You—"

"I know about Hope2O."

"—don't... Wait." His eyes scanned her face. "You know about Hope2O? How could you possibly know?" He took a step back, his expression suspicious. "How did you find out? Did Dalton know?"

"Relax." It was all she could do not to chuckle at his open skepticism. "It's nothing nefarious. Sharlene knows. She told me." He was still eyeing her suspiciously, so she quickly explained about the conversation she and Sharlene had had while he'd been off looking for the photos.

The tension seemed to drain out of him as she spoke. Finally he said, "You're not mad?"

"I found out you're generous and charitable. I learned you're doing great things to help all of mankind. Why would that make me mad?"

Worried, yes, because this was the kind of man he was. The kind who worried that his good deeds would be held against him.

"Some women would be angry that I misled them."

"You never misled me. You're just very guarded. There's a difference."

"Well, you say that now. You might feel differently when you've had time to think it over. After all, you started dating a rich man who was in line to inherit hundreds of millions of dollars. Not a man who works for an international aid organization."

"You can't honestly believe I was dating you for the money. That's not the kind of relationship we had anyway."

He shot her an odd look at that. "No. I don't suppose it is."

There was a note of finality in his voice, like he'd reached some sort of decision. Whatever it was, she wasn't sure she wanted to hear more. She couldn't take any more glimpses into his soul. She already felt as though she'd flown too close to the sun.

Fourteen

Maybe he was an idiot, but he didn't figure out something was wrong with Sydney until after they'd already checked out of the hotel and he'd driven her back to her little bungalow in Montrose. As much as he wasn't looking forward to confronting his parents, he knew he had to talk to them and had just assumed that he and Sydney would go as soon as they left the hotel. However, once he saw her clothes, he knew that wasn't an option. Dirt from his car was smeared across the back of her pale slacks and tan sweater. He'd thought he kept his car pretty clean, but apparently he was going to have to talk to the car care service he used.

Sydney was so quiet on the drive to her neighborhood that he had to wonder if something was wrong. When he pulled up in front of the house, Sydney said, "I'll just be a minute. You can wait in the car if you'd like."

"No, I'll come in," he said, not realizing at first that maybe she'd been asking him not to come in.

She opened the front door and gestured him through. It led

straight into a small living room, with an office off to the right and the kitchen straight ahead.

"Help yourself to a drink," she said, hurrying past the kitchen and gesturing toward the refrigerator. She darted into the bedroom, shutting the door behind her, leaving him standing in the living room staring blankly at the door through which she'd retreated, wondering what was up. She normally wasn't shy. She'd dressed and undressed in front of him countless times in the past four months. So why had she shut him out of the bedroom? Was she mad about the whole sleeping-with-her-boss thing?

He hadn't really thought about it when he'd had her spread out over the hood of her car. If he had, he probably would have assumed that she was fine with it. After all, she'd been the one to point out how close they were to the hotel.

While she changed, he occupied himself by looking around the tiny house. It was a bungalow probably dating back to the 1930s or so, but it had obviously been updated. The kitchen was open and modern, with a large granite-topped island floating between the living room and the kitchen. The office probably could have been used as a bedroom, but she had lined the wall with bookshelves and placed an Eames lounge chair in the center of the room. A large brown tabby cat sat curled up in the chair. When he reached out to touch it, the cat opened one eye and growled ominously.

He'd only been inside her house a handful of times, but he knew where it was because he'd picked her up there. It was decorated in mid-century modern antiques, with lots of pale wood and sleek lines. The furniture had all been lovingly cared for and looked like it might have been inherited from grandparents, though Griffin now knew it had not been.

He crossed back to her bedroom, leaning against the frame of the closed door. "I didn't know you had a cat," he called.

"Um…yeah," she called from the other side of the door. "That's Grommet."

"Like the animated dog?"

"Yeah." She opened the door. Now she was dressed in slim blue jeans and a moss-green knit sweater. "Just like that. He likes cheese."

Sydney tugged at the hem of her sweater and didn't quite meet his gaze. She looked beautiful, as she always did, but this outfit was more casual than her normal, middle-of-the-work-day professionalism.

"You ready?" he asked.

She knotted her fingers together, her expression twisting in indecision. "Here's the thing. I don't think I should go."

"What? You can't let them intimidate you like—"

"No!" she hastened to reassure him. "It's not that. I just..." She blew out a breath and seemed to be searching for words.

Sydney, who was never at a loss for words, suddenly was. Moreover, she seemed a little lost in general.

He crossed over to her, cupping her cheek in his palm and tipping her face up to his. "Hey, what's up?"

"I just think that maybe you need to do this alone."

He frowned. She still wasn't quite meeting his gaze and if she bit down any harder on her lip, she was going to start bleeding. He traced his thumb across her lower lip, gently freeing it from her teeth. "No. I need you there with me. I need a voice of reason. I need someone who's not emotionally involved. That's what you said, remember?"

"I know that's what I said, but I'm not..." Finally, she forced her gaze to his. "I don't think I can be your voice of reason anymore."

He thought of how crazy and messed up his family was. He thought of everything his father and his mother had put him through in the past few days. Hell, his entire life. And every time he'd fought them on anything, he'd done it alone. He'd never once, in his entire thirty years of life, had anyone been completely in his corner. Until now. Until Sydney.

She was everything to him now. No matter what else happened he was going to make damn sure that he didn't let her go.

He closed the distance between them and kissed her, molding his mouth to hers. Pouring into that kiss all the things he wouldn't be able to tell her until all this trouble with this family was resolved.

He lifted his mouth from hers and waited until she opened her eyes before saying, "I still need you there. No matter what."

They found his mother at the house, sitting beside his father's bed, reading him the business section of the newspaper aloud. The home health care nurse was sitting in the hall, giving them privacy. Thank God for small blessings. Most days, it was damn near impossible to have a private conversation with his parents; Griffin was relieved that today he'd have a shot at it. He went into the room where his father's hospital bed had been set up. Sydney was beside him as he walked up to the door, and she gave his hand a little tug. With a tilt of her head, she indicated she would wait in the hall, but he didn't release her hand, instead pulling her in with him. Caro sat in a wingback chair between the bed and the window that overlooked the front lawn. The head of Hollister's bed had been raised so he, too, was sitting upright.

Griffin wasn't sure if Sydney had ever even met his father, but if Hollister's fragile appearance shocked her, she didn't let on. Having her by his side, Griffin saw his father through new eyes, taking in all the things he hadn't noticed the past few visits. Hollister's skin looked pale and paper thin. His eyes were sunken. The myriad tubes and IVs hooked up to him only made him look more frail.

But Griffin didn't let that moment of empathy stop him. He marched into the room and tossed the photos of the mystery nanny down on the bed between his parents.

They both looked up at him in surprise, barely glancing at Sydney where she stood in the doorway.

"What is the meaning of this?" Caro asked, her voice cool.

"I was about to ask you the same thing," Griffin replied.

Hollister reached out a trembling hand and picked up the picture closest to him. He made a *harumphing* noise and then let the picture drop. "Is that the best—" his words were cut off by a series of hacking coughs "—you can do? A thirty-year-old picture?"

Griffin stood at the foot of his father's bed, his hands propped on his hips, staring down at his parents. There was a slight tremble in Caro's chin and she appeared to have lost all the cruel bravado that had carried her through lunch.

He felt only the slightest twinge of remorse. He didn't want to do this, but he wasn't the one who had started this, either.

"This thirty-year-old-picture is of the woman I believe wrote the letter. Dalton believed it, too. She worked here as a nanny when I was an infant. And I refuse to believe that neither of you remember anything about her. Especially since she appears to have stalked Hollister and stolen a family heirloom. Mother, if Sharlene is to be believed, before this girl—Vivian—disappeared forever, she had you so worked up, you demanded that Sharlene call the police and have her arrested. The idea that neither of you remember her at all is so preposterous as to be laughable."

For a long moment no one spoke. Hollister was glaring at Griffin, and the enmity in his gaze was strong enough to abolish the illusion that he was a fragile man. Caro had gone as white as Hollister's hospital-issued bed linens.

Finally, Griffin said, "I want some answers, and you should think very carefully before you give them. Because these may be the last words you speak to me."

Hollister gave a snort of disbelief. Caro's hands twitched nervously on the newspaper, causing it to rustle. Then she carefully folded the paper up and stood, placing it on the seat of the chair before crossing to look out the windows at the sprawling green lawns.

"This is all your father's fault."

"Of course it…is," Hollister gasped out through his coughing. "You always bl-bla-blame me. For everything."

Caro threw back her head and laughed. A desperate, maniacal laugh that seemed to echo through the room. "That's because it is always your fault. But this time especially." She spun to glare at her husband. "Why couldn't you just let it go? Why couldn't you just get the letter, feel the gut-wrenching sense of betrayal and just accept the fact that there's someone out there you don't have under your thumb? That's what you were supposed to do, damn it!"

Hollister looked at his wife, blinking in surprise. For the first time—maybe in his entire life—his expression wasn't arrogant and defiant. Instead, it was confused. "What do you mean?" He coughed again. "What I was supposed to do?"

And suddenly, Griffin got it. He understood what should have been glaringly obvious right from the very beginning. All the tension washed out of his body and he bent his neck, dropping his head forward and shaking it back and forth. "Mother, what did you do?"

"Caro?" Hollister asked, his voice sounding strangely hollow.

She turned back to the window, wrapping her arms tightly around her thin body, which suddenly looked frail, too. "I never meant for any of this to happen." She sent a pleading look over her shoulder at Hollister. "I just wanted to punish you. To hurt you like you'd done me so many times. And I knew it would drive you crazy, not knowing more about your daughter."

"So you sent the letter," Griffin said flatly. He stared at his mother, but for a long moment, she said nothing at all. Finally, he closed his eyes and scrubbed a hand down his face. "For the love of God, can't you be honest about at least this? Can't you—"

"I did." Her tone was as flat as his. "I never imagined what he would do. I never dreamed it would come to this."

"But when it did, when he first called us all into this room, showed us the letter and lay out the challenge, why not just come clean then?"

She whirled back to face them, her expression desperate. "Because I'd lost everything! He had cut me out of his will already. All I had was the hope that you'd find the girl, get everything and take pity on me."

"Mother, you—"

"Do you have any idea how hard I've worked trying to get you clues? How hard it was to keep Dalton off the right trail? How complicated this has been to try to feed you information without revealing how much I knew?"

Caro's voice was rising steadily toward hysteria. Griffin just stood there, shaking his head slowly back and forth. He was so tired of his mother's manipulations. If just once she'd stood up to Hollister, maybe he could feel more sympathy for her. But over and over again, he'd watched his mother sacrifice her pride, her dignity and her children to her own greed. She would never stand up to Hollister because doing so might jeopardize the status quo. Even this one tiny rebellion she'd tried to hide and bury beneath a wealth of lies. Another woman would have divorced Hollister long ago, but Caro was either too proud or too greedy, Griffin wasn't sure which.

Hollister's expression had sharpened into bitter distaste. "Caro, you ignorant twit," he said.

All three of them turned and stared at him. It was the same phrase the letter had used, and Griffin felt another pang of sympathy for Caro. No matter how manipulative and mean she might sometimes be, she didn't deserve to have her husband speak to her like that. Ever. Let alone in front of her son.

Griffin turned his back on his father and spoke to his mother, his voice softer now. "Mother, is there any truth to the letter at all? Does Hollister have a missing daughter, or did you just make it all up?"

Caro clenched and unclenched her hands in front of her

chest, the tears in her eyes now spilling over. "Vivian really was Dalton's nanny. She really did give birth to a girl and I believe that girl is Hollister's child. Why else would Vivian have been so obsessed with Hollister? Why else would she have taken his mother's ring?"

"She could have just been angry that you fired her. Did you think of that?"

"No," Caro shook her head. "If you're angry, you take something valuable. You steal a thousand dollars' worth of silverware that no one will notice until Christmas. You take the five hundred-dollar bills off the dresser. I wasn't wearing either ring that day. She overlooked my engagement ring with its eight-thousand-dollar diamond as well as probably ten grand in other jewelry, all so she could take Hollister's damn heirloom. That's either stupid or crazy."

He turned back to his father. "Okay then, it's on you. Did you sleep with that young woman?"

Hollister didn't even look at the picture. "Of course I did. But Vee turned out to be crazier than a June bug in July. Following me back here. Hiring on as the nanny. I refused to see her."

"So this girl, Vivian, Vee, you never even knew she was pregnant, did you?"

"If I had known, do you think we'd be having this conversation now? But don't you start thinking you've won, buddy boy. Identifying the mother was never what this challenge was about. I don't care who sent that letter." His long speech caught up with him and he once again dissolved into a fit of coughing. When he spoke again, his voice was thin. "You have to find the girl."

"No. No, I don't." Griffin looked at his father first and then back to his mother, once again shaking his head. "But if Cooper wants to, this will give him a place to start."

"What are you saying, boy?"

"I'm out," Griffin said simply.

"You're what?" Sydney asked. It was the first time she'd spoken in the entire conversation and everyone looked at her. Caro still looked tearful and broken. Hollister looked like he hadn't even realized she was there. Griffin turned and smiled at her.

"I'm done. Just like Dalton. I'm done looking for the heiress. I'm done working for Cain Enterprises. I'm tired of being a part of this sick, dysfunctional family. So I'm done." He walked back to where Sydney stood beside the door and held out his hand. She put her hand in his automatically, even though she knew she couldn't hold it long.

"Come on," he said. "Let's go."

She let him lead her out of his parents' house. He moved so fast it was like he was fleeing.

She stumbled along, taking three steps for every two of his. He knew he was walking too fast for her, but he also knew she'd be able to keep up. And he just wasn't willing to stop until they were well clear of the house, crossing the lawn back to his car. Then she dug in her heels and tugged her hand from his.

"Wait. Griffin, wait."

Griffin turned to look back at Sydney, half expecting to see that she'd stopped because she'd lost a shoe or something. But instead, she was just standing there under one of the sprawling live oaks that draped over his parents' lawn.

"What?" he asked. He wanted to keep moving. To get into his car, slam it into gear and tear down the highway. It was the same adrenaline fest he'd experienced earlier today, but instead of being fueled by anger, this time it was the sweet heady buzz of freedom.

Sydney took a step back from him. Almost as if she was afraid of him. "You're making a mistake."

"What?" This time it was flat-out confusion. What did she mean *a mistake?*

"Giving up on the search. Quitting Cain Enterprises. It's a

mistake. You need to go back in and tell them you've changed your mind."

He let out a bark of laughter. "Are you crazy? Did you hear that conversation in there? I'm not going to change my mind. I quit."

"You can't quit. You can't leave Cain Enterprises."

Sydney held her breath, waiting for Griffin's response. She knew it wasn't going to be pretty. He was hurt. He was angry.

But instead of taking out his anger on her, he gave a bark of laughter. "Hell, if Dalton can quit, I can quit."

"You may not realize it, but Cain Enterprises is who you are. What would you do if you quit?"

"Who cares what I do? We'll leave. We could travel. Go anywhere we want. Get married. We could—"

She held up her hands, cutting him off. "Whoa, whoa, whoa. Wait a second. Now you want to get married?"

He stared at her blankly for a second, and she had to wonder if he even realized he'd said it. But then he shrugged. "Sure. Let's get married." He smiled, but there was a frenzied look to his expression. "Don't you get it? I don't have to be part of that family anymore. I don't have to be a part of that cycle of misery anymore. I can do anything I want. I can marry anyone I want."

Oh, crap. This was worse than she thought. She had fully expected him to cling desperately to their relationship out of familiarity. She'd been prepared for that. She had not seen this coming. It simply hadn't occurred to her that he would try to sweep her up into his rebellion against his family, but that's exactly what he was doing. Irony of ironies, suddenly she was *his* wild oats.

Which was not at all the same thing as being the love of his life. Despite him proposing to her in what she could only imagine was a fit of delirium, he hadn't once mentioned love. And why would he? Sure, they'd been sleeping together for months, and sure, she had a key to his apartment, but neither of those things signified any real emotion on his part. Both the sex and the key were just accidents, really.

If she was a different kind of person, if she wasn't someone who needed to be needed, she might risk it. She might agree to marry him, hoping that later he'd fall for her just as hard as she'd fallen for him. But Sydney Edwards—Sinnamon Edwards—desperately needed to be loved. Really and truly. Loved for who she was. And so she couldn't risk it.

But she also couldn't tell him that, because Griffin was smooth and smart and if he thought she needed the words to convince her, he'd probably say them.

"You can't run away from your life like that," she said instead.

"Why not?" He held her at arm's length, studying her face as he asked, "What's holding me here?"

"Your job, for starters."

He looked surprised, then suddenly distrustful. "You care so much about my job?"

"Yes. I do. I care about Cain Enterprises. You do, too. You're just too stubborn to see it." She seemed to have his full attention now, so she spoke quickly, not wanting to lose this chance to convince him. "All this time you've been searching for the heiress, planning on hiring Dalton back as CEO, and you haven't seen that you would actually be just as good a CEO as he was. Better, maybe."

He dropped her hands and stepped away, leaving a gap of several feet between them. When he spoke, his voice was flat and devoid of emotion. "So, what? You think I should just stay here. Find the heiress. Stay on as CEO. Then we'll get married?"

She ignored his comment about getting married, because this time it felt more like a jab than a proposal. "What's important is that you find your sister. You have this idea in your head that you can run away to Africa and reinvent yourself, but you can't. You think that the only way you'll ever know that someone loves you for you is if you give up all your money. But that's ridiculous."

"Is it?" His voice was chilling and as lifeless as a block of ice.

"Yes. You are who you are, regardless of whether or not you have the money. And if you walk away from everything now, you're only robbing yourself of the chance to be the person you were meant to be."

"And who's that? Someone with a lot of money?"

"Someone who might have a sister out there who cares about him. Someone who is a great CEO. Think about all the people who work at Cain Enterprises who you know and care about. Jenna and Peyton and Marion. Are you really just going to walk away from them? You're just going to abandon the company? You're really going to do that?"

"So that's your big plan for the future. We keep searching for the heiress. I stay on as CEO of Cain Enterprises." Suddenly, as he spoke, his meaning was blaringly obvious. The fog had cleared. "And you'll be right there by my side. Because, presumably, once I'm worth close to half a billion dollars, you'll get over this fear of being the EA who sleeps with her boss."

Okay, so he wasn't playing dumb, he was being dumb.

"You think I'm after your money?"

"Oh, I think you win either way. You've said all along you were in this for job security. So either you get to stay on as the assistant of the CEO of a company or you end up married to the CEO. Either way, your financial security is pretty much guaranteed, right?"

"That's what you think?" she asked. "That all I care about is the money?"

"Why else would you be so damn desperate to convince me to find the heiress and to stay on as CEO?"

"Because I want what's best for you, you dumbass. Did it

honestly never occur to you that I just wanted you to make the best decision for you?"

"No. That never occurred to me. And you wanna know why? Because if you do know about Hope2O and you really understand what I'm trying to do there, then you'd understand that nothing would make me happier than funneling all that money into a worthy charity."

"Oh, I understand all right." He made her so mad, she wanted to launch herself at him and strangle him. Instead, she satisfied herself with merely stalking across the pristine lawn and getting right up in his face. "I understand perfectly well that your family has you so emotionally messed up that you think no one will ever love you for yourself alone. So you think the only way to earn redemption or respect is to pour all your money into a worthy cause."

"I don't—" He made a meager protest, but she didn't let him finish.

She was too furious to stop midrant. "I get that. And that would be so convenient for you, wouldn't it? Because then when someone fell in love with you, it would be just you on the table. And you'd never have to wonder whether or not they really loved you. And you would never have to suck it up and just learn to trust someone on their own merits. That would be perfect for you, right?"

He was stubbornly silent, refusing to acknowledge the truth to her words.

So she went on. "And maybe that would have worked out for you if your father hadn't come up with this damn contest for Cain Enterprises. But he did and it screwed up all your plans. Because regardless of whether or not you want to admit it, you care about this company. You care about these people. And if you walk away from it now, you will end up regretting it forever. You know what will happen if you don't play Hollister's game, don't you? Cooper doesn't want Cain Enterprises. He has his own empire to run. So Cain Enterprises will end up reverting to the state. Sheppard Capital will probably swoop in and dismantle it bit by bit."

"Cooper—"

"I'm not done yet," she interrupted him again. "Yes, you'll know that whatever woman you end up with down the line will really love you for you—you will damn well guarantee that because you'll both be living in sub-Saharan Africa on the salary of an international aid worker. But guess what? To guarantee your personal happiness you will have sacrificed the jobs and livelihoods of countless people you really care about."

Finally, finally, she was done with the barrage of anger that had rushed out of her. Her! Sydney, who never lost her temper. Who had never been angry at him, not even when he'd told her about the background check.

But she'd lost her temper now because he was being so damn dense about himself, about what he really needed.

And now he just stared at her, like she'd lost her ever-loving mind. So she asked, "Are you really going to sacrifice all of Cain Enterprises, just so you can have some sort of guarantee that you're loved? Are you really willing to make that sacrifice?"

"What if I am?"

"Then you're not the man I thought you were."

"And let me guess…if I am that guy, if I'm that guy who can walk away from millions of dollars, then you don't want to be with me."

"The money is not what I want. It never was."

"Answer the question, Sydney. If I walk away from Cain Enterprises, I lose you. Do I have that right?"

"That's what you don't get. You never had me to begin with."

"You sure about that? 'Cause I'm pretty sure I had you just about an hour ago."

"Nice." She laughed bitterly, even though she wanted to cry. "If you can't win an argument with logic, then throw sex back into the mix, just to make me feel cheap. You know, for someone who doesn't want to be cruel and manipulative like your family, you do a damn good job of it."

"Well, then, you're going to love this. You don't want to be the girl who sleeps with her boss to get ahead. Fine. You're not that girl anymore. You're fired."

"I guess I should have seen that coming. If you can't have what you want, then you'll damn well make sure no one else does, either." She let out a bitter laugh. "You know, if I thought you could actually get away with that, I'd sue you. I think we'll both be better off if we just pretend you never said that." She turned and started to walk away, but then turned back around and looked at him. "You want to know the real reason I would never marry you? Because you're wrong—it doesn't have anything to do with the money or whether or not you get control of Cain. It's because I saw this coming from a mile away. I knew from day one that eventually you'd get bored or frustrated and you'd push me away."

"So you pushed me away first? You just conveniently waited until I let all that money slip through my fingers before doing it."

By now she was so annoyed with him that she couldn't even respond, so she circled back around to him trying to fire her. Even though she didn't really believe he'd do it. Even though she would sue his pants off if he followed through, she couldn't believe he'd threatened it. "Besides, you know the one thing you've forgotten? You can't fire me. You already quit. You're not my boss anymore."

"Oh, I've only told my parents I quit. I'll sure as hell stay on at Cain Enterprises long enough to make sure you never work there again."

"So you'll put up with something you hate just to make me miserable?" She swallowed the welling of grief that swelled up in her throat. "Your father would be so proud."

Fifteen

She thought Griffin would come after her.

Even after all the horrible things they'd said to one another, even though her heart felt like it was being crushed under a steamroller, she honestly expected him to come after her. Even if for no other reason than the fact that she was on foot, miles from home, in River Oaks, for goodness' sake.

He didn't come after her.

He just let her walk away. Which took forever. Just walking down the block seemed to take an eternity. The whole time, she was painfully aware of him still standing there on his parents' lawn, hands fisted on his hips, watching her walk away.

Of course, she didn't turn around and check to see if he was still there. For all she knew, he may have gone back inside and poured himself a drink. But she never heard his car take off, and he never passed her on the road. So the whole interminable time she was walking past the six sprawling estates on his parents' block, she pictured him standing there behind her, watching her walk away.

That image was the only thing that kept her from crumbling to the ground in tears. Because no matter what else happened, she would not let him see her crying. It wasn't strength that kept her going. It wasn't even pride. It was pure stubbornness. He'd crushed her, but she'd been crushed before.

That was the thing about a kid like her. She'd lost everything at the age of seven. Everything she'd ever known had been ripped away from her, even though everything she'd ever known was absolute crap. But once she'd lost everything, she knew she could live through losing everything again. She might have been terrified, but she had just kept going.

So now she kept walking. Just putting one foot in front of the other until she'd finally reached the end of the block. Then she turned the corner and walked some more. Cars drove past without noticing her—not Griffin's car, but others. It was the people on foot who worried her. Twice she saw other women walking on the other side of the street. Once, it was a nanny pushing a high-end stroller that she was pretty sure cost more than her car. The second time a pair of spandex-wrapped trophy wives. Neither spared her more than a passing glance and she turned another corner. Only then did she admit that she was lost. In addition to being emotionally adrift, she actually had no idea how to get herself home.

She wandered down the block for a few minutes before stopping in front of a house with an impenetrable line of privacy shrubs hiding it from the street. Near the street, the branches of a massive live oak dipped low to the ground. She sank to the ground in the shade of the tree, grateful to be at least somewhat shielded from anyone passing by. Then she dug out her phone and pulled up the maps app. She dropped a pin at the current location and then asked for directions back to her own house. Three point eight miles. It might as well be twenty-three point eight. Yes, it would be possible for her to walk home from here, but she just didn't have the energy. She called Tasha.

"Hey, what's up?" Tasha asked. "That lazy boss of yours isn't sick again, is he?"

Sydney had intended to calmly ask for a ride home, but the instant she heard Tasha's voice, the whole story poured out.

"I'm going to kill him!" Tasha said indignantly when the story petered out. "I'm actually going to kill that jerk."

Despite herself, Sydney let out a strangled laugh. "I don't think—"

"No. Really. I think we should kill him. Between you, me, Marco, Jen and George, that's what…five of us who grew up in the foster care system before ending up with Molly. Surely one of us knows someone who grew up to be a professional hit man, right? I'm guessing Jen. She was always the toughest."

Again, Sydney laughed. "Yeah. It would probably be Jen. But don't call her just yet. What I could really use now is just a ride."

Tasha snorted. "Honey, I got in the car as soon as you called. I'll be there in fifteen minutes."

Thirteen minutes later, Sydney climbed into her foster sister's beat-up Chevy. Tasha wrapped her in a brief hug before putting the car back into gear. Tasha was a crappy driver who talked too much with her hands. This was probably the first time they'd ever been in the car together that Sydney hadn't spent the whole drive fearing for her life. Today she simply felt too numb.

For the first five minutes of the drive, Tasha plotted Griffin's murder in grisly detail. Because she was in her final year of law school, most of the discussion was about how to get away with it. Eventually, she had Sydney laughing so hard she was crying. And then just crying.

When she finally looked up, they were in the parking lot of a strip mall. Tasha had killed the engine and was frantically digging through the car's glove compartment for a tissue. Finally, she held out an old napkin.

"I really can kill him," Tasha offered.

Sydney blew her nose. "That won't be necessary."

Tasha looked down at the dash and swallowed visibly. "I've never seen you cry before."

"I don't know that anyone has." Sydney stared down at the mangled strap of her purse. She thought about saying more about Griffin—because she'd cried in front him, but that had been right after they'd had sex and she didn't really think he'd noticed. That should have been a sign right there. But her throat closed over the words. So instead she said, "I don't know what I'm going to do about my job."

"You know he can't get away with that crap. He can't fire you over any of this. We'll sue his ass. We'll—"

"I don't... I know I could totally sue him. And maybe I should. For justice or whatever. But I don't really think that he'll fire me. He'll come to his senses and realize he can't get away with it. But I don't think I can go back to work there anyway. I can't see him every day."

"You could—"

But she shook her head. "Even if I found another position in the company, I'd still know I was working for him. I don't want that."

And here it was, reason number one why sleeping with her boss was a bad idea.

For a few long seconds, she was painfully aware of Tasha studying her. Then Tasha said fiercely, "You'll get another job!"

"In this economy?" Sydney shook her head. "It could take months. Yeah, I have my savings, but—" She broke off because her savings weren't all that extensive. She'd helped three of her four foster-siblings with college tuition, but the last thing she wanted was for Tasha to feel badly. "Hey, I can put the house on the market. I'll need to find an apartment that allows cats, but Grommet and I don't need all that room. It's a great little place in a great neighborhood. I'm sure I can—"

She broke off again, this time because Tasha was chuckling.

"What?" Sydney demanded.

"I'm not going to let you sell your house!"

"But—"

"God, you're so stubborn."

"I am not."

"Of course you are." Tasha twisted in her seat. "Look, you've helped with my tuition for the past four years. I'm not going to let you sell your house."

"I didn't help that much," she protested. She'd just chipped in here and there.

"You helped enough. I can get out of my apartment lease and move in with you. We'll share the mortgage payment. We could even get by with one car if we had to. And I've still got my job at the law library. We'll make it work. You're my sister. I'm not going to let you lose your home without a fight."

Tasha's words should have made her feel better, but they only made her cry more. It turned out she had a financial safety net after all. It was just her emotions that were free falling.

Griffin had ripped all of her long-sought-after security right out from under her. Her entire adult life, she'd worked to become financially independent. She'd struggled and scraped and starved to get where she was now...or rather, where she'd been a week ago. And because she'd slept with Griffin, she'd lost it all.

She should be devastated. She should be curling into a ball on the ground in tears. And she was devastated...just not about that. The job, the money, the security. She could live without all that. So she'd have to start over. Big deal. She could do that. Even without the safety net of family to help support her through the tough times, she'd still be fine.

No, what devastated her was that she'd lost Griffin. True, she'd never really had him. Her brain had never believed they'd get to be together, but somehow, despite that, her heart had believed it. Her heart had wanted and dreamed of what her brain had never dared to imagine: a life with Griffin. Her heart would have been happy in Houston, working for Cain Enterprises, or

in sub-Saharan Africa. She would have gone anywhere to be
with him. Unfortunately, he didn't want or need her.

She'd get over losing her job, but she might never recover
from losing him.

In the end, Tasha didn't need to move in with her. The grueling search for a new job ended up being neither grueling nor
long. The day after her big fight with Griffin, she'd resigned
from Cain Enterprises. At first, he refused to even accept her
resignation. He even went so far as to offer her a stiff apology.
She didn't wait around to hear him out, but had left her letter
on her desk on the way out. Four days after that, she got a call
at home from Sheppard Capital. Sharlene offered her a job.

At first, Sydney was tempted to refuse. It smacked of charity. She didn't want a pity job merely because Griffin felt badly
about giving her no option but to quit.

"Don't be ridiculous, dear," Sharlene had said, brushing
aside her protests. "Griffin didn't call me. Dalton did. He was
furious that Griffin put you in this position. Even in the heat
of an argument, he should have known better. Dalton wanted
to hire you himself, but he doesn't start with the new company
for another three weeks, so I insisted I get first dibs. After all,
I know how hard a good assistant is to come by. Besides, I also
know what it means to be a man's assistant. To spend your
every waking moment anticipating his needs only to find out
he doesn't need you at all."

In the end, she had let Sharlene convince her. Not because
she really wanted the job, but because it was easier than fighting her. Besides, she did need a job. The pay was nearly what
she'd made at Cain Enterprises, and it was nice to go to work
somewhere where no one knew that splotchy skin and red eyes
weren't normal for her.

Sharlene's own assistant, apparently, had been wanting to
move to their office in Dallas and so, after a week of unem-
ployment, Sydney started work as Sharlene's new assistant.

A full week passed while she settled numbly into her new job. It was midway through her second week at the new job when Griffin walked into the office.

Seeing him at work was the one thing she hadn't anticipated when she'd accepted the job from Sharlene. The sight of him was like a kick to the solar plexus.

It took every ounce of willpower she had to swallow back her tears, muster her professionalism and ask politely, "Is Ms. Sheppard expecting you?"

Griffin looked her up and down without a trace of his normal easy smile. "No," he said simply. "I'm not here to see her."

That gave her a moment's pause. She hoped to hell that he was in the wrong office then because she just did not have the energy to be polite to him when all she really wanted to do was curl into a ball and cry. For about a month. Or even two.

Still, she kept a smile on her face that was at least semi-polite and asked, "Then can I direct you to someone else's office?"

"No. I'm right where I want to be." Before she ask what he meant, he pulled a business card down on the desk in front of her. "There. Will that do it?"

"What?"

"Look at the card, damn it."

His voice was hard and intractable. His face humorless.

She looked from him down to the business card. It had the familiar Cain Enterprises logo on the left-hand side. To the right of that were the words: Griffin Cain. And beneath that: President & Chief Executive Officer.

She stared at the card for a long moment before looking back up at him. "I don't understand."

"I've been working nonstop for the past two and half weeks to convince the board to name me CEO. Permanently. I groveled before my father. I called in all kinds of favors for this. I'm not quitting. I'm not leaving Cain Enterprises." With that, he walked around to her side of the desk and pulled her to her feet.

Then, before she could question him or protest, he dropped to one knee in front of her. He pulled out a ring box and flipped it open. Inside was a simple diamond solitaire. "Now, will you please marry me?"

The sight of him on his knees before her, the sight of the ring, the entire proposal…it was straight out of a fairy tale. And it killed her to have to turn him down.

"Griffin, I…" She started to shake her head, but she could barely talk past the tears.

He must have heard the denial in her voice because he stood, pulling her into his arms and cupping her face. "Don't say no."

"I can't…I can't say yes."

"Why not?"

His expression nearly broke her heart. Because he looked like he genuinely didn't know why she might say no.

She shook her head and pulled out of his arms. "Griffin, you don't really care about me."

To her surprise, he laughed. "That's ridiculous. Of course I do. I love you."

Her heart felt like it was trying to crawl right out of her and throw itself into his waiting hands. "You don't."

He grabbed her arm and pulled her back to him. "I do. I know you think you know me pretty well, but you don't get to tell me how I feel."

She swallowed her heart back down. She couldn't meet his gaze, so instead, she stared at the top button of his shirt. "You don't really mean that."

"I do."

"No. You don't. Look, I get why you might think you love me. But you really don't. It's just good sex and familiarity."

"It's great sex." He tipped her chin up so she was looking at him. "And it's love."

She forced herself to meet his gaze. "No. It's not." His arms felt so damn good around her and the sensation made it even harder to say what she had to say, but she forced the words out. "Things have been very complicated for you the past few weeks. You're confused. If you think you love me, it's just because I'm the one stable thing in your life right now and—"

Griffin interrupted her with a bark of laughter. "You think you're the one stable thing in my life?"

"Well, I—"

"Sydney, you make me crazy. You are maddening and delightful and you make me feel things no one else has ever made me feel. You tempt me beyond reason. The one thing you are not is stable."

"I—"

"You've driven me crazy ever since I first met you. Don't get me wrong, you are right about a lot of things, and you were totally right about me needing to stay on as CEO. But you are not right about why I'm asking you to marry me."

"I'm not?"

"I'm not asking you because I want stability in my life. I'm asking because I want you in my life."

"But…you don't really love me."

"What on earth makes you think I don't love you?"

"If you love me," she challenged, "why didn't you ever tell me about Hope2O?"

"If you love me why didn't you ever tell me about Sinnamon?"

For a moment, she stared at him, openmouthed. And then she realized she didn't have an answer for that.

Slowly, he smiled. "Hey, we both kept our secrets longer than we should have. We're both really private people. This crazy search for the heiress did turn everything upside down. But that's not a bad thing. If this hadn't happened, we probably would have taken a lot longer to get here. But I don't have any doubt that we still would have gotten here. I love you, Sydney. I think I've loved you ever since we first met. And if that doesn't convince you, then consider this. I spent the past two weeks flying all over the country, meeting with each member of the board to convince them to name me CEO. All so that I could make this proposal perfect. I messed up the first time I asked you to marry me. I wanted to do it right this time."

Again, he dropped to his knee in front of her and held out the ring box.

"Sydney Edwards, will you marry me?"

And suddenly, she was crying again. She, who never cried in front of anyone and would have sworn she was cried out for the rest of her life, was crying. So she never actually said yes. She just nodded until he got the hint. He stood up and kissed her through her tears.

Finally, a long time later, she looked up, smiling a little. "I don't suppose this is a good time to give you back that key to your condo."

He frowned, and it seemed to take him a moment to realize what she meant. Then he chuckled. "No. Why don't you keep that? It might come in handy when we're planning the wedding."

She pushed up on her toes and was about to kiss him again when she realized he was wearing a sweater. The same cashmere sweater she had him wear to that first board meeting. "You're wearing Dalton's sweater," she said softly.

"You said I looked good in it. So I made him give it to me. He was happy to donate to the cause. He said he'd give up all his sweaters if I'd just stop moping and come after you."

She gave his arm a playful punch. "You weren't really moping, were you? You're not the type to mope."

He smiled. "Not anymore, I'm not."

Epilogue

"Now we know. This is the girl we're looking for," Griffin said.

Sydney walked back into Griffin's living room carrying a tray of coffee mugs just in time to see him carefully place the two photos on the ottoman in front of his sectional sofa. Sydney set the tray of coffee on the end table. Griffin reached for his mug immediately, sending her a grateful smile as he did.

She felt that familiar little flutter in her heart as she returned his smile. How had she gotten so lucky?

Before she could distribute the rest of the coffees, Dalton handed one to Laney, who sat on the sofa beside him. Laney gave Dalton's leg a squeeze as she took the coffee from him, but instead of drinking it herself, she carried it over to the window where Cooper stood looking out.

Sydney had met Cooper only that morning, at Laney and Dalton's wedding. The event had been a quiet affair, done in the backyard of the Cain estate, so that Hollister's nurse could wheel him out to watch.

For now, because all three brothers were in town for the wedding, Griffin had called this meeting. He'd seemed relived that Cooper had shown up. Laney handed Cooper his coffee, giving his arm a friendly rub. He smiled down at her with more affection than he'd shown either of his brothers.

Laney returned to her spot beside Dalton, curling her feet under her as she sat. Cooper wandered over, sipping his coffee as he looked down at the pictures.

"You haven't exactly been making lightning-fast progress, have you?"

Griffin shot him an annoyed look. "I've been a little busy running the company."

A little busy was putting it mildly. Griffin had attacked the position as CEO with the same fervor he dedicated to all his projects. Hope2O wasn't suffering from neglect, either. Now that the cat was out of the bag, Sharlene had joined Hope2O's board and together they were plotting to get Dalton involved. Between the three of them, they would take good care of the charity.

Sydney ran her palm across his leg and she felt some of the tension seep out of him before Griffin added, "But, no, not particularly. Hollister's condition has stabilized, but we can't put this off forever."

"Griffin is right," Dalton said. "We've got to find this girl."

Cooper looked at them all with a raised eyebrow. "Based on nothing more than a pair of old photographs?"

Sydney scooted to the edge of the seat and reached over to turn the photos so they faced Cooper. By now, she figured she knew as much as any of them, maybe more. "We know this is the girl." She pointed to the child in the picture. "This was taken years ago, obviously. We figure she's about Griffin's age now. This woman here was her mother. When she worked for the Cains she used the name Vivian Beck, but we don't think that's her real name."

"Why?" Cooper asked.

"Because she disappeared after she was fired," Griffin explained. "We tried to track her down by social security number, but that was a dead end, too."

Dalton stared at the picture. "So we still have nothing."

"Not exactly." Sydney took another sip of her coffee. "When we showed the picture to Hollister, he called the mother Vee, not Vivian. And he admitted that when she came to Houston and got the job as the Cain nanny, she had followed him from somewhere. In a later conversation, he called her Victoria. So I looked up the company records to see where he'd been in the months before she got that job and found out that he'd just returned from—"

"Victoria," Dalton said.

Sydney looked up at him, but he and Laney were exchanging a look.

"So I was right," Laney said. "Victoria was the name of the girl's mother, in addition to being the name of a city."

Dalton nodded, his expression grim. "So that's what we know. In 1982 Hollister spent three months in Victoria, Texas. And while he was there, he met and—presumably impregnated—a young woman whose name was also Victoria. So it shouldn't be too hard to track her down. How many women named Victoria could there possibly be in Victoria, Texas?"

"Exactly," Griffin said. "Once we find the mother, we should be able to track down the daughter."

Cooper frowned. "You're sure this is the woman who wrote the letter?"

Sydney shot a sidelong look at Griffin. He'd gone back and forth on whether or not he wanted to tell his brothers that Caro had written the letter. She took his hand in hers and gave it a squeeze.

"Yes," he lied as he tapped his finger on the photo of the girl. "I'm sure this girl here is the one we're looking for."

"Well, then." Cooper took one last sip of his coffee before

setting his mug on the table. "It seems like you've got this all wrapped up. It seems like you've won."

Griffin stood before Cooper could walk out. "I didn't ask you to come just so I could rub your nose in it."

"Then why did you ask me here?"

"Neither Dalton nor I have been able to find this girl on our own. We're all tired of Hollister's games. I think we should work together—we need your help. I think we should split the money."

"You want to divide up the company three ways?"

"No. Four ways. Once we find her, we give her a quarter of it. After all, she's our sister."

* * * * *

She was his best friend.

But in the back of Jason's mind, lying in wait all these years, was curiosity. What would it be like between them?

"I've been thinking about it all afternoon and decided I'd be a pretty lousy friend if I wasn't there when you needed me."

A broad smile transformed her expression. "You don't know how much this means to me. I'll call the clinic tomorrow and make an appointment for you."

Jason shook his head. "No fertility clinic. No doctor." He hooked his fingers around the sash that held her robe closed and tugged her a half step closer. Heat pooled below his belt at the way her lips parted in surprise. "Just you and me."

Something like excitement flickered in her eyes, only to be dampened by her frown. "Are you suggesting what I think you're suggesting?"

"Let's make a baby the old-fashioned way."

Dear Reader,

When I set out to write a friends-to-lovers book I had no idea of the challenges involved in helping best friends since first grade find their forever love.

Jason and Ming have been there for each other through every challenge and success. They bring out the best in each other. Or they did until romance entered the picture.

Deciding to take a chance on love is not always easy, and it's even worse for Ming and Jason because they risk losing their best friend if the relationship goes wrong. I hope you enjoy their journey from friends to forever.

All the best!

Cat Schield

A TRICKY
PROPOSITION

BY
CAT SCHIELD

Published in Great Britain 2013
by Mills & Boon, an imprint of Harlequin (UK) Limited,
Eton House, 18-24 Paradise Road, Richmond, Surrey TW9 1SR

© Catherine Schield 2013

ISBN: 978 0 263 90471 0
ebook ISBN: 978 1 472 00597 7

51-0413

Harlequin (UK) policy is to use papers that are natural, renewable and recyclable products and made from wood grown in sustainable forests. The logging and manufacturing processes conform to the legal environmental regulations of the country of origin.

Printed and bound in Spain
by Blackprint CPI, Barcelona

Cat Schield has been reading and writing romance since high school. Although she graduated from college with a BA in business, her idea of a perfect career was writing books for Mills & Boon. And now, after winning the Romance Writers of America 2010 Golden Heart Award for series contemporary romance, that dream has come true. Cat lives in Minnesota with her daughter, Emily, and their Burmese cat. When she's not writing sexy, romantic stories for Mills & Boon® Desire™, she can be found sailing with friends on the St Croix River or in more exotic locales like the Caribbean and Europe. She loves to hear from readers. Find her at www.catschield.com. Follow her on Twitter @catschield.

To my best friend, Annie Slawik.
I can't thank you enough for all the laughter
and support. Without you I wouldn't be who I am.

One

Ming Campbell's anxiety was not soothed by the restful trickle of water from the nearby fountain or by the calming greenery hanging from baskets around the restaurant's out-door seating area. With each sip of her iced pomegranate tea she grew more convinced she was on the verge of making the biggest mistake of her life.

Beneath the table, her four-pound Yorkshire terrier lifted her chin off Ming's toes and began her welcome wiggle. Muf-fin might not be much of a guard dog, but she made one hell of an early warning system.

Stomach tightening, Ming glanced up. A tall man in loose-fitting chinos, polo shirt and casual shoes approached. Sexy stubble softened his chiseled cheeks and sharp jaw.

"Sorry I'm late."

Jason Sterling's fingertips skimmed her shoulder, sending a rush of goose bumps speeding down her arm. Ming cursed her body's impulsive reaction as he sprawled in the chair across from hers.

Ever since breaking off her engagement to his brother, Evan, six months ago, she'd grown acutely conscious of any and all contact with him. The friendly pat he gave her arm. His shoulder bumping hers as he sat beside her on the couch. The affable hugs he doled so casually that scrambled her nerve endings. It wasn't as if she could tell him to stop. He'd want to know what was eating at her, and there was no way she was going to tell him. So, she silently endured and hoped the feelings would go away or at least simmer down.

Muffin set her front paws on his knee, her brown eyes fixed on his face, and made a noise that was part bark, part sneeze. Jason slid his hand beneath the terrier's belly and lifted her so she could give his chin a quick lick. That done, the dog settled on his lap and heaved a contented sigh.

Jason signaled the waitress and they ordered lunch. "How come you didn't start without me?"

Because she was too keyed up to be hungry. "You said you were only going to be fifteen minutes late."

Jason was the consummate bachelor. Self-involved, preoccupied with amateur car racing and always looking for the next bit of adventure, whether it was a hot girl or a fast track. They'd been best friends since first grade and she loved him, but that didn't mean he didn't occasionally drive her crazy.

"Sorry about that. We hit some traffic just as we got back into town."

"I thought you were coming home yesterday."

"That was the plan, but then the guys and I went out for a couple beers after the race and our celebration went a little long. None of us were in any shape to drive five hours back to Houston." With a crooked smile he extended his long legs in front of him and set his canvas-clad foot on the leg of her chair.

"How is Max taking how far you are ahead of him in points?" The two friends had raced domestic muscle cars in events sanctioned by the National Auto Sports Association since they were sixteen. Each year they competed to see who could amass the most points.

"Ever since he got engaged, I don't think he cares."

She hadn't seen Jason this disgruntled since his dad fell for a woman twenty years his junior. "You poor baby. Your best buddy has grown up and gotten on with his life, leaving you behind." Ming set her elbow on the table and dropped her chin into her palm. She'd been listening to Jason complain about the changes in his best friend ever since Max Case had proposed to the love of his life.

Jason leaned forward, an intense look in his eyes. "Maybe I need to find out what all the fuss is about."

"I thought you were never going to get married." Sudden anxiety crushed the air from her lungs. If he fell madly in love with someone, the dynamic of their friendship would change. She'd no longer be his best "girl" friend.

"No worries about that." His lopsided grin eased some of her panic.

Ming turned her attention to the Greek salad the waitress set in front of her. In high school she'd developed a crush on Jason. It had been hopeless. Unrequited. Except for one brief interlude after prom—and he'd taken pains to assure her that had been a mistake—he'd never given her any indication that he thought of her as anything but a friend.

When he headed off to college, time and distance hadn't blunted her feelings for him, but it had provided her with perspective. Even if by some miracle Jason did fall madly in love with her, he wasn't going to act on it. Over and over, he'd told her how important her friendship was to him and how he didn't want to do anything to mess that up.

"So, what's up?" Jason said, eyeing her over the top of his hamburger. "You said you had something serious to discuss with me."

And in the thirty minutes she'd sat waiting for him, she'd

talked herself into a state of near panic. Usually she told him everything going on in her life. Well, almost everything.

When she'd starting dating Evan there were a few topics they didn't discuss. Her feelings for his brother being the biggest. Holding her own council about such an enormous part of her life left her feeling as if a chunk of her was missing, but she'd learned to adjust and now found it harder than she expected to open up to him.

"I'm going to have a baby." She held her breath and waited for his reaction.

A French fry paused midway between his plate and his mouth. "You're pregnant?"

She shook her head, some of her nervousness easing now that the conversation had begun. "Not yet."

"When?"

"Hopefully soon."

"How? You're not dating anyone."

"I'm using a clinic."

"Who's going to be the father?"

She dodged his gaze and stabbed her fork into a kalamata olive. "I've narrowed the choices down to three. A lawyer who specializes in corporate law, an athlete who competes in the Ironman Hawaii challenge every year and a wildlife photographer. Brains. Body. Soul. I haven't decided which way to go yet."

"You've obviously been thinking about this for a while. Why am I only hearing about it now?" He pushed his plate away, abandoning his half-eaten burger.

In the past she'd been able to talk to Jason about anything. Getting involved with his brother had changed that. Not that it should have. She and Jason were friends with no hope of it ever being anything more.

"You know why Evan and I broke up." She'd been troubled that Evan hadn't shared her passion for family, but she thought he'd come around. "Kids are important to me. I wouldn't do what I do if they weren't."

She'd chosen to become an orthodontist because she loved kids. Their sunny view of the world made her smile, so she gave them perfect teeth to smile back.

"Have you told your parents?"

"Not yet." She shifted on her chair.

"Because you know your mother won't react well to you getting pregnant without being married."

"She won't like it, but she knows how much I want a family of my own, and she's come to accept that I'm not going to get married."

"You don't know that. Give yourself a chance to get over your breakup with Evan. There's someone out there for you."

Not likely when the only man she could see herself with was determined never to marry. Frustration bubbled up. "How long do I wait? Another six months? A year? In two months I turn thirty-two. I don't want to waste any more time weighing the pros and cons or worrying about my mom's reaction when in my heart I know what I want." She thrust out her chin. "I'm going to do this, Jason."

"I can see that."

Mesmerizing eyes studied her. Galaxy blue, the exact shade of her '66 Shelby Cobra convertible. He'd helped her convince her parents to buy the car for her seventeenth birthday and then they'd spent the summer restoring it. She had fond memories of working with him on the convertible, and every time she drove it, she couldn't help but feel connected to Jason. That's why she'd parked the car in her garage the day she started dating his brother and hadn't taken it out since.

"I'd really like you to be on board with my decision."

"You're my best friend," he reminded her, eyes somber. "How can I be anything but supportive?"

Even though she suspected he was still processing her news and had yet to decide whether she was making a mistake, he'd chosen to back her. Ming relaxed. Until that second she hadn't realized how anxious she was about Jason's reaction.

"Are you done eating?" she asked a few minutes later, catching the waitress's eye. Jason hadn't finished his lunch and showed no signs of doing so. "I should probably get back to the clinic. I have a patient to see in fifteen minutes."

He snagged the bill from the waitress before she set it on the table and pulled out his wallet.

"I asked you to lunch." Ming held her hand out imperiously. "You are not buying."

"It's the least I can do after being so late. Besides, the way you eat, you're always a cheap date."

"Thanks."

While Jason slipped cash beneath the saltshaker, she stood and called Muffin to her. The Yorkie refused to budge from Jason's lap. Vexed, Ming glared at the terrier. She was not about to scoop the dog off Jason's thighs. Her pulse hitched at the thought of venturing anywhere near his muscled legs.

Air puffing out in a sigh, she headed for the wood gate that led directly to the parking lot. Jason was at her side, dog tucked beneath his arm, before she reached the pavement.

"Where's your car?" he asked.

"I walked. It's only two blocks."

Given that humidity wasn't a factor on this late-September afternoon, she should have enjoyed her stroll to the restaurant. But what she wanted to discuss with Jason had tied her up in knots.

"Come on. I'll drive you back." He took her hand, setting off a shower of sparks that heightened her senses.

The spicy scent of his cologne infiltrated her lungs and caused the most disturbing urges. His warm, lean body bumped against her hip. It was moments like these when she was tempted to call her receptionist and cancel her afternoon appointments so she could take Jason home and put an end to all the untidy lust rampaging through her body.

Of course, she'd never do that. She'd figure out some other way to tame the she-wolf that had taken up residence beneath her skin. All their lives she'd been the conservative one. The one who studied hard, planned for the future, organized her life down to the minute. Jason was the one who acted on impulse. Who partied his way through college and still managed to graduate with honors. And who liked his personal life unfettered by anyone's expectations.

They neared his car, a 1969 Camaro, and Jason stepped forward to open the passenger door for her. Being nothing more than friends didn't stop him from treating her with the same chivalry he afforded the women he dated. Before she could sit down he had to pluck an eighteen-inch trophy off her seat. Despite the cavalier way he tossed the award into the backseat, Ming knew the win was a source of pride to him and that the trophy would end up beside many others in his "racing" room.

"So what else is on your mind?" Jason asked, settling behind the wheel and starting the powerful engine. Sometimes he knew what she was thinking before she did.

"It's too much to get into now." She cradled Muffin in her arms and brushed her cheek against the terrier's silky coat. The dog gave her hand a happy lick.

"Give me the CliffsNotes version."

Jason accelerated out of the parking lot, the roar of the 427 V-8 causing a happy spike in Ming's heart rate. Riding shotgun in whatever Jason drove had been a thrill since the year he'd turned sixteen and gotten his first muscle car. Where other boys in school had driven relatively new cars, Jason and Max preferred anything fast from the fifties, sixties and seventies.

"It doesn't matter because I changed my mind."

"Changed your mind about what?"

"About what I was going to ask you." She wished he'd just drop it, but she knew better. Now that his curiosity had been aroused, he would bug her until he got answers. "It doesn't matter."

"Sure it does. You've been acting odd for weeks now. What's up?"

Ming sighed in defeat. "You asked me who was going to be the father." She paused to weigh the consequences of telling him. She'd developed a logical explanation that had nothing to do with her longing to have a deeper connection with him. He never had to know how she really felt. Her heart a battering ram against her ribs, she said, "I wanted it to be you."

Silence dominated until Jason stopped the car in front of the medical building's entrance. Ming's announcement smacked into him like the heel of her hand applied to his temple. That she wanted to have a baby didn't surprise him. It's what had broken up her and Evan. But that she wanted Jason to be the father caught him completely off guard.

Had her platonic feelings shifted toward romance? Desire? Unlikely.

She'd been his best friend since first grade. The one person he'd let see his fear when his father had tried to commit suicide. The only girl who'd listened when he went on and on about his goals and who'd talked sense into him when doubts took hold.

In high school, girlfriends came and went, but Ming was always there. Smart and funny, her almond-shaped eyes glowing with laughter. She provided emotional support without complicating their relationship with exasperating expectations. If he canceled plans with her she never pouted or ranted. She never protested when he got caught up working on car engines or shooting hoops with his buddies and forgot to call her. And more often than not, her sagacity kept Jason grounded.

She would have made the perfect girlfriend if he'd been willing to ruin their twenty-five-year friendship for a few months of romance. Because eventually his eye would wander and she'd be left as another casualty of his carefully guarded heart.

He studied her beautiful oval face. "Why me?"

Below inscrutable black eyes, her full lips kicked up at the corners. "You're the perfect choice."

The uneasy buzz resumed in the back of his mind. Was she looking to change their relationship in some way? Link herself to him with a child? He never intended to marry. Ming knew that. Accepted it. Hadn't she?

"How so?"

"Because you're my best friend. I know everything about you. Something about having a stranger's child makes me uncomfortable." She sighed. "Besides, I'm perfectly comfortable being a single parent. You are a dedicated bachelor. You won't have a crisis of conscience and demand your parental rights. It's perfect."

"Perfect," he echoed, reasoning no matter what she claimed, a child they created together would connect them in a way that went way beyond friendship.

"You're right. I don't want marriage or kids. But fathering your child..." Something rumbled in his subconscious, warning him to stop asking questions. She'd decided against asking him to help her get pregnant. He should leave it at that.

"Don't say it that way. You're making it too complicated. We've been friends forever. I don't want anything to change our relationship."

Too late for that. "Things between us changed the minute you started dating Evan."

Jason hadn't welcomed the news. In fact, he'd been quite displeased, which was something he'd had no right to feel. If she was nothing more than his friend, he should have been happy that she and Evan had found each other.

"I know. In the beginning it was awkward, but I never would have gone out with him if you hadn't given me your blessing."

What other choice did he have? It wasn't as if he intended to claim her as anything other than a friend. But such rational thinking hadn't stood him in good stead the first time he'd seen his brother kiss her.

"You didn't need my blessing. If you wanted to date Evan, that was your business." And he'd backed off. Unfortunately, distance had lent him perspective. He'd begun to see her not only as his longtime friend, but also as a desirable woman. "But let's get back to why you changed your mind about wanting me."

"I didn't want *you*," she corrected, one side of her mouth twitching. "Just a few of your strongest swimmers."

She wanted to make light of it, but Jason wasn't ready to oblige her. "Okay, how come you changed your mind about wanting my swimmers?"

She stared straight ahead and played with the Yorkie's ears, sending the dog into a state of bliss. "Because we'd have to keep it a secret. If anyone found out what we'd done, it would cause all sorts of hard feelings."

Not anyone. Evan. She'd been hurt by his brother, yet she'd taken Evan's feelings into consideration when making such an important decision. She'd deserved better than his brother.

"What if we didn't keep it a secret? My dad would be thrilled that one of his sons made him a grandfather," Jason prompted.

"But he'd also expect you to be a father." Her eyes soft with understanding, she said, "I wouldn't ask that of you."

He resented her assumption that he wouldn't want to be involved. Granted, until ten minutes earlier he'd never considered being a parent, but suddenly Jason didn't like the idea that his child would never know him as his father. "I don't suppose I can talk you out of this."

"My mind is set. I'm going to have babies."

"Babies?" He ejected the word and followed it up with a muttered curse. "I thought it was a baby. Now you're fielding a baseball team?"

A goofy snort of laughter escaped her. Unattractive on ninety-nine percent of women, the sound was adorable erupting from her long, thin nose. It probably helped that her jet-black eyes glittered with mischief, inviting him to join in her amusement.

"What's so funny?" he demanded.

She shook her head, the action causing the ebony curtains of hair framing her exotic Asian features to sway like a group of Latin dancers doing a rumba. "You should see the look on your face."

He suppressed a growl. There was not one damn thing about this that was funny. "I thought this was a one-time deal."

"It is, but you never know what you're going to get when you go in vitro. I might have triplets."

Jason's thoughts whirled. "Triplets?" Damn. He hadn't adjusted to the idea of one child. Suddenly there were three?

"It's possible." Her gaze turned inward. A tranquil half smile curved her lips.

For a couple, triplets would be hard. How was she going to handle three babies as a single mom?

Images paraded through his head. Ming's mysterious smile as she placed his hand on her round belly. Her eyes sparkling as she settled the baby in his arms for the first time. The way the pictures appealed to him triggered alarm bells. After his father's suicide attempt, he'd closed himself off to being a husband and a father. Not once in the years since had he questioned his decision.

Ming glanced at the silver watch on her delicate wrist. "I've got seven minutes to get upstairs or I'll be late for my next appointment."

"We need to talk about this more."

"It'll have to be later." She gathered Muffin and exited the car.

"When later?"

But she'd shut the door and was heading away, sleek and sexy in form-fitting black pants and a sleeveless knit top that showed off her toned arms.

Appreciation slammed into his gut.

Uninvited.

Unnerving.

Cursing beneath his breath, Jason shut off the engine, got out of the car and headed for the front door, but he wasn't fast enough to catch her before she crossed the building's threshold.

Four-inch heels clicking on the tile lobby floor, she headed toward the elevator. With his longer legs, Jason had little trouble keeping pace. He reached the elevator ahead of her and put his hand over the up button to keep her from hitting it.

"The Camaro will get towed if you leave it there."

He barely registered her words. "Let's have dinner."

A ding sounded and the doors before them opened. She barely waited for the elevator to empty before stepping forward.

"I already have plans."

"With whom?"

She shook her head. "Since when are you so curious about my social life?"

Since her engagement had broken off.

On the third floor, they passed a door marked Dr. Terrance Kincaid, DDS, and Dr. Ming Campbell, DDS. Another ten feet and they came to an unmarked door that she unlocked and breezed through.

One of the dental assistants hovered outside Ming's office. "Oh, good, you're here. I'll get your next patient."

Ming set down Muffin, and the Yorkie bounded through the hallway toward the waiting room. She headed into her office and returned wearing a white lab coat. When she started past him, Jason caught her arm.

"You can't do this alone." Whether he meant get pregnant or raise a child, he wasn't sure.

Her gentle smile was meant to relieve him of all obligations. "I'll be fine."

"I don't doubt that." But he couldn't shake the sense that she needed him.

A thirteen-year-old boy appeared in the hallway and waved to her.

"Hello, Billy," she called. "How did your baseball tournament go last month?"

"Great. Our team won every game."

"I'd expect nothing else with a fabulous pitcher like you on the mound. I'll see you in a couple minutes."

As often as Jason had seen her at work, he never stopped being amazed that she could summon a detail for any of her two hundred clients that made the child feel less like a patient and more like a friend.

"I'll call you tomorrow." Without waiting for him to respond, she followed Billy to the treatment area.

Reluctant to leave, Jason stared after her until she disappeared. Impatience and concern urged him to hound her until he was satisfied he knew all her plans, but he knew how he'd feel if she'd cornered him at work.

Instead, he returned to the parking lot. The Camaro remained at the curb where he'd left it. Donning his shades, he slid behind the wheel and started the powerful engine.

Two

When Ming returned to her office after her last appointment, she found her sister sitting cross-legged on the floor, a laptop balanced on her thighs.

"There are three chairs in the room. You should use one."

"I like sitting on the ground." With her short, spiky hair and fondness for natural fibers and loose-fitting clothes, Lily looked more than an environmental activist than a top software engineer. "It lets me feel connected to the earth."

"We're three stories up in a concrete building."

Lily gave her a "whatever" shoulder shrug and closed the laptop. "I stopped by to tell you I'm heading out really early tomorrow morning."

"Where to this time?"

For the past five years, her sister had been leading a team of consultants involved with transitioning their company's various divisions to a single software system. Since the branches were all over the country, she traveled forty weeks out of the year. The rest of the time, she stayed rent-free in Ming's spare bedroom.

"Portland."

"How long?"

"They offered me a permanent position."

Her sister's announcement came as an unwelcome surprise. "Did you say yes?"

"Not yet. I want to see if I like Portland first. But I gotta tell you, I'm sick of all the traveling. It would be nice to buy a place and get some appliances. I want a juicer."

Lily had this whole "a healthy body equals a healthy mind" mentality. She made all sorts of disgusting green concoctions that smelled awful and tasted like a decomposing marsh. Ming's eyes watered just thinking about them. She preferred to jump-start her day with massive doses of caffeine.

"You won't get bored being stuck in one city?"

"I'm ready to settle down."

"And you can't settle down in Houston?"

"I want to meet a guy I can get serious about."

"And you have to go all the way to Portland to find one?" Ming wondered what was really going on with her sister.

Lily slipped her laptop into its protective sleeve. "I need a change."

"You're not going to stick around and be an auntie?" She'd hoped once Lily held the baby and saw how happy Ming was as a mom, her sister could finally get why Ming was willing to risk their mother's wrath about her decision.

"I think it's better if I don't."

As close as the sisters were, they'd done nothing but argue since Ming had divulged her intention of becoming a single mom. Her sister's negative reaction had come as a complete surprise. And on the heels of her broken engagement, Ming was feeling alone and blue.

"I wish I could make you understand how much this means to me."

"Look, I get it. You've always wanted children. I just think that a kid needs both a mother and a father."

Ming's confidence waned beneath her sister's criticism. Despite her free-spirited style and reluctance to be tied down, Lily was a lot more traditional than Ming when it came to family. Last night, when Ming had told her sister she was going to talk to Jason today, Lily had accused Ming of being selfish.

But was she? Raising a child without a father didn't necessarily mean that the child would have problems. Children needed love and boundaries. She could provide both.

It wasn't fair for Lily to push her opinions on Ming. She hadn't made her decision overnight. She'd spent months and months talking to single moms, weighing the pros and cons, and using her head, not her emotions, to make up her mind about raising a child on her own. Of course, when it came right down to it, her longing to be a mother was a strong, biological urge that was hard to ignore.

Ming slipped out of her lab coat and hung it on the back of her office door. "Have you told Mom about the job offer?"

"No." Lily countered. "Have you told her what you're going to do?"

"I was planning to on Friday. We're having dinner, just the two of us." Ming arched an eyebrow. "Unless you'd like to head over there now so we can both share our news. Maybe with two of us to yell at, we'll each get half a tongue lashing."

"As much as I would love to be there to see the look on Mom's face when she finds out you're going to have a baby without a husband, I'm not ready to talk about my plans. Not until I'm completely sure."

It sounded as if Lily wasn't one hundred percent sold on moving away. Ming kept relief off her face and clung to the hope that her sister would find that Portland wasn't to her liking.

"Will I see you at home later?"

Lily shook her head. "Got plans."

"A date?"

"Not exactly."

"Same guy?" For the past few months, whenever she was in town, her sister had been spending a lot of time with a mystery man. "Have you told him your plans to move?"

"It's not like that."

"It's not like what?"

"We're not dating."

"Then it's just sex?"

Her sister made an impatient noise. "Geez, Ming. You of all people should know that men and women can be just friends."

"Most men and women can't. Besides, Jason and I are more like brother and sister than friends."

For about the hundredth time, Ming toyed with telling Lily about her mixed feelings for Jason. How she loved him as a friend but couldn't stop wondering if they could have made it as a couple. Of course, she'd blown any chance to find out when she'd agreed to have dinner with Evan three years ago.

But long before that she knew Jason wouldn't let anything get in the way of their friendship.

"Have you told him about your plans to have a baby yet?"

"I mentioned it to him this afternoon."

She was equally disappointed and relieved that she'd decided against asking Jason to help her get pregnant. Raising his child would muddle her already complicated emotions where he was concerned. It would be easier to get over her romantic yearnings if she had no expectations.

"How did he take it?"

"Once he gets used to the idea, I think he'll be happy for me." Her throat locked up. She'd really been counting on his support.

"Maybe this is the universe's way of telling you that you're on the wrong path."

"I don't need the universe to tell me anything. I have you." Although Ming kept her voice light, her heart was heavy. She was torn between living her dream and disrupting her relationships with those she loved. What if this became a wedge between her and Lily? Or her and Jason? Ming hated the idea of being pulled in opposite directions by her longing to be a mom and her fear of losing the closeness she shared with either of them.

To comfort herself, she stared at her photo wall, the proof of what she'd achieved these past seven years. Hundreds of smiles lightened her mood and gave her courage.

"I guess you and I will just have to accept that neither one of us is making a decision the other is happy with," Ming said.

Jason paced from one end of his large office to the other. Beyond his closed door, the offices of Sterling Bridge Company emptied. It was a little past six, but Jason had given up working hours ago. As the chief financial officer of the family's bridge construction business, he was supposed to be looking over some last-minute changes in the numbers for a multimillion-dollar project they were bidding on next week, but he couldn't focus. Not surprising after Ming's big announcement today.

She'd be a great mom. Patient. Loving. Stern when she had to be. If he'd voiced doubts it wasn't because of her ability to parent, but how hard it would be for her to do it on her own. Naturally Ming wouldn't view any difficulty as too much trouble. She'd embrace the challenges and surpass everyone's expectations.

But knowing this didn't stop his uneasiness. His sense that he should be there for her. Help her.

Help her what?

Get pregnant.

Raise his child?

His gut told him it was the right thing to do even if his brain warned him that he was embarking on a fool's journey. They were best friends. This was when best friends stepped up and helped each other out. If the situation was reversed and he wanted a child, she'd be the woman he'd choose to make that happen.

But if they did this, things could get complicated. If his brother found out that Jason had helped Ming become a mother, the hurt they caused might lead to permanent estrangement between him and Evan.

On the other hand, Ming deserved to get the family she wanted.

Another thirty minutes disappeared with Jason lost in thought. Since he couldn't be productive at the office, he decided to head home. A recently purchased '73 Dodge Charger sat in his garage awaiting some TLC. In addition to his passion for racing, he loved buying, fixing up and selling classic muscle cars. It's why he'd chosen his house in the western suburbs. The three-acre estate had afforded him the opportunity to build a six-car garage to house his rare collection.

On the way out, Jason passed his brother's office. Helping Ming get pregnant would also involve keeping another big secret from his brother. Jason resented that she still worried about Evan's feelings after the way he'd broken off their engagement. Would it be as awkward for Evan to be an uncle to his ex-fiancée's child as it had been for Jason to watch his best friend fall in love with his brother?

From the moment Ming and Evan had begun dating, tension had developed between Jason and his brother. An unspoken rift that was territorial in nature. Ming and Jason were best friends. They were bonded by difficult experiences. Inside jokes. Shared memories. In the beginning, it was Evan who was the third wheel whenever the three of them got together. But this wasn't like other times when Ming had dated. Thanks to her long friendship with Jason, she was practically family. Within months, it was obvious she and Evan were perfectly matched in temperament and outlook, and the closer Ming and Evan became, the more Jason became the outsider. Which was something he resented. Ming was his best friend and he didn't like sharing her.

Entering his brother's office, Jason found Evan occupying the couch in the seating area. Evan was three years older and carried more weight on his six-foot frame than Jason, but otherwise, the brothers had the same blue eyes, dark blond hair and features. Both resembled their mother, who'd died in a car accident with their nine-year-old sister when the boys were in high school.

The death of his wife and daughter had devastated their father. Tony Sterling had fallen into a deep depression that lasted six months and almost resulted in the loss of his business. And if Jason hadn't snuck into the garage one night to "borrow" the car for a joyride and found his father sitting behind the wheel with the garage filling with exhaust fumes, Tony might have lost his life.

This pivotal event had happened when Jason was only fifteen years old and had marked him. He swore he would never succumb to a love so strong that he would be driven to take his own life when the love was snatched away. It had been an easy promise to keep.

Jason scrutinized his brother as he crossed the room, his footfalls soundless on the plush carpet. Evan was so focused on the object in his hand he didn't notice Jason's arrival until he spoke.

"Want to catch dinner?"

Evan's gaze shot toward his brother, and in a furtive move, he pocketed the earrings he'd been brooding over. Jason recognized them as the pearl-and-diamond ones his brother had given to Ming as an engagement present. What was his brother doing with them?

"Can't. I've already got plans."

"A date?"

Evan got to his feet and paced toward his desk. With his back to Jason, he spoke. "I guess."

"You don't know?"

That was very unlike his brother. When it came to living a meticulously planned existence, the only one more exacting than Evan was Ming.

Evan's hand plunged into the pocket he'd dropped the earrings into. "It's complicated."

"Is she married?"

"No."

"Engaged?"

"No."

"Kids?"

"Let it go." Evan's exasperation only increased Jason's tension.

"Does it have something to do with Ming's earrings in your pocket?" When Evan didn't answer, Jason's gut clenched, his suspicions confirmed. "Haven't you done enough damage there? She's moving on with her life. She doesn't need you stirring things up again."

"I didn't plan what happened. It just did."

Impulsive behavior from his plan-everything-to-death brother? Jason didn't like the sound of that. It could only lead to Ming getting hurt again.

"What exactly happened?"

"Lily and I met for a drink a couple months ago."

"You and Lily?" He almost laughed at the odd pairing. While Evan and Ming had been perfectly compatible, Evan and Lily were total opposites. Then he sobered. "Just the once?"

"A few times." Evan rubbed his face, bringing Jason's attention to the dark shadows beneath his eyes. His brother looked exhausted. And low. "A lot."

"Have you thought about what you're doing?" When it came to picking sides, Jason would choose Ming every time. In some ways, she was more like family to him than Evan. Jason had certainly shared more of himself with her. "Don't you think

Ming will be upset if she finds out you and her sister are dating?"

Before Evan could answer, Jason's cell began to ring. With Ming's heart in danger and his brother in his crosshairs, Jason wouldn't have allowed himself to be distracted if anyone else on the planet was calling. But this was Ming's ringtone.

"We'll talk more about this later," he told his brother, and answered the call as he exited. "What's going on?"

"It's Lily." There was no mistaking the cry for help in Ming's voice.

Jason's annoyance with his brother flared anew. Had Ming found out what was going on? "What about her?"

"She's moving to Portland. What am I going to do without her?"

What a relief. Ming didn't yet know that her sister was dating Evan, and if Lily moved to Portland then her relationship with her sister's ex-fiancé would have to end.

"You still have me." He'd intended to make his tone light, but on the heels of his conversation with his brother moments before, his declaration came out like a pledge. "Do you want to catch a drink and talk about it? We could continue our earlier conversation."

"I can't. Terry and I are having dinner."

"Afterward?"

"It's been a long day. I'm heading home for a glass of wine and a long, hot bath."

"Do you want some company?"

Unbidden, his thoughts took him to an intoxicating, sensual place where Ming floated naked in warm, fragrant water. Candles burned, setting her delicate, pale shoulders aglow above the framing bubbles of her favorite bath gel. The office faded away as he imagined trailing his lips along her neck, discovering all the places on her silky skin that made her shiver.

"Jason?" Ming's voice roused him to the fact that he was standing in the elevator. He didn't remember getting there.

Damn it. He banished the images, but the sensations lingered.

"What?" he asked, disturbed at how compelling his fantasy had been.

"I asked if I could call you later."

"Sure." His voice had gone hoarse. "Have a good dinner."

"Thanks."

The phone went dead in his hand. Jason dropped the cell back into his pocket, still reeling from the direction his thoughts had gone. He had to stop thinking of her like that. Unfortunately, once awakened, the notion of making love to Ming proved difficult to coax back to sleep.

He headed to his favorite bar, which promised a beer and a dozen sports channels as a distraction from his problems. It failed to deliver.

Instead, he replayed his conversations with both Ming and Evan in his mind. She wanted to have a baby, wanted Jason's help to make that happen, but she'd decided against it before he'd had a chance to consider the idea. All because it wouldn't be fair to Evan if he ever found out.

Would she feel the same if she knew Evan was dating Lily and that he didn't care if Ming got hurt in the process? That wouldn't change her mind. Even if it killed her, Ming would want Evan and Lily to be happy.

But shouldn't she get to be selfish, too? She should be able to choose whatever man she wanted to help her get pregnant. Even the brother of her ex-fiancé. Only Jason knew she'd never go there without a lot of convincing.

And wasn't that what best friends were for?

Fifteen minutes after she'd hung up on Jason, Ming's heart was still thumping impossibly fast. She'd told herself that when he'd asked if she wanted company for a glass of wine and a hot bath, he hadn't meant anything sexual. She'd called him for a shoulder to cry on. That's all he was offering.

But the image of him sliding into her oversize tub while candlelight flickered off the glass tile wall and a thousand soap bubbles drifted on the water's surface...

"Ready for dinner?"

Jerked out of her musing, Ming spun her chair away from her computer and spied Terry Kincaid grinning at her from the doorway, his even, white teeth dazzling against his tan skin. As well as being her partner in the dental practice and her best girl friend's father, he was the reason she'd chosen to become an orthodontist in the first place.

"Absolutely."

She closed her internet browser and images of strollers disappeared from her screen. As crazy as it was to shop for baby stuff before she was even pregnant, Ming couldn't stop herself from buying things. Her last purchase had been one of those mobiles that hangs above the crib and plays music as it spins.

"You already know how proud I am of you," Terry began after they'd finished ordering dinner at his favorite seafood place. "When I brought you into the practice, it wasn't because you were at the top of your class or a hard worker, but because you're like family."

"You know that's how I feel about you, too." In fact, Terry was so much better than her own family because he offered her absolute support without any judgment.

"And as a member of my family, it was important to me that I come to you with any big life-changing decisions I was about to make."

Ming gulped. How had he found out what she was going to do? Wendy couldn't have told him. Her friend knew how to keep a secret.

"Sure," she said. "That's only fair."

"That's why I'm here to tell you that I'm going to retire and I want you to take over the practice."

This was the last thing she expected him to say. "But you're only fifty-seven. You can't quit now."

"It's the perfect time. Janice and I want to travel while we're still young enough to have adventures."

In addition to being a competitive sailor, Terry was an expert rock climber and pilot. Where Ming liked relaxing spa vacations in northern California, he and his wife went hang gliding in Australia and zip lining through the jungles of Costa Rica.

"And you want me to have the practice?" Her mind raced at the thought of all the things she would have to learn, and fast. Managing personnel and finances. Marketing. The practice thrived with Terry at the helm. Could she do half as well? "It's a lot."

"If you're worried about the money, work the numbers with Jason."

"It's not the money." It was an overwhelming responsibility to take on at the same time she was preparing for the challenge of being a single mom. "I'm not sure I'm ready."

Terry was unfazed by her doubts. "I've never met anyone who rises to the challenge the way you do. And I'm not going to retire next week. I'm looking at the middle of next year. Plenty of time for you to learn what you need to know."

The middle of next year? Ming did some rapid calculation. If everything went according to schedule, she'd be giving birth about the time when Terry would be leaving. Who'd take over while she was out on maternity leave? She'd hoped for twelve glorious weeks with her newborn.

Yet, now that the initial panic was fading, excitement stirred. Her own practice. She'd be crazy to let this opportunity pass her by.

"Ming, are you all right?" Concern had replaced delight. "I thought you'd jump at the chance to run the practice."

"I'm really thrilled by the opportunity."

"But?"

She was going to have a baby. Taking over the practice would require a huge commitment of time and energy. But Terry believed in her and she hated to disappoint him. He'd taken her under his wing during high school when she and Wendy had visited the office and shown her that orthodontia was a perfect career for someone who had an obsession with making things straight and orderly.

"No *buts*." She loaded her voice with confidence.

"That's my girl." He patted her hand. "You have no idea how happy I was when you decided to join me in this practice. There's no one but you that I'd trust to turn it over to."

His words warmed and worried her at the same time. The amount of responsibility overwhelmed her, but whatever it took, she'd make sure Terry never regretted choosing her.

"I won't let you down."

Crickets serenaded Jason as he headed up the walk to Ming's front door. At nine o'clock at night, only a far-off bark disturbed the peaceful tree-lined street in the older Houston suburb. Amongst the midcentury craftsman homes, Ming's contemporary-styled house stood out. The clean lines and geometric landscaping suited the woman who lived there. Ming kept her surroundings and her life uncluttered.

He couldn't imagine how she was going to handle the sort of disorder a child would bring into her world, but after his conversation with Evan this afternoon, Jason was no longer deciding whether or not he should help his oldest friend. It was more a matter of how he was going to go about it.

Jason rang her doorbell and Muffin began to bark in warning. The entry light above him snapped on and the door flew open. Jason blinked as Ming appeared in the sudden brightness. The scent of her filled his nostrils, a sumptuous floral that made him think of making love on an exotic tropical island.

"Jason? What are you doing here?" Ming bent to catch the terrier as she charged past, but missed. "Muffin, get back here."

"I'll get her." Chasing the frisky dog gave him something to concentrate on besides Ming's slender form clad in a plum silk nightgown and robe, her long black hair cascading over one shoulder. "Did I wake you?" he asked, handing her the squirming Yorkie.

His body tightened as he imagined her warm, pliant form snuggled beside him in bed. His brother had been a complete idiot not to give her the sun, moon and whatever stars she wanted.

"No." She tilted her head. "Do you want to come in?"

Swept by the new and unsettling yearning to take her in his arms and claim her lush mouth, Jason shook his head. "I've been thinking about what we talked about earlier today."

"If you've come here to talk me out of having a baby, you can save your breath." She was his best friend. Back in high school they'd agreed that what had happened after prom had been a huge mistake. They'd both been upset with their dates and turned to each other in a moment of weakness. Neither one wanted to risk their friendship by exploring the chemistry between them.

But in the back of Jason's mind, lying in wait all these years, was curiosity. What would it be like between them? It's why he'd decided to help her make a baby. Today she'd offered him the solution to satisfy his need for her and not complicate their friendship with romantic misunderstandings. He'd be a fool not to take advantage of the opportunity.

"I want to help."

"You do?" Doubt dominated her question, but relief hovered nearby. She studied him a long moment before asking, "Are you sure?"

"I've been thinking about it all afternoon and decided I'd be a pretty lousy friend if I wasn't there when you needed me."

A broad smile transformed her expression. "You don't know how much this means to me. I'll call the clinic tomorrow and make an appointment for you."

Jason shook his head. "No fertility clinic. No doctor." He hooked his fingers around the sash that held her robe closed and tugged her a half step closer. Heat pooled below his belt at the way her lips parted in surprise. "Just you and me."

Something like excitement flickered in her eyes, only to be dampened by her frown. "Are you suggesting what I think you're suggesting?"

"Let's make a baby the old-fashioned way."

Three

"Old-fashioned way?" Ming's brain sputtered like a poorly maintained engine. What the hell was he...? "Sex?"

"I prefer to think of it as making love."

"Same difference."

Jason's grin grew wolfish. "Not the way I do it."

Her mind raced. She couldn't have sex—make love—with Jason. He was her best friend. Their relationship worked because they didn't complicate it by pretending a friends-with-benefits scenario was realistic. "Absolutely not."

"Why not?"

"Because..." What was she supposed to give him for an excuse? "I don't feel that way about you."

"Give me an hour and I'm sure you'll feel exactly that way about me."

The sensual light in his eyes was so intense she could almost feel his hands sliding over her. Her nipples tightened. She crossed her arms over her chest to conceal her body's involuntary reaction.

"Arrogant jackass."

His cocky grin was her only reply. Ming scowled at him to conceal her rising alarm. He was enjoying this. Damn him. Worse, her toes were curling at the prospect of making love with him.

"Be reasonable." *Please be reasonable.* "It'll be much easier if you just go to the clinic. All you have to do is show up, grab a magazine and make a donation."

"Not happening."

The air around them crackled with electricity, raising the hair at the back of her neck.

"Why not?" She gathered the hair hanging over her shoulder and tugged. Her scalp burned at the harsh punishment. "It's not as if you have any use for them." She pointed downward.

"If you want them, you're going to have to get them the old-fashioned way."

"Stop saying that." Her voice had taken on a disturbing squeak.

Jason naked. Her hands roaming over all his hard muscles. The slide of him between her thighs. She pressed her knees together as an ache built.

"Come on," he coaxed. "Aren't you the least bit curious?"

Of course she was curious. During the months following senior prom, it's all she'd thought about. "Absolutely not."

"All the women I've dated. Haven't you wondered why they kept coming back for more?"

Instead of being turned off by his arrogance, she found his confidence arousing. "It never crossed my mind."

"I don't believe that. Not after the way you came on to me after prom."

"I came on to you? You kissed me."

"Because you batted those long black eyelashes of yours and went on and on about how no one would ever love you and how what's-his-name wasn't a real man and that you needed a real man."

Ming's mouth fell open. "I did no such thing. You were the one who put your arm around me and said the best way to get over Kevin was to get busy with someone else."

"No." He shook his head. "That's not how it happened at all."

Damn him. He'd given his word they'd never speak of it again. What other promises would he break?

"Neither one of us is going to admit we started it, so let's just agree that a kiss happened and we were prevented from making a huge mistake by my sister's phone call."

"In the interests of keeping you happy," he said, his tone sly and patronizing, "I'll agree a kiss happened and we were interrupted by your sister."

"And that afterward we both agreed it was a huge mistake."

"It was a mistake because you'd been dumped and I was fighting with my girlfriend. Neither one of us was thinking clearly."

Had she said that, or had he? The events of the night were blurry. In fact, the only thing she remembered with crystal clarity was the feel of his lips on hers. The way her head spun as he plunged his tongue into her mouth and set her afire.

"It was a mistake because we were best friends and hooking up would have messed up our relationship."

"But we're not hormone-driven teenagers anymore," he reminded her. "We can approach the sex as a naked hug between friends."

"A naked hug?" She wasn't sure whether to laugh or hit him.

What he wanted from her threatened to turn her emotions into a Gordian knot, and yet she found herself wondering if she could do as he asked. If she went into it without expectations, maybe it was possible for her to enjoy a few glorious nights in Jason's bed and get away with her head clear and her heart unharmed.

"Having…" She cleared her throat and tried again. "Making…" Her throat closed up. Completing the sentence made the prospect so much more real. She wasn't ready to go there yet.

Jason took pity on her inability to finish her thought. "Love?"

"It's intimate and…" Her skin tingled at the thought of just how intimate.

"You don't think I know that?"

Jason's velvet voice slid against her senses. Her entire body flushed as desire pulsed hot and insistent. How many times since her engagement ended had she awakened from a salacious dream about him, feeling like this? Heavy with need and too frustrated to go back to sleep? Too many nights to count.

"Let me finish," she said. "We know each other too well. We're too comfortable. There's no romance between us. It would be like brushing each other's teeth."

"Brushing each other's teeth?" he echoed, laughter dancing in his voice. "You underestimate my powers of seduction."

The wicked light in his eye promised that he was not going to be deterred from his request. A tremor threatened to upend the small amount of her confidence still standing.

"You overestimate my ability to take you seriously."

All at once he stopped trying to push her buttons and his humor faded. "If you are going to become a mother, you don't want that to happen in the sterile environment of a doctor's office. Your conception should be memorable."

She wasn't looking for memorable. Memorable lasted. It clogged up her emotions and made her long for impossible things. She wanted clinical. Practical. Uncomplicated.

Which is why her decision to ask him to be her child's father made so little sense. What if her son or daughter inherited his habit of mixing his food together on the plate before eating because he liked the way it all tasted together? That drove her crazy. She hated it when the different types of food touched each other.

Would her baby be cursed by his carefree nature and impulsiveness? His love of danger and enthusiasm for risk taking?

Or blessed with his flirtatious grin, overpowering charisma, leadership skills and athletic ability.

For someone who thought everything through, it now occurred to her that she'd settled too fast on Jason for her baby's father. As much as she'd insisted that he wouldn't be tied either legally or financially to the child, she hadn't considered how her child would be part of him.

"I would prefer my conception to be fast and efficient," she countered.

"Why not start off slow and explore where it takes us?"

Slow?

Explore?

Ming's tongue went numb. Her emotions simmered in a pot of anticipation and anxiety.

"I'm going to need to think about it."

"Take your time." If he was disappointed by her indecisiveness, he gave no indication. "I'm not going anywhere."

Three days passed without any contact from Ming. Was she considering his proposal or had she rejected the idea and was too angry at his presumption to speak to him? He shouldn't care what she chose. Either she said yes and he could have the opportunity to satisfy his craving for her, or she would refuse and he'd get over the fantasy of her moaning beneath him.

"Jason? Jason?" Max's shoulder punch brought Jason back to the racetrack. "Geez, man, where the hell's your head today?"

Cars streaked by, their powerful engines drowning out his unsettling thoughts. It was Saturday afternoon. He and Max were due to race in an hour. Driving distracted at over a hundred miles an hour was a recipe for trouble.

"Got something I didn't resolve this week."

"It's not like you to worry about work with the smell of gasoline and hot rubber on the wind."

Max's good-natured ribbing annoyed Jason as much as his

slow time in the qualifying round. Or maybe more so because it wasn't work that preoccupied Jason, but a woman.

"Yeah, well, it's a pretty big something."

Never in his life had he let a female take his mind off the business at hand. Especially when he was so determined to win this year's overall points trophy and show Max what he was missing by falling in love and getting engaged.

"Let me guess, you think someone's embezzling from Sterling Bridge."

"Hardly." As CFO of the company his grandfather began in the mid-fifties, Jason had an eagle eye for any discrepancies in the financials. "Let's just say I've put in an offer and I'm waiting to hear if it's been accepted."

"Let me guess, that '68 Shelby you were lusting after last month?"

"I'm not talking about it," Jason retorted. Let Max think he was preoccupied with a car. He'd promised Ming that he'd keep quiet about fathering her child. Granted, she hadn't agreed to let him father the child the way he wanted to, but he sensed she'd come around. It was only a matter of when.

"If it's the Shelby then it's already too late. I bought it two days ago." Max grinned at Jason's disgruntled frown. "I had a space in my garage that needed to be filled."

"And whose fault is that?" Jason spoke with more hostility than he meant to.

A couple of months ago Jason had shared with Max his theory that the Lansing Employment Agency was not in the business of placing personal assistants with executives, but in matchmaking. Max thought that was crazy. So he wagered his rare '69 'Cuda that he wouldn't marry the temporary assistant the employment agency sent him. But when the owner of the placement company turned out to be the long-lost love of Max's life, Jason gained a car but lost his best buddy.

"Why are you still so angry about winning the bet?" Despite his complaint, Max wore a good-natured grin. Everything about Max was good-natured these days. "You got the car I spent five years convincing a guy to sell me. I love that car."

He loved his beautiful fiancée more.

"I'm not angry," Jason grumbled. He missed his cynical-about-love friend. The guy who understood and agreed that love and marriage were to be avoided because falling head over heels for a woman was dangerous and risky.

"Rachel thinks you feel abandoned. Like because she and I are together, you've lost your best friend."

Jason shot Max a skeptical look. "Ming's my best friend. You're just some guy I used to hang out with before you got all stupid about a girl."

Max acted as if he hadn't heard Jason's dig. "I think she's right."

"Of course you do," Jason grumbled, pulling his ball cap off and swiping at the sweat on his forehead. "You've become one of those guys who keeps his woman happy by agreeing with everything she says."

Max smirked. "That's not how I keep Rachel happy."

For a second Jason felt a stab of envy so acute he almost winced. Silent curses filled his head as he shoved the sensation away. He had no reason to resent his friend's happiness. Max was going to spend the rest of his life devoted to a woman who might someday leave him and take his happiness with her.

"What happened to you?"

Max looked surprised by the question. "I fell in love."

"I know that." But how had he let that happen? They'd both sworn they were never going to let any woman in. After the way Max's dad cheated on his wife, Max swore he'd never trust anyone enough to fall in love. "I don't get why."

"I'd rather be with Rachel than without her."

How similar was that to what had gone through his father's mind after he'd lost his wife? His parents were best friends. Soul mates. Every cliché in the book. She was everything to

him. Jason paused for breath. It had almost killed his dad to
lose her.

"What if she leaves you?"

"She won't."

"What if something bad happens to her?"

"This is about what happened to your mom, isn't it?" Max
gave his friend a sympathetic smile. "Being in love doesn't
guarantee you'll get hurt."

"Maybe not." Jason found no glimmers of light in the shadows around his heart. "But staying single guarantees that I
won't."

A week went by before Ming responded to Jason's offer to
get her pregnant. She'd spent the seven days wondering what
had prompted him to suggest they have sex—she just couldn't
think of it as making love—and analyzing her emotional response.

Jason wasn't interested in complicating their friendship with
romance any more than she was. He was the one person in her
life who never expected anything from her, and she returned
the favor. And yet, they were always there to help and support
each other. Why risk that on the chance that the chemistry between them was out-of-this-world explosive?

Of course, it had dawned on her a couple of days ago that
he'd probably decided helping her get pregnant offered him a
free pass. He could get her into bed no strings attached. No
worries that expectations about where things might go in the
future would churn up emotions.

It would be an interlude. A couple of passionate encounters
that would satisfy both their curiosities. In the end, she would
be pregnant. He would go off in search of new hearts to break,
and their friendship would continue on as always.

The absolute simplicity of the plan warned Ming that she
was missing something.

Jason was in his garage when Ming parked her car in his

driveway and killed the engine. She hadn't completely decided to accept his terms, but she was leaning that way. It made her more sensitive to how attractive Jason looked in faded jeans and a snug black T-shirt with a Ford Mustang logo. Wholly masculine, supremely confident. Her stomach flipped in full-out feminine appreciation as he came to meet her.

"Hey, what's up?"

Light-headed from the impact of his sexy grin, she indicated the beer in his hand. "Got one of those for me?"

"Sure."

He headed for the small, well-stocked fridge at the back of the garage, and she followed. When he bent down to pull out a bottle, her gaze locked on his perfect butt. Hammered by the urge to slide her hands over those taut curves, she knew she was going to do this. Correction. She *wanted* to do this.

"Thanks," she murmured, applying the cold bottle to one overheated cheek.

Jason watched her through narrowed eyes. "I thought you didn't drink beer anymore."

"Do you have any wine?" she countered, sipping the beer and trying not to grimace.

"No."

"Then I'm drinking beer." She prowled past racing trophies and photos of Jason and Max in one-piece driving suits. "How'd your weekend go?"

"Come upstairs and see."

Jason led the way into the house and together they ascended the staircase to Jason's second floor. He'd bought the home for investment purposes and had had it professionally decorated. The traditional furnishings weren't her taste, but they suited the home's colonial styling.

He'd taken one of the four bedrooms as his man cave. A wall-to-wall tribute to his great passion for amateur car racing. On one wall, a worn leather couch, left over from his college days, sat facing a sixty-inch flat-screen TV. If Jason wasn't racing his Mustang or in the garage restoring a car, he was here, watching NASCAR events or recaps of his previous races.

He hit the play button on the remote and showed Ming the clip of the race's conclusion.

The results surprised her. "You didn't win?" He'd been having his best season ever. "What happened?"

His large frame slammed into the old couch as he sat down in a disgruntled huff. A man as competitive as Jason had a hard time coming in second. "Had a lot on my mind."

The way his gaze bore into her, Ming realized he blamed her for his loss. She joined him on the couch and jabbed her finger into his ribs. "I'm not going to apologize for taking a week to give your terms some thought."

"I would've been able to concentrate if I'd known your answer."

"I find that hard to believe," she said, keeping her tone light. Mouth Sahara dry, she drank more beer.

He dropped his arm over the back of the couch. His fingertips grazed her bare shoulder. "You don't think the thought of us making love has preoccupied me this last week?"

"Then you agree that we run the risk of changing things between us."

"It doesn't have to." Jason's fingers continued to dwell on her skin, but now he was trailing lines of fire along her collarbone. "Besides, that's not what preoccupied me."

This told Ming all she needed to know about why he'd suggested they skip the fertility clinic. For Jason this was all about the sex. Fine. It could be all about the sex for her, too.

"Okay. Let's do it." She spoke the words before she could second-guess herself. She stared at the television screen. It would be easier to say this next part without meeting his penetrating gaze. "But I have a few conditions of my own."

He leaned close enough for her to feel his breath on her neck. "You want me to romance you?"

As goose bumps appeared on her arms, she made herself

laugh. "Hardly. There is a window of three days during which we can try. If I don't get pregnant your way, then you agree to do it my way." Stipulating her terms put her back on solid ground with him. "I'm not planning on dragging this out indefinitely."

"I agree to those three days, but I want uninterrupted time with you."

She dug her fingernails beneath the beer label. In typical Jason fashion, he was messing up her well-laid plans.

She'd been thinking in terms of three short evenings of fantastic sex here at his house and then heading back home to relive the moments in the privacy of her bedroom. Not days and nights of all Jason all the time. What if she talked in her sleep and told him all her secret fantasies about him? What if he didn't let her sleep and she grew so delirious from all the hours of making love that she said something in the heat of passion?

"You're crazy if you think our families are going to leave us alone for three days."

"They will if we're not in Houston."

This was her baby. She should be the one who decided where and when it was conceived. The lack of control was making her edgy. Vulnerable.

"I propose we go somewhere far away," he continued. "A secluded spot where we can concentrate on the business at hand."

The business at hand? He caressed those four words with such a high degree of sensuality, her body vibrated with excitement.

"I'll figure out where and let you know." At least if she took charge of where they went she wouldn't have to worry about her baby being conceived in whatever town NASCAR was racing that weekend.

She started to shift her weight forward, preparing to stand, when Jason's hand slid across her abdomen and circled around to her spine.

"Before you go."

He tugged her upper half toward him. The hand that had been skimming her shoulder now cupped the back of her head. She was trapped between the heat of his body and his strong arm, her breasts skimming his chest, nipples turning into buds as desire plunged her into a whirlpool of longing. The intent in his eyes set her heart to thumping in an irregular rhythm.

"What do you think you're doing?" she demanded, retreating from the lips dipping toward hers.

"Sealing our deal with a kiss."

"A handshake will work fine."

Her brusque dismissal didn't dim the smug smile curving his lips. She put her hand on his chest. Rock-hard pecs flexed beneath her fingers. The even thump of his heart mocked her wildly fluctuating pulse.

"Not for me." He captured and held her gaze before letting his mouth graze hers. With a brief survey of her expression, he nodded. "See, that wasn't so bad."

"Right." Her chest rose and fell, betraying her agitation. "Not bad."

"If you relax it will get even better." He shifted his attention to her chin, the line of her jaw, dusting his lips over her skin and making her senses whirl.

"I'm not ready to relax." She'd geared up to tell him that she'd try getting pregnant his way. Getting physical with him would require a different sort of preparation.

"You don't have to get ready." His chest vibrated with a low chuckle. "Just relax."

"Jason, how long have we known each other?"

"Long time." He found a spot that interested him just below her ear and lingered until she shivered. "Why?"

Her voice lacked serenity as she said, "Then you know I don't do anything without planning."

His exhalation tickled her sensitive skin and made holding still almost impossible. "You don't need to plan. Just let go."

Right. And risk him discovering her secret? Ever since she'd decided to ask his help in getting pregnant, she'd realized that what she felt for him was deeper than friendship. Not love. Or not the romantic sort. At least she didn't think so. Not yet. But it could become that sort of love if they made love over and over and over.

And if he found out how her feelings had changed toward him, he'd bolt the way he'd run from every other woman who'd tried to claim his heart.

Ming tensed to keep from responding to the persuasive magic of his touch. Just the sweep of his lips over her skin, the strength of his arms around her, raised her temperature and made her long for him to take her hard and fast.

"I'll let go when we're out of town," she promised. Well, lied really. At least she hoped she was lying. "What are you doing?"

In a quick, powerful move, he'd shifted her onto her back and slid one muscular leg between her thighs. Her body reacted before her mind caught up. She bent her knees, planted her feet on the couch cushions and rocked her hips in the carnal hope of easing the ache in her loins.

"While you make arrangements for us to go away, I thought you'd feel better if you weren't worried about the chemistry between us."

His heat seeped into her, softening her muscles, reducing her resistance to ash. "No worries here. I'm sure you're a fabulous lover." She trembled in anticipation of just how fabulous. With her body betraying her at his every touch, she had to keep her wits sharp. "Otherwise, why else would you have left a trail of broken hearts in your wake?"

Jason frowned. "I didn't realize that bothered you so much."

"It doesn't."

He hummed his doubt and leaned down to nibble on her earlobe. "Not sure I believe you."

With her erogenous zones on full red alert, she labored to keep her legs from wrapping around his hips. She wanted to feel him hard and thick against the thudding ache between her thighs. Her fingernails dug into the couch cushions.

"You're biting your lip." His tongue flicked over the tender spot. "I don't know why you're fighting this so hard."

And she didn't want him to find out. "Okay. I'm not worried about your sexual prowess. I'm worried that once we go down this path, there'll be no turning back."

"Oh, I see. You're worried you're going to fall in love with me."

"No." She made a whole series of disgruntled, dismissive noises until she realized he was teasing her. Two could play at this game. "I'm more concerned you'll fall in love with me."

"I don't think that's going to happen."

"I don't know," she said, happy to be on the giving end of the ribbing. "I'm pretty adorable."

"That you are." He scanned her face, utterly serious. "Close your eyes," he commanded. "We're going to do this."

She complied, hoping the intimacy they shared as friends would allow her to revel in the passion Jason aroused in her and keep her from worrying about the potential complications. Being unable to see Jason's face helped calm the flutters of anxiety. If she ignored the scent of sandalwood mingled with car polish, she might be able to pretend the man lying on top of her was anyone else.

The sound of his soft exhalation drifted past her ears a second before his lips found hers. Ming expected him to claim her mouth the way he had fifteen years ago and kiss her as if she was the only woman in the world he'd ever wanted. But this kiss was different. It wasn't the wild, exciting variety that had caused her to tear at Jason's shirt and allow him to slip his hand down the bodice of her dress to bare her breasts.

Jason's lips explored hers with firm but gentle pressure. If she'd worried that she'd be overcome with desire and make a complete fool of herself over him, she'd wasted her energy.

This kiss was so controlled and deliberate she wondered if Jason was regretting his offer to make love to her.

An empty feeling settled in her chest.

"See," Jason said, drifting his lips over her eyelids. "That wasn't so bad."

"I never expected it would be."

"Then what are you so afraid of?"

What if her lust for him was stronger than his for her? What if three days with him only whet her appetite for more?

"The thought of you seeing me naked is one," she said, keeping her tone light to hide her dismay.

His grin bloomed, mischievous and naughty. "I've already seen you naked."

"What?" Lust shot through Ming, leaving her dazzled and disturbed. "When?"

"Remember that family vacation when we brought you with us to Saint John? The outdoor shower attached to my bedroom?"

"Everyone was snorkeling. That's why I came back to the villa early." She'd wanted the room Jason ended up with because of the outdoor shower. Thinking she was alone, she'd used it. "You spied on me?"

"More like stumbled upon you."

She shoved at his beefy shoulder but couldn't budge him. "Why did you have to tell me that?"

"To explain why you have no need to be embarrassed. I've seen it all before." And from his expression, he'd liked what he saw.

Ming flushed hot. Swooning was impossible if she was lying down, right?

"How long did you watch me?"

"Five, maybe ten minutes."

Her mouth opened, but no words came out. Goose bumps erupted at the way his gaze trailed over her. Was she wrong about the kiss? Or was she the only one who caught fire every time they touched?

He stood and offered her his hand. She let him pull her to her feet and then set about straightening her clothes and finger-combing her hair.

Already she could feel their friendship morphing into something else. By the time their three days together were up, she would no longer be just his friend. She would be his ex-lover. That would alter her perspective of their relationship. Is that really what she wanted?

"I've been charting my cycle for the last six months," she said, uncaring if he'd be disinterested in her feminine activities. "The next time I ovulate is in ten days. Can you get away then?"

"Are you sure you want to go through with this?"

Had he hoped his kiss would change her mind? "I really want this baby. If sleeping with you is the only way that's going to happen, I'm ready to make the sacrifice."

He grinned. "Make the arrangements."

Four

Ming had chosen Mendocino, California, for her long weekend with Jason because the only person who knew it was her favorite getaway spot was Terry's daughter, Wendy, her closest girlfriend from high school. Wendy had moved to California with her husband seven years earlier and had introduced Ming to the town, knowing she would fall in love with the little slice of New England plopped onto a rugged California coast. The area featured some of the most spectacular scenery Ming had ever seen, and every year thereafter she returned for a relaxing long weekend.

That all had ended two years ago. She'd arrived early in September for a few days of spa treatments and soul-searching. Surrounded by the steady pulse of shore life, she lingered over coffee, browsed art galleries and wine shops, and took a long look at her relationship with Evan. They'd been going out for a little over a year and he'd asked her to decide between becoming a fully committed couple or parting ways.

That long weekend in Mendocino she'd decided to stop feeling torn between the Sterling brothers. She loved Evan one way. She loved Jason another. He'd been nothing but supportive of her dating Evan and more preoccupied than ever with his career and racing hobby. Ming doubted Jason had even noticed that Evan took up most of her time and attention. Or maybe she just wished it had bothered him. That he'd tell his brother to back off and claim Ming as his own.

But he hadn't, and it had nagged at her how easily Jason had let her go. She'd not viewed a single one of his girlfriends as casually. Each new love interest had meant Jason had taken his friendship with Ming even more for granted.

In hindsight, she understood how she'd fallen for Evan. He'd showered her with all the attention she could ever want.

Despite how things worked out between them, she'd never regretted dating Evan or agreeing to be his wife. So what if their relationship lacked the all-consuming passion of a romance novel. They'd respected each other, communicated logically and without drama. They'd enjoyed the same activities and possessed similar temperaments. All in all, Evan made complete sense for her as a life partner. But had everything been as perfect as it seemed?

A hundred times in the past six months she'd questioned whether she'd have gone through with the wedding if Evan hadn't changed his mind about having kids and ended their engagement.

They'd dated for two years, been engaged for one.

Plenty of time to shake off doubts about the future.

Plenty of time to decide if what she felt for Evan was enduring love or if she'd talked herself into settling for good enough because he fit seamlessly into her picture of the perfect life.

They were ideally suited in temperament and ideology. He never challenged her opinions or bullied her into defending her beliefs. She always knew where she stood with him. He'd made her feel safe.

A stark contrast to the wildly shifting emotions Jason aroused in her.

The long drive up from San Francisco gave Ming too much time to think. To grow even more anxious about the weekend with Jason. Already plagued by concern that letting him help her conceive a baby would complicate their relationship, now she had to worry that making love with him might just whip up a frenzy of emotions that would lead her to disappointment.

Knowing full well she was stalling, Ming stopped in Mendocino and did some window-shopping before she headed to the inn where she and Jason would be staying. To avoid anyone getting suspicious about the two of them doing something as unusual as heading to California for the weekend, they'd travelled separately. Ming had flown to San Francisco a few days ago to spend some time with Wendy. Jason had headed out on Friday morning. As much as Ming enjoyed visiting with her friend, she'd been preoccupied with doubts and worries that she couldn't share.

Although Wendy was excited about Ming's decision to have a baby, she wouldn't have approved of Ming's choice of Jason as the father. So Ming kept that part of her plans to herself. Wendy had been there for all Ming's angst in the aftermath of the senior prom kiss and believed she had wasted too much energy on a man who was never going to let himself fall in love and get married.

Add to this her sister's disapproval, and the fact that the one person she'd always been able to talk to when something was eating at her was the source of her troubles, and Ming was drowning in uncertainty.

The sun was inching its way toward the horizon when Ming decided she'd dawdled long enough. She paid the gallery owner for the painting of the coast she'd fallen in love with and made arrangements to have it shipped back to her house. Her feet felt encased in lead as she headed down the steps toward her rental car.

She drove below the speed limit on the way to the inn. Gulls wheeled and dove in the steady winds off the Pacific as the car rolled down the driveway, gravel crunching beneath the tires. Silver Mist Inn was composed of a large central lodge and a collection of small cottages that clung to the edge of the cliffs. The spectacular views were well matched by the incredible cuisine and the fabulous hospitality of the husband-and-wife team who owned the inn and spa.

Rosemary was behind the check-in desk when Ming entered the lodge. "Hello, Ming," the fifty-something woman exclaimed. "How wonderful to see you."

Ming smiled. Already the relaxing, familiar feel of the place was sinking into her bones. "It's great to see you, too, Rosemary. How have you been?"

Her gaze drifted to the right of reception. The lodge's main room held a handful of people sipping coffee, reading or talking while they enjoyed the expansive views of the ocean. Off to the left, a door led to a broad deck that housed lounge chairs where waitresses were busy bringing drinks from the bar.

"Busy as always." Rosemary pushed a key toward Ming. "Your friend checked in three hours ago. You're staying in Blackberry Cottage."

The change of plans revived Ming's earlier uneasiness. "I booked my regular room in the lodge."

Rosemary nodded. "After your friend saw all we had to offer, he wanted to upgrade your accommodations. It's a little bigger, way more private and the views are the best we have."

"Thank you." Ming forced her lips into a smile she wasn't feeling.

Why had Jason disrupted her arrangements? Whenever she vacationed here, she always stayed in the same room, a comfortable suite with a large balcony that overlooked the ocean. This weekend in particular she'd wanted to be in familiar surroundings.

Ming parked her car beside the one Jason had rented and

retrieved her overnight bag from the trunk. Packing had taken her three hours. She'd debated every item that had gone into the carry-on luggage.

What sort of clothes would set the correct tone for the weekend? She'd started with too much outerwear. But the purpose of the trip wasn't to wander the trails by the cliffs but to explore Jason's glorious, naked body.

So, she'd packed the sexy lingerie she'd received as a bridal shower gift but never gotten the chance to wear. As she'd folded the silky bits of lace and satin, she realized the provocative underwear sent a message that Ming hoped to drive Jason wild with passion, and that struck her as very nonfriendlike.

In the end, she'd filled the suitcase with leggings and sweaters to combat the cool ocean breezes and everyday lingerie because she was making too big a deal out of what was to come.

Ming entered the cottage and set her suitcase by the front door. Her senses purred as she gazed around the large living room decorated in soothing blues and golds. Beyond the cozy furnishings was a wall of windows that revealed a deck gilded by the setting sun and beyond, the indigo ocean.

To her right something mouthwatering was cooking in the small, well-appointed kitchen. An open door beside the refrigerator led outside. Nearing the kitchen, she spied Jason enjoying the ocean breezes from one of the comfortable chairs that flanked a love seat on the deck.

For an undisturbed moment she observed him. He was as relaxed as she'd seen him in months, expression calm, shoulders loose, hands at ease on the chair's arms. A sharp stab of anticipation made her stomach clench. Shocked by the excitement that flooded her, Ming closed her eyes and tried to even out her breathing. In a few short hours, maybe less, they would make love for the first time. Her skin prickled, flushed. Heat throbbed through her, forging a path that ended between her thighs.

Panic followed. She wasn't ready for this. For him.

Telling her frantic pulse to calm down, Ming stepped onto the deck. "Hi."

Jason's gaze swung her way. A smile bloomed. "Hi yourself." He stood and stepped toward her. "You're later than I expected."

His deep voice and the intense light in his eyes made her long to press herself into his arms and pretend they were a real couple and that this was a magical getaway. She dug her nails into her palms.

"It's been over a year since I've seen Wendy. We had a lot to catch up on."

"What was her take on your decision to have a baby?"

"Total support." Ming slipped past him and leaned her elbows on the railing. As the sapphire-blue ocean churned against rugged cliffs, sending plumes of water ten feet into the air, she put her face into the breeze and let it cool her hot cheeks. "After the week I had, it was a relief to tell someone who didn't go all negative on me."

"I wasn't negative."

Ming tore her gaze from the panorama and discovered Jason two feet away. Attacked by delicious tingles, she shook her head. "No, but you created trouble for me, nonetheless."

"Did you tell her about us?"

Ming shook her head. "We're supposed to keep this a secret, remember? Besides, she never liked you in high school."

"Everybody liked me in high school."

Although he'd been a jock and one of the most popular guys in school, Jason hadn't been mean to those less blessed the way his football buddies had been.

"Don't you mean all the girls?" Blaming nerves for her disgruntled tone, Ming pressed her lips together and redirected her attention to the view. The sun was still too bright to stare at, but the color was changing rapidly to orange.

"Them, too." Jason reached out and wrapped the ends of her scarf around his fists.

He tugged, startling her off balance, and stepped into her space. Her hormones shrieked in delight as the scent of cologne and predatory male surrounded her. She gulped air into her lungs and felt her breasts graze his chest. A glint appeared in his eyes, sending a spike of excitement through her.

"Something smells great in the kitchen. What's for dinner?" she asked, her voice cracking on the last word. Her appetite had vanished in the first rush of desire, but eating would delay what came later.

"Coq au vin." Although his lips wore a playful smile, his preoccupation with her mouth gave the horseplay a sexual vibe. He looked prepared to devour her in slow, succulent bites. "Your favorite. Are you hungry?"

He looked half-starved.

"I haven't eaten since breakfast." Her stomach had been too knotted to accept food.

"Then I'd better feed you." He softened his fists and let her scarf slip through his fingers, releasing her. "You'll need your strength for what I have planned for you tonight."

Freed, Ming couldn't move. The hunger prowling through her prevented her from backing to a safe distance. His knowing smirk kept her tongue-tied. She silently cursed as she trailed after him into the kitchen.

"I found a really nice chardonnay in town." He poured two glasses of wine and handed one to Ming. "I figured we'd save the champagne for later."

Great. He was planning to get her liquored up. She could blame the alcohol for whatever foolish thing she cried out in the heat of passion. She swallowed half the pale white wine in a single gulp and made approving noises while he pulled a wedge of brie out of the fridge. Grapes. Crackers. Some sort of pâté. All the sort of thing she'd served him at some point. Had he paid attention to what she liked? Asking herself the question had an adverse effect on her knees and led to more dangerous ruminating. What else might he have planned for her?

"Dinner should be ready in half an hour." He had everything assembled on a plate and used his chin to gesture toward the deck. "It's a gorgeous night. Let's not waste the good weather."

Early September in northern California was a lot cooler than what they'd left behind in Houston, and Ming welcomed the break from the heat. "It really is beautiful." She carried their glasses outside. "We should take a long walk after dinner."

Jason set down the plate and shot her a look. "If you have any strength in your legs after I'm done with you, we'll do that."

Despite the hot glance that accompanied his suggestive words, she shivered. Is this how the weekend was going to go? One long flirtation? It took them away from their normal interaction. Made her feel as if they'd grown apart these past few years and lost the comfortable intimacy they'd once shared.

"You're cold. Come sit with me and I'll warm you up."

Her scattered wits needed time to recover before she was ready to have his arms around her. "I'll grab my wrap."

"Let me get it."

"It's on my suitcase by the door."

How was she supposed to resist falling under his spell if he continued being so solicitous? This was the Jason she'd glimpsed with other women. The one she'd longed to have for her own. Only this Jason never stayed to charm any one woman for more than a few months, while Ming had enjoyed her fun-loving, often self-involved friend in her life for over twenty years. She sighed. Was it possible for him to be the thoughtful, romantic lover and a great friend all in one?

Was she about to find out? Or would making love with him complicate her life? Was he close to discovering she'd harbored a secret, unrequited crush on him for years? At best he'd not take it seriously and tease her about it. At worst, he'd put up walls and disappear the way he always did when a girlfriend grew too serious. Either way, she wasn't ready for his pity or his alarm.

Jason returned with her dark blue pashmina. "I put your suitcase in the bedroom."

Foolishly her heart jerked at the last word. Every instinct told her to run. Altering their relationship by becoming sexually intimate was only going to create problems.

Then he was wrapping the shawl around her and grazing her lips with his. All thoughts of fleeing vanished, lost in the heat generated by her frantic heart.

She put a hand on his arm. "Jason—"

He put a finger against her lips and silenced her. "Save it for later."

The twinkle in his eye calmed some of the frenzy afflicting her hormones. She reminded herself that he was way more experienced in the art of seduction, having had vast numbers of willing women to practice on. He liked the chase. It was routine that turned him off. And right now, he was having a ball pursuing her. Maybe if she stopped resisting, he'd turn down the charisma.

So, she took half a dozen slow, deep breaths and forced herself to relax. Nibbling cheese, she stared at their view and kept her gaze off the handsome man with the dazzling blue eyes. But his deep voice worked its way inside her, its rumble shaking loose her defenses. She let him feed her grapes and crackers covered with pâté. His fingers skimmed her lips, dusted sensation over her cheeks and chin. By the time they were bumping hips in the small kitchen while transferring coq au vin and potatoes to plates, pouring more wine and assembling cutlery, Ming had gotten past her early nerves.

This was the Jason she adored. Funny, completely present, a tad bit naughty. The atmosphere between them was as easy as it had ever been. They'd discussed Terry's offer to take over the practice. Her sister's decision to buy a house in Portland. And stayed away from the worrisome topic of what was going to happen after dessert.

"This is delicious," Ming murmured, closing her eyes in

rapture as the first bite of coq au vin exploded on her taste buds. "My favorite."

"I thought you'd appreciate it. Rosemary told me the restaurant was known for their French cuisine." Jason had yet to sample the dinner.

She indicated his untouched plate. "Aren't you hungry?" He sure looked half-starved.

"I'm having too much fun watching you eat."

And just like that the sizzle was back in the room. Ming's mouth went dry. She bypassed her wine and sipped water instead. After her first glass of the chardonnay, she'd barely touched her second. Making love to Jason for the first time demanded a clear head. She wanted to be completely in the moment, not lost in an alcoholic fog.

"How can watching me eat be fun?" She tried to make her tone light and amused, but it came out husky and broken.

"It's the pleasure you take in each bite. The way you savor the flavors. You're usually so matter-of-fact about things, I like knowing what turns you on."

He wasn't talking about food. Ming felt her skin heat. Her blood moved sluggishly through her veins. Even her heart seemed to slow. She could feel a sexy retort forming on her tongue. She bit down until she had it restrained. They were old friends who were about to have sex, not a man and a woman engaged in a romantic ritual that ended in passionate lovemaking. Ming had to be certain her emotions stayed out of the mix. She could count on Jason to do the same.

"The backs of my knees are very ticklish." She focused on cutting another bite of chicken. "I've always loved having my neck kissed. And there's a spot on my pelvis." She paused, cocked her head and tried to think about the exact spot. "I guess I'll have to show you when we get to that point." She lifted her fork and speared him with a matter-of-fact gaze. "And you?"

His expression told her he was on to her game. "I'm a guy.

Pretty much anywhere a beautiful woman touches me, I'm turned on."

"But there has to be something you really like."

His eyes narrowed. "My nipples are very sensitive."

She pressed her lips together to keep from laughing. "I'll pay special attention to them," she said when she trusted her voice.

If they could talk like this in the bedroom, Ming was confident she could emerge from the weekend without doing something remarkably stupid like mentioning how her feelings for him had been evolving over the last few months. She'd keep things casual. Focus on the physical act, not the intimacy. Use her hands, mouth and tongue to appreciate the perfection of Jason's toned, muscular body and avoid thinking about all those tiresome longings she'd bottled up over the years.

Savor the moment and ignore the future.

While Jason cleared the dishes from the table, Ming went to unpack and get ready for what was to come. Her confidence had returned over dinner. She had her priorities all in a row. Her gaze set on the prize. The path to creating a baby involved being intimate with Jason. She would let her body enjoy making love with him. Emotion had no place in what she was about to do.

Buoyed by her determination, Ming stopped dead in the doorway between the living room and bedroom. The scene before her laid waste to all her good intentions. Here was the stuff of seduction.

The centerpiece of the room was a king-size bed with the white down comforter pulled back and about a hundred red rose petals strewn across the white sheets. Candles covered every available surface, unlit but prepared to set a romantic mood when called upon. Piano music, played by her favorite artist, poured from the dresser, where portable speakers had been attached to an iPod. Everything was perfect.

Her chest locked up. She could not have designed a better setting. Jason had gone to a lot of trouble to do this. He'd planned, taken into account all her favorite things and executed all of this to give her the ideal romantic weekend.

It was so unlike him to think ahead and be so prepared. To take care of her instead of the other way around. It was as if she was here with a completely different person. A thoughtful, romantic guy who wanted something more than three days of great sex and then going back to being buddies. The sort of man women fell for and fell for hard.

"What do you think?"

She hadn't heard Jason's approach over the thump of her heart. "What I think is that I can't do this."

Jason surveyed the room, searching for imperfections. The candles were vanilla scented, her favorite. The rose petals on the bed proclaimed that this weekend was about romance rather than just sex. The coq au vin had been delicious. Everything he'd done was intended to set the perfect stage for romance.

He'd given her no indication that he intended to rush her. He'd promised her a memorable weekend. She had to know he'd take his time with her, drive her wild with desire. This wasn't some spontaneous hookup for him. He took what they were about to do seriously.

What the hell could possibly be wrong?

"I'm sorry," she said into the silence. Sagging against the door frame, she closed her eyes and the weight of the world appeared to descend on her.

"I don't understand."

"I don't, either." She looked beautiful and tragic as she opened her eyes and met his gaze. "I want to do this."

He was very glad to hear that because anticipation had been eating him alive these past few days. He wanted her with an intensity he'd never felt before. Maybe that was because ever since he'd kissed her, he'd been fantasizing about this moment. Or maybe he'd never worked this hard to get a woman into bed before.

"Being a mom is all I think about these days. I know if I want your help to get pregnant, we have to do it this weekend." Ming lapsed into silence, her hunched shoulders broadcasting discomfort.

"I didn't realize making love with me required so much sacrifice on your part." He forced amusement into his tone to keep disappointment at bay.

Her words had cut deep. When he'd insisted they make her baby this way instead of going to a clinic, he thought this would be the perfect opportunity to satisfy his longing for her. The kiss between them a few days earlier confirmed the attraction between them was mutual. Why was she resisting when the vibe between them was electric? What was she afraid of?

"I didn't mean it that way." But from her unhappy expression his accusation hadn't been far off.

"No?" Jason leaned against the wall and fought the urge to snatch her into his arms and kiss her senseless. He could seduce her, but he didn't want just her body, he wanted... "How exactly did you mean it?"

"Look, we're best friends. Don't you think sleeping together will make things awkward between us?"

"Not possible. It's because we're just friends that it will work so great." He sounded as if he was overselling used cars of dubious origin. "No expectations—"

"No strings?"

He didn't like the way she said that. As if he'd just confirmed her worst fears. "Are you worried that I'm in this just for the sex?" She wasn't acting as if she hoped it would lead to something more.

"Yes." She frowned, clearly battling conflicting opinions. "No."

"But you have some sort of expectation." Jason was surprised that his flight response wasn't stimulated by her question. Usually when a woman started thinking too much, it was time to get out.

"Not the sort you mean." She gave her head a vigorous shake. "I know perfectly well that once we have sex—"

"Make love."

"Whatever." She waved her hand as if she was batting away a pesky fly. "That once we…become intimate, you will have your curiosity satisfied—"

"Curiosity?" The word exploded from him. That's not how he'd describe the hunger pulsing through him. "You think all I feel is curiosity?"

She gave him a little shoulder shrug. Frustration clawed at him. The bed was feet away. He was damned tempted to scoop her up in his arms and drop her onto the softly scented sheets. Give her a taste of exactly what he was feeling.

He pushed off the wall and let his acute disappointment and eight-inch height advantage intimidate her into taking a step back. "And what about you? Aren't you the least bit curious how hot this thing between us will burn?"

"Oh, please. I'm not one of the women you date."

The second she rolled her eyes at him, Jason knew he'd hit a soft spot. Ming overthought everything. She liked her life neat and orderly. That was great for her career, but in her personal life she could use a man who overwhelmed her senses and short-circuited her thoughts. His brother hadn't been able to do it. Evan had once complained that his fiancée had a hard time being spontaneous and letting go. He'd never come right out and said that she'd been reserved in bed. Evan had too much respect for Ming to be so crass, but Jason had been able to read between the lines.

"What is that supposed to mean?"

"Has it ever occurred to you to look at the sort of women you prefer to date?"

"Beautiful. Smart. Sexy."

"Needy. Clinging. Terrified of abandonment." She crossed her arms over her chest and stared him down as no one else did. "You choose needy women to get your ego stroked and then, when you start to pull away because they're too clingy, they fear your abandonment and chase you."

"That's ridiculous." Jason wasn't loving the picture she was painting of him. Nor was this conversation creating the romantic mood he'd hoped for, but he refused to drop the subject until he'd answered her charges.

"Jennifer was a doctor," he said, listing the last three women he'd dated. "Amanda owned a very successful boutique and Sherri was a vice president of marketing. Independent, successful women all."

"Jennifer had daddy issues." She ticked the women off on her fingers. "Her father was a famous cardiologist and never let her feel as if she was good enough even though she finished second in her class at med school. Amanda was a middle child. She had four brothers and sisters and never felt as if her parents had time for her. As for Sherri, her mom left when she was seven. She had abandonment issues."

"How did you know all that?"

Ming's long-suffering look made his gut tighten. "Who do you think they come to when the relationship starts to cool?"

"What do you tell them?"

"That as wonderful as you are, any relationship with you has little chance of becoming permanent. You are a confirmed bachelor and an adrenaline junky with an all-consuming hobby who will eventually break their heart."

"Do they listen to you?"

"The healthy ones do."

"You know, if we weren't such old and dear friends, I might be tempted to take offense."

"You won't," she said confidently. "Because deep down you know you choose damaged women so eventually their issues will cause trouble between you and you have the perfect excuse to break things off."

Deep down he knew this? "And here I thought I dated them because they were hot." About then, Jason realized Ming had picked a fight with him. "I don't want to talk about all the women I've dated." But it was too late.

Ming wore the mulish expression he'd first encountered on the playground when one of his buddies had shoved her off the swings.

"This weekend was a mistake." She slipped sideways into the bedroom and headed straight for her suitcase.

To Jason's bafflement, she used it as a battering ram, clearing him from her path to the front door.

"You're leaving?"

"You thought conceiving a baby should be memorable, but the only thing I'm going to remember about being here with you is this fight."

"We're not fighting." She was making no sense, and Jason wasn't sure how trying to provide her with a romantic setting for their first time together had sparked her wrath. "Where do you think you're going?"

"Back to San Francisco. There's a midnight flight that will put me back in Houston by morning."

How could she know that unless…? "You'd already decided you weren't going to stay."

"Don't be ridiculous." Her voice rang with sincerity, but she was already out the door and her face was turned away from him. "I just happened to notice it when I was booking my flight."

Ming was approaching the trunk of her rental car as Jason barreled through the front door and halted. His instincts told him to stop her. He was reasonably certain he could coax her mood back to romance with her favorite dessert and a stroll through the gardens, but her words had him wondering about his past choices when it came to relationships.

In the deepening twilight, a full harvest moon, robust and orange from the sunset, crested the trees. A lovers' moon. Pity it would go to waste on them.

Jason dug his fingers into the door as Ming turned her car

around. Was giving her time to think a good idea? He was gambling that eventually she'd remember that she needed him to get pregnant.

Five

Ming hadn't been able to sleep on the red-eye from San Francisco to Houston. The minute her car had reached the Mendocino city limits, she'd begun to feel the full weight of her mistake. She had three choices: convince Jason to use a clinic for her conception, give up on him being her child's father or stop behaving like a ninny and have sex with him. Because it was her nature to do so, she spent the flight home making pro and con lists for each choice. Then she weighted each item and analyzed her results.

Logic told her to head for the nearest sperm bank. Instead, as soon as the wheels of the plane hit the runway, she texted him an apology and asked him to call as soon as he was able.

The cab from the airport dropped her off at nine in the morning. She entered her house and felt buffeted by its emptiness. With Lily in Portland and Muffin spending the weekend with Ming's parents, she had the place to herself. The prospect depressed her, but she was too exhausted to fetch the active Yorkshire terrier.

Closing the curtains in her room, she slid between the sheets but didn't fall asleep as soon as her head touched the pillow. She tortured herself with thoughts of making love with Jason. Imagined his strong body moving against her, igniting her passion. Her body pulsed with need. If she hadn't panicked, she wouldn't feel like a runaway freight train. She'd be sated and sleepy instead of wide awake and horny.

Ming buried her face in the pillow and screamed her frustration until her throat burned. That drained enough of her energy to allow her to sleep. She awakened some hours later, disoriented by the dark room, and checked the clock. It was almost five. She pushed to a sitting position and raked her long hair away from her face. Despite sleeping for six hours, she was far from rested. Turbulent dreams of Jason returned her to that unfulfilled state that had plagued her earlier.

If not for the evocative scents of cooking, she might have spent what remained of the day in bed, but her stomach growled, reminding her she hadn't had anything to eat except the power bar she'd bought at the airport. She got dressed and went to the kitchen to investigate.

"Something smells great." Ming stepped off the back stairs and into her kitchen, surprising her sister.

The oven door closed with a bang as she spun to face Ming. "You're home." Lily's cheeks bore a rosy flush, probably put there by whatever simmered on the stove.

Even though both girls had learned to cook from their mother, only Lily had inherited their mother's passion for food. Ming knew enough to keep from starving, but for her cooking was more of a necessity than an infatuation.

"You're cooking."

"I was craving lamb."

"Craving it?" The dish was a signature item Lily prepared when she was trying to impress a guy. It had been over a year since she'd made it. "I thought you were going to be house hunting in Portland this weekend."

"I changed my mind about spending the weekend."

"Does this mean you're changing your mind about moving?" Ming quizzed, unable to contain the hope in her voice.

"No." Lily pulled a bottle of wine from the fridge and dug in a drawer for the corkscrew. "How come you're home so early? I thought you were gone all weekend."

Ming thought of the chardonnay she and Jason had shared. How he'd fed her grapes and how she'd enjoyed his hands on her skin. "I wasn't having any fun so I thought I'd come home." Not the whole truth, but far from a lie. "I didn't get a chance to tell you before you left town last week, but Terry wants to sell me his half of the practice. He's retiring."

"How are you going to manage a baby and the practice all by yourself?"

"I can handle it just fine."

"I think you're being selfish." Lily's words, muffled by the refrigerator door, drove a spear into Ming's heart. She pulled a bowl of string beans out and plunked them on the counter. "How can you possibly have enough time for a child when you're running the practice?"

"There are a lot of professional women who manage to do both." Ming forced back the doubts creeping up on her, but on the heels of her failure with Jason this weekend, she couldn't help but wonder if her subconscious agreed with Lily.

What if she couldn't do both well? Was she risking complete failure? No. She could do this. Even without a partner in her life to help her when things went wrong, or to celebrate the triumphs?

She was going to be awfully lonely. Sure, her parents would help when they could, but Lily was moving and Jason had his racing and his career to occupy him. What was she thinking? She would have her child and the practice to occupy her full attention. What about love? Marriage?

She brushed aside the questions. What good did it do to

focus on something she couldn't control? Planning and organization led to success, and she was a master of both.

With her confidence renewed, she poured wine from the bottle Lily had opened. As it hit her taste buds, she made a face. She checked the label and frowned at her sister.

"Since when do you drink Riesling?"

"I'm trying new things."

"This is Evan's favorite wine."

"He recommended it so I bought a bottle."

"Recently?"

"No." Her sister frowned. "A while ago. Geez, what's with all the questions? I tried a type of wine your ex liked. Big deal."

Lily's sharpness rocked Ming. Was her sister so upset with her that it threatened to drive a wedge between them?

Ming set down her wineglass. "I'm going to run over to Mom and Dad's and pick up Muffin. Is there anything you need me to get while I'm out?"

"How about a bottle of wine you prefer?"

Flinching at her sister's unhappy tone, Ming grabbed her keys and headed for the door. "You know, I'm not exactly thrilled with your decision to move to Portland, but I know it's something you feel you have to do, so I'm trying to put aside my selfish wish for you to stay and at least act like I'm supportive."

Then, without waiting for her sister's reply, Ming stepped into her garage and shut the door firmly behind her. With her hands shaking, she had a hard time getting the key into the ignition of the '66 Shelby Cobra. She'd chosen to drive the convertible tonight, hoping the fresh air might clear away all the confusion in her mind.

The drive to her parents' house was accomplished in record time thanks to the smoothly purring 425 V8 engine. She really should sell the car. It was an impractical vehicle for a mother-to-be, but she had such great memories of the summer she and Jason had spent fixing it up.

After her spat with Lily, she'd planned to join her parents for dinner, but they were meeting friends at the country club, so Ming collected her dog and retraced her path back to her house. A car sat in her driveway. In the fading daylight, it took her a second to recognize it as Evan's.

Because she and Jason were best friends and she knew there'd be occasions when she'd hang out with his family, Ming had made a decision to keep her interactions with Evan amicable. In fact, it wasn't that hard. Their relationship lacked the turbulent passion that would make her hate him for dumping her. But that didn't mean she was okay about him showing up without warning.

Ming parked the convertible in the garage. Disappointment filled her as she tucked Muffin under her arm and exited the car. She'd been hoping Jason had stopped by. He hadn't called her or responded to her text.

When she entered the house, the tension in the kitchen stopped her like an invisible wall. What the heck? Evan and her sister had chosen opposite sides of the center island. An almost empty wine bottle sat between them. Lily's mouth was set in unhappy lines. Her gaze dropped from Evan to the bowl of lettuce on the counter before her.

"Evan, this is a surprise." Ming eyed the vase of flowers beside the sink. Daisies. The same big bunch he always gave her after they'd had a difference of opinion. He thought the simple white flower represented a sweet apology. He was nothing if not predictable. Or maybe not so predictable. Why had he shown up on her doorstep without calling?

Lily didn't look Ming's way. Had her sister shared with Evan her dismay about Ming's decision to have a baby? Stomach churning, she set Muffin down. The terrier headed straight for her food bowl.

"What brings you here?" Ming asked.

"I came by to… Because…" He appeared at a loss to explain his reason for visiting.

"Are you staying for dinner? Lily's making rack of lamb. I'm sure there's enough for three, or I should say four, since usually she makes it for whomever she's dating at the time."

Evan's gaze sliced toward Lily. "You're dating someone?"

"Not dating exactly, just using him for sex." Ming lowered her voice. "Although I think she's ready to find someone she can get serious about. That's why she's moving to Portland."

"And the guy she's seeing." Since Lily refused to look up from the lettuce she was shredding, Evan directed the question at Ming. "She can't get serious about him?"

"She says they're just friends." The Yorkie barked and Ming filled Muffin's bowl. "Isn't that right, Lily?"

"I guess." Lily's gaze darted between Ming and Evan.

"So, when are you expecting him to show?"

"Who?"

"The guy you're preparing the lamb for."

"There's no guy," Lily retorted, her tone impatient. "I told you I was craving lamb. No big deal."

Ming felt the touch of Evan's gaze. She'd been using Lily's love life to distract him from whatever purpose he had for visiting her tonight. Something about Evan had changed in the past year. The closer they got to their wedding, the more he'd let things irritate him. A part of her had been almost relieved when he called things off.

What was he doing here tonight? She glanced at the daisies. If he was interested in getting back together, his timing was terrible.

"I'm going to head upstairs and unpack," she told them, eager to escape. "Evan, make sure you let me know if Lily's mystery man shows up. I'm dying to meet him."

"There's no mystery man," her sister yelled up the stairs at her.

Ming set her suitcase on the bed and began pulling clothes out of it. She put everything where it belonged, hamper and dry cleaning pile for the things she'd worn, drawers and hangers for what she hadn't. When she was done, only one item remained. A white silk nightie. Something a bride might wear on her wedding night. She'd bought it in San Francisco two days ago specifically for her weekend with Jason.

Now what was she supposed to do with it?

"Ming?"

She spun around at the sound of Evan's voice. "Is Lily's date here?"

His gaze slid past her to the lingerie draped over the foot of her bed. He stared at it for a long moment before shifting his attention back to her.

"I've wanted to talk to you about something."

Her pulse jerked. He was so solemn. This couldn't be good. "You have? Let's go have dinner and chat."

He put up his hands as she started for the door. "This is something we need to discuss, just us."

Nothing that serious could ever be good. "You know, I'm in a really good place right now." She pulled her hair over one shoulder and finger-combed it into three sections. "The practice is booming. Terry wants me to buy him out." Her fingers made quick work of a braid and she snagged a scrunchy off her nightstand. "I'm happy."

"And I don't want that to change. But there's something you need to know—"

"Dinner's ready."

Ming cast her sister a grateful smile. "Wonderful. Come on, Evan. You're in for a treat." She practically raced down the stairs. Her glass of wine was on the counter where she'd left it and Ming downed the contents in one long swallow. Wincing at the taste, she reached into her wine cooler and pulled out a Shiraz.

Over dinner, Evan's sober expression and Lily's preoccupation with her own thoughts compelled Ming to fill the awkward silence with a series of stories about her trip to San Francisco and amusing anecdotes about Wendy's six-year-old daughter.

By the time the kitchen was cleaned up and the dishwasher happily humming, she was light-headed from too much wine and drained from carrying the entire conversation.

Making no attempt to hide her yawns, Ming headed upstairs and shut her bedroom door behind her. In the privacy of her large master suite, she stripped off her clothes and stepped into the shower. The warm water pummeled her, releasing some of the tension from her shoulders. Wrapped in a thick terry-cloth robe, she sat cross-legged on her window seat and stared out over her backyard. She had no idea how long her thoughts drifted before a soft knock sounded on her door.

Lily stuck her head in. "You okay?"

"Is Evan gone?"

Lily nodded. "I'm sorry about what I said to you earlier."

"You're not wrong. I am being selfish." Ming patted the seat beside her. "But at the same time you know that once I decide to do something, I give it my all."

Lily hugged Ming before sitting beside her on the window seat. "If anyone is going to be supermom it's you."

"Thanks." Ming swallowed past the tightness in her throat. She hated fighting with Lily. "So, what's up with Evan?"

"What do you mean?"

"When I came in tonight, he looked as grim as I've ever seen him. I figured he was explaining why he showed up out of the blue." Ming knew her sister had always been partial to Jason's older brother. Often in the past six months, Ming thought Lily had been the sister most upset about the broken engagement. "You two became such good friends these last few years. I thought maybe he'd share with you his reason for coming here tonight."

"Do you think Jason told him that you want to have a baby?"

"He wouldn't do that." Ming's skin grew warm as she imagined where she'd be right at this moment if she hadn't run out on Jason. Naked. Wrapped in his arms. Thighs tangled. Too happy to move. "I know this sounds crazy, but what if Evan wants to get back together?"

"Why would you think he'd want to do that?" Lily's voice rose.

"I don't. Not really." Ming shook her head. "It's just that after I told Jason I wanted to get pregnant, he was so insistent that I'm not over Evan."

"Are you?" Her sister leaned forward, eyebrows drawn together. "I mean Evan broke up with you, not the other way around."

Ming toyed with the belt of her robe. The pain of being dumped eased a little more each day, but it wasn't completely gone. "It really doesn't matter how I feel. The reasons we broke up haven't changed."

"What if they did? What if the problems that came between you were gone? Out of the picture?" Lily was oddly intent. "Would you give him another chance?"

Ming tried to picture herself with Evan now that she'd tasted Jason's kisses. She'd settled for one brother instead of fighting for the other. That was a mistake she wouldn't make again. She'd rather be happy as a single mom than be miserable married to a man she didn't love.

"I've spent the last six months reimagining my life without Evan," she told her sister. "I'd rather move forward than look back."

At a little after 8:00 p.m., Jason sat in his car and stared at Ming's house. When she'd left him in Mendocino, his pride had kept him from chasing after her for a little over two hours. He'd come to California to spend the weekend with Ming, not to pace a hotel room in a frenzy of unsatisfied desire. Confident she wouldn't miraculously change her mind and return to him, Jason had gotten behind the wheel and returned to the San Francisco airport, where he'd caught a 6:00 a.m. flight back to Houston.

He hadn't liked the way things had been left between them, and her text message gave him hope she hadn't, either. After catching a few hours of sleep, he'd come here tonight to talk her into giving his strategy one last shot.

But the sight of his brother's car parked in Ming's driveway distracted him. What the hell was Evan doing here? Had he come to tell Ming that he was dating her sister? If so, Jason should get in there because Ming was sure to be upset.

He had his hand on the door release when her front door opened. Despite the porch light pouring over the couple's head, he couldn't see Lily's expression, but her body language would be visible from the moon.

Ming's sister was hung up on his brother. And from the way Evan slid his hands around her waist and pulled her against him for a deep, passionate kiss, the feeling was mutual.

It took no more than a couple of seconds for an acid to eat at Jason's gut. He glanced away from the embracing couple, but anger continued to build.

What the hell did Evan think he was doing? Didn't he care about Ming's feelings at all? Didn't he consider how hurt she'd be if she saw him kissing Lily? Obviously not. Good thing Jason was around to straighten out his brother before the situation spun out of control.

A motor started, drowning out Jason's heated thoughts. Evan backed out of the driveway. Jason had missed the chance to catch his brother in the act. Cursing, he dialed Evan's number.

"Jason, hey, what's up?"

"We need to talk."

"So talk." Considering the fact that Evan had just engaged in a long, passionate kiss, he wasn't sounding particularly chipper.

"In person." So he could throttle his brother if the urge arose. "O'Malley's. Ten minutes."

The tension in Jason's tone must have clued in his brother to Jason's determination because Evan agreed without protest. "Sure. Okay."

Jason ended the call and followed his brother's car to the neighborhood bar. He chose the parking spot next to Evan's and was standing at his brother's door before Evan had even turned off the engine.

"You and Lily are still seeing each other?" Jason demanded, not allowing his brother to slide from behind the wheel.

"I never said I was going to stop."

"Does Ming know?"

"Not yet."

"She'll find out pretty quickly if you keep kissing Lily in full view of Ming's neighbors."

"I didn't think about that." Evan didn't ask how Jason knew. "I was sure Ming wouldn't see us. She'd gone up to her room."

"So that made it okay?" Fingers curling into fists, Jason stabbed his brother with a fierce glare. "If you intend to flaunt your relationship, you need to tell her what you and Lily are doing."

"I started to tonight, but Lily interrupted me. She doesn't want Ming to know." And Evan didn't look happy about it. "Can we go inside and discuss this over a beer?"

Considering his mood, Jason wasn't sure consuming alcohol around his brother was a wise idea, but he stepped back so Evan could get out of the car. With an effort Jason unclenched his fists and concentrated on soothing his bad temper. By the time they were seated near the back, Jason's fury had become a slow burn.

"Why doesn't Lily want Ming to know?" Jason sat with his spine pressed against the booth's polished wood back while Evan leaned his forearms on the table, all earnest and contrite.

"Because I don't think she intends for it to go anywhere."

If Evan wasn't running the risk of hurting Ming all over again, Jason could have sympathized with his brother's pain. "Then you need to quit seeing her."

"I can't." Despite the throb in his brother's voice, the corners of his mouth relaxed. "The sex is incredible. I tell myself a hundred times a day that it's going nowhere and that I should get out before anyone is hurt, but then I hear her voice or see her and I have to…" He grimaced. "I don't know why I'm telling you this."

"So you two are combustible together." Resentment made Jason cross. He and Ming had great chemistry, too, but instead of exploring some potentially explosive lovemaking, they were at odds over what effect this might have on their friendship.

"It's amazing."

"But…?" Jason prompted.

"I don't know if we can make it work. We have completely different ideas about what we want." Evan shook his head. "And now she's moving to Portland."

Which should put an end to things, but Jason sensed the upcoming separation was causing things to heat up rather than cool down.

"Long-range relationships don't work," Jason said.

"Sometimes they do. And I love her." Something Evan looked damned miserable about.

"Is she in love with you?"

"She claims it's nothing but casual sex between us. But it sure as hell doesn't feel casual when we're at it."

Love was demonstrating once again that it had no one's best interests at heart. Evan was in love with Lily, but she obviously didn't feel the same way, and that made him unhappy. And finding out that her ex-fiancé was in love with her sister was going to cause Ming pain. Nothing good came of falling in love.

"All the more reason you should quit seeing Lily before Ming finds out."

"That's not what I want."

"What *you* want?"

Jason contemplated the passion that tormented his brother. The entire time Evan and Ming were dating, not once had Evan displayed the despair that afflicted him now.

"How about what's good for Ming?" Jason continued.

"Don't you think you did enough damage to her when you broke off your engagement two weeks before the wedding?"

"Yeah, well, that was bad timing on my part." Evan paused for a beat. "We weren't meant to be together."

"You and Lily aren't meant to be together, either."

"I don't agree." Evan sounded grim. "And I want a chance to prove it. Can I count on you to keep quiet?"

"No." Seeing his brother's expression, Jason relented. "I'm not going to run over there tonight and tell her. Talk to Lily. Figure this out. You can have until noon tomorrow."

As his anger over Evan's choice of romantic partner faded, Jason noticed the hollow feeling in his chest was back. He sipped the beer the waitress had set before him and wondered why Ming had chosen to pick a fight with him in California instead of surrendering to the heat between them.

Was she really afraid their relationship would be changed by sex? How could it when they'd been best friends for over twenty years? Sure, there'd been sparks the night of senior prom, but they'd discussed the situation and decided their friendship was more important than trying to date only to have it end badly.

And what they were about to do wasn't dating. It was sex, pure and simple. A way for Ming to get pregnant. For Jason to purge her from his system.

For him to satisfy his curiosity?

Maybe her accusation hadn't been completely off the mark. He wouldn't be a guy if he hadn't looked at Ming in a bathing suit and recognized she was breathtaking. From prom night his fingers knew the shape of her breasts, his tongue the texture of her nipples. The soft heat of her mouth against his. That wasn't something he could experience and then never think about again.

But he wasn't in love with her. He'd never let that happen. Their friendship was too important to mess up with romance. Love had almost killed his father. And Evan wasn't doing too well, either.

Nope. Better to keep things casual. Uncomplicated.

Which didn't explain why he'd offered to help Ming get pregnant and why he'd suggested they do it the natural way. And Jason had no easy answer.

Six

By Sunday afternoon Ming still hadn't heard from Jason, and his lack of response to her phone calls and texts struck her as odd. She'd apologized a dozen times. Why was he avoiding her? After brunch with Lily, she drove to Jason's house in the hope of cornering him and getting answers. Relief swept her as she spied him by the 'Cuda he'd won off Max a few months ago. She parked her car at the bottom of the driveway and stared at him for a long moment.

Bare except for a pair of cargo shorts that rode low on his hips, he was preoccupied with eliminating every bit of dust from the car's yellow paint. His bronzed skin glistened with a fine mist of water from the hole in the nearby garden hose. The muscles across his back rippled as he plunged the sponge into the bucket of soapy water near his bare feet.

Ming imagined gliding her hands over those male contours, digging her nails into his flesh as he devoured her. The fantasy inspired a series of hot flashes. She slid from behind the wheel and headed toward him.

"I think you missed a spot," she called, stopping a couple feet away from the back bumper. Hearing the odd note in her own voice brought about by her earlier musing, she winced. When he frowned at her, she pointed to a nonexistent smudge on the car's trunk.

Since waking at six that morning, she'd been debating what tack to take with Jason. Did she scold him for not calling her back? Did she pretend that she wasn't hurt and worried that he'd ignored her apologies? Or did she just leave her emotional baggage at the door and talk to him straight like a friend?

Jason dropped the sponge on the car's roof and set his hands on his hips. "I'm pretty sure I didn't."

She eyed the car. "I'm pretty sure you did." When he didn't respond, she stepped closer to the car and pointed. "Right here."

"If you think you can do better..." He lobbed the dripping sponge onto the trunk. It landed with a splat, showering her with soapy water. "Go ahead."

Unsure why he got to act unfriendly when she'd been the one to apologize only to be ignored, she picked up the sponge and debated what to do with it. She could toss it back and hope it hit him full in the face, or she could take the high road and see if they could talk through what had happened in California.

Gathering a calming breath, she swept the sponge over the trunk and down toward the taillights. "I've left you a few messages," she said, focusing on the task at hand.

"I know. Sorry I haven't called you back."

"Is there a reason why you didn't?"

"I've been busy."

Cleaning an already pristine car was a pointless endeavor. So was using indirect methods to get Jason to talk about something uncomfortable. "When you didn't call me back, I started wondering if you were mad at me."

"Why would I be mad?"

Ming circled the car and dunked the sponge into the bucket. Jason had retreated to the opposite side of the 'Cuda and was spraying the car with water. Fine mist filled the air, landing on Ming's skin, lightly coating her white blouse and short black skirt. She hadn't come dressed to wash a car. And if she didn't retreat, she risked ruining her new black sandals.

"Because of what happened in Mendocino."

"You mean because you freaked out?" At last he met her gaze. Irritation glittered in his bright blue eyes.

"I didn't freak...exactly."

"You agreed we'd spend three days together and when you got there, you lasted barely an hour before picking a fight with me and running out. How is that not freaking?"

Ming scrubbed at the side mirror, paying careful attention to the task. "Well, I wouldn't have done that if you hadn't gone all Don Juan on me."

"Don Juan?" He sounded incredulous.

"Master of seduction."

"I have no idea what you're talking about."

"The roses on the bed. The vanilla candles. I'm surprised you didn't draw me a bubble bath." In the silence that followed her accusation, she glanced up. The expression on his face told her that had also been on his agenda. "Good grief."

"Forgive me for trying to create a romantic mood."

"I didn't ask for romance," she protested. "I just wanted to get pregnant."

In a clinic. Simple. Uncomplicated.

"Since when do you have something against romance? I seem to remember you liked it when Evan sent you flowers and took you out for candlelit dinners."

"Evan and I were dating." They'd been falling in love.

She picked up the bucket and moved to the front of the car. This time Jason stayed put.

"I thought you'd appreciate the flowers and the candlelight."

Ming snorted. "Men do stuff like that to get women into bed. But you already knew we were going to have sex. So what was with the whole seduction scene?"

"Why are you making such an issue out of this?"

She stopped scrubbing the hood and stared at him, hoping she could make him understand without divulging too much. "You created the perfect setting to make me fall in love with you."

"That's not what I was doing."

"I know you don't plan to make women fall for you, but it's what happens to everyone you date." She applied the sponge to the hood in a fury. "You overwhelm them with romantic gestures until they start picturing a future with you and then you drop them because they want more than you can give them."

The only movement in his face was the tic in his jaw. "You make it sound like I deliberately try to hurt them."

"That's not it at all. I don't think you have any idea what it's like when you turn on the Sterling charm."

"Are you saying that's what I did to you?"

It was the deliberate nature of what he'd done that made her feel like a prize to be won, not a friend to be helped. Another conquest. Another woman who would fall in love with him and then be dumped when she got too serious. When she wanted too much from him.

"Yes. And I don't get why." She dropped the sponge into the bucket and raked her fingers through her damp hair, lifting the soggy weight off her neck and back so the breeze could cool her. "All I wanted was to have a baby. I didn't want to complicate our friendship with sex. Or make things weird between us." Dense emotions weighed on her. Her shoulders sagged beneath the burden. She let her arms fall to her sides. "That's why I've decided to let you off the hook."

"What do you mean?"

"I'm going forward as originally planned. I'll use an anonymous donor and we can pretend the last two weeks never happened."

"I'm tired of pretending."

Before she'd fully processed his statement, chilly water rained down on her. Ming shrieked and stepped back.

"Hey." She wiped water from her eyes and glared at Jason. "Watch it."

"Sorry." But he obviously wasn't.

"You did that on purpose."

"I didn't."

"Did, too."

And abruptly they were eight again, chasing each other around her parents' backyard with squirt guns. She grabbed the sponge out of the bucket and tossed it at his head. He dodged it without even moving his feet, and a smattering of droplets showered down on her.

The bucket of water was at her feet. Seconds later it was in her hands. She didn't stop to consider the consequences of what she was about to do. How long since she'd acted without thought?

"If you throw that, I'll make sure you'll regret it," Jason warned, his serious tone a stark contrast to the dare in his eyes.

The emotional tug-of-war of the past two weeks had taken a toll on her. Her friendship with Jason was the foundation that she'd built her life on. But the longing for his kisses, the anticipation of his hands sliding over her naked flesh... She was on fire for him. Head and heart at war.

"Damn you, Jason," she whispered.

Soapy water arced across the six feet separating them and landed precisely where she meant it to. Drenched from head to groin, Jason stood perfectly still for as long as it took for Ming to drop the bucket. Then he gave his head a vigorous shake, showering soapy droplets all around him.

Ming watched as if in slow motion as he raised the hose in his hand, aimed it at her and squeezed the trigger. Icy water sprayed her. Sputtering with laughter, she put up her hands and backed away. Hampered by her heels from moving fast enough to escape, she shrieked for Jason to stop. When the deluge continued, she kicked off her shoes and raced for the house.

Until she stood dripping on Jason's kitchen floor, it hadn't occurred to her why she hadn't made a break for her car. The door leading to the garage slammed shut.

Shivering in the air-conditioning, Ming whirled to confront Jason.

He stalked toward her. Eyes on fire. Mouth set in a grim line. She held her ground as he drew near. Her trembling became less about being chilled and more about Jason's intensity as he stepped into her space and cupped her face in his hands.

"I'm sorry about California…"

The rest of her words were lost, stopped by the demanding press of his lips to hers. Electrified by the passion in his kiss, she rose up on tiptoe and wrapped her arms around his neck and let him devour her with lips, tongue and teeth.

Yes. This is what she'd been waiting for. The crazy wildness that had gripped them on prom night. The urgent craving to rip each other's clothes off and couple like long-lost lovers. Fire exploded in her loins as pulse after pulse drove heat to her core.

She drank from the passion in his kiss, found her joy in the feint and retreat of his tongue with hers. His hands left her face and traveled down her throat to her shoulders. And lower. She quaked as his palms moved over her breasts and caressed her stomach. Before she knew what he was after, he'd gathered handfuls of her blouse. She felt a tremor ripple through his torso a second before he tore her shirt open.

Flinging off her ruined shirt, Ming arched her back and pressed into his palms as he cupped her breasts through her sodden bra and made her nipples peak. Between her thighs an ache built toward a climax that would drive her mad if she couldn't get him to hurry. Impatience clawed at her. She needed his skin against hers. Reaching behind her, Ming released her bra clasp.

Jason peeled it away and drew his fingertips around her

breasts and across her aching nipples. "Perfect." Husky with awe, his voice rasped against her nerves, inflaming her already raging desire.

He bent his head and took one pebbled bud into his mouth, rolling his tongue over the hard point before sucking hard. The wet pulling sensation shot a bolt of sensation straight to where she hungered, wrenching a gasp from Ming.

"Do that again," she demanded, her fingers biting into his biceps. "That was incredible."

He obliged until her knees threatened to give out. "I've imagined you like this for so long," he muttered against her throat, teeth grazing the cord in her neck.

"Like what, half-naked?"

"Trembling. On fire." He slipped his hand beneath her skirt and skimmed up her thigh. "For me."

Shuddering as he closed in on the area where she wanted him most, Ming let her own fingers do some exploring. Behind the zipper of his cargo shorts he was huge and hard. As her nails grazed along his length, Jason closed his eyes. Breath escaped in a hiss from between his clenched teeth.

Happy with his reaction, but wanting him as needy as he'd made her, she unfastened his shorts and dived beneath the fabric to locate skin. A curse escaped him when she sent his clothes to pool at his feet. She grasped him firmly.

Abandoning his own exploration, he pulled her hands away and carried them around to his back. His mouth settled on hers again, this time stealing her breath and her sense of equilibrium. She was spinning. Twirling. Lost in the universe. Only Jason's mouth on hers, his arms banding her body to his, gave her any sense of reality.

This is what she'd been missing on the couch in his den and on the deck in California. The line between friend and lover wasn't just blurred, it was eradicated by hunger and wanton impulses. Hesitations were put aside. There was only heat and urgency. Demand and surrender.

Her back bumped against something. She opened her eyes as Jason's lips left hers.

"I need you now," she murmured as he nibbled down her neck.

"Let's go upstairs."

Her knees wouldn't survive the climb. "I can't make it that far."

"What do you have in mind?"

His kitchen table caught her eye. "How about this?"

Her knees had enough strength to back him up five feet. He looked surprised when she shoved him onto one of the four straight-back chairs.

"I'm game if you are."

She hadn't finished shimmying out of her skirt when she felt his fingers hook in the waistband of her hot pink thong and begin drawing it down her thighs. Naked, she stared down at him, her heart pinging around in her chest.

There was no turning back from this moment.

Jason's fingers bit into her hips as she straddled the chair. Meeting his gaze, she positioned herself so the tip of him grazed her entrance. Looking into his eyes, she could see straight to his soul. No veils hid his emotions from her.

She lowered herself, joining them in body as in spirit, let her head fall back and gloried at the perfection of their fit.

He'd died and gone to heaven. With Ming arched over his arm, almost limp in his grasp, he'd reached a nirvana of sorts. The sensation of being buried inside her almost blew the top of his head off. He shuddered, lost in a bewildering maze of emotions.

"This is the first time," he muttered, lowering his lips to her throat, "I've never done this before."

She tightened her inner muscles around him and he groaned. Her chest vibrated in what sounded like a laugh. With her fingers digging into his shoulders, she straightened and stared deep into his eyes.

"I have it on good authority," she began, leaning forward to draw her tongue along his lower lip, "that this is not your first time." She spoke without rancor, unbothered by the women he'd been with before.

He stroked his hands up her spine, fingers gliding over her silken skin, feeling the ridges made by her ribs. "It's the first I've ever had sex without protection."

"Really?" She peered at him from beneath her lashes. "I'm your first?"

"My only."

The instant the words were out, Jason knew he'd said too much. Delight flickered in her gaze. Her glee lasted only for the briefest of instances, but he'd spotted it, knew what he'd given away.

"I like the sound of that."

"Only because I am never going to get anyone but you pregnant."

Her smile transformed her from serene and mysterious to animated and exotic. "I like the sound of that, too." This time when she kissed him, there was no teasing in her actions. She took his mouth, plunged her tongue deep and claimed him.

Fisting a hand in her hair, Jason answered her primal call. Their tongues danced in familiar rhythm, as if they hadn't had their first kiss over a decade before. He knew exactly how to drive her wild, what made her groan and tremble.

"I'll let you in on a little secret," she whispered, her breath hot in his ear. "You're my first, too."

Incapable of speech as she explored his chest, her clever fingers circling his nipples, nails raking across their sensitive surface, he arched his brow at her in question.

"I've never had sex on a kitchen chair before." She rotated her hips in a sexy figure eight that wrenched a groan from his throat. "I rather like it."

Pressure built in his groin as she continued to experiment with her movements. Straddling his lap, she had all the control she could ever want to drive him mad. Breath rasping, eyes half-closed, Jason focused on her face to distract himself from the pleasure cascading through his body. In all the dreams he'd had of her, nothing had been this perfect.

Arching her back, she shifted the angle of her hips and moved over him again. "Oh, Jason, this is incredible."

"Amazing." He garbled the word, provoking a short laugh from her. "Perfect."

"Yes." She sat up straight and looked him square in the eyes. "It's never been like this."

"For me, either."

Deciding they'd done enough talking, Jason kissed her, long and deep. Her movements became more urgent as their passion burned hotter. His fingers bit into her hips, guiding her. A soft cry slipped from her parted lips. Jason felt her body tense and knew she was close. That's all it took to start his own climax. Gaze locked on her face, he held back, waiting for her to pitch over the cliff. The sheer glory of it caught him off guard. She gave herself completely to the moment. And called his name.

With his ears filled with her rapture, he lost control and spilled himself inside her. They were making more than a baby. They were making a moment that would last forever. The richness of the experience shocked him. Never in a million years would he have guessed that letting himself go so completely would hit him with this sort of power.

Shaking, Jason gathered Ming's body tight against his chest and breathed heavily. As the last pulses of her orgasm eased, he smoothed her hair away from her face and bestowed a gentle kiss on her lips.

"I'm glad I was your first," she murmured, her slender arms wrapped around his neck.

He smiled. "I'm glad you're my only."

* * *

Taking full advantage of Jason's king-size bed, Ming lay on her stomach lengthwise across the mattress. With her chin on his chest, her feet kicking the air, she watched him. Naked and relaxed, he'd stretched out on his back, his hands behind his head, eyes closed, legs crossed at the ankle. An easy smile tipped the corners of his lips upward. Ming regarded his satisfied expression, delighted that she'd been the one to bring him to this state. Twice.

While her body was utterly drained of energy, the same couldn't be said for her mind. "Now that we have that out of the way, perhaps you can explain why you've been avoiding me for two days."

Jason's expression tightened. "Have you talked to your sister?"

"Lily?" Ming pushed herself into a sitting position. "We had brunch before I came here. Why?"

His lashes lifted. "She didn't tell you."

She had no idea what he was talking about. "Tell me what?"

"About her and Evan." Jason looked unhappy. "They've been seeing each other."

"My sister and your brother?" Ming repeated the words but couldn't quite get her mind around the concept. "Seeing each other...you mean dating?"

Her gaze slid over Jason. Two weeks ago she'd have laughed at anyone who told her she and Jason were going to end up in bed together. The news of Evan and Lily was no less unexpected.

"Yes." He touched her arm, fingers gentle as they stroked her skin. "Are you okay?"

His question startled her. But it was the concern on his face that made her take stock of her reaction. To her dismay she felt a twinge of discomfort. But she'd be damned if she'd admit it.

"If they get married we'll end up being brother and sister." She was trying for levity but fell short of the mark.

Jason huffed out an impatient breath. "Don't make light of this with me. I'm worried that you'll end up getting hurt."

Ming's bravado faded. "But it can't be that serious. Lily is moving to Portland. She wouldn't be doing that if they had a future together." Her voice trailed away. "That's why she's leaving, isn't it? They're in love and my sister can't break it off and stick around. She needs to move thousands of miles away to get over him."

"I don't know if your sister is in love with Evan."

"But Evan's in love with her."

Jason clamped his mouth shut, but the truth was written all over his face.

Needing a second to recover her equilibrium, Ming left the bed and snagged Jason's robe off the bathroom door. She put it on and fastened the belt around her waist. By the time she finished rolling up the sleeves, she felt calmer and more capable of facing Jason.

"How long have you known?" Ming heard the bitterness in her voice and tried to reel in her emotions. Evan hadn't exactly broken her heart when he'd ended their engagement, but that didn't mean she hadn't been hurt. She'd been weeks away from committing to him for the rest of her life.

"I've known they were going out but didn't realize how serious things had gotten until I spoke with Evan last night." Jason left the bed and came toward her. "Are you okay?"

"Sure." Something tickled her cheek. Ming reached up to touch the spot and her fingers came away wet. "I'm fine."

"Then why are you crying?"

Her heart pumped sluggishly. "I'm feeling sorry for myself because I'm wondering if Evan ever loved me." She stared at the ceiling, blinking hard to hold back the tears. "Am I so unlovable?"

Jason's arms came around her. His lips brushed her cheek. "You're the furthest thing from unlovable."

Safe in his embrace, she badly wanted to believe him, but

the facts spoke loud and clear. She was thirty-one, had never been married and was contemplating single motherhood.

"One of these days you'll find the right guy for you. I'm sure of it."

Hearing Jason's words was like stepping on broken glass. Pain shot through her, but she had nowhere to run. The man her heart had chosen had no thought of ever falling in love with her.

Ming pushed out of Jason's arms. "Did you really just say that minutes after we finished making love?"

His expression darkened. "I'm trying to be a good friend."

"I get that we're never going to be a couple, but did it ever occur to you that I might not be thinking about another man while being naked with you?" Her breath rushed past the lump in her throat.

"That's funny." His voice cracked like a whip. "Because just a second ago you were crying over the fact that my brother is in love with your sister."

Ming's mouth popped open, but no words emerged. Too many statements clogged the pathway between her brain and her lips. Everything Jason had said to her was perfectly reasonable. Her reactions were not. She was treating him like a lover, not like a friend.

"You're right. I'm a little thrown by what's happening between Lily and Evan. But it's not because I'm in love with him. And I can't even think about meeting someone and starting a relationship right now."

"Don't shut yourself off to the possibility."

"Like you have?" Ming couldn't believe he of all people was giving her advice on her love life. Before she blurted out her true feelings, she gathered up all her wayward emotions and packed them away. "I'd better get home and check on Muffin."

"I'm sure Muffin is fine." Jason peered at her, his impatience banked. "Are you?"

"I'm fine."

"Why don't I believe you?"

She wanted to bask in his concern, but they were in different places in their relationship right now. His feelings for her hadn't changed while she was dangerously close to being in love with him.

"No need to worry about me." Ming collected her strength and gave him her best smile. Crossing to his dresser, she pulled out a T-shirt. "Is it okay if I borrow this since you ruined my blouse?"

Jason eyed her, obviously not convinced by her performance. "Go ahead. I don't want to be responsible for any multicar pile-ups if you drive home topless." His tone was good-natured, but his eyes followed her somberly as she exchanged shirt for robe and headed toward the door.

"I'll call you later," she tossed over her shoulder, hoping to escape before unhappiness overwhelmed her.

"You could stay for dinner." He'd accompanied her downstairs and scooped up her black skirt and her hot pink thong before she could reach them, holding them hostage while he awaited her answer.

"I have some case files to look over before tomorrow," she said, conscious of his gaze on her as she tugged her underwear and skirt from his hands.

"You can work on them after dinner. I have some reports to go over. We can have a study date just like old times."

As tempting as that sounded, she recognized that it was time to be blunt. "I need some time to think."

"About what?"

"Things," she murmured, knowing Jason would never let her get away with such a vague excuse. Like how she needed to adjust to being friends *and* lovers with Jason. Then there was the tricky situation with her sister. She needed to get past being angry with Lily, not because she was dating Ming's ex-fiancé, but because her sister might get what Ming couldn't: a happily-ever-after with a man who loved her.

"What is there to think about?" Jason demanded. "We made love. Hopefully, we made a baby."

Her knees knocked together. Could she be pregnant already? The idea thrilled her. She wanted to be carrying Jason's child. Wanted it now more than ever. Which made her question her longing to become a mother. Would she be as determined if it was any other man who was helping her get pregnant? Or was she motivated by the desire to have something of Jason otherwise denied to her?

"I hope that, too." She forced a bright smile.

His bare feet moved soundlessly on the tile floor as he picked up her ruined blouse and carried it to the trash. Slipping back into her clothes, she regarded him in helpless fascination.

In jeans and a black T-shirt, he was everything she'd ever wanted in a man, flaws and all. Strong all the time, sensitive when he needed to be. He demonstrated a capacity for tenderness when she least expected it. They were incredible together in bed and the best of friends out of it.

"Or are you heading home to fret about your sister and Evan seeing each other?"

"No." But she couldn't make her voice as convincing as she wanted it to sound. "Evan and I are over. It was inevitable that he would start dating someone."

She just wished it hadn't happened with her sister.

Ming lifted on her tiptoes and kissed Jason. "Thanks for a lovely afternoon." The spontaneous encounter had knocked her off plan. She needed to regroup and reassess. Aiming for casual, she teased, "Let me know if you feel like doing it again soon."

He grabbed her hand and pushed it against his zipper. "I feel like doing it again now." His husky voice and the intense light in his eyes made her pulse rocket. "Stay for dinner. I promise you won't leave hungry."

The heat of him melted some of the chill from her heart. She leaned into his chest, her fingers curving around the bulge in his pants. He fisted his hand in her hair while his mouth slanted over hers, spiriting her into a passionate whirlwind. This afternoon she'd awakened to his hunger. The power of it set her senses ablaze. She was helpless against the appeal of his hard body as he eased her back against the counter. On the verge of surrendering to the mind-blasting pleasure of Jason's fingers sliding up her naked thigh, his earlier words came back to her.

One of these days you'll find the right guy for you.

She broke off the kiss. Gasping air into her lungs, she put her hands on Jason's chest and ducked her head before he could claim her lips again.

"I've really got to go," she told him, applying enough pressure to assure him she wasn't going to be swayed by his sensual persuasion.

His hands fell away. As hot as he'd been a moment ago, when he stepped back and plunged his hands into his pockets, his blue eyes were as cool and reflective as a mountain lake.

"How about we have dinner tomorrow?" she cajoled, swamped by anxiety. As perfect as it was to feel his arms tighten around her, she needed to sort out her chaotic emotions before she saw him again.

"Sure." Short and terse.

"Here?"

"If you want." He gave her a stiff nod.

She put her hand on his cheek, offered him a glimpse of her longing. "I want very much."

His eyes softened. "Five o'clock." He pressed a kiss into her palm. "Don't be late."

Seven

Ming parked her car near the bleachers that overlooked the curvy two-mile track. Like most of the raceways where Jason spent his weekends, this one was in the middle of nowhere. At least it was only a couple of hours out of Houston. Some of the tracks he raced at were hundreds of miles away.

Jason was going to be surprised to see her. It had been six or seven years since she'd last seen him race. The sport didn't appeal to her. Noisy. Dusty. Monotonous. She suspected the thrills came from driving, not watching.

So, what was she doing here?

If she was acting like Jason's "friend," she would have remained in Houston and spent her Saturday shopping or boating with college classmates. Driving over a hundred miles to sit on a metal seat in the blazing-hot sun fell put her smack dab in the middle of "girlfriend" territory. Would Jason see it as such? Ming took a seat in the stands despite the suspicion that coming here had been a colossal mistake.

The portion of track in front of her was a half-mile drag

strip that allowed the cars to reach over a hundred miles an hour before they had to power down to make the almost ninety-degree turn at the end. The roar was impressive as twenty-five high-performance engines raced past Ming.

Despite the speed at which they traveled, Jason's Mustang was easy to spot. Galaxy-blue. When he'd been working on the car, he'd asked for her opinion and she'd chosen the color, amused that she'd matched his car to his eyes without him catching on.

In seconds, the cars roared off, leaving Ming baking in the hot sun. With her backside sore from the hard bench and her emotions a jumble, it was official. She was definitely exhibiting "girlfriend" behavior.

And why? Because the past week with Jason had been amazing. It wasn't just the sex. It was the intimacy. They'd talked for hours. Laughed. She'd discovered a whole new Jason. Tender and romantic. Naughty and creative. She'd trusted him to take her places she'd never been, and it was addictive.

Which is why she'd packed a bag and decided to surprise him. A single day without Jason had made her restless and unable to concentrate.

Ming stood. This had been a mistake. She wasn't Jason's girlfriend. She had no business inserting herself into his guy time because she was feeling lonely and out of sorts. She would just drive back to Houston and he'd never know how close she'd come to making a complete fool of herself over him.

The cars roared up the straightaway toward her once again. From past experience at these sorts of events, she knew the mornings were devoted to warm-up laps. The real races would begin in the afternoon.

She glanced at the cars as they approached. Jason's number twenty-two was in the middle of the pack of twenty-five cars. He usually saved his best driving for the race. As the Mustang reached the end of the straightaway and began to slow down for the sharp turn, something happened. Instead of curving to the left, the Mustang veered to the right, hit the wall and spun.

Her lungs were ready to burst as she willed the cars racing behind him to steer around the wreckage so Jason didn't suffer any additional impact. Once the track cleared, his pit crew and a dozen others hurried to the car. Dread encased Ming's feet in concrete as she plunged down the stairs to the eight-foot-high chain-link fence that barred her from the track.

With no way of getting to Jason, she was forced to stand by and wait for some sign that he was okay. She gripped the metal, barely registering the ache in her fingers. The front of the Mustang was a crumpled mess. Ming tried to remind herself that the car had been constructed to keep the driver safe during these sorts of crashes, but her emotions, already in a state of chaos before the crash, convinced her he would never hear how she really felt about him.

"Wow, that was some crash," said a male voice beside her. "Worst I've seen in a year."

Ming turned all her fear and angst on the skinny kid with the baseball cap who'd come up next to her. "Do you work here?"

"Ah, yeah." His eyes widened as the full brunt of her emotions hit him.

"I need to get down there, right now."

"You're really not supposed—"

"Right now!"

"Sure. Sure." He backed up a step. "Follow me." He led her to a gate that opened onto the track. "Be careful."

But she was already on the track, pelting toward Jason's ruined car without any thought to her own safety. Because of the dozen or so men gathered around the car, she couldn't see Jason. Wielding her elbows and voice like blunt instruments, she worked her way to the front of the crowd in time to see Jason pulled through the car's window.

He was cursing as he emerged, but he was alive. Relief slammed into her. She stopped five feet from the car and watched him shake off the hands that reached for him when he swayed. He limped toward the crumpled hood, favoring his left knee.

Jason pulled off his helmet. "Damn it, there's the end of my season."

It could have been the end of him. Ming sucked in a breath as a sharp pain lanced through her chest. It was just typical of him to worry about his race car instead of himself. Didn't he realize what losing him would do to the people who loved him?

She stepped up and grabbed his helmet from his hands, but she lost the ability to speak as his eyes swung her way. She loved him. And not like a friend. As a man she wanted to claim for her own.

"Ming?" Dazed, he stared at her as if she'd appeared in a puff of smoke. "What are you doing here?"

"I came to watch you race." She gripped his helmet hard enough to crack it. "I saw you crash. Are you okay?"

"My shoulder's sore and I think I did something to my knee, but other than that, I'm great." His lips twisted as he grimaced. "My car's another thing entirely."

Who cares about your stupid car? Shock made her want to shout at him, but her chest was so tight she had only enough air for a whisper. "You really scared me."

"Jason, we need to get the car off the track." Gus Stover and his brother had been part of Jason's racing team for the past ten years. They'd modified and repaired all his race cars. Ming had lost track of how many hours she and Jason had spent at the man's shop.

"That's a good idea," she said.

"A little help?" Jason suggested after his first attempt at putting weight on his injured knee didn't go so well.

Ming slipped her arm around his waist and began moving in the direction of the pit area. As his body heat began to warm her, Ming realized she was shaking from reaction. As soon as they reached a safe distance from the track, Jason stopped walking and turned her to face him.

"You're trembling. Are you okay?"

Not even close. She loved him. And had for a long time. Only she'd been too scared to admit it to herself.

"I should be asking you that question," she said, placing her palm against his unshaven cheek, savoring the rasp of his beard against her skin. She wanted to wrap her arms around him and never let go. "You should get checked out."

"I'm just a little banged up, that's all."

"Jason, that was a bad crash." A man in his late-thirties with prematurely graying hair approached as they neared the area where the trailers were parked. He wore a maroon racing suit and carried his helmet under one arm. "You okay?"

"Any crash you can walk away from is a good one." Leave it to Jason to make light of something as disastrous as what she'd just witnessed. "Ming, this is Jim Pearce. He's the current points leader in the Texas region."

"And likely to remain on top now that Jason's done for the season."

Is that all these men thought about? Ming's temper began to simmer again until she saw the worry the other driver was masking with his big, confident grin and his posturing. It could have been any of these guys. Accidents didn't happen a lot, but they were part of racing. This was only Jason's second in the entire sixteen years he'd been racing. If something had gone wrong on another area of the track, he might have ended up driving safely onto the shoulder or he could have taken out a half dozen other cars.

"Nice to meet you." As she shook Jim's hand, some of the tension in her muscles eased. "Were you on the track when it happened?"

"No. I'm driving in the second warm-up lap." His broad smile dimmed. "Any idea what happened, Jason? From where I stood it looked like something gave on the right side."

"Felt like the right front strut rod. We recently installed Agent 47 suspension and might have adjusted a little too aggressively on the front-end alignment settings."

Jim nodded, his expression solemn. "Tough break."

"I'll have the rest of the year to get her rebuilt and be back better than ever in January."

Ming contemplated the hours Jason and the Stover brothers would have to put in to make that happen and let her breath out in a long, slow sigh. If she'd seen little of him in the past few months since he'd made it his goal to take the overall points trophy, she'd see even less of him with a car to completely rebuild.

"The Stovers will get her all fixed up for you." Jim thumped Jason on the back. "They're tops."

As Jim spoke, Jason's car was towed up to the trailer. The men in question jumped off the truck and began unfastening the car.

"What happened?" Jason called.

"The strut rod pulled away from the helm end," Gus Stover replied. "I told you the setting was wrong."

His brother, Kris, shook his head. "It's so messed up from the crash, we won't know for sure until we get her on the lift."

"Do you guys need help?" Jason called.

Jim waved and headed off. Ming understood his exit. When Jason and the Stovers started talking cars, no one else on the planet existed. She stared at the ruined car and the group of men who'd gathered to check out the damage. It would be the talk of the track for the rest of the weekend.

"Looks like you've got your hands full," she told Jason, nodding toward a trio of racers approaching them. "I'm going to get out of here so you can focus on the Mustang."

"Wait." He caught her hand, laced his fingers through hers. "Stick around."

She melted beneath the heat of his smile. "I'll just be in the way."

"I need you—"

"Jason, that was some crash," the man in the middle said.

Ming figured she'd take advantage of the interruption to escape, but Jason refused to relinquish her hand. A warm feeling set up shop in her midsection as Jason introduced her. She'd expected once his buddies surrounded him, he wouldn't care if she took off.

But after an hour she lost all willpower to do so. Despite the attention Jason received from his fellow competitors, he never once forgot that she was there. Accustomed to how focused Jason became at the track, Ming was caught off guard by the way he looped his arm around her waist and included her in the conversations.

By the time the car had been packed up later that afternoon, she was congratulating herself on her decision to come. They sat side by side on the tailgate of his truck. Jason balanced an icepack on his injured knee. Despite the heat, she was leaning against his side, enjoying the lean strength of his body.

"What prompted you to come to the track today?" he questioned, gaze fixed on the Stover brothers as they argued over how long it would take them to get the car ready to race once more.

The anxiety that had gripped her before his crash reappeared and she shrugged to ease her sudden tension. "It's been a long time since I've seen you race." She eyed the busted-up Mustang. "And now it's going to be even longer."

"So it seems."

"Sorry your season ended like this. Are you heading back tonight?"

"Gus and Kris are. I've got a hotel room in town. I think I'll ice my knee and drive back tomorrow."

She waited a beat, hoping he'd ask her to stay, but no invitation was forthcoming. "Want company?"

"In the shape I'm in, I'd be no use to you." He shot her a wry smile.

As his friend, she shouldn't feel rejected, but after accepting that she was in love with him and being treated like his girlfriend all day, she'd expected he'd want her to stick around. She recognized that he was in obvious pain and needed a restful night's sleep. A friend would put his welfare above her own desires.

"Then I guess I'll head back to Houston." She kissed him on the cheek and hopped off the tailgate.

He caught her wrist as her feet hit the ground. "I'm really glad you came today."

It wasn't fair the way he turned the sex appeal on and off whenever it suited him. Ming braced herself against the lure of his sincere eyes and enticing smile. Had she fallen in love with his charm? If so, could she go back to being just his friend once they stopped sleeping together?

She hoped so. Otherwise she'd spend the rest of her life in love with a man who would never let himself love her back.

"Supporting each other is what friends are for," she said, stepping between his thighs and taking his face in her hands.

Slowly she brought her lips to his, releasing all her pent-up emotions into the kiss. Her longing for what she could never have. Her fear over his brush with serious injury. And pure, sizzling desire.

After the briefest of hesitations, he matched her passion, fingers digging into her back as he fed off her mouth. The kiss exhilarated her. Everything about being with Jason made her happy. Smiling, she sucked his lower lip into her mouth and rubbed her breasts against his chest. As soon as she heard his soft groan, she released him.

Stepping back, Ming surveyed her handiwork. From the dazed look in his eyes, the flush darkening his cheekbones and the unsteady rush of breath in and out of his lungs, the kiss had packed a wallop. A quick glance below his belt assured her he would spend a significant portion of the evening thinking about her. Good.

"Careful on the drive home tomorrow," she murmured, wiping her fingertip across her damp lips in deliberate seduction. "Call me when you get back."

And with a saucy wave, she headed for her car.

The sixty-eight-foot cruiser Jason had borrowed for Max's bachelor party barely rocked as it encountered the wake of the large powerboat that had sped across their bow seconds earlier. Cigar in one hand, thirty-year-old Scotch in the other, Jason tracked the boat skimming the dark waters of Galveston Bay from upstairs in the open-air lounge. On the opposite rail, Max's brothers were discussing their wives and upcoming fatherhood.

"She's due tomorrow," Nathan Case muttered, tapping his cell phone on his knee. "I told her it was crazy for me come to this bachelor party, but she was determined to go out dancing with Missy, Rachel and her friends."

Nathan's aggrieved tone found a sympathetic audience in Jason. Why were women so calm about the whole pregnancy-and-giving-birth thing? Ming wasn't even pregnant, and Jason was already experiencing a little coil of tension deep in his gut. He hadn't considered how connected he'd feel to her when he'd agreed to father her baby. Nor could he stop wondering if he'd feel as invested if they'd done it her way and he'd never made love to her.

"I'm sure Emma knows what she's doing," Sebastian Case said. Older than Max and Nathan by a few years, Sebastian was every inch the confident CEO of a multimillion-dollar corporation.

"I think she's hoping the dancing will get her contractions started." Nathan stared at the cell phone as if he could make it ring by sheer willpower. "What if her water breaks on the dance floor?"

"Then she'll call and you can meet her at the hospital." Sebastian's soothing tones were having little effect on his agitated half brother.

"You're barely into your second trimester," Nathan scoffed. "Let's see how rational you are when Missy hasn't been able to see her feet for a month, doesn't sleep more than a few hours a night and can't go ten minutes without finding a bathroom."

Sebastian's eyes grew distant for a few seconds as if he was imagining his wife in the final weeks before she was due.

"Do you know what you're having?" Even as Jason asked Nathan the question, he realized that a month ago he never would have thought to inquire.

"A boy."

Jason lifted his Scotch in a salute. "Congratulations."

"You're single, aren't you?" Sebastian regarded him like a curiosity. "How come you're not downstairs with Max and his buddies slipping fives into the ladies' G-strings instead of hanging out with a couple old family men?"

Because he wasn't feeling particularly single at the moment.

Jason raised the cigar. "Charlie said no smoking in the salon."

"But you're missing the entertainment." Nathan gestured toward the stairs that led below.

Some entertainment. Max might be downstairs with a half dozen of their single friends and a couple of exotic dancers someone had hired, but Jason doubted his best friend was having any fun. Max wasn't interested in any woman except Rachel.

Up until two weeks ago Jason hadn't understood what had come over his friend. Now, after making love with Ming, his craving for her had taken on a life of its own. His body stirred at the memory of her dripping wet in his kitchen. The way her white blouse had clung to her breasts, the fabric rendered sheer by the water. He wasn't sure what he would have done if she'd denied him then. Gotten down on his knees and begged?

Probably.

Jason shoved aside the unsettling thought and smirked at Nathan. "When you're free to hit a strip club any night of the week, the novelty wears off. You two are the ones who should be downstairs."

"Why's that?" Nathan asked.

"I just assumed with your wives being pregnant…"

Sebastian and Nathan exchanged amused looks.

"That our sex lives are nonexistent?" Sebastian proposed. He looked as relaxed and contented as a lion after consuming an antelope.

The last emotion pestering Jason should be envy. He was the free one. Unfettered by emotional ties that had the potential to do damage. Unhampered by monotony, he was free to sleep with a different woman every night of the week if he wanted. He had no demanding female complicating his days.

"Did it surprise either of you that Max is getting married?" Jason asked.

Sebastian swirled the Scotch in his glass. "If I had to wager which one of you two would be getting married first, I would have bet on you."

"Me?" Jason shook his head in bafflement.

"I thought for sure you and Ming would end up together."

"We're close friends, nothing more."

Sebastian's thumb traced the rim of his glass. "Yeah, it took me a long time to see what was waiting right under my nose, too."

Rather than sputter out halfhearted denials, Jason downed the last of his drink and stubbed out the cigar. The Scotch scorched a trail from his throat to his chest.

"I think I'll go see if Max needs rescuing."

They'd been cruising around Galveston for a little over an hour and Jason was as itchy to get off the boat as Nathan. He wanted to blame his restlessness on the fact that the bachelor party meant a week from now his relationship with his best buddy would officially go on the back burner as Max took on his new responsibilities as a husband. But Max had been splitting his loyalty for three months now, and Jason was accustomed to being an afterthought.

No, Jason's edginess was due to the fact that like Nathan, Sebastian and Max, he'd rather be with the woman he was intimate with than whooping it up with a bunch of single guys and a couple of strippers.

What had happened to him?

Only two weeks ago he'd been moaning that Max had abandoned him for a woman. And here he was caught in the same gossamer net, pining for a particular female's companionship.

He met Max on the narrow stairs that connected the salon level to the upper deck, where Nathan and Sebastian remained.

"Feel like getting off this boat and hooking up with our ladies?" Max proposed. "I just heard from Rachel. They've had their fill of the club."

Jason glanced at his watch. "It's only ten-thirty. This is your bachelor party. You're supposed to get wild one last time before you're forever leg-shackled to one woman."

"I'd rather get wild with the woman I'm going to be leg-shackled to." Max punched Jason in the shoulder. "Besides, I don't see you downstairs getting a lap dance from either Candy or Angel."

"Charlie said no smoking in the salon. I went upstairs to enjoy one of the excellent cigars Nathan brought."

"And this has nothing to do with the warning you gave Ming tonight?"

Jason cursed. "You heard that?"

"I thought it was cute."

"Jackass." Swearing at Max was a lot easier than asking himself why he'd felt compelled to tell Ming to behave herself and not break any hearts at the club. He'd only been half joking. The thought of her contemplating romance with another man aroused some uncomfortably volatile emotions.

"And it doesn't look like she listened to you."

"What makes you say that?"

Max showed him his cell phone screen. "I think this guy's pretty close to having his heart broken."

Jason swallowed a growl but could do nothing about the frown that pulled his brows together when he glimpsed the photo of Ming dancing with some guy. Irritation fired in his gut. It wasn't the fact that Ming had her head thrown back and her arms above her head that set Jason off. It was the way the guy had his hands inches from her hips and looked prepared to go where no one but Jason belonged.

Max laughed. "I know Nathan and Sebastian are ready to leave. Are you up for taking the launch in and leaving the boys to play by themselves?"

Damn right he was. "This is your party. Where you go, I go."

Eight

Rachel Lansing, bride-to-be, laughed at the photo her fiancé sent her from his bachelor party. Sitting across the limo from her, Ming wasn't the least bit amused. Her stomach had been churning for the last half an hour, ever since she'd found out that there were exotic dancers on the boat. And her anxiety hadn't been relieved when she hadn't spotted Jason amongst the half dozen men egging on the strippers. He could be standing behind Max, out of the camera's range.

She had no business feeling insecure and suspicious. It wasn't as if she had a claim to Jason beyond their oh-so-satisfying baby-making activities. Problem was, she couldn't disconnect her emotions. And heaven knew she'd been trying to. Telling herself over and over that it was just sex. Incredibly hot, passionate, mind-blowing sex, but not the act of two people in love. Just a couple of friends trying to make a baby together.

Whom was she kidding?

For the past two weeks, she'd been deliriously happy and anxiety-ridden by turn. Every time he slid inside her it was a struggle not to confide that she was falling in love with him, and her strength was fading fast. Already she was rationalizing why she and Jason should continue to be intimate long after she was pregnant.

It was only a matter of time before she confessed what she truly wanted for her future and he'd sit her down and remind her why they'd made love in the first place. Then things would get awkward and they'd start to avoid each other. No. Better to stay silent and keep Jason as her best friend rather than lose him forever.

"If you're worried about Jason, Max texted me and said he's on the upper deck with Nathan and Sebastian." Rachel gave Ming a reassuring smile.

"I'm not worried about Jason," Ming hastily assured her as she sagged in relief. She mustered a smile. "No need for me to be. We're just friends. Have been for years."

A fact Rachel knew perfectly well since the four of them had gone out numerous times since she and Max had gotten engaged. Ming had no idea why she had to keep reminding people that she and Jason were not an item.

"Jason's a great guy."

"He sure is." Ming saw where this was going and knew she had to cut Rachel off. "But he's the sort of guy who isn't ever going to fall in love and get married."

Rachel cocked her head. "Funny, that's what I thought about Max and yet he lost his favorite car to Jason over a wager that he wouldn't get married." Her blue eyes sparkled with mischief. "What's to say Jason won't change his mind, too?"

Ming smiled back, but she knew there was a big difference between the two men. Max hadn't found his father trying to kill himself because he was so despondent over the loss of his wife and daughter. And after getting the scoop about how Max and Rachel had met five years earlier, Ming suspected the reason Max had been so down on love and marriage was that he'd already lost his heart to the woman of his dreams.

"I don't know," Ming said. "He's pretty set in his ways. Besides, you weren't around when my engagement to Jason's brother ended. It made me realize that I'm happier on my own."

"Yeah, before Max, I was where you are. All I have to say is that things change." Rachel nudged her chin toward her soon-to-be-sisters-in-law. "Ask either of those two if they believed love was ever going to happen for them. I'll bet both of them felt the way you do right now."

Ming glanced toward the back of the limo, where Emma, nine months pregnant and due any second, and Missy, four months pregnant and radiant, sat side by side, laughing. They had it all. Gorgeous, devoted men. Babies on the way. Envy twisted in Ming's heart.

She sighed. "I'm really happy for all of you, but love doesn't find everyone."

"If you keep an open mind it does."

The big diamond on Rachel's hand sparkled in the low light. Ming stared at it while her fingers combed her hair into three sections. As she braided, she mused that being in love was easy when you were a week away from pairing your engagement ring with a wedding band. Not that she begrudged any of the Case women their happiness. Each one had gone through a lot before finding bliss, none more so than Rachel. But Ming just wasn't in a place where she could feel optimistic about her own chances.

She was in love with a man who refused to let his guard down and allow anyone in, much less her. Because she couldn't get over her feelings for Jason, she'd already lost one man and almost made the biggest mistake of her life. And as of late, she was concerned that having Jason father her child was going to lead to more heartache in the future.

Ming mulled Rachel's words during the second half of the forty-five-minute drive from downtown Houston to the Galveston marina where the men would be waiting. Maybe she should have gone home from the club like Rachel's sister, Hailey, instead of heading out to meet up with Jason. They'd made no plans to rendezvous tonight. She was starting to feel foolish for chasing him all the way out here.

If Jason decided to stay on the yacht with the bachelor party instead of motoring back to the dock on the launch with Max and his brothers, would she be the odd girl out when the couples reunited? Her chest tightened. Ming closed her eyes as they entered the marina parking lot.

The limo came to a stop. Ming heard the door open and the low rumble of male voices. She couldn't make her eyes open. Couldn't face the sight of the three couples embracing while she sat alone and unwanted.

"What's the matter? Did all the dancing wear you out?"

Her eyes flew open at Jason's question. His head and shoulders filled the limo's open door. Heart pounding in delight, she clasped her hands in her lap to keep from throwing herself into his arms. That was not how friends greeted each other.

"I'm not used to having that much fun." She scooted along the seat to the door, accepting Jason's hand as her foot touched the pavement. His familiar cologne mingled with the faint scent of cigars. She wanted to nuzzle her nose into his neck and breathe him in. "How about you? Did you enjoy your strippers?"

"They preferred to be called exotic dancers." He showed her his phone. "They weren't nearly as interesting as this performance."

She gasped at the picture of herself dancing. How had Jason gotten ahold of it? So much for what happens at a bachelorette party stays at a bachelorette party. She eyed the women behind Jason. Who'd ratted her out?

"It was just some guy who asked me to dance," she protested.

"Just some guy?" He kept his voice low, but there was no denying the edge in his tone. "He has his hands all over you."

She enlarged the image, telling herself she was imagining the possessive glint in Jason's eye. "No he doesn't. And if this had been taken five seconds later you would have seen me shove him away and walk off the dance floor."

"Whoa, sounds like a lover's spat to me," Rachel crowed.

Confused by the sparks snapping in Jason's blue eyes, Ming realized a semicircle of couples had formed five feet away. Six faces wore various shades of amusement as they looked on.

Jason composed his expression and turned to face the group. "Not a lover's spat."

"Just a concerned friend," Max intoned, his voice dripping with dry humor.

"Come on, we're all family here." Sebastian's gesture encompassed the whole group. "You can admit to us that you're involved."

"We're not involved." Ming found her voice.

"We're friends," Jason said. "We look out for each other."

"I disagree," Max declared, slapping Jason on the back. "I think you've finally realized that your best friend is the best thing that ever happened to you." He glanced around to see if the others agreed with him. "About time, too."

"You don't know what you're talking about." Jason was making no attempt to laugh off his friend's ribbing.

Ming flinched at Jason's resolute expression. If he'd considered moving beyond friendship, Max would be the one he'd confide in. With Jason's adamant denial, Ming had to face the fact that she was an idiot to hope that Jason might one day realize they belonged together.

"Oh!"

All eyes turned to Emma, who'd bent over, her hand pressed to her round belly.

"Are you okay?" Nathan put his arm around her waist. "Was it a contraction?"

"I don't know. I don't think so." Emma clutched his arm. "Maybe you'd better take me home."

To Ming's delight everyone's focus had shifted to Emma. What might or might not be going on between Ming and Jason was immediately forgotten. As Nathan opened the passenger door for Emma, she looked straight at Ming and winked. Restraining a grin, Ming wondered how many times Emma had used the baby in such a fashion.

"Alone at last," Jason said, drawing her attention back to him. "And the night is still young."

Ming shivered beneath his intense scrutiny. "What did you have in mind?"

"I was thinking maybe you could show me your dancing skills in private."

"Funny. I was thinking maybe you could give me a demonstration of the techniques you picked up from your strippers tonight."

"Exotic dancers," he corrected, opening the passenger door on his car so she could get in. "And I didn't pick up anything because I wasn't anywhere near their dancing."

The last of her tension melted away. "I don't believe you," she teased, keeping her relief hidden. She leaned against his chest and peered up at him from beneath her lashes. "Not so long ago you wouldn't have missed that kind of action."

"Not so long ago I didn't have all the woman I could handle waiting for me at home."

"Except I wasn't waiting for you." Lifting up on tiptoe, she pressed her lips to his and then dropped into the passenger seat.

"No, you were out on the town breaking hearts."

The door shut before her retort reached Jason's ears. Was he really annoyed with her for dancing with someone? Joy flared and died. She was reading too much into it.

"So, where are we heading?" Jason turned out of the marina parking lot and got them headed toward the bridge off the island.

"You may take me home. After all that heartbreaking, my feet are sore." She tried to smile, but her heart hurt too much. "Besides, Muffin is home alone."

"Where's Lily?"

"Supposedly she's out of town this weekend."

"Why supposedly?"

"Because I drove past Evan's house and her car was in the driveway."

"You drove past Evan's house?" Jason shifted his gaze off the road long enough for her to glimpse his alarm. "Are you sure that was a good idea?"

She bristled at his disapproving tone. "I was curious if my sister had lied to me."

"You were curious." He echoed her words doubtfully. "Not bothered that they're together?"

"No."

"Because you two were engaged not that long ago and now he's dating your sister."

"Why do you keep bringing that up?" Her escalating annoyance came through loud and clear. She'd known Jason too long not to recognize when he was picking a fight.

"I want you to be honest with yourself so this doesn't blow up between you and your sister in the future."

"You don't think I'm being honest with myself?"

"Your sister is dating the man who broke off your engagement two weeks before the wedding. I think you're trying too hard to be okay with it."

He took her hand and she was both soothed and frustrated by his touch. No matter what else was happening between them, Jason was her best friend. He knew her better than anyone. Sometimes better than she knew herself. But the warm press of his fingers reminded her that while he could act like a bossy boyfriend, she came up against his defenses every time she started to play girlfriend.

"Right now I've got my hands full with you." Ming wasn't exaggerating on that score. "Can we talk about something else? Please?"

The last thing she wanted was to argue with him when her hopes for the evening required them to be in perfect accord.

"Sure." Even though he agreed, she could tell he wasn't happy about dropping the subject. "What's on your mind?"

"I have the house to myself until late Sunday if you want to hang out."

"That sounds like an invitation to sleep over."

She made a sandwich of his hand and hers and ignored the anxious flutter in her stomach.

"Maybe it is." Flirting with Jason was fun and dangerous. It was easy to lose track of reality and venture into that tricky romantic place best avoided if she wanted their friendship to remain uncomplicated.

Or maybe she was too far gone for things to ever be the same between them again.

The part of her that wanted them to be more than just friends was growing stronger every day. It was a crazy hope, but she couldn't stop the longing any more than Jason could get past his reluctance to fall in love.

"Ming…"

She heard the wariness in his voice and held up her hand. They hadn't spent a single night together this whole week. That had been a mutual decision based on practicality. Neither of them wanted Evan to pop over late one night and find her at Jason's house. Plus, Lily had been in Houston all week and would have noticed if Ming had stayed out all night.

But she was dying to spend the night snuggled in his arms. And the craving had nothing to do with making a baby.

"Forget I said anything." Her breath leaked out in a long, slow sigh. "This past week has been fun. But you and I both know I'm past my prime fertility cycle. It makes no sense for us to keep getting together when I'm either pregnant or I'm too late in my cycle to try."

"Wait. Is that what this week has been about?" He sounded put out. "You're just using me to make a baby?"

Startled, she opened her mouth to deny his claim and realized he was trying to restore their conversation to a lighter note by teasing her. "And a few weeks from now we'll see if you've succeeded." She faked a yawn. "I guess I'm more tired than I thought."

Jason nodded and turned the topic to the bachelorette party. Ming jumped on board, glad to leave behind the tricky path they'd been treading.

By the time he turned the car into her driveway, she'd man-handled her fledgling daydreams about turning their casual sex into something more. She was prepared to say good-night and head alone to her door.

"Call me tomorrow," he told her. "I've got to go shopping for Max and Rachel's wedding present."

"You haven't done that yet?"

"I've been waiting for you to offer to do it for me."

Robbed of a dreamy night in Jason's arms and the pleasure of waking up with him in the morning, Ming let her irritation shine. "You said no about going in on a gift together, so you're on your own."

"Please come shopping with me." He put on his most appealing smile. "You know I'm hopeless when it comes to department stores."

How could she say no when she'd already agreed to help him before they'd started sleeping together. It wasn't fair to treat him differently just because she felt differently toward him.

"What time tomorrow?"

"Eleven? I want to be home to watch the Oilers at three."

"Fine," she grumbled.

With disappointment of her own weighing her down, she plodded up the stairs and let herself into her house. Muffin met her in the foyer. She danced around on her back legs, wringing a small smile from Ming's stiff lips.

"I'll take you out back in a second." She waited by the front door long enough to see Jason's headlights retreating down her driveway, then headed toward the French doors that led from her great room to the pool deck.

While the Yorkie investigated the bushes at the back of her property, Ming sat down on a lounge chair and sought the tranquility often gained by sitting beside her turquoise kidney-shaped pool. She revisited her earlier statement to Jason. It made no sense for them to rendezvous each afternoon and have the best sex ever if all they were trying to do was make a baby. Only, if she was completely honest with herself, she'd admit that a baby isn't all she wanted from Jason.

Her body ached with unfulfilled desire. Her soul longed to find the rhythm of Jason's heart beating in time with hers. From the beginning she'd been right to worry that getting intimate with her best friend was going to lead her into trouble. But temptation could be avoided for only so long when all you've ever wanted gets presented to you on a silver platter. She would just have to learn to live with the consequences.

Finding nothing of interest in the shrubbery, Muffin came back to the pool, her nails clicking on the concrete. Sympathetic to her mistress's somber mood, the terrier jumped onto Ming's lap and nuzzled her nose beneath Ming's hand.

"I am such an idiot," she told the dog, rubbing Muffin's head.

"That makes two of us."

Jason hadn't even gotten out of Ming's neighborhood before he'd realized what a huge error he'd made. In fact, he hadn't made it to the end of her block. But just because he'd figured it out didn't mean returning to Ming wasn't an even bigger mistake. So, he'd sat at a stop sign for five minutes, listening to Rascal Flatts and wondering when his life had gotten so damned complicated. Then, he'd turned the car around, used his key to get into Ming's house and found her by the pool.

"Let's go upstairs," he said. "We need to talk."

Ming pulled her hair over one shoulder and began to braid it. "We can't talk here?"

Was she being deliberately stubborn or pretending to be dense?

Without answering, he pivoted on his heel and walked toward the house. Muffin caught up as he crossed the threshold. Behind him, Ming's heels clicked on the concrete as she rushed after him.

"Jason." She sounded breathless and uncertain. She'd stopped in the middle of her kitchen and called after him as he got to the stairs. "Why did you come back?"

Since talking had only created problems between them earlier, he was determined to leave conversation for later. Taking the stairs two at a time, he reached her bedroom in record time. Unfastening his cuffs, he gazed around the room. He hadn't been up here since he'd helped her paint the walls a rich beige. The dark wood furniture, rich chestnut bedspread and touches of sage green gave the room the sophisticated, expensive look of a five-star hotel suite.

"Jason?"

He'd had enough time to unfasten his shirt buttons. Now, as she entered the room, he let the shirt drop off his shoulders and draped it over a chair. "Get undressed."

While she stared at him in confounded silence, he took Muffin from her numb fingers and deposited the dog in the hallway.

"She always sleeps with me," Ming protested as he shut the door.

"Not tonight."

"Well, I suppose she can sleep on Lily's bed. Jason, what's gotten into you?"

His pants joined his shirt on the chair. With only his boxer briefs keeping his erection contained, he set his hands on his hips.

"You and I have been best friends for a long time." Since she wasn't making any effort to slip out of that provocative halter-top and insanely short skirt, he prowled toward her. "And

I've shared with you some of the hardest things I've ever had to go through."

She made no attempt to stop him as he tugged at the thin ribbon holding up her top, but she did grab at the fabric as it began to fall away from her breasts. "If you're saying I know you better than anyone except Max, I'd agree."

Jason hooked his fingers in the top and pulled it from her fingers, exposing her small, perfect breasts. His lungs had to work hard to draw in the air he required. Damn it. They had been together all week, but he still couldn't get over how gorgeous she was, or how much he wanted to mark her as his own.

"Then it seems as if I'm doing our friendship an injustice by not telling you what's going on in my head at the moment."

Reaching around her, he slid down the zipper on her skirt and lowered it past her hips. When it hit the floor, she stepped out of it.

"And what's that?"

Jason crossed his arms over his chest and stared into her eyes. It was nearly impossible to keep his attention from wandering over her mostly naked body. Standing before him in only a black lace thong and four-inch black sandals, she was an exotic feast for the eyes.

"I didn't like seeing you dancing with another man."

The challenge in her almond-shaped eyes faded at his admission. Raw hope rushed in to replace it. "You didn't?"

Jason ground his teeth. He should have been able to contain the truth from her. That he'd admitted to such possessive feelings meant a crack had developed in the well-constructed wall around his heart. But a couple weaknesses in the structure didn't mean he had to demolish the whole thing. He needed to get over his annoyance at her harmless interaction with some random guy. Besides, wasn't he the one who'd initially encouraged her that there was someone out there for her?

To hell with that.

Taking her hand, he drew her toward the bed.

"Not one bit." It reminded him too much of how he'd lost her to his brother. "It looked like you were having fun without me."

"Did it, now?" His confession had restored her confidence. With a sexy smile, she coasted her nails from his chest to the waistband of his underwear. "I guess I was imagining that you were otherwise occupied with your exotic dancers. Did they get you all revved up? Is that why we're here right now?"

He snorted. "The only woman I have any interest in seeing out of her clothes is you."

Heaven help him—it was true. He hadn't even looked at another woman since this business of her wanting to become a mother came up. No. It had been longer than that. Since his brother had broken off their engagement.

The level of desire he felt for her had been eating at him since last weekend when she'd kissed him good-bye at the track. That had been one hell of a parting and if his knee hadn't been so banged up he never would've let her walk away.

This isn't what he'd expected when he'd proposed making love rather than using a clinic to help her conceive. He'd figured his craving for her was strictly physical. That it would wane after his curiosity was satisfied.

What he was feeling right now threatened to alter the temper of their friendship. He should slow things down or stop altogether. Yeah. That had worked great for him earlier. He'd dropped her off and then raced back before he'd gotten more than a couple blocks away.

Frustrated with himself, he didn't give her smug smile a chance to do more than bud before picking her up and dumping her unceremoniously on the bed. Without giving her a chance to recover, he removed first one then the other of her shoes. As each one hit the floor, her expression evolved from surprised to anticipatory.

It drove him crazy how much he wanted her. Every cell in his body ached with need. Nothing in his life had ever compared. Was it knowing her inside and out that made the sexual chemistry between them stronger than normal?

While he snagged her panties and slid them down her pale thighs, she lifted her arms above her head, surrendering herself to his hot gaze. The vision of her splayed across the bed, awaiting his possession, stirred a tremor in his muscles. His hands shook as he dropped his underwear to the floor.

Any thought of taking things slow vanished as she reached for him. A curse made its way past his lips as her confident strokes brought him dangerously close to release.

"Stop." His harsh command sounded desperate.

He took her wrist in a firm grip and pinned it above her head. Lowering himself into the cradle between her thighs, he paused before sliding into her. Two things were eating at him tonight: that picture of her dancing and her preoccupation with Evan and Lily's romance.

"You're mine." The words rumbled out of him like a vow. Claiming her physically hadn't rattled his safe bachelor existence, but this was a whole different story.

"Jason." She waggled her hips and arched her back, trying to entice him to join with her, but although it was close to killing him, he stayed still.

"Say it." With his hands keeping her wrists trapped over her head and his body pinning hers to the mattress, she was at his mercy.

"I can't…" Her eyes went wide with dismay. "…say that."

"Why not?" He rocked against her, giving her a taste of what she wanted.

A groan erupted past her parted lips. She watched him through half-closed eyes. "Because…"

"Say it," he insisted. "And I'll give you what you want."

Her chest rose and fell in shallow, agitated breaths. "What I want…"

He lowered his head and drew circles around her breast with his tongue. His willpower had never felt so strong before. When she'd started dating his brother, he'd been in the worst sort of hell. Deep in his soul, Jason had always believed if she'd choose anyone, she'd pick him. They were best friends. Confidants. Soul mates. And buried where neither had ventured before prom night was a flammable sexual chemistry.

Both of them had been afraid at the power of what existed between them, but he'd been the most vocal about not ruining their friendship. So vocal, in fact, she'd turned to his brother before Jason had had time to come to his senses.

"Mine." He growled the word against her breast as his mouth closed around her nipple.

She gasped at the strong pull of his mouth. "Yours." She wrapped her thighs around his hips. "All yours."

"All mine."

Satisfied, he plunged into her. Locked together, he released her wrists and kissed her hard and deep, sealing her pledge before whisking them both into unheard of pleasure.

Nine

Moving slowly, her legs wobbly from the previous night's exertions, Ming crossed her bedroom to the door, where Muffin scratched and whined. She let the Yorkie in, dipping to catch the small dog before Muffin could charge across the room and disturb the large, naked man sprawled facedown in the middle of the tangled sheets.

"Let's take you outside," she murmured into the terrier's silky coat, tearing her gaze away from Jason.

Still shaken from their passionate lovemaking the night before, she carefully navigated the stairs and headed for the back door. After cuddling against Jason's warm skin all night, the seventy-degree temperature at 7:00 a.m. made her shiver. She should have wrapped more than a silky lavender robe around her naked body.

While Muffin ran off to do her business and investigate the yard for intruders, Ming plopped down on the same lounge she'd occupied the night before and opened her mind to the thoughts she'd held at bay all night long.

What the hell had possessed Jason to demand that she admit to belonging to him? Battling goose bumps, she rubbed at her arms. The morning air brushed her overheated skin but couldn't cool the fire raging inside her. *His.* Even now the word made her muscles tremble and her insides whirl like a leaf caught in a vortex. She dropped her face into her hands and fought the urge to laugh or weep. He made her crazy. First his vow to never fall in love and never get married. Now this.

Muffin barked at something, and Ming looked up to find her dog digging beneath one of the bushes. Normally she'd stop the terrier. Today, she simply watched the destruction happen.

What was she supposed to make of Jason's territorial posturing last night? Why had he reacted so strongly to the inflammatory photo? She'd understand it if they were dating. Then he'd have the right to be angry, to be driven to put his mark on her.

Jason hadn't changed his mind about falling in love. Initially last night he hadn't even wanted to spend the night. So, what had brought him back? It was just about the great sex, right? It wasn't really fair to say he only wanted her body, but he'd shown no interest in accepting her heart.

Ming called Muffin back to the house and started a pot of coffee. She wasn't sure if Jason intended to head home right away or if he would linger. She hoped he'd stick around. She had visions of eating her famous cinnamon raisin bread French toast and drinking coffee while they devoured the Sunday paper. As the day warmed they could go for a swim in her pool. She'd always wanted to make love in the water. Or they could laze in bed. It would be incredible to devote an entire day to hanging out.

Afternoon and evening sex had been more fun and recreational than serious and committed. Ming could pretend they were just enjoying the whole friends-with-benefits experience. Sleeping wrapped in each other's arms had transported them into "relationship" territory. Not to mention the damage done to her emotional equilibrium when Jason admitted to feeling jealous.

She brought logic to bear on last night's events, and squashed the giddy delight bubbling in her heart. She'd strayed a long way from the reason she was in this mess in the first place. Becoming a mom. Time to put things with Jason in perspective. They were friends. Physical intimacy might be messing with their heads at this point, but once she was pregnant all sex would cease and their relationship would go back to being casual and supportive.

"I started coffee," she announced as she stepped into her bedroom and stopped dead at the sight of the person standing by her dresser.

Lily dropped something into Ming's jewelry box and smiled at her sister. "I borrowed your earrings. I hope that's okay."

"It's fine." From her sister, Ming's gaze went straight to the bed and found it empty. Relief shot through her, making her knees wobble. "I thought you were in Portland."

"I came back early."

Since Lily wasn't asking the questions Ming was expecting, she could only assume her sister hadn't run into Jason. "Ah, great."

Where the hell was he?

"How come Jason's car is in the driveway?" Lily asked.

Ming hovered near the doorway to the hall, hoping her sister would take the hint and come with her. "Max's bachelor party was last night. He had a little too much to drink so I drove him home and brought the car back here."

Too late she realized she could have just said he was staying in the guest room. That would at least have given him a reason to be in the house at this hour. Now he was trapped until she could get away from Lily.

Her sister wandered toward the window seat. "I put an offer in on a house."

"Really?" What was going to happen between her and Evan if she was moving away?

Lily plopped down on the cushioned seat and set a pillow in her lap, looking as if she was settling in for a long talk. "You sound surprised."

Ming shot a glance toward the short hallway, flanked by walk-in closets, that led to her bathroom. He had to be in there.

"I guess I was hoping you'd change your mind." She pulled underwear and clothes from her dresser and headed toward the bathroom. "Let me get dressed and then you can tell me all about it."

Her heart thumped vigorously as she shut the bathroom door behind her.

Jason leaned, fully clothed and completely at ease, against her vanity. "I thought you said she was spending the weekend with Evan."

"She was." Ming frowned when she realized he clearly thought she'd lied to him. "Something must have happened. She seems upset." Ming dropped her robe and stepped into her clothes, ignoring his appreciative leer. "Did she see you?"

"I was already dressed and in here when I heard you start talking." Readying himself to make a break for it.

"You were leaving?" Ming shouldn't have been surprised. Last night was over. Time to return their relationship to an easygoing, friendly place. Hadn't she been thinking the same thing? So why did her stomach feel like she'd been eating lead? "Did you intend to say goodbye or just sneak out while I was downstairs with Muffin?"

"Don't be like that."

"Why don't you tell me exactly how I'm supposed to be."

Not wanting her sister to get suspicious, Ming returned to the bedroom without waiting for Jason's answer. Her heart ached, but she refused to give in to the pain pressing on the edge of her consciousness.

Since Lily seemed entrenched in Ming's room, she sat beside her sister on the window seat. To catch Lily's attention, Ming put her hand on her knee. "Tell me about the house."

"House?"

"The one you put an offer in on."

"It's just a house."

"How many bedrooms does it have?"

"Two."

Curious about whatever was plaguing her sister, Ming was distracted by Muffin investigating her way toward the bathroom. "Nice neighborhood?"

"I think I made a huge mistake."

"Then withdraw the offer." She held her breath and waited for the terrier to discover Jason and erupt in a fit of barking.

"Not the house. The guy I've been seeing."

With an effort, Ming returned her full attention to her sister. "I thought you were just friends."

"It's gone a little further than that."

"You're sleeping together?" She asked the question even though she suspected the answer was yes.

Although the fact that her ex-fiancé was dating her sister continued to cause Ming minor discomfort, she was relieved that her strongest emotion was concern for her sister. When jealousy had been her first reaction to the realization that Lily and Evan were involved, Ming had worried that she was turning into a horrible person.

And lately, on top of all her other worries, Ming had started to wonder how Evan would feel if he found out about her and Jason. Something that might just happen if they weren't more careful.

"Yes. But it's not going anywhere."

Ming's gaze strayed to the bathroom door she hadn't completely closed. Muffin had yet to return to the bedroom. What was going on in there?

"Because you don't want it to?"

"I guess."

That tight spot near Ming's heart eased a little. "You guess? Or you know?" When her sister didn't answer, Ming asked, "Do you love him?"

"Yes." Lily stared at her hands.

Ming's throat locked up, but she couldn't blame her sister for falling for Evan. The heart rarely followed a logical path. And it must be tearing Lily apart to love the man who'd almost married her sister.

"I think you should forget about moving to Portland."

"It's not that simple."

Time to rattle her sister's cage a little. "Funny, Jason told me Evan's dating someone, but his situation is complicated, too." Ming gave a little laugh. "Maybe you two should get together and compare notes."

"I suppose we should." Lily gave her a listless smile.

Was there a way for Ming to give her sister permission to have a future with Evan? "You know, I was glad to hear that Evan had found someone and was moving on with his life."

"Really?" Despite Lily's skeptical tone, her eyes were bright with hope.

"He and I weren't mean to be. It happens."

"That's not how you felt six months ago."

"I'm not going to say that having him break off our engagement two weeks before the wedding was any fun, but I'd much rather find out then that we weren't meant to be than to get married and try to make it work only to invest years and then have it fail."

Ming's cell phone rang. She plucked it off the nightstand and answered it before Lily could respond.

"If I'm going to be stuck in your bathroom all morning, I'd love a cup of coffee and some breakfast."

"Good morning to you, too," she said, mouthing Jason's name to Lily. "How are you feeling?"

"Tired and a little aroused after checking out the lingerie drying in your shower."

"Sure, I can return your car." She rolled her eyes in Lily's direction. "Are you sober enough to drive me back here?"

"I guess I don't need to ask what excuse you gave your sister for why my car is at your house." Jason's voice was dry.

"I can follow you over there and bring you back," Lily offered.

"Hey, Lily just offered to follow me to your house so I can drop the car off."

"You're a diabolical woman, do you know that?"

"I'm sure it's no bother," Ming continued. "We're going to make breakfast first though."

"French toast with cinnamon raisin bread?"

"That's right. Your favorite." And one of the few things Ming enjoyed cooking. "Pity you aren't here this morning to have some."

"Just remember that paybacks can be painful."

"Oh, I didn't realize you needed your car to go shopping for Max and Rachel's wedding gift this morning. I'll see you in fifteen minutes." She disconnected the call. "I'm going to run Jason's car over to him and then I'll come back and we can make breakfast."

"Are you sure you don't want me to drive you over there?"

"No. I think the fresh air will do him some good."

She escorted Lily to the kitchen and settled her with a cup of green tea before she headed for the front door. Jason was already in the car when she arrived.

"Lily sounded upset this morning," Jason said. "Did I hear her say she put an offer on a house?"

"In Portland. But she seems really unsure what her next move is." She drove the car into the parking lot of a coffee shop in her neighborhood and cut the engine. "She's conflicted about going." She paused a beat. "Did you know they're sleeping together?"

Silence filled the space between her and Jason. Ming listened to the engine tick as it cooled, her thoughts whirling.

"Yes." He was keeping things from her. That wasn't like him.

"And you didn't tell me?"

"I didn't want you to get upset."

"I'm not upset." Not about Lily and Evan.

Last weekend she'd discovered what she really wanted from Jason. It wasn't a baby she would raise on her own. It was a husband who'd adore her and a bunch of kids to smother with love. She was never going to have that with him, and accepting that was tearing her apart.

"Well, you don't look happy."

"I want my sister to stay in Houston." The air inside the car became stuffy and uncomfortable. Ming shoved open the door and got out.

By the time she reached the Camaro's front bumper, Jason was there, waiting for her. "What happens if Lily and Evan decide to get married?"

Then she would be happy for them. "Evan and I were over six months ago."

"You and Evan broke up six months ago."

"Are you insinuating I'm not over him?"

"Are you?" He set his hand on his hips, preventing her from going past.

"Don't be ridiculous." She tried to sidestep him, but he shifted to keep her blocked. "Would I be sleeping with you if I was hung up on your brother?"

"If I recall, the only reason you're sleeping with me is so you can get pregnant."

She should be relieved that he believed that. It alleviated the need for complicated explanations. But what had happened between them meant so much more to her than that she couldn't stay silent.

"Perhaps you need to think a little harder about that first afternoon in your kitchen." She leaned into his body, surrendering her pride. "Did it seem as if all I was interested in was getting pregnant?"

"Ming." The guilt in his voice wrenched at her. He cupped her shoulders, the pressure comforting, reassuring.

She stared at his chest and hoped he wouldn't see the tears burning her eyes. "I knew it was going to get weird between us."

"It's not weird."

"It's weird." She circled around him and headed to the passenger side. "I should probably get back."

For a moment Jason stood where she'd left him. Ming watched him through the windshield, appreciating the solitude to collect her thoughts. It was her fault that their relationship was strained. If she'd just stuck with her plan and used a clinic to get pregnant, she wouldn't have developed a craving for a man who could never be hers. And she wouldn't feel miserable for opening herself to love.

As Jason slid behind the wheel, she composed her expression and gathered breath to tell him that they needed to go back to being friends without benefits, but he spoke first.

"Last night." He gripped the steering wheel hard and stared straight ahead. "I crossed the line."

To fill the silence that followed his confession, Jason started the Camaro, but for once the car's powerful engine didn't make him smile.

"Because of what you wanted me to say." Ming sounded irritated and unsure.

"Yes." Moments earlier, he'd considered skirting the truth, but she'd been honest about her feelings toward him.

"Then why did you?"

Making love to her had flipped a switch, lighting him up like a damned merry-go-round. He kept circling, his thoughts stuck on the same track, going nowhere. He liked that they were lovers. At the same time he relied on the stability of their friendship. So far he'd been operating under the belief that he could have it both ways. Now, his emotions were getting away from him. Logic told him lust and love were equally powerful and easily confused. But he'd begun to question his determination to never fall in love.

"Because it's how I feel."

"And that's a bad thing?"

He saw the hope in her eyes and winced. "It isn't bad. We've been close a long time. My feelings for you are strong." How did he explain himself without hurting her? "I just don't want to lead you on and I think that's what I did."

"Lead me on?" She frowned. "By making me think that you wanted to move beyond friendship into something…more?" Her fingers curled into fists. "I'm not sure who I'm more angry with right now. You or me."

If he'd known for sure that sleeping with her would complicate their friendship, would he have suggested it? Yes. Even now he wasn't ready to go back to the way things were. He had so much he longed to explore with Ming.

If he was honest with himself, he'd admit that helping her get pregnant was no longer his primary motivation for continuing their intimate relationship. He'd have to weigh a deeper connection with Ming against the risk that someday one of them would wake up and realize they were better off as friends. If emotions were uneven, their friendship might not survive.

"Do you want to stop?" He threw the car into gear and backed out of the parking spot.

"You're making me responsible for what does or doesn't happen between us? How is that fair?"

Below her even tone was a cry for help. Jason wanted to pull her close and kiss away her frown. If today they agreed to go back to the way things were, how long would he struggle against the impulse to touch her the way a lover would?

"I want you to be happy," he told her. "Whatever that takes."

"Do you?" She looked skeptical. "Last night I wanted you to stay, but you got all tense and uncomfortable." A deep breath helped get her voice back under control. When she continued, she seemed calmer. "I know it's because you have a rule against spending the night with the women you see."

"But I spent last night with you."

"And this morning you couldn't put your clothes on fast enough." She stared at him hard enough to leave marks on his face.

"So what do you want from me?"

"I'd like to know what you want. Are we just friends? Are we lovers?"

Last night he'd denied their relationship to his friends and felt resistance to her suggestion that he stay the night with her. As happy as Max and his brothers were to be in love with three terrific women, Jason could only wonder about future heartbreak when he looked at the couples. He didn't want to live with the threat of loss hanging over his head, but he couldn't deny that the thought of Ming with another man bugged him. So did her dismay that Evan had fallen in love with Lily.

"I won't deny that I think we're good together," he said. "But you know how I feel about falling in love."

"You don't want to do it."

"Can't we just keep enjoying what we have? You know I'll always be there for you. The chemistry between us is terrific. Soon you'll be busy being a mom and won't have time for me." He turned the car into her driveway and braked but didn't put the Camaro in Park. He needed to get away, to mull over what they'd talked about today. "Let's have dinner tomorrow."

"I can't. It's the Moon Festival. Lily and I are having dinner with our parents tomorrow. I'm going to tell them my decision to have a baby, and she's going to tell them she's moving." Ming sighed. "We promised to be there to support each other."

Jason didn't envy either sister. Helen Campbell was a stubborn, opinionated woman who believed she knew what was best for her daughters. At times, Ming had almost collapsed beneath the weight of her mother's hopes and dreams for her.

She hadn't talked about it, but Jason knew the breakup of her engagement had been a major blow to Ming's mother.

"What about Tuesday?" he suggested.

She put her hand on the door release, poised to flee. "It's going to be a hectic week with Max and Rachel's wedding next weekend."

Jason felt a sense of loss, but he didn't understand why. He and Ming were still friends. Nothing about that had changed.

"What's wrong?"

"It's too much to go into now."

Jason caught her arm as she pushed the door open and prevented her from leaving. "Wait."

Ming made him act in ways that weren't part of his normal behavior. Today, for example. He'd hid in her bathroom for fifteen minutes while she and her sister had occupied the bedroom. There wasn't another woman on earth he would have done that for.

Now he was poised to do something he'd avoided with every other woman he'd been involved with. "You're obviously upset. Tell me what's going on."

"I feel like an idiot." Her voice was thick with misery. "These last couple weeks with you have been fantastic and I've started thinking of us as a couple."

Her admission didn't come as a complete shock. Occasionally over the years he too had considered what they'd be like together. She knew him better than anyone. He'd shared with her things no one else knew. His father's suicide attempt. How he'd initially been reluctant to join the family business. The fact that the last words he'd spoken to his little sister before she'd died had been angry ones.

"Even knowing how you feel about love—" She stopped speaking and blinked rapidly. "Turns out I'm just like all those other women you've dated. No, I'm worse, because I knew better and let myself believe…" Her chin dropped toward her chest. "Forget it, okay?"

Was she saying she was in love with him? Her declaration hit him like a speeding truck. He froze, unable to think, unsure what to feel. Had she lost her mind? Knowing he wasn't built for lasting relationships, she'd opened herself up to heartbreak?

And where did they go from here? He couldn't ask her to continue as they'd been these past two weeks. But he'd never had such mind-blowing chemistry with anyone before, and he was a selfish bastard who wasn't going to give that up without a fight.

"Saturday night, after the wedding, we're going to head to my house and talk. We'll figure out together what to do." But he suspected the future was already written. "Okay?"

"There's nothing to figure out." She slid out of the car. "We're friends. Nothing is going to change that."

But as he watched her head toward her front door, Jason knew in the space of a few minutes, everything had changed.

Ten

Ming caught her sister wiping sweaty palms on her denim-clad thighs as she stopped the car in front of her parents' house and killed the engine. She put her hand over Lily's and squeezed in sympathy.

"We'll be okay if we stick together."

Arm in arm they headed up the front walk. No matter what their opinions were about each other's decisions, Ming knew they'd always form a unified front when it came to their mother.

Before they reached the front door, it opened and a harlequin Great Dane loped past the handsome sixty-year-old man who'd appeared in the threshold.

"Dizzy, you leave that poor puppy alone," Patrick Campbell yelled, but his words went unheeded as Dane and Ming's Yorkie raced around the large front yard.

"Dad, Muffin's fine." In fact, the terrier could run circles around the large dog and dash in for a quick nip then be gone again before Dizzy knew what hit her. "Let them run off a little energy."

After surviving rib-bruising hugs from their father, Ming and Lily captured the two dogs and brought them inside. The house smelled like heaven, and Ming suspected her mother had spent the entire weekend preparing her favorite dishes as well as the special moon cakes.

Ming sat down at her parents' dining table and wondered how the thing didn't collapse under the weight of all the food. She'd thought herself too nervous to eat, but once her plate was heaped with a sample of everything, she began eating with relish. Lily's appetite didn't match hers. She spent most of the meal staring at her plate and stabbing her fork into the food.

After dinner, they took their moon cakes outside to eat beneath the full moon while their mother told them the story of how the festival came to be.

"The Mongolians ruled China during the Yuan Dynasty," Helen Campbell would begin, her voice slipping naturally into storytelling rhythm. She was a professor at the University of Houston, teaching Chinese studies, language and literature. "The former leaders from the Sung dynasty wanted the foreigners gone, but all plans to rebel were discovered and stopped. Knowing that the Moon Festival was drawing near, the rebel leaders ordered moon cakes to be baked with messages inside, outlining the attack. On the night of the Moon Festival, the rebels successfully overthrew the government. What followed was the establishment of the Ming dynasty. Today, we eat the moon cakes to remember."

No matter how often she heard the tale, Ming never grew tired of it. As a first-generation American on her mother's side, Ming appreciated the culture that had raised her mother. Although as children both Ming and Lily had fought their mother's attempts to keep them attached to their Chinese roots, by the time Ming graduated from college, she'd become fascinated with China's history.

She'd visited China over a dozen times when Helen had returned to Shanghai, where her family still lived. Despite growing up with both English and Chinese spoken in the house, Ming had never been fluent in Mandarin. Thankfully her Chinese relatives were bilingual. She couldn't wait to introduce her own son or daughter to her Chinese family.

Stuffed to the point where it was difficult to breathe, Ming sipped jasmine tea and watched her sister lick sweet bean paste off her fingers. The sight blended with a hundred other memories of family and made her smile.

"I've decided to have a baby," she blurted out.

After her parents exchanged a look, Helen set aside her plate as if preparing to do battle.

"By yourself?"

Ming glanced toward Lily, who'd begun collecting plates. Ever since they'd been old enough to reach the sink, it was understood that their mother would cook and the girls would clean up.

"It's not the way I dreamed of it happening, but yes. By myself."

"I know how much you want children, but have you thought everything through?" Her mother's lips had thinned out of existence.

"Helen, you know she can handle anything she sets her mind to," her father said, ever supportive.

Ming leaned forward in her chair and looked from one parent to the other. "I'm not saying it's going to be a picnic, but I'm ready to be a mom."

"A single mom?" Helen persisted.

"Yes."

"You know my thoughts on this matter." Her mother's gaze grew keen. "How does Jason feel about what you're doing?"

Ming stared at the flowers that surrounded her parents' patio. "He's happy for me."

"He's a good man," her mother said, her expression as tranquil as Ming had ever seen it. "Are you hoping he'll help you?"

"I don't expect him to." Ming wondered if her mother truly

understood that she was doing this on her own. "He's busy with his own life."

Patrick smiled. "I remember how he was with your cousins. He's good with kids. I always thought he'd make a great father."

"You did?" The conversation had taken on a surreal quality for Ming. Since he never intended to get married, she'd never pictured Jason as a father. But now that her dad had mentioned it, she could see Jason relishing the role.

"What I meant about Jason…is he going to help you make the baby?" her mother interjected.

"Why would you think that?"

"You two are close. It seems logical."

Ming kept her panic off her face, but it wasn't easy. "It would mess up our friendship."

"Why? I'm assuming you're going to use a clinic."

This was all hitting a little too close to home. "That's what I figured I'd do." Until Jason came up with the crazy notion of them sleeping together. "I'd better give Lily a hand in the kitchen."

Leaving her parents to process what she'd told them, Ming sidled up to her sister.

"I shared my news." She started rinsing off dishes and stacking them in the dishwasher. "Are you going to tell them you've bought a house in Portland?"

"I changed my mind."

"About the house or Portland?"

"Both."

"Evan must be thrilled." The words slipped out before Ming realized what she was saying. In her defense, she was rattled by her father's speculation about Jason being a great dad and her mother's guess that he was going to help her get pregnant.

"Evan?" Lily tried to sound confused rather than anxious, but her voice buckled beneath the weight of her dismay. "Why would Evan care?"

The cat was out of the bag. Might as well clear the air. "Because you two are dating?"

Ming was aware that keeping a secret about her and Jason while unveiling her sister's love life was the most hypocritical thing she'd done in months.

"Don't be ridiculous."

"Evan admitted it to Jason and he told me."

"I'm sorry I didn't tell you."

"Don't you think you should have?" She didn't want to resent Lily for finding happiness.

"I honestly didn't think anything was going to happen between us."

"Happen between you when, exactly?" Ming's frustration with her own love life was bubbling to the surface. "The first time you went out? The first time he kissed you?"

"I don't want this to come between us."

"Me, either." But at the moment it was, and Ming couldn't dismiss the resentment rumbling through her.

"But I don't want to break up with him." Beneath Lily's determined expression was worry. "I can't."

Shock zipped across Ming's nerve endings. "Is it that serious?"

"He told me he loves me."

"Wow." Ming exhaled in surprise.

It had taken almost a year of dating for Evan to admit such deep feelings for her. As reality smacked her in the face, she was overcome by the urge to curl into a ball and cry her eyes out. What was wrong with her? She wasn't in love with Evan. She'd made her peace with their breakup. Why couldn't she be happy for her sister?

"Do you feel the same?"

Lily wouldn't meet her gaze. "I do."

"How long have you been going out?"

"A couple months. I know it seems fast, but I've been interested in Evan since high school. Until recently, I had no idea he saw me as anything more than your baby sister. Emphasis on the *baby*." Lily's lips curved down at the corners.

There was a five-year difference in their ages. That gap would have seemed less daunting as Lily moved into her twenties and became a successful career woman.

"I guess he's seen the real you at last."

"I want you to know, I never meant for this to happen."

"Of course you didn't."

"It's just that no one has control over who they fall in love with."

What Lily had just told Ming should have relieved her own guilt over what she and Jason were doing. Evan had moved on. He was in love. If he ever discovered what was happening between her and Jason, Evan should be completely accepting. After all, he'd fallen for her sister. All Ming was doing was getting pregnant with Jason's child. It wasn't as if they were heading down the path to blissfully-ever-after.

Struck by the disparity between the perfect happiness of every couple she knew and the failure of her own love life, Ming's heart ached. Her throat closed as misery battered her. Her longing for a man she could never have and her inability to let him go trapped her. It wasn't enough to have Jason as her best friend. She wanted to claim him as her lover and the man she'd spend the rest of her life committed to. On her current path, Ming wasn't sure how she was ever going to find her way out of her discontent, but since she wasn't the sort who moldered in self-pity, she'd better figure it out.

Unwinding in her office after a hectic day of appointments, Ming rechecked the calendar where she'd been keeping track of her fertility cycle for the past few months. According to her history, her period should have started today.

Excitement raced through her. She could be pregnant. For a second she lost the ability to breathe. Was she ready for this? Months of dreaming and hoping for this moment hadn't prepared her for the reality of the change in her life between one heartbeat and the next.

Ming stared at her stomach. Did Jason's child grow inside her? She caught herself mid-thought. This was her child. Not hers and Jason's. She had to stop fooling herself that they were going to be a family. She and Jason were best friends who wanted very different things out of life. They were not a couple. Never would be.

"Are you still here?" Terry leaned into the room and flashed his big white smile. "I thought you had a wedding rehearsal to get to."

Ming nodded. "I'm leaving in ten minutes. The church is only a couple miles away."

"Did those numbers I gave you make you feel better or worse?"

Earlier in the week Terry had opened up the practice's books so she could see all that went into the running of the business. Although part of her curriculum at dental school had involved business courses that would help her if she ever decided to open her own practice, her college days were years behind her.

"I looked them over, but until I get Jason to walk me through everything, I'm still feeling overwhelmed."

"Understandable. Let me know if you have any questions."

After Terry left, Ming grabbed her purse and headed for the door. Until five minutes ago, she'd been looking forward to this weekend. Max and Rachel were a solid couple.

Thanks to Susan Case, Max's mother, the wedding promised to be a magical event. After both Nathan and Sebastian had skipped formal ceremonies—Nathan marrying Emma on a Saint Martin beach and Sebastian opting for an impromptu Las Vegas elopement—Susan had threatened Max with bodily harm if she was denied this last chance at a traditional wedding.

Most brides would have balked at so much input from their future mother-in-law, but Rachel's only family was her sister, and Ming thought the busy employment agency owner appreciated some of the day-to-day details being handled by Max's mother.

When Ming arrived at the church, most of the wedding party was already there. She set her purse in the last pew and let her gaze travel up the aisle to where the minister was speaking to Max. As the best man, Jason stood beside him, listening intently. Ming's breath caught at the sight of him clad in a well-cut dove-gray suit, white shirt and pale green tie.

Was she pregnant? It took effort to keep her fingers from wandering to her abdomen. When she'd embarked on this journey three weeks ago, she'd expected that achieving her goal would bring her great joy and confidence. Joy was there, but it was shadowed by anxiety and doubt.

She wasn't second-guessing her decision to become a mom, but she no longer wanted to do it alone. Jason would freak out if he discovered how much she wanted them to be a real family. Husband, wife, baby. But that's not how he'd visualized his future, and she had no right to be disappointed that they wanted different things.

As if her troubled thoughts had reached out to him, Jason glanced in her direction. When their eyes met, some of her angst eased. Raising his eyebrows, he shot her a crooked grin. Years of experience gave her insight into exactly what he was thinking.

Max couldn't be talked out of this crazy event.

She pursed her lips and shook her head.

You shouldn't even try. He's found his perfect mate.

"Are you two doing that communicating-without-words thing again?"

Ming hadn't noticed Missy stop beside her. With her red hair and hazel eyes, Sebastian's wife wore chocolate brown better than anyone Ming had ever met.

"I guess we are." Ming's gaze returned to Jason.

"Have you ever thought about getting together? I know you

were engaged to his brother and all, but it seems as if you'd be perfect for each other."

"Not likely." Ming had a hard time summoning energy to repeat the tired old excuses. She was stuck in a rut where Jason was concerned, with no clue how to get out. "We're complete opposites."

"No one is more different than Sebastian and I." Missy grinned. "It can be a lot of fun."

Based on the redhead's saucy smile, Ming had little trouble imagining just how much fun the newlyweds were having. She sighed. Prior conversations with Emma, Missy and Rachel had shown her that not everyone's road to romance was straight and trouble-free, but Ming knew she wasn't even on a road with Jason. More like a faint deer trail through the woods.

"He doesn't want to fall in love."

Missy surveyed the three Case men as the minister guided them into position near the front of the church. "So make him."

Rather than lecture Missy about how hopeless it was to try changing Jason's mind about love and marriage, Ming clamped her lips together and forced a smile. What good would it do to argue with a newly married woman who was a poster child for happily ever after?

As she practiced her walk up the aisle on Nathan's arm, she had a hard time focusing on the minister's instructions. Casting surreptitious glances at Jason, standing handsome and confident beside Max, she fought against despair as she realized there would never be a day when the man she loved waited for her at the front of the church. She would never wear an elegant gown of white satin and shimmering pearls and speak the words that would bind them together forever.

"And then you separate, each going to your place." The minister signaled to the organist. "Here the music changes to signal that the bride is on her way."

While everyone watched Rachel float up the aisle, her happiness making it appear as if her feet didn't touch the ground,

Ming stared down at the floor and fought against the tightness in her throat. She was going to drive herself mad pining for an ending that could never be.

Twenty minutes later, the wedding party was dismissed. They trooped back down the aisle, two-by-two, with Nathan and Ming bringing up the rear.

"How's Emma doing?" she asked. Nathan's wife was five days past her due date.

"She's miserable." Nathan obviously shared his wife's discomfort. "Can't wait for the baby to come."

"I didn't see her. Is she here tonight?"

"No." A muscle jumped in his jaw. "I told her to stay home and rest up. Tomorrow is going to be a long day." Nathan scowled. "But if I know her, she's working on the last of her orders to get them done before the baby arrives."

Nathan's wife made some of the most unique and beautiful jewelry Ming had ever seen. Missy's wedding set was one of her designs. From what Jason had told her, Max and Rachel's wedding rings had been created by Emma as well.

"I'm worried she's not going to slow down even after the baby arrives," Nathan continued, looking both exasperated and concerned. "She needs to take better care of herself."

"Why, when she has you to take care of her?"

Nathan gave her a wry grin. "I suppose you're right. See you tomorrow."

Smiling thoughtfully at Nathan's eagerness to get home to his wife, Ming went to fetch her purse. When she straightened, she discovered Jason standing beside her. He slipped his fingers through hers and squeezed gently.

"I missed you this week."

Shivers danced along her spine at his earnest tone. "I missed you, too."

More than she cared to admit. Although they'd talked every day on the phone, their conversations had revolved around the dental practice financials and other safe topics. They hadn't discussed that Evan was in love with Lily, and Ming wasn't sure Jason even knew.

"I don't suppose I could talk you into coming home with me tonight," he murmured, drawing her after the departing couples.

Although tempted by his offer, she shook her head. "I promised Lily we'd hang out, and I have an early appointment to get my hair and makeup done tomorrow." She didn't like making up excuses, but after what she'd started to suspect earlier, the only thing she wanted to do was take the pregnancy test she'd bought on the way to the church and see if it was positive. "Tomorrow after the reception."

Jason walked her to her car and held her door while she got behind the wheel. He lingered with his hand on the door. The silence between them grew heavy with expectation. Ming's heart slowed. The crease between his brows told her that something troubled him.

She was the first to break the silence. "Evan's in love with Lily and she's decided to stay in Houston."

"How do you feel about that?"

"I'm thrilled."

"I mean about how Evan feels about her."

With a determined smile she shook her head. "I'm happy for him and Lily."

"You're really okay with it?"

"I'm going to be a mom. That's what I'm truly excited about. That's where I need to put all my energy."

"Because you know I'm here if you want to talk."

"Really, I'm fine," she said, keeping her voice bright and untroubled. She knew he was just being a good friend, but she couldn't stop herself from wishing his concern originated in the same sort of love she felt for him. "See you at the restaurant."

He stared at her for a long moment more before stepping back. "Save me a seat."

And with that, he closed her car door.

Eleven

Jason had never been so glad to be done with an evening. Sitting beside Ming while toast after toast had been made to the bride and groom, he'd never felt more alone. But it's what he wanted. A lifetime with no attachments. No worries that he'd ever become so despondent over losing a woman that he'd want to kill himself.

Logic and years of distance told him that his father had been in an extremely dark place after the death of his wife and daughter. But there was no reason to believe that Jason would ever suffer such a devastating loss. And if he did, wasn't he strong enough to keep from sinking into a hole and never coming out?

And yet, his reaction to that photo of her dancing hadn't exactly been rational. Neither had the way he'd demanded that she declare herself to be his. Oh, he'd claimed that he didn't want to lead her on. The truth was he was deathly afraid of losing her.

"I'm heading home." Ming leaned her shoulder against his.

Her breath brushed his neck with intoxicating results. "Can you walk me to my car?"

"I think I'll leave, too." The evening was winding down. Sebastian and Missy had already departed.

As soon as they cleared the front door, he took her hand. Funny how such a simple act brought him so much contentment. "Did I mention you look beautiful tonight?"

"Thank you." Only her eyes smiled at him. The rest of her features were frozen into somber lines.

They reached her car and before he could open her door, she put a hand on his arm. "This is probably not the best place for this…" She glanced around, gathered a breath and met his gaze. Despite her tension, joy glittered in her dark eyes. "I'm pregnant."

Her declaration crushed the air from his lungs. He'd been expecting it, but somehow now, knowing his child grew inside her, he was beyond thrilled.

"You're sure?"

"As sure as an early pregnancy test can be." Her fingers bit into his arm. "I took one at the restaurant." She laughed unsteadily. "How crazy is that? I couldn't even wait until I got home."

Jason wrapped his arms around her and held her against him. A baby. Their baby. He wanted to rush back into the restaurant and tell everyone. They were going to be parents. Reality penetrated his giddy mood. Except she didn't want to share the truth with anyone. She intended to raise the child on her own.

"I'm glad you couldn't wait," he told her, his words muffled against her hair. "It's wonderful news."

From chest to thigh, her long, lean body was aligned with his. How many months until holding her like this he'd feel only her rounded stomach? Or would he even get to snuggle with her, her head resting on his shoulder, her arms locked around his waist?

"Of course, this means…"

Knowing what was coming next, Jason growled. "You aren't seriously going to break up with me on the eve of Max's wedding."

"Break up with you?" She tipped her head back so he could see her smile, but she wouldn't meet his eyes. "That would require us to be dating."

But they'd sworn never to explore that path. Would they miss a chance to discover that the real reason they were such good friends was because they were meant to be together?

Are you listening to yourself? What happened to swearing you'd never fall in love?

Frustrated by conflicting desires, Jason's hold on her tightened. Her breath hitched as he lowered his head and claimed her mouth. Heat flared between them. Their tongues tangled while delicious sensations licked at his nerves. She was an endless feast for his senses. A balm for his soul. She challenged him and made him a better person. And now she was pregnant with his child. They could be happy together.

All he needed to do was let her in.

He broke off the kiss and dragged his lips across her cheek. What existed in his heart was hers alone. He could tell her and change everything.

The silence between them lengthened. Finally, Ming slid her palm down his heaving chest and stepped back.

"We're just good friends who happen to be sleeping together until one of us got pregnant," she said, her wry tone at odds with her somber eyes.

"And we promised nothing would get in the way of our friendship."

She sagged against him. "And it won't."

"Not ever."

Our baby.

Jason's words the previous night had given her goose bumps.

Almost ten hours later, Ming rubbed her arms as the sensation lingered.

My baby.

She tried to infuse the declaration with conviction, but couldn't summon the strength. Not surprising, when his claim filled her with unbridled joy. It was impossible to be practical when her heart was singing and she felt lighter than air.

Pulling into the parking lot of the salon Susan Case had selected based on their excellent reputation, Ming spent a few minutes channeling her jubilation over her baby news into happiness for Rachel and Max. It was easy to do.

The bride was glowing as she chatted with her sister, Hailey, Missy and Susan. As Ming joined the group, two stylists took charge of Rachel, escorting her to a chair near the back. Rachel had let her hair grow out from the boyish cut she'd had when Ming had first met her. For her wedding look, the stylists pinned big loops of curls all over her head and attached tiny white flowers throughout.

Unaccustomed to being the center of attention, Rachel endured being fussed over with good grace. Watching the stylists in action, Ming was certain the bride would be delighted with the results.

Because all the bridesmaids had long hair, they were styled with the front pulled away from their face and soft waves cascading down their back. When the four girls lined up so Susan could take a photo, the resulting picture was feminine and romantic.

Although the wedding wasn't until four, the photographer was expecting them to be at the church, dressed in their wedding finery by one. With a hundred or more photos to smile for and because she'd skipped breakfast after oversleeping, Ming decided she'd better grab lunch before heading to the church. She ended up being the last to arrive.

Naturally her gaze went straight to Jason. Standing halfway up the aisle, model-gorgeous in his tuxedo, he looked far

more stressed than the groom. Ming flashed back to their senior prom, the evening that marked the beginning of the end
for her in terms of experiencing true love.

"Don't you look handsome," she exclaimed as he drew near.
Over the years, she'd had a lot of practice pretending she wasn't
infatuated with him. That stood her in good stead as Jason
pulled her into his arms for a friendly hug.

"You smell as edible as you look," he murmured. "Whose
insane idea was it to dress you in a color that made me want
to devour you?"

For her fall wedding, Rachel had chosen strapless empire
waist bridesmaid dresses in muted apple green. They would all
be carrying bouquets of orange, yellow and fuchsia.

Ming quivered as his sexy voice rumbled through her. If he
kept staring at her with hungry eyes, she might not be able to
wait until after the wedding to get him alone. A deep breath
helped Ming master her wayward desires. Today was about
Max and Rachel.

"Susan proposed apple green, I believe." She'd never know
how she kept her tone even given the chaos of her emotions.

"Remind me to thank her later."

Ming restrained a foolish giggle and pushed him to arm's
length so she could check him out in turn. "I like you in a tux.
You should wear one more often."

"If I'd known how much fun it would be to have you undress
me with your eyes, I would have done so sooner."

"I'm not undressing—" She stopped the flow of words as
Emma waddled within earshot.

"I don't know what you're planning on taking off," the very
pregnant woman said as she stepped into the pew beside them,
"but I'd start with what he's wearing."

Jason smirked at Ming, but there was no time for her to respond because the photographer's assistant called for the wedding party to come to the front of the church.

With everyone in a festive mood, it was easy for Ming to

laugh and joke with the rest of Rachel's attendants as they posed for one photo after another. The photographer's strict schedule allowed little time for her to dwell on how close she'd been to her own wedding six months earlier, or whether she might be in this same position months from now if things continued to progress with Lily and Evan.

But in the half-hour lull between photos and ceremony, she had more than enough quiet to contemplate what might have been for her and to ponder the future.

She kept apart from the rest of the group, not wanting her bout of melancholy to mar the bride and groom's perfect day. Shortly before the ceremony was supposed to start, Jason approached her and squeezed her hand.

"You look pensive."

"I was just thinking about the baby."

"Me, too." His expression was grave. "I want to tell everyone I'm the father."

Ming's heart convulsed. Last night, after discovering she was pregnant, she'd longed to stand at Jason's side and tell everyone they were having a baby. Of course, doing it would bring up questions about whether or not they were together.

"Are you sure this is a good idea?"

"The only reason you wanted to keep quiet was because you didn't want to hurt Evan. But he's moved on with your sister."

"So you decided this because Evan and Lily are involved?"

"It isn't about them. It's about us. I'm going to be in the child's life on a daily basis." His expression was more determined than she'd ever seen it. "I think I should be there as his dad rather than as Uncle Jason."

He'd said *us*.

Only it wasn't about her and Jason. Not in the way she wanted. Ming's heart shuddered like a damaged window battered by strong winds. At any second it could shatter into a thousand pieces. She loved the idea that he wanted to be a father, but she couldn't ignore her yearning to have him be there for her as well.

"Come on, you two," Missy called as the wedding party began moving into position near the church's inner door. "We're on."

Jason strode to his position in line and Ming relaxed her grip on her bouquet before the delicate stems of the Gerber daisies snapped beneath the intensity of her conflicting emotions.

As maid of honor, Rachel's sister, Hailey, was already in place behind Max and his parents. The music began signaling the trio to start down the aisle. The groom looked relaxed and ready as he accompanied his parents to their places at the front of the church.

The bright flowers in Ming's hands quivered as she stood beside Nathan. He appeared on edge. His distress let Ming forget about her own troubles.

"Are you okay?" she asked.

Lines bracketed his mouth. "I tried to convince Emma to stay home. Although she wouldn't admit it, she's really having a difficult time today. I'm worried about her."

"I'm sure it's natural to be uncomfortable when you're past your due date," Ming said and saw immediately that her words had little effect on the overprotective father-to-be. "She'll let you know if anything is wrong."

"I'm concerned that she won't." He glanced behind him at the bride. "She didn't want anything to disturb your day."

Rachel put her hand on Nathan's arm, her expression sympathetic. "I appreciate both of you being here today, but if you think she needs to be at home, take her there right after the ceremony."

Nathan leaned down and grazed Rachel's cheek with his lips. "I will. Thank you."

He seemed marginally less like an overwound spring as they took their turn walking down the aisle. It might have helped that his wife beamed at him from the second row. Ming's stomach twisted in reaction to their happiness. Even for someone who wasn't newly pregnant and madly in love with a man who refused to feel the same way, it was easy to get overwhelmed by emotions at a wedding. Holding herself together became easier as she watched Rachel start down the aisle.

The bride wore a long strapless dress unadorned by beading or lace. Diamond and pearl earrings were her only jewelry. Her styling was romantic and understated, allowing the bride's beauty and her utter happiness to shine.

With her father dead and her mother out of her life since she was four, Rachel had no one to give her away. Ming's sadness lasted only until she realized this was the last time Rachel would walk alone. At the end of the ceremony, she would be Max's wife and part of his family.

Ming swallowed past the lump in her throat as the minister began talking. The rest of the ceremony passed in a blur. She was roused out of her thoughts by the sound of clapping. Max had swept Rachel into a passionate kiss. The music began once more and the happy couple headed back down the aisle, joined for life.

Because they'd been the last up the aisle, Nathan and Ming were the last to return down it. They didn't get far, however. As they drew near Emma, Ming realized something was wrong. Nathan's wife was bending forward at the waist and in obvious pain. When Nathan hastened to her side, she clutched his forearm and leaned into his strength.

"I think it might be time to get to the hospital," she said, her brown eyes appearing darker than ever in her pale face.

"How long has this been going on?" he demanded.

"Since this morning."

Nathan growled.

"I'm fine. I wanted both of us to be here for Rachel and Max. And now I'd like to go to the hospital and give birth to our son."

"Stubborn woman," Nathan muttered as he put a supporting arm around his wife and escorted her down the aisle.

"Do you want us to come with you?" Max's mother asked, following on their heels. She reached her hand back to her husband.

"No." Emma shook her head. "Stay and enjoy the party. The baby probably won't come anytime soon." But as she said it, another contraction stopped her in her tracks.

"I'm going to get the car." Handing his wife off to Ming, Nathan raced out of the church.

Ming and Emma continued their slow progress.

"Has he always been like this?" Ming asked, amused and ever so envious.

"It all started when my father decided to make marrying me part of a business deal Nathan was doing with Montgomery Oil. Since then he's got this crazy idea in his head that I need to be taken care of."

"I think it's sweet."

Emma's lips moved into a fond smile. "It's absolutely wonderful."

By the time Ming got Emma settled into Nathan's car and returned to the church, half the guests had made it through the reception line and had spilled onto the street. Since she wasn't the immediate family of the bride and groom, she stood off to one side and waited until the wedding party was free so she could tell them what had happened to Nathan and Emma.

"The contractions seemed fairly close together," Ming said in answer to Susan Case's question regarding Emma's labor. "She said she'd started having them this morning, so I don't know how far along she is."

"Hopefully Nathan will call us from the hospital and let us know," Max's father said.

Sebastian nodded. "I'm sure he will."

"In the meantime," Max said, smiling down at his glowing wife, "we have a reception to get to."

A limo awaited them at the curb to take the group to The Corinthian, a posh venue in downtown Houston's historica district. Ming had never attended an event there, but she'd heard nothing but raves from Missy and Emma. And they were right. The space took its name from the fluted Corinthian columns that flanked the long colonnade where round tables of ten had been placed for the reception. Once the lobby for the First National Bank, the hall's thirty-five-foot ceilings and tall windows now made it an elegant place to hold galas, wedding receptions and lavish birthday parties.

Atop burgundy damask table cloths, gold silverware flanked gilded chargers and white china rimmed with gold. Flickering votive candles in glass holders nestled amongst flowers in Rachel's chosen palette of gold, yellow and deep orange.

Ming had never seen anything so elegant and inviting.

"Susan really outdid herself," Missy commented as she and her husband stopped beside Ming to admire the view. "It almost makes me wish Sebastian and I hadn't run off to Las Vegas to get married." She grinned up at her handsome husband. "Of course, having to wait months to become his wife wouldn't have been worth all this."

Sebastian lifted her hand and brushed a kiss across her knuckles. The heat that passed between them in that moment made Ming blink.

She cleared her throat. "So, you don't regret eloping?"

Missy shook her head, her gaze still locked on her husband's face. "Having a man as deliberate and cautious as Sebastian jump impulsively into a life-changing event as big as marriage was the most amazing, romantic, sexy thing ever."

"He obviously knew what he wanted," Ming murmured, her gaze straying to where Jason laughed with Max's father.

Sebastian's deep voice resonated with conviction as he said, "Indeed I did."

Twelve

Keeping Ming's green-clad form in view as she chatted with their friends, Jason dialed his brother's cell. Evan hadn't mentioned skipping the wedding, and it was out of character for him to just not show. When voice mail picked up, Jason left a message. Then he called his dad, but Tony hadn't heard from Evan, either. Buzzing with concern, Jason slid the phone back into his pocket and headed for Ming.

She was standing alone, her attention on the departing Sebastian and Missy, a wistful expression on her face. Their happiness was tangible. Like a shot to his head, Jason comprehended Ming's fascination. Despite her insistence that she wasn't cut out for marriage, it's what she longed for. Evan had ended their engagement and broken her heart in the process. Her decision to become a single mom was Ming's way of coping with loneliness.

How had he not understood this before? Probably because he didn't want it to be true. He hated to think that she'd find someone new to love and he'd lose her all over again.

Over dinner, while Rachel and Max indulged the guests by kissing at every clinking of glassware, Jason pondered his dinner companion and where the future would take them after tonight. He'd been happier in the past couple of weeks than he'd been in years. It occurred to him just how much he'd missed the closeness that had marked their relationship through high school.

He wasn't ready to give up anything that he'd won. He wanted Ming as the best friend whom he shared his hopes and fears with. He wanted endless steamy nights with the sexy temptress who haunted his dreams. Most of all, he wanted the family that the birth of their baby would create.

All without losing the independence he was accustomed to.

Impossible.

He wasn't foolish enough to think Ming would happily go along with what he wanted, so it was up to Jason to figure out how much he was comfortable giving up and for her to decide what she was willing to live with.

By the time the dancing started, Jason had his proposition formed. Tonight was for romance. Tomorrow morning over breakfast he would tell her his plan and they would start hashing out a strategy.

"Hmm," she murmured as they swayed together on the dance floor. "It's been over a decade since we danced together. I'd forgotten how good you are at this."

"There are things I'm even better at." He executed a spin that left her gasping with laughter. "How soon can we get out of here?"

"It's barely nine." She tried to look shocked, but her eyes glowed at his impatience.

"It's the bride and groom's party." In the crush on the dance floor, he doubted if anyone would notice his hand venturing over her backside. "They have to stick around. We can leave anytime."

Her body quivered, but she grabbed his hand and repositioned it on her waist. "I don't think Max and Rachel would appreciate us ducking out early."

Jason glanced toward the happy newlyweds. "I don't think they'll even notice."

But in the end, they stayed until midnight and saw Max and Rachel off. The newlyweds were spending the night at a downtown hotel and flying on Monday to Gulf Shores, Alabama, where Max owned a house. The location had seemed an odd choice to Jason until he heard the story of how Max and Rachel met in the beach town five years earlier.

As the guests enjoyed one last dance, Jason slid his palm into the small of Ming's back. "Did your sister say anything about Evan's plan to miss the wedding today?"

A line appeared between Ming's finely drawn eyebrows. "No. Did you try calling him?"

"Yes. And I spoke with my dad, too. He hadn't heard from him. This just isn't like Evan."

"Let me call Lily and see if she knows what's going on." Ming dialed her sister's cell and waited for her to pick up. "Evan didn't make the wedding. Did he tell you he was planning on skipping it?" Ming met Jason's eyes and shook her head.

"Find out when she last spoke to him."

"Jason wants to know when you last heard from him. I'm going to put you on speaker, okay?"

"Last night."

It was odd for his brother to go a whole day without talking to one of them. "Is something going on with him?"

"Last night he proposed." Lily sounded miserable.

"Wow," Ming exclaimed, her excitement sounding genuine.

"I told him I couldn't marry him."

Anxiety kicked Jason in the gut. "I guess I don't need to ask how he took that."

Twice he'd seen Evan slip into the same self-destructiveness their father had once exhibited. The first time as a senior in high school when his girlfriend of three years decided to end things a week after graduation. Evan had spent the entire summer in a black funk. The second time was about a year before he and Ming had started dating. His girlfriend of two years had dumped him and married her ex-boyfriend. But Jason suspected neither of those events had upset Evan to the extent that losing Lily would.

"I don't understand," Ming said. "I thought you loved him."

"I do." Lily's voice shook. "I just can't do that to you."

Ming looked to Jason for help. "I don't blame either of you for finding each other."

While the sisters talked, Jason dialed his brother again. When he heard Evan's voice mail message, he hung up. He'd already left three messages tonight. No need to leave another.

"Do you mind if I stop by Evan's before I head home?" Jason quizzed Ming as he escorted her to where she'd left her car. "I'll feel better if I see that he's all right."

"Sure."

"Just let yourself in. I shouldn't be more than fifteen minutes behind you."

But when he got to his brother's house, he discovered why Evan hadn't made it to the wedding and hadn't called him back. His brother was lying unconscious on his living room floor while an infomercial played on the television.

An open bottle of pain pills was tipped over on the coffee table. Empty. In a flash Jason became a fifteen-year-old again, finding his father passed out in the running car, the garage filled with exhaust. With a low cry, Jason dropped to his knees beside his brother. The steady rise and fall of Evan's chest reassured Jason that his brother wasn't dead. Sweat broke out as he grabbed his brother's shoulder and shook.

"Evan. Damn it. Wake up." His throat locked up as he searched for some sign that his brother was near consciousness. Darkness closed over his vision. He was back in the shadow-filled garage, where poisonous fumes had raked his throat and filled his lungs. His chest tightened with the need to cough. His brother couldn't die. He had to wake him. With both hands on Evan's shoulders, Jason shook him hard. "Evan."

A hand shoved him in the chest, breaking through the walls of panic that had closed in on Jason.

"Geez, Jason." His brother blinked in groggy confusion. "What the hell?"

Chest tight, Jason sat on the floor and raked his fingers through his hair. Relief hadn't hit him yet. He couldn't draw a full breath. Oxygen deprivation made his head spin. He dug the heels of his palms against his eyes and felt moisture.

Grabbing the pill bottle, he shook it in his brother's face. "How many of these did you take?"

"Two. That's all I had."

And if there had been more? Would he have taken them? "Are you sure?"

Evan batted away his brother's hand. "What the hell is wrong with you?"

"You didn't make the wedding. So I came over to check on you. Then I saw you on the floor and I thought..." He couldn't finish the thought.

"I didn't make the wedding because I wasn't in the mood."

"And these?"

"I went for a bicycle ride this morning to clear my head and took a spill that messed up my back. That's why I'm lying on the floor. I seized up."

"I left three messages." Jason's hands trembled in the aftermath of the adrenaline rush. "Why didn't you call me back?"

"I turned my phone off. I didn't want to talk to anyone." Evan rolled to his side and pushed into a sitting position. "What are you doing here?"

"Lily said she turned down your proposal. I thought maybe you'd done something stupid."

But Evan wasn't listening. He sucked in a ragged breath. "She's afraid it'll hurt her sister if we get married." He blinked three times in rapid succession. "And she wouldn't listen to me when I said Ming wouldn't be as upset as Lily thinks."

Jason couldn't believe what he was hearing. Was this Evan's way of convincing himself he wasn't the bad guy in this scenario? "How do you figure? It's only been six months since your engagement ended."

Evan got to his feet, and Jason glimpsed frustration in his brother's painful movements. "I know you think I messed up, but I did us both a favor."

"How do you figure?" Jason stood as well, his earlier worry lost in a blast of righteous irritation.

"She wasn't as much in love with me as you think she was."

Jason couldn't believe his brother was trying to shift some of the blame for their breakup onto Ming. "You forget who you're talking to. I know Ming. I saw how happy she was with you."

"Yeah, well. Not as happy as she could have been."

"And whose fault was that?" He spun away from Evan and caught his reflection in the large living room windows. He looked hollow. As if the emotion of a moment before had emptied him of all energy.

"I worked hard at the relationship," he said, his voice dull.

"And Ming didn't?"

A long silence followed his question. When Jason turned around, his brother was sitting on the couch, his head in his hands.

"Ming and I were a mistake. I know that now. It's Lily I love." He lifted his head. His eyes were bleak. "I don't know how I'm supposed to live without her."

Jason winced at his brother's phrasing. His cell rang. Ming was calling.

"Is everything okay with Evan?" The concern in her soft voice was a balm to Jason's battered emotions. "It's been almost a half an hour."

He couldn't tell her what he thought was going on while

Evan could overhear. "He threw his back out in a bicycle-riding accident this morning."

"Oh, no. There should be some ice packs in his freezer."

"I'll get him all squared away and be there in a half an hour."

"Take your time. It's been a long couple of days and I'm exhausted. Wake me when you get here."

He ended the call and found himself smiling at the image of Ming asleep in his bed. This past week without her had been hell. Not seeing her. Touching her. He hadn't been able to get her out of his mind.

"Ming told me to put you on ice." Talking to her had lightened his mood. He needed to get his brother settled so he could get home. "Do you want me to bring the ice packs to you here or upstairs?'

"What the hell do I care?"

Evan's sharp retort wasn't like him. Lily's refusal had hit him hard. Fighting anxiety over his brother's dark mood, Jason bullied Evan upstairs and settled him in his bed. Observing his brother's listless state, Jason was afraid to leave him alone.

"Are you going to be okay?"

Evan glared at him. "Why aren't you gone?"

"I thought maybe I should stick around a bit longer."

"Sounds like Ming is waiting for you." Evan deliberately looked away from Jason, making him wonder if Evan suspected what Jason and Ming had been up to.

"She is."

"Then get out of here."

Jason headed for the door. "I'll be back to check on you in the morning."

"Don't bother. I'd rather be alone."

The fifteen-minute drive home offered Jason little time to process what had happened with Evan. What stood out for him was his brother's despair at losing the woman he loved.

He stepped from his garage into the kitchen, and stood in the dark, listening. The silence soothed him, guided him toward the safe place he'd created inside himself. The walled fortress that kept unsettling emotions at bay.

He glanced around the kitchen and smiled as his gaze landed on the chair where he and Ming had made love for the first time. Just one of the great moments that had happened in this room. In almost every room in the house.

He had dozens of incredible memories featuring Ming, and not one of them would be possible if he hadn't opened the doors to his heart and let himself experience raw, no-holds-barred passion.

But desire he could handle. It was the other strong feelings Ming invoked that plagued him. Being with her these past few weeks had made him as happy as he ever remembered. He couldn't stop imagining a life with her.

And this morning he'd been ready to make his dreams reality.

But all that had changed tonight when he'd mistaken what was going on with Evan and relived the terror of the night he'd found his father in the garage. The fear had been real. His pledge to never fall in love—the decision that had stopped making sense these last few weeks—became rational once more.

He couldn't bear to lose Ming. If they tried being a couple and it didn't work out, the damage done to their friendship might never heal. Could he take that risk?

No.

Jason marched up the stairs, confident that he was making the right decision for both of them. He'd expected to find her in his bed, but the soft light spilling from the room next door drew him to the doorway. In what had been his former den, Ming occupied the rocking chair by the window, a stuffed panda clutched against her chest, her gaze on the crib. Encased in serenity, she'd never looked more beautiful.

"Where's all your stuff?" she asked, her voice barely above a whisper.

"It's in the garage."

Gone was the memorabilia of his racing days. In its place stood a crib, changing table and rocker. The walls had been painted a soft yellow. The bedding draped across the crib had pastel jungle animals parading between palm trees and swinging from vines.

She left the chair and walked toward him past the pictures that had graced her childhood bedroom. He'd gotten them from her parents. Her father was sentimental about things like that.

"Who helped you do this?"

"No one." His arms went around her slim form, pulling her against his thudding heart. He rested his chin on her head. "Except for the paint and new carpet. I hired those out."

"You picked all this out by yourself?"

Jason had never shopped for a Christmas or birthday present without her help, and Ming was obviously having a hard time wrapping her head around what he'd accomplished in such a short time.

"Do you like it?" he prompted, surprised by how much he wanted her approval.

"It's perfect."

Nestled in Jason's arms, Ming wouldn't have believed it was possible to fall any deeper in love with him, but at that moment she did. The room had been crafted with loving care by a guy who was as comfortable in a department store as a cat in a kennel of yapping dogs.

He was an amazing man and he would be a terrific father. She was lucky to have such a good friend.

Jason's arms tightened. "I'm glad you like the room. It turned out better than I expected."

"I love you." The courage to say those words had been building in her ever since Jason told her he wanted to go public about his part in her pregnancy. She'd always been truthful with Jason. She'd be a fool and a coward to hide something so important from him.

He tensed.

She gestured at the room. "Seeing this, I thought…" Well, that wasn't true. She'd been reacting emotionally to Jason's decision to be an active father and to his decorating this room to surprise her. "I want to be more than your best friend. I want to be a family with you and our baby."

Fear that he'd react badly didn't halt her confession. As her love for him strengthened with each day that passed, she knew she was going to bare her soul at some point. It might as well be sooner so they could talk it through. "I know that's not what you want to hear," she continued. "But I can't keep pretending I'm okay with just being your best friend."

When his mouth flattened into a grim line, Ming pulled free of his embrace. Without his warmth, she was immediately chilled. She rubbed her arms, but the cold she felt came from deep inside.

"Evan knew how you felt, didn't he?" Jason made it sound like an accusation. "Tonight. He told me you weren't as in love with him as I thought."

"Why did he tell you that?"

"I assumed because he was justifying falling for Lily."

"I swear I never gave him any reason to suspect how I felt about you. I couldn't even admit it to myself until I saw you crash. You've always been so determined not to fall in love or get married." Ming's eyes burned as she spoke. "I knew you'd never let yourself feel anything more for me than friendship, so I bottled everything up and almost married your brother because I was completely convinced you and I could never be."

He was silent a long time. "I haven't told you what happened with Evan tonight."

"Is he okay?"

"When I got to his house I found him on the floor with an empty bottle of painkillers beside him. I thought he was so upset over Lily refusing to marry him that he tried to kill himself."

Ming's heart squeezed in sympathy. The wound he'd suffered when he'd found his father in the garage with the car running had cut deeper than anyone knew. The damage had been permanent. Something Jason would never be free from.

"Did he?" She'd been with Evan for three years and had never seen any sign of depression, but Jason's concern was so keen, she was ready to believe her ex-fiancé had done something to harm himself.

"No. He'd only taken a couple." A muscle jumped in Jason's jaw. He stared at the wall behind her, his gaze on a distant place. "I've never seen him like this. He's devastated that Lily turned him down."

"They're not us."

"What does that mean?" Annoyance edged his voice, warning her that he wasn't in the mood to listen.

She refused to be deterred. "Just because they might not be able to make it work doesn't mean we can't."

"Maybe. But I don't want to take the risk." He gripped her hands and held on tight.

"Have you considered what will happen if we go down that road and it doesn't work out between us? You could come to hate me. I don't want to lose my best friend."

Ming had thought about it, but she had no easy answer. "I don't want to lose you, either, but I'm struggling to think of you as just my best friend. What I feel for you is so much deeper and stronger than that."

And here's where things got tricky. She could love Jason to the best of her ability, but he was convinced that loving someone meant opening up to overwhelming loss, and she couldn't force him to accept something different. But she could make him face what he feared most.

"I love you," she said, her voice brimming with conviction. "I need you to love me in return. I know you do. I feel it every time you touch me." She paused to let her words sink in. "And because we love each other, whether you want to admit it or not, our friendship is altered. We're no longer just best friends. We're a whole lot more."

Through her whole speech he regarded her with an unflinching stare. Now he spoke. "So, what are you saying?"

"I'm saying what you're trying to preserve by not moving our relationship forward no longer exists."

A muscle jumped in his jaw as he stared at her. Silence surrounded them.

"Is this an ultimatum?"

Was it? When she started, she hadn't meant it to be.

"No. It's a statement of intent. Our friendship as it once was is over. I love you and I want us to be a family."

"And if I don't accept that things have to change?"

She made no attempt to hide her sadness. "Then we both lose."

Half an hour after her conversation with Jason, Ming plopped onto her window seat and stared at the dark backyard. She didn't bother changing into a nightgown and sliding between the sheets. What was the point when there was no way she was going to be able to sleep? Her conversation with Jason played over and over in her mind.

Could she have handled it better? Probably not. Jason was never going to relish hearing the truth. He liked their relationship exactly the way it was. Casual. Comfortable. Constant. No doubt he'd resent her for shaking things up.

Dawn found her perched on a stool at the breakfast bar, her gaze on the pool in her backyard. She cradled a cup of coffee in her hands.

"You're up early." Lily entered the kitchen and made a beeline for the cupboard where she kept the ingredients for her healthy breakfast shake. "Couldn't sleep?"

"You're an idiot." Ming knew it wasn't fair to take her frustration out on her sister, but Lily was throwing away love.

Her sister leaned back against the countertop. "Good morning to you, too."

"I'm sorry." Ming shook her head. Her heart hurt. "I'm sitting here thinking how lucky you are that Evan wants to marry you. And it just makes me so mad that you turned him down."

"Are you sure that's what you're mad about?"

Ming blinked and focused her gaze on Lily. "Of course."

"The whole time you were with Evan I was miserable."

Seeing where her sister was going, Ming laughed. "And you think I'm unhappy because Evan loves you?"

"Are you?"

"Not even a little."

"Then why are you so upset?"

With shaky hands, Ming set her cup down and rubbed her face. "I'm pregnant."

After all the arguments she'd had with her sister, the last thing Ming expected was for Lily to rush over and hug her. Ming's throat closed.

"Aren't you going to scold me for doing the wrong thing?" Ming asked.

"I'm sorry I've been so unsupportive. It wasn't fair of me to impose my opinions on you. I'm really happy for you." Lily sounded sincere. "Why didn't you didn't tell me you'd gone to the clinic?"

"Because I didn't go."

"Then how…?" Lily's eyes widened. "Jason?"

"Yes." Ming couldn't believe how much it relieved her to share the truth.

"Have you thought about what this is going to do to Evan?" It was natural that this would be Lily's reaction. She loved Evan and wanted to protect him.

"I was more worried about it before I knew he'd moved on with you." Ming crossed her arms. "But now you've turned down his proposal, and neither Jason nor I want to keep his involvement a secret."

"Why did you have to pick Jason?" Lily shook her head.

Ming refrained from asking Lily why Evan had picked her. "When I decided to have a baby, I wasn't keen on having a stranger's child. Jason understood, and because he's my best friend, he agreed to help."

"So you slept with him."

Ming's cheeks grew warm. "Yes."

"Does that mean you two are a couple?"

"No. As much as I want more, I understood that us being together was a temporary thing. Once I got pregnant, we'd stop."

"But now you're in love with him." Not a question, a statement. "Does he know?"

"I told him last night."

Lily squeezed Ming's hands. "How did he react?"

"Exactly how I'd expected him to." Ming put on her bravest smile. "He has his reasons for never falling in love."

"What are you talking about? He loves you."

"I know, but he won't admit to anything stronger than friendship."

"A friend he wants to sleep with." Lily's smile was wry.

"We have some pretty fabulous chemistry." The chuckle that vibrated in Ming's chest was bittersweet. "But he won't let it become anything more."

"Oh, Ming."

"It's not as if I didn't know how he feels." Ming slid off her stool and looped her arm through Lily's. She tugged her sister toward the stairs. "It just makes it that much more important for you to accept Evan's proposal." Closing her ears to her sister's protests, Ming packed Lily an overnight bag and herded her into the garage. "One of us deserves to be madly in love."

Fifteen minutes later, they pulled up in front of Evan's house. The longing on Lily's face told Ming she'd been right to meddle. She scooped up her sister's overnight bag and breezed up the front walk, Lily trailing slowly behind.

"Are you sure about this?" Lily questioned as they waited for Evan to answer the door.

"Positive. What a horrible sister I would be to stand in the way of your happiness."

Evan opened his door and leaned on it. He looked gray beneath his tan. "Ming? What are you doing here?"

"My sister tells me she turned down your marriage proposal."

His gaze shot beyond Ming to where Lily lingered at the bottom of his steps, but he said nothing.

Not being able to fix what was wrong in her own love life didn't mean she couldn't make sure Lily got her happily-ever-after. "She claims she turned you down because she thinks I would be hurt, but I'm moving on with my life and I don't want to be her excuse for not marrying you." Ming fixed her ex-fiancé with a steely gaze. "Do you promise you'll love her forever?"

"Of course." Evan was indignant.

Fighting to keep her composure intact, Ming headed down the steps to hug her sister. Confident they were out of Evan's hearing, she whispered, "Don't you dare come home until you've got an engagement ring on your finger."

Lily glanced at Evan. "Are you going to take your own advice and go talk to Jason?"

Ming shook her head. "Too much has happened over the last few days. We both need some time to adjust."

"He'll come around. You'll see."

But Ming didn't see. She merely nodded to pacify her sister. "I hope you're right."

Finding Evan passed out last night had reaffirmed to Jason how much better off he was alone. After such a powerful incident, Ming was convinced he'd never change his mind.

"Hey, Dad." It was late Sunday morning when Jason opened his front door and found his father standing there. "What's up?"

"Felt like having lunch with you."

From his father's serious expression, Jason wondered what he was in for, but he grabbed his keys and locked the house. "Where to?"

"Where else?"

They drove to his dad's favorite restaurant, where the pretty brunette hostess greeted Tony by name and flirted with him the whole way to the table.

"She's young enough to be your daughter," Jason commented, eyeing his father over the menu.

Tony chuckled. "She's young enough to be my granddaughter. And there's nothing going on. I love my wife."

When Tony had first announced that he was marrying Claire, Jason had a hard time believing his father had let himself fall in love again. But he'd reasoned that fifteen years of grieving was more than enough for anyone, and there was no question that Claire made his father happy. But his father's optimistic attitude toward love didn't stop Jason from wondering what would happen if Claire left.

Would his father collapse beneath the weight of sadness again? There was no way to know, and Jason hoped he never had to find out. "So, what's on your mind, Dad?"

"I spoke with Evan earlier today. Sounds like he and Lily are engaged."

"Since when?"

"Since this morning. Apparently Ming dropped her sister off and told her not to come home until she was engaged." Tony grinned. "I always loved that girl."

"Good for Evan. He was pretty beat up about Lily last night."

"He said you weren't doing too great, either."

Jason grimaced. "I found Evan on his living room floor, an empty bottle of pain pills next to him and I assumed..."

"That he'd tried to kill himself the way I had when you were fifteen." Tony looked older than his sixty-two years. The vibrancy had gone out of his eyes and the muscles in his face were slack. "That was the single darkest moment of my life, and I'm sorry you had to be the one to experience it with me."

"If I hadn't you'd be dead." They'd never really talked about what had happened. As a teenager Jason had been too shocked by almost losing a second parent to demand answers. And since Evan had been away at college, the secret had remained between Jason and his father while questions ate away Jason's sense of security.

"Looking back, I can't believe I allowed myself to sink so low, but I wasn't aware that I needed help. All I could see was a black pit with steep sides that I couldn't climb out of. Every day the hole seemed deeper. The company was months away from layoffs. I was taking my professional worries out on your mother, and that was eating me up. Then the car accident snatched her and Marie away from us. I was supposed to have driven them to the dress rehearsal for Marie's recital that night, but I was delayed at the office." Tony closed his eyes for a few seconds before resuming. "Those files could have waited until morning. If I had put my family first, they might still be alive. And in the end, all my work came to nothing. The job we'd bid went elsewhere and the company was on the verge of going under. I was to the point where I couldn't live with my failure as a husband, father or businessman."

So, this was the burden his father had carried all these years. Guilt had driven him to try to take his life because he'd perceived himself a failure?

And just like that, Jason's doctrine citing the dangers of falling in love lost all support.

"I thought you were so desperately in love with Mom that you couldn't bear to live without her anymore."

"Her death was devastating, but it wasn't why I started drinking or why I reached the point where I didn't want to go on. It was the guilt." His father regarded Jason in dismay. "Is that why you and Ming never dated? Were you afraid you'd lose her one day?"

"We didn't date because we're friends."

"But you love her."

"Of course I love her." And he did. "She's my—"

His father interrupted to finish. "Best friend." He shook his head in disgust. "Evan had another bit of news for me." Tony leaned his forearms on the table and pinned Jason with hard eyes. "Something Lily told him about Ming."

Now Jason knew why his father had shown up at his house. "She's pregnant."

"And?"

"The baby's mine."

So was Ming. His. Just as he'd told her the night of Max's bachelor party. He'd claimed her and then pushed her away because of a stupid pledge he'd made at fifteen. Had he really expected her to remain his best friend just because that's how it had always been for them?

And now that he knew the truth behind his father's depression, Jason could admit that he wanted the same things she did. Marriage. Children. The love of a lifetime.

But after he pushed her away last night, would she still want those things with him?

Jason's chair scraped the floor as he got to his feet. He threw enough money on the table to cover their tab and gestured for his father to get up. "We have to go."

"Go where?" Tony followed his son out the door without receiving an answer. "Go where?" he repeated, sliding behind the wheel of his BMW.

"I have an errand to run. Then I'm going to go see Ming. It's way past time I tell her how I really feel."

Ming swam beneath the pool's surface, stroking hard to reach the side before her breath gave out. After leaving Evan's house hours earlier, she'd been keyed up. After cleaning her refrigerator and vacuuming the whole upstairs, she'd decided to burn off her excess energy, hoping the cool water would calm both her body and her mind.

The exercise did its job. By the time she'd completed her twentieth lap, her thoughts had stopped racing. Muffin awaited her at the edge of the pool. As soon as Ming surfaced, the Yorkie raced forward and touched her nose to Ming's. The show of affection made her smile.

"What would I do without you?" she asked the small dog and received a lick in response.

"I've been asking myself the same question since you left last night."

A shadow fell across her. Ming looked up, her stomach flipping at the determined glint in Jason's blue eyes. Relief raced through her. The way their conversation had ended the previous night, she'd worried their friendship was irrevocably damaged.

"Luckily you aren't ever going to find that out." She accepted Jason's hand and let him pull her out of the water.

He wrapped her in a towel and pulled her against him. Dropping his lips to hers, he kissed her slow and deep. Ming tossed aside all the heartache of the past twelve hours and surrendered to the powerful emotions Jason aroused.

"I was wrong to dump all that stuff about Evan on you last night," he told her.

"I'm your friend. You know I'm always there for you."

"I know I take that for granted."

He took her by the hand and led her inside. To Ming's delight he pulled her toward the stairs. This wasn't what she'd expected from him after she confessed her feelings. She figured he'd distance himself from her as he'd done with women in the past.

But when they arrived in her bedroom, he didn't take her in his arms or rip the covers off the mattress and sweep her onto the soft sheets.

Instead, he kissed her on the forehead. "Grab a shower. I have an errand to run and could use your help."

An errand? Disappointment sat like a bowling ball in her stomach. "What sort of an errand?"

"I never got Max and Rachel a wedding present."

"Oh, Jason." She rolled her eyes at him.

"I'm hopeless without you," he reminded her, nudging her in the direction of the bathroom. "You know that."

"Does it have to be today?"

"They're leaving for Alabama tomorrow morning. I want them to have it before then." He scooped up the Yorkshire terrier and the dog's stuffed squirrel toy. "Muffin and I will be waiting for you downstairs."

"Fine."

Half an hour later Ming descended her stairs and found Jason entertaining Muffin with a game of fetch. She'd put on a red sundress with thin straps and loved the way Jason's eyes lit up in appreciation.

She collected the Yorkie's leash and her purse and headed out the front door. When she spotted the car in front of her house, she hesitated. "Why are you driving the 'Cuda?"

"I told you, I never got Max and Rachel a wedding present."

Understanding dawned. "You're giving him back the car?"

"The bet we made seems pretty stupid in light of recent events."

"What recent events?"

He offered her his most enigmatic smile. "Follow me and you'll find out."

When they arrived at Max and Rachel's house, Jason didn't even have a chance to get out of the car before the front door opened. To his amusement, Max looked annoyed.

"Why are you driving the 'Cuda?" he demanded as Jason slowly got to his feet. "Do you have any idea what the car's worth?"

"I don't, since you never told me what you paid for it." Jason took Ming's hand as she reached his side and pulled her close.

"Look, I'm sorry that I didn't get you anything for your wedding. Ming was supposed to help me pick something, but she backed out at the last minute."

"Jason." She bumped her hip against him in warning. "You are perfectly capable of shopping on your own."

"No, he's not," Max put in.

"No, I'm not. So, here." Jason held out the keys.

"You're giving me back the 'Cuda?" Max's thunderstruck expression was priceless.

"I realize now that I had an unfair advantage when we made the bet. You were already in love with Rachel, just too stubborn to realize it."

Max took the keys and nodded. "Being stubborn when it comes to love means you lose out on all sorts of things."

Jason felt the barb hit home. He had missed a lot with Ming. If he hadn't been so determined never to be hurt, she might have married his brother, and Jason could have ended up with a lifetime of pain.

Rachel had come out to join them. She snuggled against her husband's side and looked fondly at the bright yellow car. "What's going on?"

"Jason's giving me back the 'Cuda," Max explained with a wry grin. "Can I interest you in a ride?"

To Jason's surprise, the blonde's cheeks turned pink. Unwilling to delve too deeply into whatever subtext had just passed between husband and wife, he reached for the passenger seat and pulled out a box wrapped in white-and-silver paper and adorned with a silver bow.

"And because the car is a really lousy wedding present," he continued, handing the gift to Rachel, "I got this for you."

Rachel grinned. "I think the car is a lovely present, but thank you for this."

Jason shut the 'Cuda's door and gave the car one last pat. "Take good care of her," he told Max.

"I intend to." Max leaned down and planted a firm kiss on his wife's lips.

"I meant the car," Jason retorted, amused.

"Her, too."

After spending another ten minutes with the newlyweds, Ming and Jason returned to her car.

"What was that about?" she asked, standing beside the driver's door. "You didn't need me to help deliver the car. You could have had Max come pick it up."

"It was symbolic." He could feel her tension growing and decided he'd better tell her what was on his mind before she worked herself into a lather. "I won the car because I bet against love. It sits in my garage, a testament to my stubbornness and stupidity. So I decided to give it back to Max. Apparently in addition to its financial value it has some sentimental value to him, as well."

Her lips curved. "I'm happy to hear you admit that you were idiotic and pigheaded, but what caused your enlightenment?"

He leaned against the car and drew her into his arms.

"My dad swung by my house earlier and we had a long talk about what happened after my mother and sister died."

She sighed and relaxed against him. "You've talked with him about it before, haven't you?"

"We talked about his depression, but I never understood what was at the root of him trying to take his life."

"I thought it was because he was so much in love with your mom that he couldn't live without her."

"That's what I believed. Turns out I didn't know the whole story."

"There's more?"

"Today I found out why he was so depressed after my mother and sister died. Apparently he stayed at work when he was supposed to drive them the night they died. He thinks if he'd chosen his family over the business they might still be alive. It was eating him up."

"You mean he felt guilty?"

Jason nodded. "Guilty because he'd failed her. Not devastated by loss. All these years I was wrong to think love only led to pain." He watched Ming's expression to gauge her reaction to his tale. "When my dad fell in love with Claire, I thought he was nothing more than an optimistic fool." Jason winced. He'd spoken up against his father marrying her and a rift had formed between them. "Then Max fell in love with Rachel. Until he met her, he'd had a block of ice where his heart should be."

"But Rachel's great."

Jason nodded. "And she's perfect for Max, but when he fell head over heels for her, I was even more convinced that love made everyone else crazy and that I was the only sane one."

It scared her how firmly he clung to his convictions. "And now your brother has gone mad for Lily."

"That he has." He gave her a sheepish smile. "Max and his brothers. My dad. Evan. They're all so damned happy."

"You're happy."

"When I'm with you." He set his forehead against hers. "I've been a stubborn idiot. All this time I've been lying to myself about what I wanted. I thought if you and I made love, I could keep things the way they were between us and manage to have the best of both worlds."

"Only I had to go and fall in love with you."

"No. You had to go and tell me you wanted us to be together as a family." At last he was free to share with her what lay in his heart. "Did you know when you chose me to help you get pregnant that a baby would bind us together forever?"

"It crossed my mind, but that isn't why I decided on you." She frowned defensively. "And I'd like to point out that you agreed to help me. You also had to realize that any child I gave birth to would be part of us."

"From the instant you said you wanted me to be your baby's father, all I could think about was how much I wanted you." He took her hand and kissed her palm, felt her tension ease

"After prom night I ran from the way I felt about you. It went against everything I believed. I've been running for the last fifteen years."

"And what is it you want?"

"You. More than anything. Marry me. I want to spend the rest of my life showing you how much I love you." He produced a diamond ring and held it before her eyes.

Heart pounding, she stared at the fiery gem as he took her left hand and slid the ring onto her finger. It fit perfectly.

"Yes. Yes. Of course, yes."

Before she finished her fervent acceptance, he kissed her. As his lips moved with passionate demand against hers, she melted beneath the rush of desire. He took his time demonstrating how much he loved her until his breath was rough and ragged. At last he lifted his head and stared into her eyes. Her stark joy stopped his heart.

Grinning, he hugged her hard. "And just in case you're worried about everyone's reaction, I cleared this with your sister and parents and my brother. The consensus seems to be that it's about time we take things from friends…"

"To forever." She laughed, a glorious sound of joy. "How lucky can a girl be?" she murmured. "I get to marry my best friend and the man I adore."

Jason cupped her face and kissed her gently. "What could be better than that?"

Ming lifted onto her tiptoes and wrapped her arms around his neck. "Not one single thing."

Epilogue

One year later

Bright afternoon sunshine glinted off the brand new paint on the galaxy blue Mustang parked in the driveway. Ming adjusted the big red bow attached to the roof and waved goodbye to the Stover brothers, who'd dropped the repaired race car off moments before. With her anniversary present for Jason looking absolutely perfect, she glanced toward the colonial's front door. The delivery had not been particularly quiet and she was surprised her husband of one year hadn't come out to see what the commotion was about.

She headed inside and paused in the foyer. From the family room came the sounds of revving engines so she followed the sound. Jason sat on the couch in front of the sixty-inch TV absorbed in a NASCAR race. Muffin slept on the back of the couch near his shoulder.

"Jason?"

Muffin's head came up and her tail wagged, but Jason didn't

react at all. She circled the couch and discovered why he hadn't heard the delivery. He was fast asleep. So were their twin three-month-old sons, Jake and Connor, one on either side of him, snuggled into the crooks of his arms.

Ming grinned at the picture of her snoozing men and hoped his nap meant Jason would have lots of energy later tonight because she had plans for him that required his full strength. But right now she was impatient to show him his gift.

"Jason." She knelt between his knees and set her hands on his thighs. Muffin stretched and jumped down to lick Connor's cheek. "Wake up and see what I got you for our anniversary." When her words didn't rouse him, she slid her palms up his thigh. She was more than halfway toward her goal when his lips twitched upward at the corners.

"Keep going."

"Later."

He sighed, but didn't open his eyes. "That's what you always say." But despite his complaint, his smile had blossomed into a full-blown grin.

"And I always come through." She stood and slapped his knee. "Now come see your present."

She scooped up Jake and waited until Jason draped Connor over his shoulder and got to his feet before she headed back through the house. Muffin raced ahead of them to the foyer. Tingling with anticipation, Ming pulled open the front door and stepped aside so Jason could look out. The shock on his face when he spotted the car was priceless.

"You had the Mustang repaired?" He wrapped his free arm round her waist and pulled her tight against him.

"I did." She smiled up at him and his lips dropped onto hers for a passion-drenched kiss that curled her toes. When he let her breath again, she caught his hand and dragged him down the steps. "I think you should start racing again."

He hadn't been anywhere near the track since he'd crashed the Mustang over a year ago. Between getting married, her taking over the dental practice and the birth of their twins, they'd been plenty busy.

"Are you sure that's what you want?" Jason ran his hand along the front fender with the same appreciation he'd lavished on her thigh the previous night. "It'll take me away some weekends."

"I never wanted you to stop doing what you love."

"What I love is being your husband and a father to Jake and Connor."

"And I love that, too." She nudged her body against his. "But racing is your passion, and Max is bored to death without you to compete against."

He coasted his palm over her hip and cupped her butt, drawing her up on her toes for a slow, thorough kiss. The babies began to fuss long before Ming was done savoring her husband's fabulous technique and they broke apart with matching regretful sighs.

"More of that to come later," she assured him, soothing Jake.

While they were distracted, a car had pulled up behind the Mustang. Max and Rachel got out. "Get a room you two," Max called good-naturedly, picking up the excited terrier.

"That's the plan," Ming retorted, handing off her son to Rachel.

"Great to see you guys." Jason switched Connor to his other arm so he could give Max a man hug. "Are you staying for dinner?"

"They're staying," Ming said. "We're leaving. They're going to babysit while we celebrate our anniversary." Since the twins were born, uninterrupted time together was pretty much nonexistent, and Ming was determined that she and Jason should make a memorable start to their second year of marriage.

Jason eyed Max. "Are you sure you're up for this?"

"I think I could use a little parenting practice."

"I'm pregnant," Rachel announced, beaming.

While Jason congratulated Max, and Rachel cooed over

Jake, Ming marveled at her good fortune. She'd married her best friend and they had two healthy baby boys. Her practice was thriving. Lily and Evan were getting married in the spring. Everything that had been going wrong a little over a year ago was now sorted out. It wasn't perfect, but it was wonderful.

Jason looked over and caught her watching him. The blaze that kindled in his eyes lit an answering inferno deep inside her. For twenty-five years he'd been her best friend and that had been wonderful, but for the rest of her life he was going to be her husband and that was perfect.

* * * * *

A sneaky peek at next month...

Desire

PASSIONATE AND DRAMATIC LOVE STORIES

My wish list for next month's titles...

In stores from 19th April 2013:

☐ A Wedding She'll Never Forget – Robyn Grady

& Millionaire in a Stetson – Barbara Dunlop

☐ Beguiling the Boss – Joan Hohl

& A Trap So Tender – Jennifer Lewis

☐ One Secret Night – Yvonne Lindsay

& Project: Runaway Heiress – Heidi Betts

2 stories in each book - only £5.49!

Available at WHSmith, Tesco, Asda, Eason, Amazon and Apple

Just can't wait?

Special Offers

Every month we put together collections and longer reads written by your favourite authors.

Here are some of next month's highlights— and don't miss our fabulous discount online!

Australia
OUTBACK FANTASIES

Margaret WAY Barbara HANNAY Leah MARTYN

On sale 19th April

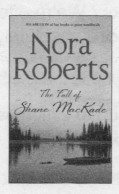

Nora Roberts
The Fall of Shane MacKade

On sale 3rd May

THE CORRETTIS
Sins

CAROL MARINELLI
SARAH MORGAN

On sale 3rd May

Save 20%
on all Special Releases

Find out more at
www.millsandboon.co.uk/specialreleases

Visit us
Online

0513/ST/MB414

Mills & Boon® Online

Discover more romance at
www.millsandboon.co.uk

- 🌹 **FREE** online reads
- 🌹 **Books** up to one month before shops
- 🌹 **Browse our books** before you buy

...and much more!

---

or exclusive competitions and instant updates:

 Like us on **facebook.com/romancehq**

 Follow us on **twitter.com/millsandboonuk**

 Join us on **community.millsandboon.co.uk**

isit us Online   Sign up for our FREE eNewsletter at
www.millsandboon.co.uk